R A V E R

By

STEPHEN JAYDELL

Copyright © 2013 Stephen Jaydell
All rights reserved.
ISBN: 9798668174935

2nd Edition

PROLOGUE

Illuminated by high frequency super-bright flashes, strobing freeze-framed hands punch the air as the tie-dyed dungaree ravers chant "ah-seed" to the never-ending four-four kick drum and acid-house squelches. War of the Worlds style, the pitch-black countryside is ripped apart by two high powered light-sabre green lasers sweeping toward the brightly lit big wheel and spinning waltzers. Scanning across the multi-coloured silhouetted horizon the euphoric rush caresses his spine, tingles his skull and a sense of love fills his heart. Alive like never before, he's loving life and loving everyone. He's lived a half-life, surreal and unreal and make believe, an urban daydream clouded by hazy chemical cocktails. Eyes closing, his thoughts drift to the night-time darkness. Mind splintering, he's faced with black-and-white snap-shot pictures of tower-blocks and skinheads, riots and Police brutality. Nostrils flaring with childhood smells of ginger-bread spices, stewing tea and curried goat, guilt, remorse and regret creep slowly from the shadows of his mind. Fight the darkness, fight the fear, get back on the up from the down. Squeezing his eyes tightly shut, the "move-your-body" metronome echoes around him and once again takes him higher.

That was then, this is now...

Knock-knock. No answer. Looking over the open walkway around the estate, he hears the opening bars of that Guy Called Gerald track echoing from an open window in the other block, "ahhh-ha-ha-yeah, voodoo-ray, voodoo-ray." A smile curls at the corner of his mouth. He remembers moving thirty thousand ravers to that very tune just a few of weeks ago.

He knocks again, harder this time. Still no answer.

Looking through the window, he can tell someone's inside. Facing the door he smashes his foot against the lock. Bursting open, the door slams against the inside wall before bouncing back. Turning away he covers his mouth as an unbearable smell burns his nostrils. Edging in, he can just about see through the kitchen door, three-quarter closed. Eyes dart to the balcony door, smashed and bloodied. Slowly pushing the door ajar, he scans the torn apart room. Signs of a struggle. He spots a pile of papers on the table, chewed up with scribbles all over them. Beyond that, past the table he sees the body on the floor.

Lump in the throat, tears roll down his face.

1. Spin Back

"You can't foresee it, it happens bit by bit, until complete craziness surrounds you and you're doing exactly what you don't want to do with people you can't stand... the people you hated when you were ten years old."

John Lennon

17, HAMILTON HOUSE
GREENWICH, LONDON
LATE SUMMER, 1989

Probing the fried egg wound deep inside, I feel the crispy edge and the sticky sunny-side-up middle. Pushing my finger deeper, I flinch as the exquisitely beautiful pain engulfs my soul. Damn, this is no normal post-high headache, nah man, this is an axe through the head kind of hurt. Head pounding with echoes of the night of my life, my cerebral cortex shrivels around my decaying mind, each neuron slowly detaching from the mothership, gradually disintegrating into nothingness. I'm not stupid though, I know my pain is the inevitable outcome of brain-cell genocide inflicted by the deliciously toxic chemical cocktail I've been consuming relentlessly for god knows how long. So, I accept this is my new reality, my real life, the Ecstasy fuelled dream I thought I remembered from way back when has long since left me.

Like so many things.

Squinting through blurry-bloodshot eyes, I make out a shadow, a dark shape moving and drifting around my mind. Adrenalin surging, images of Police and gangsters, villains and heroes flash across my mind. Whispering voices of skinheads and yardies, geezers and hooligans plotting and planning echo inside my skull. I recognise him, I've always known him, it's the devil, lucifer himself. Smiling a demented smile, horns grow from his shape-changing skull while thick black blood drips slowly from his razor-sharp vampire teeth. Burning-red, his sinister-evil eyes stare deep into my soul, reading me like a book, judging me, condemning me. Satan, the duppy-king, has eventually arrived, ready to drag me kicking and screaming to the lake of fire. Ominously approaching, his long skeletal fingers wrap themselves around my scrawny neck, intent on drowning me in my personal sea of self-pity. Wanting me so bad, he'll make promises, offer me bribes and gifts, eternal life with my choice of a thousand virgins, anything to make sure I go willingly. Yeah man, eventually, after a thousand years of denial, I'll submit to him and, in-turn, be fucked by Beelzebub with his man-woman cock-pussy, before dying a hundred times over. His son and heir, prince to the king of evil, I know I'll give him all he wants and be assimilated into one of his evil minions, converted into a dark angel ready to bring even more havoc to the world.

I told you, this shit's heavy…

Even though I know he's not really here, not in real life anyway, I can't look. I know he's a figment of my imagination, a creation of my warped mind but still, I'm scared, scared of him and scared of me. That's what the devil is yeah, he's not a physical reality, nah, he's just a cognitive construct called guilt, built to control us. Maybe I'm already dead, maybe I died when what happened actually happened on the night of nights, the single best and worst moment of my shitty life. Maybe I'm already part of the dark lord's army, a soldier of doom, captain of calamity, the admiral of darkness. Yeah, I like that, catchy. Either way, I know my card's marked, it always has been. I've always felt kind of different, something odd about me but I can never quite put my finger on it…

SPLASH.

Ice-cold water jerks me back to consciousness and my eyes spring open before squinting as the light stabs into me.

"Welcome back sweetheart," the Interrogator says, sarcastically.

I fucking drenched now and, worse, he's still here, wherever the fuck "here" and whoever the fuck "he" is. But, I do actually know him, my captor, my jailor, my fear, my pain, my regret, my pain-in-the-fucking-arse. I know he won't ever leave me alone, that's for sure.

"Listen ya' dutty rasclat, you got to con-cen-trate, ya hear me," the Interrogator urges doing a shit Jamaican accent because he know it winds me up.

Head spinning, light-headed and queasy, I hold my breath until the inevitable retching eases off but the room's spinning and my stomach's doing double back flips. I can't go over it yet again, bit by bit, detail after detail, man, reliving what happened and why it happened is just too hard. But, he said it will be good for me, cathartic he said. Not even sure what the fuck that means, something to do with God, I think, the Catholics or something. My eyes chase an invisible wasp buzzing around the room until I eventually focus on the flea-bitten sofa where echoes from the past flash through my mind. I see memories of her lying there loving me, wanting me, beckoning me towards her wide-open legs and her glistening wetness. I can't face her though, can't face the truth, can't face my reality so look everywhere but there, coffee table, council issue safety glass of the balcony door, windows stained brown allowing only thin shards of sunlight to pierce into room. This place stinks. Disgusting, stomach churning hand-over-my-mouth stench of decaying sweat and dirt hangs heavy in the air and the evil, scum-bucket, snake-in-the-grass stink of sex stings my nostrils and makes my eyes water. An undercurrent of deceit washes around my ankles like a shallow pool of dread, reminding me of him, the cunt, and her the slag and them, the pair of back-stabbing mother fuckers. Eyes falling, the gravity of the coffee table is too much. Littered with half empty beer cans, cigarette butts, torn business cards used for roaches and scorched tin-foil squares, it's disgusting like a dirty cum-filled whore dragging on a cigarette after being fucked in the ass, yet, as beautiful as a delicate rose gently wilting under freshly formed dew drops. Throat drying up, my tongue swells as rancid bile juice pumps into my mouth.

"You want that shit, don't you?" the Interrogator asks seductively, already knowing the answer. *'You dirty bastard.'*

Yeah, I do want it, I yearn for it, my special treat, my comfort, my goodness, my reward. But, I'm not going to admit anything to him, though, no way. Knowing how much I want it, he'll take it away and tease me with it, use it as leverage, use it as power, use it to tease even more out of me. But, my eyes are drawn to the brown leather belt snaking across the coffee table, weaving it's way in between the debris of a thousand nightmares. Slithering and shimmering, it rises like a cobra hissing and seething, ready to strike. Shake my head and it's gone, it's not real, I know it's not real, but god damn, hallucinations? What the fuck? Next to the dormant cobra rests two orange syringes and a charred teaspoon. My balls contract and tingle as an ice-cold shiver of excitement rushes through my body. Heavy lids slide over my bloodshot eyes as I savour the beautiful goodness the zammo-from-grange-hill-when-he-becomes-a-skagg-head paraphernalia will soon bring. Smiling a coy simile, I throw a wink towards the orange daughters of doom, otherwise known as the surgical twins of inevitability. That's right bitches, later on we'll have a little dance, get a bit smoochy, get a bit naughty, proper dirty…

"Now then, enough of this mind-bending bullshit, let's get down to business," the Interrogator, otherwise known as he-who-must-be-obeyed, says. *"I want everything, right. Absolutely everything. From the very beginning."*

Always from the beginning, over and over and god damn over. Even though he said it'll help, it doesn't feel like it's helping at all, but, once it's done it's done and he can leave me alone. Right then, deep breath, hold tight, here we go, Devious Dee is in the house and tonight we're going to go back, way back, back to the old-school…

ST. SAVIOURS SECONDARY SCHOOL
BRIXTON, LONDON
SEPTEMBER, 1965

The swinging sixties some call it, and we're there, right at in the middle of it, fashion, football, music, miniskirts, the Beatles, mods and rockers. The world is ours, all we got to do is reach out and take it. Hopes and dreams and smiles and good times. My journey to now starts on my first day at school, the summer before the world cup, yeah, that's it, the first day in secondary school. The child killer and his mad-bitch-girlfriend are on the evening news every day, Hindley and something-or-other, killing kids up North, in the mountains. At the same time, the Kray Twins are all over the newspapers, gangsterising all over the place and killing "Jack-the-fucking-hat", now, that's a cool name. Dark times man, like society is somehow losing it's innocence. Anyway, we are the top dogs in our year, controlling things for sure and when I say we, I mean Me, of course, my spar Super and "him", Paul, otherwise known as "cunt".

"Paul?" the Interrogator probes, reminding me of my pain, simultaneously changing the channel on my head-television.

In a flash, the colour and vibrancy of the sixties vanishes, replaced instead with the pain of the here and now. Black and white, stark and cold, all about me-me-me-greed-is-good-selfish-ambition. Stomach churning, tumbling over and over, I sit transfixed, staring down a stream of emptiness. Mind drifting, I wander through the darkness of my regret thinking, dwelling and reminiscing, wondering what might have been. Squeezing my eyes tight together, concentrating hard, I see the wooden box in the corner of the room and the "on" switch next to the shiny grey screen. Reaching out, I pause as my maimed hand trembles inches from the switch.

Go on, do it, do it, do it.

SWITCH.

Shards of multi-coloured light explode through the cathode-ray tubes deep within my cerebral cortex, searing a nineteen-sixty-six super-nova rainbow back into my mind. Warming memories flood through my core and, once again, I feel peace. Happy thoughts, good thoughts, love and peace…

The very first morning, we wait in the classroom for ages before the teacher arrives, what's his name now, Cunningham or Stringer or something, a tiny-little bloke into science or maths. An odd looking mother-fucker, big nose, curly black hair, Jewish I think he was, thick black rimmed glasses and a white science coat. Oh, and slippers, yeah man, he wore them all day long, rain or shine. Actually, when it rained, he tied plastic bags to his feet with elastic bands around his ankles. Madness. Into the classroom, we sit at the back of class. That's right, saps at the front, potential rude-boys at the middle, and us, at the very back, surveying our kingdom. We own the class, damn, we own the whole year, in fact we owned the whole entire school. Nobody dare mess with us, well, not with Super anyway. Big, bad and scary, even back then, he looks more like fifteen than eleven. So, that first morning, Me and Super are sitting there giggling as the crazy fool of a teacher struggled to get control of the class when this skinny white kid walks in, just as plastic-bag-foot is about to take the register. The whole class stares at the white kid, but he's cool and calm, bowling in like a miniature gangster, like he owns the place.

'Erm-hum, and who-wah exactly, are you-wah then?' the teacher sings in a weird accent, patronising and rhetorical at the same time. 'Late, on your-wah first day?'

The class falls silent, staring, shocked and amazed. They hadn't seen anything like this back in primary school, just painting and playtime back then. Nah, Paul's super cool, dressed Roger Daltry style with tight trousers, upside-down tie and pointy black shoes, not like me and Super in hand-me-downs. A cool dude, even for a white kid. 'Not to worry, better late than never boss,' he says, gliding into the classroom like he's on a skateboard or hovercraft or something. Confident and cocky, arrogant almost, he winks at us while he's giving it large, the cheeky bastard. Planting himself down at an empty desk just in front of us, the whole class plus the little-Jewish teacher stare in awe as he leans back and stretches his arms out. The teacher? Shit, his little fat face flushes red then purple as steam jets out of his ears cartoon style. Ranting and raving, he grabs Paul by the scruff of the neck and wrestles him out of his chair before flinging him out of the classroom, telling him to go see the Head. Damn, the Headmasters' office on your first day at school, not even in school, not even through the very first register on the very first day. That's cold, man.

At break-time me and Super go looking for him, we'll be the centre of attention thank you very much, not no cheeky little wanna-be-a-mod like him. Eventually we find him and Super roughs him up a bit, nothing too heavy, just a peanutted tie and a few claps around his head. He doesn't fight back but, at the same time, he doesn't run off either, nah, he stands his ground, trying to reason with us. From then on, we sort of hang out together. Coming from the Frontline, we'd never hung around with kid like him before but I'm cool man, in fact, I like being different. Nearly all the kids at school keep themselves to themselves, blacks with blacks, whites with whites, Irish with Irish and Italian with Italian. Everyone apart from us, we broke the mould, we're different, we are the living embodiment of the swinging sixties. Later that same week, Paul comes around to Momma's house and listen to some records. In spite of him being into the Rolling Stones and all that "no satisfaction" crap, he can feel the vibe. I play him some of Pop's old rhythm and blues tunes, Prince Buster and Lord Creator too. Yeah man, simple, tuneful, soul-full tunes, not like the repetitively squelchy acid-man eardrum-assault the kids are listening to nowadays.

I must admit, for a wanna-be-mod, Paul's got soul.

Still a cunt though.

Back at school, there's an end of year disco, celebrating the end of the first year and also the football World Cup. The school hall's decorated with red, white and blue bunting and balloons, with national flags draped around the walls. We meet Paul at the school gates where his mum drops him off. Flanked by the grey concrete science block on the right and the sixth form common room on the left, we stroll along the concourse towards the hall without a care in the world. We'd completed a whole year of secondary school so feel like we've achieved something, we're big-men yeah, bowling along like we're in some kind of movie or something. Me in the middle, Super to my right and Paul at the other side, we walk in slow motion as an awesome super-cool soundtrack plays in the background. Under the bridge connecting each side of the school we head for the entrance to the main hall. Barging through the swing-doors, we enter and look around at the empty dancefloor. Disco lights shining brightly, the cheap twin-disco-deck sound system plays pop tunes, all "rising sun" and "my generation" bullshit. Various groups of kids hang around the edges of the hall while the teachers huddle in the corners, drinking orange squash out of plastic cups, no doubt spiked with Vodka or something, just enough to get them through the couple of hours of purgatory. We walk in and all eyes are on us, not surprising though, we look clean, crisp and tidy. Yeah man, I can't remember what I'm wearing but Paul has a sharp dark blue suit, white shirt and a thin cut bright red tie. Super has brown flared trousers and a purple silk shirt unbuttoned to his belly button, which I think belonged to his mum back in the nineteen-fifties, given the size of those fly-away collars. On the prowl like young lions, we roam around making sure everyone sees us. Paul gets chatting to a girl in the year above, and, as quick as anything, they're kissing and he's grabbing her arse. Full of confidence, he'll chat to anyone and everyone, no matter who or how old they are. Later in the evening, we get drunk, yeah man, I almost forgot about that. A few older kids have a bottle of gin, I think, so we get pissed up on gin and orange, tasted like complete and utter shit but got us fucked up. After a few cups of that disgusting crap, I'm swaying as the hall spins round and around while the chart hits of the day echo and phase in the background. Pissed-up confident, we're world beaters, untouchable, indestructible...

Damn.

Until what happened, I felt untouchable, full of confidence, king of the world. I wish what happened didn't have happen, but I know it did, and all I feel now is regret and doom, sadness and loneliness. All I do is sit here listening to Him, reminiscing the good old days through rose tinted Ray-Bans...

Anyway, back to the disco.

Pissed up, a few of us make our way through to the back of the hall into the main part of the school. Dark and dangerous, quiet and secretive, like a magnet drawing us in, we find the storeroom where the stock for the tuck shop is locked away. Only one thing to do in those circumstances, you know it, Super kicks the door in and we rob the shit out of it. Grunting, sweating and frothing at the mouth, we're in hysterics as he kicks the door something like twenty times until it bursts open. Once inside, we stuff our fat faces to the verge of puking, then form a human conveyor-belt, passing the goods into the hall. Ten minutes later, the disco's full of kids eating chocolate bars and drinking fizzy pop. The teachers must have thought we were deranged!

Still, happy times man, happy times.

Me, Super and Paul were tight. Every day after school and at weekends too we hang-out together wandering around the town, "town" being the centre of Brixton around the market and Electric Avenue. In and out of all the shops and round and around the market stalls, we'd dare each other to shoplift any old crap, fruit, washing line pegs, anything and everything. I got caught once by a stall-monger who chases me down for ages like a long-distance Ethiopian runner or something. Dodging in and out of parked cars, I trip over a curb and he lands on top of me, gives me a hiding and drags me back home. When he tells Momma what I've done, she claps me around the head and sends me to my room. I'm not allowed to hang around with Paul anymore after that, a bad influence on me apparently. 'Listen now bwai,' Momma yells. 'Don't be hanging around with that wretched lickle white bwai, ya' hear.' I think she secretly knows we still hang out, I see it in her eyes and a wry smile when she's scolding me. So, rather than come around and knock for me, we meet at the end of my road at the corner of Atlantic Road.

During the summer of the World Cup, I start running errands for the local bad-man drug dealer, Cristobal Campbell, who we know as Crissy. Strolling around the

Frontline shaft-like with his dreads bound up with a red, gold and green sweatband, he wears a long black leather coat and a proper rude boy swagger. Everyone on the Frontline knows and respects him, young kids like me, fellow rude-boys, shop-keepers, market-stall mongers even mums pushing babies in pushchairs know him. Yeah man he is "the" Frontline-man, the original gangster, the yard-man, the rude-boy protecting the neighbourhood, keeping everyone in check.

The "Frontline", shit man, I haven't called it that for ages. We are at war, you see. The urban youth of South London versus the establishment, the local council, the Police and the government. While the whole of London is the battleground, the square mile around Railton Road, from Brixton Market to Coldharbour Lane to Herne Hill is the actual Frontline, the trenches of urban warfare, the no-mans land of hope.

Crissy gets the youngsters, or "pickney youts" as he calls us to run down the shops for him, picking up a ginger beer or a half ounce of shag. 'Keep the change my-yout,' he says in his super-cool way. I don't accept that though, nah man, no way, I'll kiss my teeth, shake my head and tell him "ten bob". What's that worth nowadays, maybe fifty pence? So, we barter for a while until he gives me a little bit more, or, of even greater value, a pat on the head. Little old me negotiating with the baddest bad-man drug dealer on the Frontline, can you believe it? I reckon he likes my front, maybe I remind him of himself when he was a kid. After a while, I start running proper errands for him, between his flat on the Angel Town estate and the Windsor Pub on Leesons Road, fetching and carry brown paper bags, always brown paper bags. Crissy has a single golden rule, no looking inside, never, and I never did. But, even at twelve years old, I'm the original rude-boy Devious Dee, so "never" doesn't really mean never, not forever-never. I never look, not even a peak until the day of the World Cup final, England versus Germany. I remember it like it's yesterday, yeah man, what a day. It's funny what you can remember, what you can see and smell and taste, what you feel. Warm and hazy and beautiful …

MOMMA'S HOUSE
SALTOUN ROAD
BRIXTON, LONDON
JULY, 1966

As usual, I leave the house early. Up, dressed, bowl of cornflakes and I'm out the door heading into town to meet Paul and Super at the Record Shack in Brixton Market. Gets to the end of my road and I spot Crissy, probably coming home from a late-night dance or all-night card game or something. After a quick "what're you doing out so early" chit-chat, he sends me on an errand. No problem, I reckon I can do it quickly and be back in time to meet Paul and Super afterward. Twenty minutes later, brown paper bag collected, I'm leaving Angel Town with my head down looking as normal and inconspicuous as possible. Making my way back to the Frontline and the Windsor pub, I see Paul and Super up ahead. Bored of waiting, they come looking for me and straight away they're on me with a barrage of questions. What's in the bag? What do I do on these errands? What's in the bag? What's Crissy really like? What's in the bag? Why haven't I ever looked? On and on and on, they rabbit on like a pair of old women. I play it cool though, errands are something and nothing especially for a rube-boy like me. Secretly though, I'm loving the fact I'm the big man, Crissy's lackey, future line-man in the making. Stopping just before the Windsor Pub, just at the corner of Shakespeare and Leesons Road, I know what's coming, of course I do, I've known it's coming from the very first day I started running errands. Yeah man, I've known we'd end up here, at this very moment in time, fate or something. Paul dares me, the mother fucking snake. Crissy trusts me, tells me never to look, and I don't want to mess with him, no way, so I'll never look. He trusts me and everyone knows it, gives me some status, some importance, some meaning. "Look, der go Crissy's pickney yout", they'll say as I pass by with no problems and a rude-boy bounce. But, Paul being Paul, goes on and on and on, dare-dare-fucking-dare. Super's goading me too, calling me a pussy-hole and dickhead. Both of them chat on and on and on, relentlessly goading me, goad-goad-goad. The pair of utter wankers.

But, what else can I do?

I'm weak and feeble and untrustworthy.

Even way back then.

Gently, delicately and carefully I open it. Heads down we peer in. Holy fuck, jam-packed full of dark green weed, moist and beautifully fragrant. Scared I might drop it, it might jump out or the air might damage it in some way, I scrunch it closed straight away. I've always secretly known what's inside, but, at that very moment, I'm scared and excited at the same time. Scared by the gravity of it all, excited because I know I've crossed the line. Paul says we should take some, reckons Crissy would never know, especially if we take just a little. We have a right old barney there and then, right on the street. Half ten in the morning, holding a large bag of weed and we have a stand up argument about ripping off the baddest man on the planet. The more they argue, the more I refuse. You know what though, deep down inside I want to skank the shit out of Crissy and show him I'm not scared of him, that I'm my own man, someone he can rely on and respect.

Five minutes later…

Into the pub, I head towards the back and Crissy's usual table. Dropping the bag off as normal, I collect my keep-the-change-for-going cash plus the all-important pat on the head. Nice and steady, I head back out of the pub and, once out of sight, I'm walking quicker, then jogging, then running a full-on sprint. Running so fast, I get a stitch so bad and feel like puking. Eventually I catch up with Super and Paul at Shakespeare Road, well away from prying eyes, just under the railway arch. Turning my pocket out, I've got a golf-ball sized batch of weed, maybe a bit less. While I'm in the pub, Super blags a cigarette from an old chap on Railton Road and Paul buys some matches and Rizzla from the corner shop. We head straight to the lush greenness of Brockwell Park, find a tree and plot underneath. Resting back in the shade of the midday sun, we're secretive and undercover as Super attempts to roll a joint. "Attempts" being the key word here, it's the worst spliff you've ever seen, bent up and loose, a total disgrace, but still, a spliff, just about. He says he's seen one of his many "uncles" rolling a joint a few months ago, when he peeks into the kitchen from the top of the stairs to spy on his Momma. In silence, we sit for ages just staring at it, not really believing we're about to smoke some weed like big men, at twelve years old. Eventually, Super sparks it up. Inhaling long and deep, he coughs his lungs up and heaves to be sick. Smoke's coming out of everywhere, his nose, his mouth, his ears, it's fucking hilarious. We take turns, not really inhaling to begin with, but, by the end, we're smoking it for real. Coughing and falling about the place, we're pissing ourselves laughing while the world whirls by. By the time we smoke the second spliff, we can't stand up. Little kids playing in the park, we just roll around on the grass, dizzy and giggly, giddy and happy, free, with no worries or stress, life's nothing short of golden. Although innocent and naïve, turns out, right there, on that sunny afternoon, we took a leap from the top of the tower-block of fate and left our childhood behind. No turning back, we've taken our first steps into a cynical and sordid hyperspace. Yeah, unbeknown to us, at that very moment, we commenced our journey through space and time toward our destiny.

As the afternoon drifts on, stoned out of our minds, we walk into town and around the market, trying to mellow out from the weed induced brain-fuck. That doesn't work though, we just laugh and giggle our way around, joyful tears running down our aching cheeks. Ready for the England match, everyone's in party mood, pissed-up, happy, chatting to each other with a community feeling of real togetherness. Union Jacks fly proudly everywhere as well as bunting wafting across the streets. Yeah man, the "Union Jack" was a flag of the people back then, until the National Front get hold of it, raping and bastardising it.

Heading back to my house to watch the match, we sneak Paul straight into the front room, avoiding Momma who always stays in the kitchen. We watch the tail end of the first half while Pops sits in his chair supping his brown ale. Usually working nights, I only ever saw him at tea-time before he leaves for work. Normally, we're deadly quiet during the day while he slept, with us tip-toeing around, whispering like ninjas. Soon as he gets up ready for his night shift, we're full of life, full of noise and going crazy. He must have thought we're like that all the time, a house full of maniacs or something. Throughout the World Cup he refuses to watch any England matches, 'on principle' he says. He and Momma used to argue all the time about one day going back home, he wants to, Momma doesn't. Once Jamaica gained independence a few years before, he wanted to go back saying it'd changed, less poverty, fewer troubles, more opportunities. Momma's happy here though, she likes her life, loves her job, even if it's just mopping up other folks shit and sick in the hospital. Even now, when I close my eyes, I still see Mommas face smiling at me with love and warmth and joy and awe and tenderness…

Damn.

We're in the front room watching the match while Momma and Aunt Gertrude are in the kitchen yelling for us to hold it down and stop the "bloodclat foolishness". Aunt Gertrude has little baby Delroy there too, he must be maybe six months old or something, but man, he screams and cries all the time. Momma must have been pregnant with Marlon then. Anyway, when England score the winner, man, we're leaping around, hugging each other and going mental, Pops too. Chasing outside, the whole neighbourhood's out, screaming and cheering and running around like lunatics. Kids and grown-ups alike, everyone's happy, joyful, exploding with pride. We end up doing a massive conga up and down the street for ages and ages.

An unbelievable day start to finish.

We break up from school a week or so later for the summer holidays and split our time between hanging around the Frontline and going "up town" to London's west-end, Carnaby Street and Soho. Yeah man, we stroll around taking in the sights and enjoy being young free and single. Super scams whoever he can, I eye-up the fit Mod girls and Paul checks out the latest fashions in the super-cool boutique shops. I like the Mods, yeah, soul-boys who shave their hair off and get into reggae, somehow becoming known as 'rude-boys'. I don't get the Rockers though, dirty, grubby greasers into crap music, fighting and glue-sniffing. I carry on working for Crissy throughout the summer and we have a nice little business going, yeah man. I'm running errands, fetching and carrying his stash, while at the same time skimming some for ourselves. We smoke some and sell the rest to the other kids hanging around the Frontline. Yeah man, we're selling to kids way older than us but, with Super ready to deal with any problems, and everyone knowing I juggle for Crissy, nobody dares mess with us.

But, we both know, all good things must come to an end.

The day Crissy found out about our little enterprise, man, a dark day for sure. Everything changed then, forever…

CRISTOBAL CAMPBELLS FLAT
GABRIEL HOUSE, LOUGHBOROUGH ESTATE, BRIXTON, LONDON
LATE 1960's

As usual, I go collect the brown paper bag from Angel Town and, as usual, I go through the same bullshit routine. Something like this…

Bowl through the estate, big man on the scene yeah.

Nod to the rude-boys hanging around outside the stairwell.
Easy-nah-man.
Climb the stairs to the sixth floor.
Head along the corridor.
Quick look either way, making sure I'm not followed.
Knock-knock-knock on the door.
Wait for ages.
Knock again.
'Who dat?' the fit-as-fuck-woman-with-no-name yells.
'It's Devon,' I whisper.
Then silence.
I knock again.
'Who dare?'
'T'cha, it's Devon. Devon from Railton,' I whisper, louder.
'Who?'
'Fucking hell, Devon. Crissy sent me,' I yell.
Then more silence.
'You on your own bwai?' she says, getting serious.
'Nah, me got a whole heap of Babylon out here with me.'
That's the code.
If I'm with the Police, it's unlikely I'll say as much, so, if I say "nah, I'm on my own," she'll know there's a problem, double bolt the door and fling the stash over the balcony.
Clever really.
Door unlocked, she shows me into the kitchen and I stare first at her perky breasts, then her shapely arse as she disappears into the front room. Late teens, maybe early twenties, she's got a shoulder length loose curl afro and a great body. Tidy, very tidy. All summer she's wearing white micro-shorts with navy blue trim and a skimpy pink vest top, showing off her toned stomach and cute as fuck bellybutton. Shit, I'm like a dog with two dicks, spunking all over the ceiling in my bedroom thinking about her. Anyway, she comes back in with the brown paper bag and asks me if I want a drink. Without fail, every time, I'll always say yeah, just to carry on eyeing her up. She smiles before fixing me up a Sarsaparilla. I drink it slowly while she stands there

staring at me drinking. Yeah man, I'm staring right back at her all the while thinking about her sucking my dick while I play with her clit. Eventually, she shows me out, telling me to 'be safe nah bwai', and 'go see Cristobal right away.'

I never found out who she was, not even her name. Maybe Crissy's woman or daughter or something but either way, she's fucking fit, and my first real love.

So anyway, back to that day.

THE day.

Super and Paul wait outside the flat in the stairwell as I have wet dreams about little-miss-micro-shorts. As usual, we hunch under the stinking urine-ridden stairwell, full of skagg-head/glue-head remains. Scorched tin-foil used to burn heroin with loads of half burnt matches and scrunched-up-rock-hard bags of industrial adhesive. Taking our share of weed, being careful never take too much, we set off for the Windsor Pub. Through the door, I bounce over to Crissy, showing him my entire repertoire of maximum confidence and coolness. With a cloud of thick white smoke hanging above his head, he's sitting next to a younger guy I've never seen before. A little nod and I push the bag onto the table nudging the half drunken pint of Guinness aside. As normal, he leans over to give me the "keep-the-change-for-going" cash, but, instead of dropping some coins onto the table, his face switches. Screwed up and angry, frowning and scary, he grabs my wrist tight, like a vice. When I close my eyes, even now, I can see his face, his eyebrows vee down below his bulging forehead while his top lip stretches across his teeth. The harder he grips, the more scared I am and the more I shit myself. I feel dizzy and sick and my mind spins as dé-jà-vu thoughts whizz around me.

'Ya' think you can rob me, pickney?' he seethes.

Shit.

I'm just a kid, he can't mash me up, he can't hit a kid, surely not. What about the witnesses, the old boys playing backgammon or the drunken Irish guy always propping up the bar drinking stout and black? Grabbed by scruff of the neck, I'm pulled in between him and the younger guy. He's late teens, muscular with a slim face and protruding cheek bones with a white boy roman nose and the beginnings of a moustache. He looks like a villain and, as it turns out, he's indeed a massive villain, the biggest of them all to be honest. A few years later, "Samurai Sam" as he became to be known, will become the daddy of all gangsters, the grandfather of evil, the governor general of crime, the original Uzi carrying, mother fucking, fuck-you-up-in-a-split-second-never-think-twice Yardie. Holy shit, such a bad man he'll fuck Al Capone in the arse then slit his throat. The Kray twins? He'll make them fuck each other in the ass before smashing their heads in with a claw-hammer…

'Now, bwai,' Crissy yells in a stage whisper. 'Sit there and think pickney, contemplate the situation.' The coolest man in the universe, he softly grabs his pint and sips in silence. Looking towards the old-boys playing backgammon over the other side of the bar, I know I'm invisible, nobody can see me, nobody can save me, nobody can rescue me. Finishing his drink with an over-pronounced "ah", Crissy stares deep into me. 'You know what I'm chatting about?' she asks with a serious tone.

I come clean straight away, no point in lying, I know he knows. Looking disappointed, gutted even, he asks me why, so I tell him, all of it, one hundred percent of the truth. Nodding away, he laughs an exaggerated laugh. I'm smiling too, I'm getting away with it, he might even be proud of me. Suddenly, he stops laughing and switches back to his serious face. 'Here me now pickney, respect fa' ya juggling and ting, t'cha, reminds me of me when I a youth.'

'Crissy, honestly…' I plead.

'Hush-nah-man, can't have ya' teething from me,' his voice is deep and angry. 'If I let that pass, where will it end?'

'But Crissy…'

'T'cha, every wanna-be rude bwai will be at it, and a whole heap of tribulation flung my way.'

Frozen, I can't speak.

'So, I got to take action yeah, got be seen to be dealing with it, you understand?' He looks deadly serious, more serious than I've ever seen him before.

I nod an inevitable nod.

'You got to learn a hard lesson, son. You understand?'

Tears well in my eyes but I force myself not to cry. I can't be seen to be a pussy in front of him.

'You know who this is?' he says, nodding slowly towards the young guy. 'Him named Sam-you-ell, you hear of him?'

Tongue swelling, mouth dry, I shrug my shoulders and shake my head.

'Nah-man, course you haven't, he discrete yeah, a professional. He deals with problems, problems, like you.'

Like a magnet, my eyes are drawn back to the youth. Primed, ready to go, ready for anything, he's nodding in agreement with his introduction. Trying hard to resist, somehow our eyes meet. Dead eyes, holy shit, they're deep and dark and glazed over like a sharks. Reaching down beneath his seat, he shows me a massive sword, glistening in the half-light of the pub. Captivated by it, it holds my gaze. Beautiful, elegant, and majestic, I can't help but stare. It speaks to me you know, properly speaks in a whispering angel voice: 'I will be gentle, oh son of Adam… I will be swift and smooth… my ice-cold sleekness will glide through the air and bring you peace…' Tripping my tits off, I turn back to Crissy. I want to say sorry, promise never to do anything like this again, plead for mercy but I can't. All I can muster is 'please.'

What a pussy.

They both laugh. Wankers.

'Which one?' Sam growls, grabbing my arm. 'Pick one.'

I can't speak.

He looks at Crissy, then back at me. 'Rasclat tea-leaf, pick one yeah, or I'll do both,' he says.

'Cristobal, please, I promise.'

Crissy nods. Thank God, he understands. 'Devon, son,' he says, placing his hand on my knee all gentle and calm and caring. 'Pick one of your tea-leaf brothers to take a beating, or Sam-you-ell will deal with you quick time.'

'Pick, fool, or I'll stripe ya' bloodclat face,' Sam continues, raw aggression filling the end of his sentence.

Relieved I'm not having an arm cut off, there's no way can I choose between Paul and Super, who can do that?

'I can't man, I can't choose.' I say.

Leaning in, his head smashes into mine. Stars spin around my eyes as my head bounces off Crissy's shoulder.

'Easy-rude boy, calm it down yeah,' Crissy says looking around the pub, everyone staring deep into their pints.

'Tea'f, choose-nah,' Sam growls, impatient and angry.

'I can't choose, man. Do me, I'll take a beating,' I plead, offering myself up in the hope they'll look kindly on me for being brave and give me a pass. They both laugh though, loudly, like I've suggested I stick my head up my own arse. Crissy tells me I'm brave, but, I still got to choose.

A minute later, I leave through the swing doors. Turning right, Paul and Super are waiting at the end of the road, as they normally do. Sam-you-ell follows a few paces behind. As we approach, I mouth 'run', but they both look at me like I'm a weirdo. Sam barges me out of the way and belts Super in the face, maybe five or six times. Lightning fast hooks and upper-cuts, he's devastatingly quick man.

'What did I do, what did I do?' Super yells, trying to fight back. To be fair, he catches Sam with a jab but, shit, that just makes things worse. Grabbing the back of his head with one hand, he smashes Super in the face with the other before flinging him to the ground. I try pulling at his arm but he backhands me, telling me to 'fuck-arf.' Ten seconds later, Super's curled up on the floor, bruised and beaten, whining like an injured puppy-dog. Sam-you-ell turns to Paul, then me and says if there's a next time, he'll take "his steel" to us. He goes on to say if we want to sell any weed, we must buy it from Crissy, just like anyone else. Eye-balling us for what seems like an age, he turns and walks back towards the Windsor, bowling down the road calm and super-cool.

Scared and petrified and in awe all at the same time, my heart pounds. Blagging it, I tell them who Sam-you-ell is and say he wanted to meet the up and coming youth, and I had no idea he was going to do what he did. Super's up for plotting his revenge, fantasising about waiting in the shadows late one night with a hammer and caving his skull in before setting fire to his dead body.

The crazy-fool.

From that day, I still juggle for Crissy, but never stole from him, ever. Instead of thieving our stash, we buy an eighth of an ounce at a time and sell it on. Crissy never mentioned it again, almost like it never happened but I still see Sam-you-ell on the Frontline now and again and he'll throw me a nod and a wink and ask if I'm 'alright'. Yeah, we under Crissy's wing now, Sam's too, and everyone knows it. That day, I promised myself never to cross Crissy, or, more importantly, Sam-you-ell ever again, and I didn't.

Well, sort of didn't…

2. Rumble in the Jungle

"All you suckers, everybody. Stop talking and pay attention. I told you, I told you all that I am the greatest of all time. Never again make me the underdog. I didn't dance, I told you I didn't dance. I just wanted him to lose all his power."

Cassius Clay

THE KITCHEN
17, HAMILTON HOUSE
GREENWICH, LONDON
LATE SUMMER, 1989

Echoes of kids playing outside in the street merge with the reggae and calypso tunes echoing between the bay-windowed terraced townhouses with steps leading up to each front door. The pungent smell of Mommas curried goat tingles my nostrils as my thoughts drift like soft fluffy clouds crawling slowly across a hazy-blue late summer sky. I float back to the clichés of youth, back to simple, innocent times. Relaxed and light-headed, trippy almost, (in a good way), the suns beautifully golden rays shine down and warm my face, massaging my aching brain. It's warmer back then, not like now where it's cold and dark and shit, confused and jumbled up and all gone wrong…

  Pupils gradually adjusting to the new reality, my eyes open fully. Dirty-grey net curtains hang lifeless across the half dirty/half steamed-up windows. Through the window, I can just about make out the river Thames winding west towards the City of London the unmistakable spires of Tower Bridge then on toward Big Ben in the distance. I see the dome of Saint Pauls Cathedral casting a shadow on "the City" with its spivs and wide-boys, just like shit-cunt Paul. Freezing cold and shaking, my arms wrap tightly around my body. It doesn't help though. Chaos and craziness isn't me, especially after what happened. Inside this flat is safety, outside, in the stark, cold, harsh reality of London, in the no-one-knows-your-name-or-gives-a-shit world, it's the opposite of safety, the epitome of threat and harm. The formula is easy, inside equals control, outside equals chaos. Sanity versus reality, the most simple of simple dilemmas. Too much shit going on outside, unpredictable things and unreliable people. Too many "variables" as Paul would say. Mistakes from the past hiding in shadowy doorways and sneaky-peaky eyes in dark stairwells are ready to test me and take their revenge. Fuck that, better off inside with him than outside on my own.

"Boo-fucking-hoo. Just listen to yourself," the Interrogator says, scornfully. *"Scared of your own shadow."*

He's right, he's always fucking right. I don't give a shit though, I'm not going outside, no chance. Fuck knows what's out there. I'm staying here. My eyes are drawn to the hallway and the front door. The couple of inches of council issue wood and simple brass lock is the membrane between the safety of the inside and the Pandora's-box of madness on the outside.

"You actually think you have a choice to be here," the Interrogator asks, no doubt rhetorically.

I do have a choice, of course I do. All I got left is "choice" or free-will or whatever you call it. I can leave, if I really want to.

"Yeah? Try it, see what happens," the Interrogator threatens, slow and meaningfully.

I believe him, he must be feared. Must hide it though, can't let him see my fear otherwise he'll feast on it and devour my soul. Even so, he can't talk to me like that, I'm a grown man of thirty-four years, an adult, not some snotty nose little kid. But, all this posturing with him is tiring, exhausting and mother fucking draining. I close my eyes and he's gone.

"Oi, wake up cock sucker," the Interrogator nudges. *'No time for sleeping or day-dreaming,"* he teases. *"You're just fucked up mate. Fucked. Up. Accept it, deal with it."*

Yeah, that about sums me up. My whole entire life condensed into two simple words, "fucked" and "up". Things were good for a while though, yeah, really good. King of the world, master of the universe, I had money, cars, girls, respect, meaning, but chucked it all away and fucked everything up. Things got out of hand, got too big too soon, I couldn't control any of what happened, just too complicated, like a spider's web, all tangled up, sticky and scary. Shit just happens, like it's always meant to happen, like my life's on rails. The railway tracks from Herne Hill back to Brixton, I can't get off, can't change direction. You can't change the future, can't alter your fate, your destiny. What's meant to be will be, and all that crap.

"Fate? Gets you off the hook, all convenient and tidy, right?" the Interrogator says, conclusively and definitively. *"But it's not like that is it? YOU fucked things up and now you're in here with ME going through this SHIT,"* he spits, fatalism stretching through his voice.

It wasn't me, man, none of it.

Shit just happens.

"You could have stopped at any time, just walked away. But, you're weak and feeble and fucking fragile," the Interrogator says, crushing me with words.

Weak and feeble and fragile, yeah, maybe now, but, back in the day, back in the old-school, shit man, I'm the man, THE man! Bad boy Devon, Devious Dee in the house. Not bad meaning bad, bad meaning good, in a Run DMC way.

Let me tell you...

Crissy and Samurai Sam continue to run things on the Frontline, Sam more than Crissy actually. Yeah, he becomes a legend, "Samurai Sam", king of the Yardies, striding around Railton Road handing out beatings to all and sundry. He becomes the top man, the most feared and respected rude boy in the whole of London. Crissy is the figurehead for sure, the Chairman or non-Executive Director, but Sam, well, he's the Chief Executive, the go getter, the main fucking man. I still see the fit girl at Crissy's flat for a while, but eventually, like everyone in my life, she's gone. After her a new guy about Sam's age begins running things, a Rasta named Claude. An always-serious-never-smiling dreadlock guy, he's cold man, cold as ice, all about the business, pure business. We keep the same door-knocking routine as before, but there's no sarsaparilla, no softness, no caring, no hot pants and definitely no perky breasts. Claude's all about the money, and he don't trust me one bit, I see it in his eyes, yeah man. Looking at me like he wants to pull my arms off and launch me over the balcony, there's a weirdness about him. Demented eyes, his pupils are sort of off-centre and ever so slightly cross-eyed. Claude can say "fuck you" without uttering a single word. Behind his eyes, he has a sort of inevitable aura, like he knows when his time's due to come, like he's in control of everyone and everything. Little did I know back then, our futures are intertwined and inextricably linked.

Dreadlocks and gangsters aside, as the years roll by, we built a nice little business, Me, Super and Paul. We deal to the youngsters around the Frontline while Sam serves everyone else. We got a load of regular customers so have cash, girls and clothes galore. We are unstoppable, we own the future, at least we did back then. Yeah, back then was a time of hope, real hope, even for the likes of me and Super. It wasn't ever about black or white though, nah, it's about rich versus poor, the haves versus have-nots, the inner cities versus the suburbs.

The nineteen-seventies, damn, what a fucked-up decade for sure. Not like the sixties, nah, the sixties were the best, everything changed in the sixties. Music, colour television, Concorde, Carnaby Street and the Kings Road, Woodstock, Martin Luther King getting a peace prize, the Beetles, Twiggy and Mary Quant mini-skirts, (yeah man), Hippies, LSD and Man on the god damn Moon. Imagine, walking on the moon and looking back towards earth, seeing literally all of mankind in one blink, being able to see the entire history of our species with just one look? How do you deal with that? Some say it's a hoax, a massive piss take just to get one up on the Russians, but, man, that is one big lie to keep secret.

Anyway, the seventies are different.

The Beatles breaking up, Hendrix topping himself, Glam-fucking Rock? South African racialism, Cambodia and Poll-Pot whoever the fuck that is, killing all manner of man with the Americans supporting him. Shit man, the whole fucking world's fucked. All the hope and excitement of the sixties fade away, even Carnaby Street changes from genuine coolness to superficial bandwagon make believe coolness in a can. The Sixties stretched possibilities whereas the seventies sprung it right back to where it was before, a negative reaction to the positive action. Mods are out of fashion, so they crop their hair and called themselves 'rude-boys'. Paul does the same, grade two all over he said. Super takes the piss telling him to black himself up like the Minstrels or something. The funny thing, well, the sad, almost tragic thing is most of these mod-come-rude-boys will eventually turn into football hooligans or racist national-front fronters. The Irish troubles are all over the news too, with their religious tribulations. We sent the army into Belfast to keep the peace and they sent bombs and mayhem over here to mainland England, a proper fuck-off-and-mind-your-own-business message if ever I heard one. Around that time, a few Irish kids join our year at school. Talking with a weird accent, eye-this and bee-jesus that, the Irish girls are fascinated by me and Super, wanting to touch our skin and feel our hair. Can you believe it? We're like rock stars or something. Apparently, the Police over there turned bad, start smashing up the Catholics, or Protestants? I can't remember, but I know they both believe in Jesus and in God, the same God, the exact same God the Jewish and the Muslims pray too as well. The same God, yet they're fighting each other and blowing shit up? Where in the bible does it talk about blowing shit up?

Blowing shit up? Blows my fucking mind more like.

Hell, hark at me, on my soap box, giving it large, putting the world to rights. Bit late for that now though, I've no idea about this religion bullshit or any thoughts of God. Nah, I know I'm heading deep-south, down below, partying for eternity with the prince of darkness, the king of evil, the devil himself.

Where did I get to?

DEAN STREET
SOHO, LONDON
EARLY 1970's

Saturday nights, we do our normal tour of Soho till late, looking into the red-light porno shops and the pretty girls for sale in the part-open doorways. By the time we decide to head home, the tube trains have stopped running, so we hail a taxi. But, they not stopping for three little shits like us, no way. Super suggests we walk the couple of miles down to the Elephant and Castle where we can get a proper taxi-cab, and not one of these Hackney Carriage black-cabs that dominate the west-end. Walking across London Bridge, just our luck there's no taxi's whatsoever, so, we continue heading south for about a mile or so, eventually passing an old-fashioned pub. Well after closing time, it's heaving with a proper lock-in-after-hours-knees-up going on. The George and Dragon or something, the outside is tiled floor to head height with dark green tiles, with frosted windows above. A typical London pub, apart from the union jack in the window, we both know what that means. Instinctively we increase our stride and pick up the pace. An Elvis tune blares out through the doorway with loads of folk inside singing along. Just as we go by, we hear some ranting and raving so turn around to see a group of cockney geezers hanging out of the doorway hollering in our direction. One of them steps forward and shouts "fark-off back home on ya' banana-boat," or something. Super, as normal, gets angry and aggressive, brave and manly. Having spent the evening eyeing up the pretty girls in Soho, he's frustrated and wound up, gritting his teeth and clenching his fists. Meanwhile, the pissed up publionians are shouting and jeering and making monkey noises. Paul tells us to keep walking and pulls us on but Super's not having any of it, nah, he's shouting back, motioning them forward, goading them on. Then, glistening through the dark night-time sky, a pint-glass floats through the air in a perfect, beautiful super-slow-motion parabolic arc. More follow, lots more. Like glass magnets, we're leaping around, dodging them as they smash around our feet. A bit of a joke to begin with, them flinging and us dodging, I even hear a few of them laughing as we theatrically leap around. It'd be funny, if it wasn't so messed up. More and more pissed-up folk spill out of the pub, but, this time, they're younger blokes with red-braces, Fred Perry T-shirts and Doc Martin boots, stereotypical national fronters. Then, it gets serious. They charge toward us and we have it away quick-time down the road then through an estate and in and out of the railway-arched side streets. I hear them shouting and screaming while more and more of them appear from nowhere. The whole estate has awoken from it's suburban coma and are chasing us. No clue where are, we just keep running and running. Me and Paul are sweating and panting while Super, with zero effort, keeps up with us while laughing his head off. Eventually, we turn onto Newington Causeway and see the beacon of civilisation, a late-night bus. Chasing it down, we jump on the open platform at the back and head straight upstairs to give the chasing mass of hate the finger and moony our arses through the back window. Picking up speed, the national front-fuck-wits fade into the distance and we breathe a sigh of relief. Twenty minutes later we jump off at Stockwell and walk back to Brixton from there.

What a night.

I had enough troubles with the fronters around this time, in fact, I sort of made my name on the Frontline because of them. Yeah yeah, I totally get the irony. In the last year of secondary school, I must have been maybe sixteen years old and everyone's hyper with rumours the National Front are planning a march through Brixton. They're living a lie, the fronters, a glossy veneer with a massive deceit inside. They march under the banner "against racism and fascism" whereas in fact they're marching for racism, not against it. They understood exactly what they're doing, oh yeah, real calculated and clever. They rope in local church and council leaders too, make it look respectable, real and genuine. The rest of the crowd are disaffected or un-informed dickheads marching like brainless ants, looking for anything to give them purpose to their dull, piss-boring lives. Turns out, the march wasn't through Brixton but through London's west-end, near Charing Cross station and Trafalgar Square. Me, Super and Paul plus a few others decide to go up there and see what it's about. Once there, we see swarms of Police standing around, nervous and tetchy, directing the marching folk down the Strand into Trafalgar Square. The road has barriers all along the edge, with lots of citizens and tourists standing around watching. Barging our way to the front, we stand at the edge of the pavement and sense a palpable air of anticipation. A weird nervous energy builds around us while in the distance we can hear a base-drum banging and a rumble of rowdy crowds yelling and jeering and screaming. Coming into view, I see a massive crowd, Roman Empire style, crawling towards us with Union Jacks and other banners waving above their heads. It's so loud, the noise is scary to be honest. As they go by, we start shouting and booing, joe-public citizens and tourists too. The marching hoards shout back, pure hate and disgust in their voices. Then, trouble. Scuffles at first, then it escalates and ultra-violence kicks off big time. Police, fronters, citizens, kids, tourists, shop-keepers, taxi-drivers, newspaper vendors, homeless tramps, everyone, literally everyone's rampaging. We throw some punches and a few kicks before getting out of there quick time.

Heavy shit man. Apparently, a man got killed.

Heading back to the safety of Brixton, we come out of the train station and bounce through the market onto Electric Avenue. Up ahead in the distance we spot a group of white kids, maybe seven or eight of them, about our age, each of them looking like stereotypically fronters. Seeing us approach, they spread across the pavement. The lad in the middle, looks like their leader, nods his head, stretches his chest out and steps forward. 'You lot should fark-off the other way,' he says, looking us up and down. Three of us versus seven of them? Even though I can handle myself and of course we got Super, still tough odds. A surge of adrenaline pumps through me. Fuck it, if a tear up is necessary, then bring it on. I'm not about to turn around or cross the street, fuck that, this is our neighbourhood and we run tings! Turning to Super, his eyes are practically popping out of his head, he's totally up for it, of course he is, he lives for this kind of shit. I look at Paul and to be fair, even he looks up for it. We continue toward them with our chests bursting through our t-shirts when one of them, not the leader, but a big lumbering cocksucker bolts forward. Ugly as fuck in a red and black checked shirt with ripped jeans, he steams in but Super steps up and chins him with a devastating right cross. The best punch I've ever seen, a proper Joe Lewis style windmill of fuck-you, a lightning bolt of angry, a storm of Incredible-Hulk strength. The lumbering cocksuckers head cracks to the side, knees buckle and he's on the floor, totally out cold. The others stand in silence, jaws dropping, looking shit scared because they've just realised, they've made a massive mistake. Super stands motionless, guard up in southpaw stance, nodding his head and smiling. Soaking it up for a few seconds, he starts screaming 'come on, come on then.' Their leader, McMahon, I learnt his name when the Police came to Mommas house the next day to question me about it, stands firm though. Brave for sure, but equally, stupid as fuck. 'You and me, straighter, here and now,' he shouts, pointing at me. Volcano's burning in his eyes and veins popping out of his neck, Super edges further forward but I pull him back. Mister brave and/or stupid has offered me out, not him.

I can't back down.

Wanting to land the first blow, I launch a flying kick and get him in the stomach and we land together on the pavement. Grappling and rolling around, he's strong, strong as an Ox. Paul and Super are shouting me on as the fronters shout for him. Eventually, I'm on top, straddling him, pinning his arms down to the floor. Face screwed up, pure hate in his eyes, the dirty bastard spits in my face. Next thing I know I'm on my side, then on my back and he's on top of me grunting like a dog head butting me in the face. I'm getting done, big time. Panicking, I reach down and somehow grab his balls. Squealing like a flea-bitten dirty dog, he rolls off onto his side and we both struggle to our feet, staring at each other. Bell ringing, we're back in our corners, end of round one. Grabbing hold of me, Paul wipes the blood from my nose and tells me to be brave while Punching my arm, Super tells me to stop being a pussy and to deal with him quick time because his Momma will have his tea ready by now and he's starving hungry. A crowd has gathered across the street, mostly rude-boys from Railton Road and a few shop keepers. I know I got to big it up, grit my teeth and kick the living shit out of this racist motherfucker.

Seconds out, round two…

We fight for ages, a series of quick battles then we regroup. Round after round, he won't be beaten, nor will I. We end up along Coldharbour Lane near the Somerleyton Estate. With my eye swollen and nose bloody, he's mashed up with lumps and bumps all round his head. Grabbing a milk bottle, he smashes it on the wall near the entrance walk-way and smiles. Damn, I'm not getting stabbed, not there and not by him, so I look around for a tool. Somebody, god knows who, passes me a tennis racket, can you believe it, a fucking tennis racket? Lurching forward, I lash him across his head and the frame cracks into two. Blood squirts everywhere, half his face is covered in a dark red, phantom-of-the-opera style blood-mask. Screaming, he crouches down and covers his head so lash him another four, maybe five times. 'Alright, alright, you've done me, you've done me,' he yells, looking horrendous, in a right state. His buddies help him to his feet and they head up the walk-way ramp into the Estate shouting fuck know what about "next time". Straight away, I'm freezing, shivery-shaking and absolutely exhausted. Super and Paul grab me around my shoulders and my head starts to throb. I see Crissy with Claude across the street back towards the railway bridge watching. 'Easy-nah, rude boy,' Crissy shouts, tapping his chest with his right hand. A wave of pride gushes over me, washing away the pain. A hundred feet tall, I'm the big man on the Frontline, ridding the neighbourhood of the dirty racist fools. Next morning, the Police come around, hammering on Momma's door, saying they've received a complaint from a mister and missus McMahon in relation to an alleged assault on their son. Momma sends them packing, telling them I've been home in bed all day yesterday with a fever. Front door slamming shut behind them, she's ramping at me about Babylon coming around her yard and disturbing the family. Vexed, she claps me about the head and tells me never to bring tribulation to her door again, or she'll pack a bag for me and send me out onto the street. After the fight, I'm well known around Frontline and get enough respect. Yeah man, rude-boys pat me on the back while pickneys yell my name. Talk of the town, I'm the crown prince of the Frontline, ambassador of Brixton, the guy who stood up to the racialists, single handed beat up a gang of fronters. We all became well known actually, Super for mashing up youths who don't pay us and Paul for being our mate. Yeah, rude-boys call him "duppy-bwai-lemon", for looking like a ghost and for being a lemon.

Yeah man, life on the Frontline's cool and consistent.

With no job to go to, I leave school a few months later and every day becomes the same. Super usually comes around mid-morning and I'm still be in bed, so he lets himself in. Sitting opposite me on Marlon's bed, he skins up and after a few joints, we have tea and toast. The only variation to our mellow life is fried egg sandwiches on Fridays and signing-on at the unemployment office every Tuesday. During the week Paul grafts nine-to-five at his olds-mans office in the City for not much more way less than what we made on the dole, doing fuck all and juggling our business. He didn't mind though, he referred to it as an "investment", once he's served his apprenticeship, he'll be on five times what he's on now, and within another two years, twenty times, plus a massive annual bonus. Most days me and Super stroll around the Frontline, selling weed to whoever we can while chit-chatting with all the rude-boys, keeping up our visibility, making sure everyone knows we're still about. Surviving inner city London is all about reputation, you see. After hustling and bustling and sharing stories with other rude-boys about how shit things were, I'll pick little Marlon up from School at half past three. Walking him home, he's be in between me and Super grabbing us by our hands and we'll swing up way up into the air, 'faster and faster, higher and higher,' he screams with excitement. Eventually, we get home and I'll get him his dinner before Momma gets home from work at the hospital at about six.

Marlon must have been five or six by then, maybe older.

Shit man, I miss him.

My little Marlon.

My baby brother…

3. Walking on Sunshine

"Living isn't everything, but you know the feeling love can bring. When you're floating through your cloud, baby don't shout too loud. The sky's the limit and you just keep on walking on…"

Eddie Grant

THE FRONT ROOM
17, HAMILTON HOUSE
GREENWICH, LONDON
LATE SUMMER, 1989

Savouring precious memories of my baby brother Marlon, I wipe a tear of liquid regret from my cheek. Damn, I see his smiling face when he's little and young and fragile and innocent and my heart breaks. I think about him all the time, all day, every day. I dwell on what happened, about what if what happened didn't have to happen or if it happened to me instead, I'd have taken that any day rather this mental nightmare. Can't think straight, can't keep re-living this nightmare over and over and over. When I close my eyes, I see it like it's a full-length feature film, actually, more like a pirate-video nasty, images I can't forget, can't rid from my mind. Hell must be like this, maybe this is hell, trapped in this shithole flat with Him, a waiting room between real-life and eternal darkness. Not sure I believe in heaven or hell though, if you believe in heaven you must believe in God, and if you believe in God, then you got to believe in the Devil. One can't exist without the other, mutually dependent or "symbiotic" as Paul would say.

Can't believe that, no way man, not after what I've done.
Religion?
Momma dragged me and Marlon down to Church every Sunday, Pops too. We get dressed up in our Sunday Best, and march down there, singing our hearts out to praise the Lord before going home for Sunday dinner. Curried goat, sometimes spiced mutton, always plantain and rice and black-peas, the only time where we spend any proper time together. After happy families, I'm straight back to my life on the Frontline, ducking and diving and juggling. Marlon's just the same, soon as we finish dinner he's be back to his runnings with the little pickney youth friends. I miss him, so badly I can feel it like my stomach, like my intestines are in a vice. It's hard to say and I don't want to say it, but he's

responsible for what happened, not me. He made the decision, he took the risk, it's on him, not me. Even so, I wish I could rewind the cassette tape of my past, spin-back the history of time and change what happened, do things differently.

Story of my life.

"It's called regret, dickhead," the Interrogator says, pointing out the obvious, as he always does.

Well yeah, if that's what it is, then that's what I'm feeling. I don't need you reminding me of it. I can't take any more of this mind-warping trippy shit, call it regret if you like, I don't know, but I tell you one thing, I wish it didn't happen. I understand what I've done and what I've caused and my part in it all, but don't try and trick me into a confession. In any case, you're as much to blame as me. Nobody planned it this way, it went too far, way too far…

Buzz.

Stomach churning, I squeeze my burning eyes together and rub my palms over my face. Exhausted, I haven't slept properly ages, weeks, months even. My thoughts blur and fade, get all mixed up and fucked, I know that much for sure. When my eyes are closed and my breathing's heavy, my realities merge and mix. With every breath I take, (every move I make), I sink further into this sofa. Man, it's so comfy, I've forgotten how comfy this feels. One thing I do remember though, with crystal clarity, is Shirley and the Saturday night sex-sessions we'd have right here on this very sofa. Yeah, wanting and urging for me, she's heavy breathing and panting with little beads of sweat on her top lip as her wetness glistens and pulses ever so slightly. Her eyes are locked on to mine and I see us growing old, sitting arm in arm in Greenwich park with a blanket over our knees.

You see, I was wanted, once.

Buzzz…

I remember feeding my baby boy right here on this sofa too, three in the morning then falling asleep with him in my arms while my princess sleeps deeply next door. Looking into his face, I've see his future, he's happy and strong and good looking. He's in a Savile Row three-piece suit doing high finance, big-city deals, being paid by the hour for his genius. He's grown into a man and I'm proud, I've always been proud. With that, the cloud of shit above my head evaporates as a wave of happiness washes over me, I can feel it, it's exquisite. Breathing deeply, my brainwaves flatten as contentment flows around me like a soft summer breeze.

Buzzzzzzzzz...

What the fuck?

The buzzing vibrates through my bones. Eyes wide open, heart-rate pumping, fuck. Fear shudders through me and every pore pumps with sweat...

Buzzzzzz.

The room vibrates and shakes and the light above my head flickers, dims, then fades. The darkness in the corner grows as shadows move into the centre of the room. It's happening again, look to the light, always the light, love is the key. Squeezing my eyes together, blocking out the blackness, I sense movement, something rustling. Even though I'm scared, fuck it, got to open my eyes. Total darkness, a cloak of ice-cold ambiance wraps tightly around my shoulders as my breath hangs in the air. Eyes drawn to the far wall, nah, that can't be right, can't be real. Pulsing in and out, the wall bulges and stretches, almost as if it's breathing, like it's alive. My fingers scratch deep into the sofa as my heart rate races. The buzzing continues and the floor vibrates like the whole tower-block is a giant dildo. Shaking my core, my vision zigzags back and forth around the room. This shits not real. Hand-shaped shapes stretch, eventually ripping through the wall as long, bony fingers reach out and probe the air. Something forms behind the wallpaper, looks like a head or a skull with a pointed Roman nose and sunken eye-sockets. It's bulging through, forehead first while what looks like a jaw-bone opens wide, so wide, too wide. Long fingers tear through the wall and feel into the centre of the room, feeling for me, seeking me out. My eyes trace up from the skeletal fingers across the arm to the large shoulder now edging into the room. Following the arm and shoulder, the skull rips into the room as piercing petrified screams reverberate around my head. Burning red evil eyes appear inside the skull and immediately sear into my soul. Terror strikes me as the razor-sharp vampire teeth sparkle in the darkness and the mouth opens unfeasibly wide. Razor-sharp fangs grow, and, as they do, the screaming intensifies. Multiple arms reach out from behind the skull and move towards me. This can't be happening, it can't be real, but it's right there in front of me, I can see it. Love is the key, tell myself over and over, say it like a prayer, a mantra to all that is good and holy. The vampire monster comes toward me, scuttling on a mish-mash of arms and hands where it should have legs and feet, like a giant spider from the waist down. I'm paralysed, can't move, can't scream, can't even think. It's bony arms grow even further, extending and reaching for me. Razor-sharp nails find me and tear at my sweat stained t-shirt, scratching my skin. Shit, I'm infected. It's awful and horrendous and shit-scary. Why me, why now, why? The room continues to shake while the buzzing and screaming reaches a crescendo, pneumatically drilling into my inner cranium as blood drips from my eardrums. I can't take it. The building shakes like a Richter-force-ten earthquake and the ground beneath me splits open to reveal searing hot molten lava, bubbling and spitting. This is it, this is the end, my end, the end of time. The noise is deafeningly loud, way too loud, ear burstingly loud. The god damn devil, Satan himself is here, here to take me.

I fucking knew it.

Then.

A gigantic nuclear-bomb is detonated, exploding searing hot super-white light through my eyes into my optical nerve. The thousand degree blast tears skin and muscle tissue from my bones, evaporates memories from my prefrontal cortex and detaches my mortal soul from my decrepit body.

I am, quite literally, obliterated.

Then.

Nothing.

Darkness and silence surround me.

Is this being dead?

Eyes slowly opening.

Skeleton's gone and peace fills my heart. I realise love is indeed the key, it always has been. Beautifully clean and pure shards of ultra bright light edge into the room beneath and around the walls, defeating the forces of darkness. The light grows brighter and brighter and my heart lifts, mood changes and eye-brows arch. The walls shudder and wobble before zooming away to reveal the moon and the stars and the majesty of infinite space. Unreal, I'm floating in an anti-gravity void, surrounded by moons and stars and distant alien planets. "Dev-onnnn," I hear them calling me. I don't know who's calling, but it's familiar and calming and I'm not afraid anymore. "Devvvvv-onnnnnn," they call again, their chorus sweet and angelic and beautifully harmonic. Maybe I'm dead and ascending to heaven with the chorus of angles guiding me, showing me the way. A thousand thoughts dart through my mind but I'm okay, I'm free, happy and content. I've finally found peace…

Then.

Eyes springing open, I'm transported back to this reality.

Leaping from the sofa struggling to find the light switch I crash against the coffee table. Fuck. Reaching out in all directions, I eventually find it, flick, the room fills with stark white light from the shade-less bulb hanging from the centre of the room. My broken heart sinks even deeper. The starkness of the light makes everything feel more dirty, more dingy and definitely more shit.

Nightmares? Vampires and angels? Aliens and stars?

I got to find a way of dealing with this madness…

Stomach churning, hunger pangs spasm.

"Hungry?" the Interrogator says, seemingly genuine. *"Bit of brown then, see you through the night?"*

Hmm, brown?

Need to play it cool.

Shouldn't really, but, when in Rome. Yeah, fuck it, go on then, you've twisted my arm. Perching on the edge of the sofa, I pick up the empty cigarette packet and shake out a small, inch long paper wrap. Opening it delicately, my heart flutters. The gorgeous dirty-white powder peppered with flecks of brown shimmers like gold bullion. It's so sexy, I can't wait. Grabbing the roll of silver foil, I tear a piece three or four inches square and carefully slide a small amount of the powder into the middle. Pursing my lips to kiss it, I allow saliva to dribble onto the powder. It spheres and beads and rests on top, refusing to be absorbed. Securing the foil tray in my left hand, with my right, I reach out and grab my trusty biro pen pipe, chard and scorched at one end. Moving it slowly towards my mouth, lips tighten and heart rate jumps. Grabbing the lighter, my balls tighten in anticipation. Yeah baby, soon come my darling. Flick, the lighter burns brightly as I gently caress the dancing orangey-blue flame up and down the foil, being careful not to burn my precious concoction. As it bubbles, creamy-white clouds of goodness drift slowly upward. Quick-quick, double quick, must hoover it up. The vile-yet-bitter-sweet taste vortex's through the pipe. Yeah man, come to daddy. Slithering around my mouth, it eases down my throat, filling my lungs, consuming my soul. I feel it's warmth.

Hmmm, gooooooooodnessssssssss…

Thoughts of vampires and aliens dissolve into nothingness. Lids falling, eyes rolling back, I drift into heaven. Tilting back, I hear echoes of pleasure seeping out. Shrinking, alice-in-wonderland style, the entirety of the world consumes me. I'm comfortably insignificant, a tiny speck of sand on the beach of infinity. I'm nobody, invisible, anonymous, safe. A familiar warmness forms around the back of my neck, massaging my aching temples as a tingling crown of beautifulness morphs across the top of my head. King of the world, master of the universe, I feel amazing, connected to every single living thing in existence. The pleasure crown pierces my mind and pumps in the glorious life-force-energy of the galaxy. I'm Jesus and Abraham, Buddha and Muhammad, saviour of the world, curing mankind, making the world a better place. Wobbling, shuddering and rushing, I suck-up the remaining fumes and gently place the paraphernalia back down on the coffee table. Orgasmic waves pulsate through me as I float gently sideways.

Soooo elegant and sophisticated…

And sooooo god damn….

GoooooOOOOOOODDDDDD.

Laying on the sofa, the heaviness of the nightmares lift, and I feel light, weightless almost. I feel myself rising and begin to hover, then slowly glide towards the ceiling. Rotating, back glued to the ceiling, I'm looking back down towards the sofa and the shrivelled-up body of a premature baby laying there, helpless and weak, nearly dead but not quite. It's a sorry, gut wrenching sight.

Ultimate sadness.

I know who it is, you do too.

Gravity forces my pity-tears to rain on it's forehead, my own tears splashing on my own forehead. What have I become? Freeze frame pictures of my childhood flash before me, happy images of when I was strong, manly and in control.

Then.

Shaking uncontrollably, eyes open.

What the fuck?

Grabbing my hooded top, the black one with a day-glow-yellow smiley face on the front, I pull it over my head. Warmth oozes into my ribs before the ice-cold shakes quickly return.

"Look at you, look at what you've become." the Interrogator says, judgementally. *'Browning, dreaming and panicking. And you tell me you're not responsible?"* the Interrogator quizzes, already knowing I know he knows the answer. *"Don't bother with an answer, it's rhetorical, dickhead."*

Rhetoric-what? Shakespeare shit? What you on about? I'm

the victim here, none of this is my doing. Look at what I've lost, what I once had and now haven't. Just leave me alone…

Back alone with my thoughts, I stare through the window at the urban scenery. Busy but still, empty but full, it's life but not a real life, a life without purpose. Like me, the world is all alone.

Poor, lonely, fucked up world.

Poor, lonely, fucked up skagg-head, heroin addicted me.

"Keep going," the Interrogator says, encouragingly. *"Tell me about the Frontline, about the riots."*

Arms wrapping around my thinning torso, I feel myself rock back and forth, forcing comfort into my sorry soul. Closing my eyes, my mind flicks through the pages of my life, the encyclopaedia of crap, the bible of total and utter bullshit. I'm transported to Greenwich Park, it's summer and the sun shines bright. A warming, gentle breeze wafts against my face while golden rays of sunlight penetrate me, warming my core. She's with me, my baby boy too, my brand-new son and heir. We sit on a soft and luscious picnic rug near the gates of the Royal Observatory, overlooking the Naval College at the bottom of the hill. Laughing and joking, we share smiles and love and laugher and happiness. We eat strawberries from each others finger tips and sip cold white wine from crystal glasses before sharing a small kiss. Smiling, I watch my boy gurgle and giggle as I tickle his tummy, and look toward her and she's staring at me with love in her eyes. This is perfect, as close to heaven on earth as any man will ever get.

Maybe I died that day, that day of days. Maybe this, right here, right now is my own hell, my personal purgatory maybe, hells waiting room. I miss them, they're my life, without them and without her I am literally nothing. Eyes slowly opening again, the sunny warmness of Greenwich Park fades into the grim coldness of now and this shitty flat. The darkness of my personal cell returns to surround me, trap me and confound me. I'm incredibly sad, the saddest, loneliest man on earth, too sad to live but too pussy to die. I know I must push on, get this over with, get to the end quicker…

BRIXTON
LONDON
EARLY APRIL, 1981

The riot, or the "uprising" is when the world changed forever. We were heard for the very first time, which brought us hope and optimism. Yeah, we've risen and everyone around the world takes notice, we have a voice, anything is possible, anything. Nobody knows for sure how it started, but the media say it's orchestrated and contrived, that agitators and racists made it happen deliberately. Others think the Government led a massive conspiracy to clear-out all the squats and the drugs from the Frontline. Either way, they hold a public enquiry afterwards with an old-school pro-establishment judge and loads of politicians and councillors giving evidence. Unsurprisingly, they conclude it was as a result of heavy-handed Policing, poor housing, poverty and a lack of jobs leading to a build-up of resentment from the "urban youth".

For fucks sake, they don't know shit.

I know the truth.

Marlon and his pickney friends had a hand in it…

He and a fuck-wit kid from Peckham had been rumbling for months before, over a girl or some kind of he-said-she-said handbags at dawn bullshit. Anyway, a whole load of Peckham boys come down to the Friday night disco thing at the Community Centre run by Reverend what's-his-name. The Peckham gang give Marlon and his mates a beating, with Marlon getting a black eye and broken rib for his trouble. They have tit-for-tat scraps and skirmishes for a few weeks after until Marlon, the brave little solider, heads to the North Peckham estate on his own and waits for their head boy. They have a bruising fight, a proper straightener apparently, ending up with Marlon smashing him across the head with an iron bar, then biting his nose clean off. Yeah, scuffling on the floor, Marlon's on his back having the shit head-butted out of him so all he can do is reach up and bite onto the fools nose. Takes a chunk out of his face and the Peckham pussyclat has to have plastic surgery and skin graft. Marlon comes home mashed-up with a deep cut on his head, crying, convinced he's killed him and sure the Police will be around to arrest him any time soon. He wants to pack his bags and do one, vanish abroad or up north but I tell him the Peckham people are wrong-uns for sure, dirty scumbags, thieves and robbers in fact, but never snitches or grasses. I convince him otherwise. But, as he predicted, the Police do indeed come hunting and start harassing everyone on the Frontline even more than usual. They're sus-stopping us all the time, systematically asking everyone if they know him, me too.

Sus-stopping, otherwise known as the "suspected persons" law allows Police to stop whoever they want in order to conduct a body-search. All they need is "reasonable cause", which is easy, and goes something like this:

PC Pete: "Hey PC John, I believe that young fellow over yonder, strolling down the street seemingly minding his own business looks suspicious, do you agree?"

PC John: "Absolutely right PC Pete, I certainly do, he might have drugs or a weapon on his person, let's initiate a sus-stop on behalf of queen and country."

Fools.

The fight at the North Peckham estate sorted things out with the Peckham gang, for a while at least, but a friend of a friend arranged for a final, once and for all, winner takes all royal-rumble gang-fight. Marlon gets a crew together and they have a massive fight at Brixton train station. Properly hardcore with knives and shit, enough citizens get themselves hurt including mister no nose who gets himself stabbed by one of his own. Yep, one of his own gang lunges at Marlon with a knife but gets his own boy instead. Mister unlucky or what, mashed up by Marlon then stabbed by his own friend. The Police arrive and the fighting youth scatter in all directions with Marlon and mister unlucky being chased through the market. When the Police eventually get hold of mister unlucky, they arrest him for disturbing the peace. Damn, they don't know he's been injured and is bleeding to death.

Later that night, the Frontline's rife with rumour of a kid being stabbed by the Police and, once the sun sets, the local youth turn on the Police, flinging stones and all manner of shit. It's reported on the News at Ten and the newspapers as nothing more than a skirmish. But, little did everyone know, it was the glowing embers in the soon to come south London inferno.

During the following week, the Police flood the entire Frontline, both uniformed and plain clothes absolutely everywhere…

Street corners, Police.

Walking down the road, Police.

Unmarked cars, Police.

Hiding in bushes, Police.

Fucking everywhere, Police.

I'm sus-stopped maybe twenty times that week, probably more. Super thinks it's due to our rumble with who we thought were under-cover Police, a pair of fucked-up muscle-bound twins who paid us a visit at the scrap yard a week before.

Yeah man, I haven't thought about that for ages.

Got myself a job working at the scrap yard on Coldharbour Lane. It's steady work and not too hard, and even though the early mornings are tough, I actually really enjoy it. Anyway, I'm in the office making a cup of tea after grafting hard all morning on a piece of shit Ford Cortina when two weird looking blokes, twins by the look of them, burst through the door. They knock me about a bit, wrap me up with gaffer-tape and fire loads of questions at me about Super. Where's he at, where's he live, what time is he due down here. A proper interrogation by proper hardcore professionals, I can't work out whether they're National Front or Special Branch. So anyway, I'm bound-up and they're standing there eye-balling me, having a whale of a time, telling me about the elaborate ways they intend to torture me. Their best suggestion is to take a hammer my arms and legs, cut me all over and pour bleach into the wounds before setting my body on fire so that even my mother can't identify me. Charming! But, for the first time in my life, I'm really, properly, petrified scared. Right there, thinking about what they'll do to me, I found real fear or should I say it found me. Weird, I experience an out of body thing, feels like I've been there before, like I've seen this scene before, like I'm watching it in a movie and me isn't really me. Dé-jà-vu or something, voodoo-ray magic for sure. My mind floods with scenes of sadism, torture and utter depravity, and of Momma's crying face when she goes to identify my remains…

But.

Boom, my hero and saviour appears from nowhere. Chest bulging, shirt ripping over his cartoon over-sized pectorals, fury burning in his eyes as electricity sparks between his figures and lightening cracks off his shoulders blades. Here he comes, champion of the world, the one and only…

S U P E R.

Bursting through the doorway, he's grunting like a caged animal with a barbed wire leash. Clockwork-orange "ultra-violence" explodes as the left twin pounces. Super, deftly dodging backward, swings a big heavy rusty chain. Swooshing through the air, he connects and the twin topples. Head bowed, looking at his pray sprawled on the floor, Super is the man, the man of all men. He's a gladiator, a king, a god and a monster, yeah man, Super to the rescue, come now rude boy! His eyes slowly move from his felled prey to the other twin, and a broad smile stretches across his face. Yeah, he's loving it, he's in his element, he fucking lives for these moments. The twin stands nailed to the floor staring at his out-cold brother, his bottom lip trembling. Moving like lightning he dives at Super and they both collide out of the doorway in a blur of punches and kicks. Pushing myself up, I edge around the felled twin and over to the doorway. Out in the yard, Super and the other twin are grappling in the mud and oil, clumping each other over and over. Like a ravaged dog, the twin's on top, screaming and punching. As calm as you like, Super tilts his head and looks over at me. Still taking licks, our eyes meet and I somehow read his mind. Hands still tied behind my back I leap out of the cabin and run towards them. Without breaking my stride, I launch a boot towards the twin's head and connect with loud crack echoing off nearby buildings. Flying over the top, I land a couple of feet away, crunching my collar bone. Looking to my right, I see Super roll the oily twin over and start pounding the him in the head. Eventually, Super gets up, stares at the oily twin before walking over to me. Meanwhile, the other chain-felled twin hobbles out of the cabin and goes to his now unconscious oily brother. After waking him, they stumble arm in arm out of the yard into a nice-looking black Mercedes. Thirty seconds later, the back window winds down and the barrels of a shot gun poke through. Pop-pop, we dive for cover as they let off two shots before wheel-spinning off.

Super, my hero.

Man on fire.

Brave as a lion, strong as an ox, stupid as fuck.

Why Super, I hear you ask?

It's easy, "Super" is short for Superman.

Six years old, he climbs a tree to fetch a ball, (or something), falls and hurts his arm then carries on playing football for a few hours before going home for his dinner. In pain all evening, his Momma ends up taking him to hospital where they find out he's broken his wrist and has to stay hospital in for a couple of days while they re-set it and put a pin in. When he comes home, he has to wear a plaster-cast over his hand right up to his armpit. Funny, we draw cocks and balls and swear-words all over it. Bored shitless in hospital, a nurse gives him a dog-eared comic book, he loves it and goes absolutely mental for comics. Posters in his bedroom, he spends every penny he has on new comics and this filthy sky-blue Superman T-Shirt he wore all the time. Soon after, he starts calling himself Clark Kent, saying him playing football with a broken arm is a sure sign he's super-human. Playing along and taking the piss, we call him Superman and then Super, and it just sort of stuck…

Anyhow.

Back to the night when the Peckham idiot-fool got stabbed by his own man, and the uprising begins for real. Me and Shirley, Paul and Sammie and Super and Chantelle have a night-out in London's west-end before heading to the Albany Empire in Deptford for an after-hours dance. The dance proves to be rubbish so we end up back here. Just as well too, I'd rather be here with her than back on the Frontline battling with the Police. Next morning, blurry eyed and hung over, we see pictures in the newspaper of random youths on Railton Road throwing stones and battling with the Police. Panicking, thinking about Momma, I got to get back quickly and find out what the fuck's happening. Weaving our way through the south London traffic, Super, me and Paul eventually reach the Frontline. The whole area is locked down like a military state with Police all over the place. Loads of youths are hanging around too, the usual faces plus lots I've never ever seen before. Both the Police and the youths look primed, ready for the big kick off. Soon as I get out of the car I feel the vibe, this is pre-war, the drawing of battle lines with them setting out their stall, trying to assert their authority. Yeah, both teams mentally preparing themselves, allowing the adrenalin to build, the emotion to take over, the primeval urge swell.

Let me break it down for you.

In the red corner, we have the Frontline youths of Brixton plus other random strangers and outsiders, probably mutants from Croydon or somewhere. Whereas, in the white corner, (yep, white), hailing from the middle-class-semi-detached-well-spoken-picket-fenced-keeping-up-with-the-Jones suburbs, we have the Metropolitan Police, Old Bill himself. We know what's going to happen, of course we do, they do too. Hyper-excited, we're eager to mash-up some heads, settle old scores, get our own back, have our voices heard and just revel in utter chaos. Anarchy in the UK, yeah man, of course.

This is our time.

Stopping off first to check on my Momma and then Super's Momma, we spend ages hunting around for Marlon and his pals. After an age, we spot them on Atlantic Road. Pumped up like little kids on Christmas Eve, they're wide-eyed and totally up for it. I tell them to go home and get off the Frontline, but they won't listen, of course not, they want the chaos. Sensing the opportunity to make some serious money, Super, me and Paul head to Crissy's flat at Angel Town. With so many rude-boys hanging around the neighbourhood, we need some stock and get busy dealing quick time. As long as we keep out the way of Samurai Sam and avoid the Police, we'll clean up and make a mint. Through into the front room, Crissy, Claude and a rude-boy Jamaican named Snakehead, Crissy's cousin or nephew or something, are sitting there looking serious and solemn. Some polite chit-chat and a speech from Crissy about being careful, we get our shit and drive around to our usual customers dropping it off. Me and Paul wait in the car as Super goes into the taxi-cab office on Railton Road, (always good customers), dropping off a quarter-weight. Re-appearing at the doorway, he comes out and a couple of plain clothed Police appear from nowhere, grab him up and pin him against the wall, classic sus-stop tactics. Super lashes out, (of course), and both officers proceed to kick the shit out of him, giving him a proper hiding before chucking him in the back of a Police wagon, along with maybe six other officers. The inevitable rocking starts and the van shifts from side to side, heads, bones and skulls being crushed inside. He suffered some damage I reckon, serious Doc-Martin-in-the-head pain for sure. A few rude-boys hanging around came over to watch and it kicks off big-time.

It's a bit of a laugh to begin with, both sides goading each other and the occasional skirmish but nothing too heavy. Then, later on, around teatime, the Police come on strong, raiding the pool hall and mashing up enough youth and 'line-man alike. Outside the pool hall, we're fighting with the Police foot to foot, fist to fist, jaw to jaw. You know what, they're giving as good as they get with truncheons raised and boots flying. Couple of minutes later, a Police car parked just up the road gets torched, petrol bomb I think, orange flames licking against blackening windows. Glancing around at the blatant violence on both sides, watching the carnage and the utter chaos, I know nothing will be the same again, ever. With Super locked up in the van, we somehow get split up from Marlon who, it turns out, eventually hooks up with Delroy, Auntie Gertrude's boy. Me, Paul and Ashley, poor Ashley, head into Brixton town centre away from the main fighting on Railton and Atlantic Roads. Worried sick, I think about going to look for Marlon and maybe check on Mommas house, but don't want to get embroiled in the fighting, besides, there's money to be made robbing the shops in the town centre. Once there, we stand outside the Record Shack in the market, eating patties and drinking ginger beer, watching the Police chase down Railton Road towards the epicentre. I hear the rioting from maybe half a mile away, like a weird football crowd noise, just like when the home team scores a goal, but with the occasional crash and bang, then cheers, sirens and bell.

With the sun setting and the darkness of the night approaching, it gets a whole lot more serious. The rioters, as we did earlier, head for the shops on the high street, ready for some serious looting. Claude's in the middle of it, leading the charge like Churchill or something, but there no sign of Snakehead or Samurai Sam. Rumour has it, Crissy gets picked up by the Police and the Home Office early evening so probably missed everything. Following the rioting swarm, we end up on the high street too, yeah man, unlimited, cash free shopping. Unlike earlier in the afternoon, most shops have closed-up, so we crack through the front door or smash a window and take what we want. Some shops remain open though, can you believe it, so we just walk in and take what we want, the shopkeepers don't even try to stop us. I feel like Robin Hood, taking back what's ours. Yeah man, we've been oppressed for years and had the piss taken out of us from time, so we deserve it. We drift in and out of the shops taking all types of shit, most of it actual real-life shit, shit we don't need like toasters, kettles, girls clothes and general tit-tat-tacky crap. Paul gets himself some brandy and I get myself a brand new suit, a flared nine-teen-seventies style bad-man suit in brilliant white. Very cool, even if I say so myself. I'm talk of the town, lording it all over the place like a nineteen-seventies bad-man, all the rude-boys high fiving me and patting me on the back.

Later in the evening, when the fighting dies down a bit, we head to a party at a flat at Angel Town. A night to remember with everyone partying, celebrating, having fun like never before, like a whole heap of worry has been lifted and pressure released. The flat's rammed full of rude-boys and sexy girls along with a massive sound system laying down some serious baselines. There's a young boy in an army uniform and purple beret excellently toasting over the top, chatting about Police-officers and sus-stops. Marlon finds his way there too, walking in looking like complete shit, his t-shirt's dirty and stained and his hair's practically white with soot. A quick freshen up in the toilet, t-shirt turned inside out and he's good to go but, he's quiet, withdrawn and sort of melancholic. Tells me he got caught up in the centre of riot and had to fight his way out, man fighting man, Police versus rude-boy going toe-to-toe in total chaos.

I feel for him.

It's at that very party me and Claude hook up properly. Turns out Crissy did get arrested earlier in the day, ending up with him doing time for possession with intent to supply. After that, he's deported back to Jamaica due to an outstanding warrant. Over the next year or so, Claude and Snakehead go to war over the business Crissy left behind. Man, it's brutal and savage and completely disgusting, taking it in turn to fuck each other up in increasingly dark ways. Bad times man, dirty, dark, evil, gutter-snipe times. Claude versus Snakehead, David versus Goliath.

Kicks off way before the uprising when Samurai Sam diversified, becoming a big-time heroin dealer. He's got no time for selling weed locally around Brixton, nah man, he's big time, big money, big business, front page news. Crissy hates chemicals, especially skagg, saying anything that holds a man so tight he'll rather jack-up than fuck some pussy can't be right. So, Crissy disowns Sam and they go their separate ways. Amicable and civil with no problems, they sort of split the Frontline up, Crissy dealing natural, while Sam deals everything else, and I mean, everything. Skagg, whores, protection-rackets, skagg, gambling-dens, whores, skagg, guns, whores and of course, skagg. Sam is smart, smartest of them all. Rumour is he pays a whole heap of Police to keep him out of trouble, and to sort out any competition without him having to lift a finger. But, occasionally, he will indeed "lift a finger" and punish anyone who steps out of line by chopping them up or taking a sub-machine gun and shooting the fuck out of their front door. Yeah man, he'll fuck you up any which way he can. I hear nowadays he's living in Belgium running an entire wholesale business, yeah, big-time importer mixing with big time gangsters in Amsterdam and Turkey.

Meanwhile, Claude and Snakehead are running the Frontline together, sharing things out neat and tidy. But, as Snakehead is family with Crissy, he wants to run things on his own. It's a massive problem because Claude being Claude, he wants it too, him being Crissy's number two right hand man from time. The war begins with them arguing about who sells what and where, then the odd fight and skirmish but nothing too serious. Then, one day, one mad day, Snakehead and his Yardie-crew, (he shipped them over from Tivoli Gardens a few months before), kidnaps Claude and gives him the beating of his life. Yeah man, seriously dark evil shit. They torture him before branding his head with a red-hot iron. Claude won't be beaten though, nah, defiant to the end. Ends up with him being chucked over the balcony of a tower block in Peckham, ninth or tenth floor, can't be sure, but anyway, a fucking long way down. He's ruined, cracked skull, both arms broken, a leg too, pelvis, ribs, spleen (whatever the fuck that is), punctured lung and something to do with his liver or kidneys. In a coma for a week, then on life support for another two weeks, in total he spends a couple of months in hospital. It doesn't stop there neither. Snakehead is sadistic yeah, pure evil, pure badness, a cold-hearted villain never to be crossed, never. Even after the over-the-balcony incident, he wasn't done, no way, not by a long shot. While Claude's in hospital, Snakehead gets to his girlfriend, kidnaps her and, apparently, rapes her at gunpoint. In Police protection now, new identity, new name, living god knows where now. Even after that, Snakehead still isn't done. A sick motherfucker who knows no boundaries, he breaks into Claudes flat, robs everything, completely guts it before setting it on fire. Proper blazing inferno, the fire brigade evacuate the whole tower-block. With Claude in hospital and the council not giving a shit, it becomes a derelict squat-come-drug-den-whore-house. Holy shit, in the blink of an eye, Claudes life is rubbed out, scribbled over, eliminated.

Nowadays he walks with a limp, even though most people think he's just bowling like some type of rude boy. The injuries aren't just physical though, nah, the whole sorry episode damages him mentally and psychologically. I don't know the difference between the two, but either way, he's fucked up. When he eventually gets out of hospital, he's a shell of a man, a walking zombie, doesn't want to live but doesn't want to die. Zero motivation, zero hope, he's scared of his own shadow, paranoid and freaked out. Snakehead warns us to keep away from him, says anyone helping him will be dealt with. We all know what "dealt with" means, oh yeah, we know alright. But, I can't see Claude like that though, it's not right, I owe it to Crissy and to Claude to see him right. Shirley offers to take him in for a few weeks over here in Greenwich, far away from Snakehead and the Frontline. Even though he doesn't want to come over, he's proud yeah, but, eventually, he reluctantly submits. On a chemist-load of pain-killers and tranquilisers, he's spaced out and vague, and visits Greenwich hospital every day for physiotherapy. Me and Shirley can hear him crying during the night, sobbing away to himself or waking up screaming. I go in, sit on the side of his bed and comfort him while he nods back off. Next morning, he's none the wiser or, as I like to think of it, knows exactly what's going on but too proud to mention it.

A few months later he gets himself a flat about a mile away from here in Deptford. A year or so after that, he finds himself a job too, working the doors at Cheeks nightclub on New Cross Road. With the scar over the right-hand side of his forehead from Snakeheads ironing and with his dreads cut off he looks seriously fucked up and nobody messes with him. Reality is, he's scared of his own shadow, which of course makes him an excellent bouncer, seeing problems before they arise and pacifying punters, rather than smashing them up. After a while, he ends up managing some chaps running the doors at other south London clubs and becomes legitimate too, respectable, on a level, limited company this, accountant that.

"You mentioned Shirley," the Interrogator interjects, changing the subject to the subject I'm most scared of.

Yeah, I did. Might as well tell you about her, but I can't talk about what happened though, not yet, not now. Maybe the early days when we were young and happy, before what happened, happened…

Paul somehow knows the owner of a new club underneath

Charing Cross station and gets us on the opening night guest list. Before the club, we head to a bar in Soho where we meet three very tidy girls, Shirley being one of them. We get chatting and, after a prolonged drunken session of flirting, we invite them with us. The club's okay, a bit too new-romantics for me though, so after a couple of hours we head to an after-hours party somewhere deep-south, fuck knows where, and end up going on to her flat. Her flat is just like this one, in fact exactly the same, a carbon copy, but, "her" flat is clean and fresh and full of life, full of hope, full of love, full of passion. Not like this flat, full of decaying putrefying shit and regret and sadness, an empty soulless shell, just like me…

That's all I am now, that's what I've become.

Talking all night long about everything and nothing, we have a connection straight away, something real and tangible. It's no normal lets-see-your-fanny type thing, nah, we are deep and meaningful and real. As the sun comes up, we kiss for ages, tender and soft and gentle. She's beautiful and pretty and sexy, with such a kind heart. Totally getting me, she sees through the bloodclat-rasclat-Frontline Devon to the real me. I've never shared the real me with anyone, not even myself to be honest. Sounds corny, a cliché even, but, shit man, it's true and the only way to explain how I feel. Until her, I never really thought about who I was, who I want to be or what hopes and dreams I have. No ambition, I had no idea how good I could be, what I could become. You see, we're never encouraged to think about the future, about what we can become. If you're poor and from an inner-city council estate, any ambition is kicked out of you before it has any time to develop or grow. Not with belts and canes, oh no, more sophisticated than that, teachers, toy makers, journalists and politicians condition your thinking by limiting your horizons. They give you a single one-hour career lesson aged fifteen and ask what do you want to be, joiner, train driver, shop worker? It's never lawyer, doctor or architect, nah, good jobs are reserved for the middle classes who yield to the control of the gentry, the upper class, the ruling minority. Toy makers make toys for the masses like toy utility belts or toy tools so you can pretend to be a plumber. The newspapers report to good old joe-public, electrician or milkman or bus driver, they normalise the normal, they don't celebrate the unusual, the novel or the rich. Yeah man, those who really run the world are the rolled-up-trouser-funny-handshake-arse-bandits at Eton or some other public school.

Anyway, hark at me, getting all political…

So anyway, sitting right here talking with Shirley, I gain a new outlook on life, on who I want to be. We start seeing each other steadily and holy shit, things are good, really good, so fucking god-damn good, I never knew how good. Plus, going steady and spending more time down here means I spend less time in Brixton, which cool, exactly what I need. Over time, staying down here more and more I drift from my life on the Frontline and forge a new life here, with Shirley. Not long after the riots, Paul comes down less and less, deciding instead to knuckle down with his City job. Things are good for him too, bought himself a Porsche, can you believe it? From a dented-up Triumph Dolomite to bright red Porsche in the space of eighteen months. Tells me about a deal he's setting up, buying another company, laying off a load of people and selling an office block or something. Reckons he'll pocket a whole heap of cash by "liquidating the asset," he calls it. I think he refers to it like that so that he doesn't have to think about the fellas he's just sacked, them having to go home and look their wives and kids in the eyes telling them daddies lost his job. The brave hunter-gatherer, the bread-winner, the man of the house not being able to provide for his kids will take anyway his manliness, make him a pussy, a fairy, not a real man. Paul revels in it though, getting off on the power to crush another mans soul, just because he can, the fucking mug.

Before long, me and Shirley are living together like proper grown-ups, sharing towels, taking it in turn to cook and all that domesticated stuff. I can't travel back to Brixton every day so leave the scrap yard, besides, I want a start afresh, hold things down and do things right by Shirley. Get myself a "proper job" as a postman, yep a postman. Devious Dee in the place, walking the streets delivering giro-cheques and gas bills to little old ladies. Even though the early mornings are a killer, it's easy work and I'm always finished by lunchtime, which is convenient as me and Claude ran our pirate radio station, Dream FM, out of a tower block in Lewisham. More of that later. For now, everything's good, for the first time ever, life's good and steady and I'm truly happy.

At the beginning of eighty-two Shirley falls pregnant. A shocker, a proper bolt-of-lightning-santa-clause-make-believe-fairy-tale, but it's true, I'm to be a dad. I'll leave a long-lasting legacy on the world, my son and heir. He's six now, or seven and a bobby-dazzler with a heart-breaker smile, my pride and joy. Every time I look at him my heart literally skips a beat. Every dad must say that, but damn, it's so true. He's me and I'm him. I miss him so much. I'll say here and now, I'm so sorry he's seen what he's seen, for what he will see in the future. No matter what happens, I want him to know, I love him. I love him forever, properly forever ever. I love him until the last star in the universe stops shining.

I'll love him until the very end of time…

4. We Don't Care

"We're going for a good game of football, a good punch up and a good piss up. We love fighting, we love football…"

Harry the Dog

17, HAMILTON HOUSE
GREENWICH, LONDON
LATE SUMMER, 1989

The truth.

Heroin is my favourite past time. That damn powder brings me gorgeous, cum-bursting-out-of-my-cock beautifulness, yeah man. The millisecond blink-of-an-eye time just after the hit, just when the "ahh" has gone but you're still in the "hmm" moment, yeah, that's the moment. The perfectly satisfied, glorious, never want for anything anymore moment, the very first time virginial moment. That's what I'm seeking, it's what all junkies are trying to find, the holy-grail, the single, ultra-sexy speck in time, the grain of sand on the beach of external beautifulness, yeah, it don't get better than that.

I love it and it loves me.

Scorched foil down.

Rush building.

Leaning back, eyelids descending, I inhale deeply. Clean, fresh air fills my lungs and the rush reaches its crescendo. Face tingling, a crown of orgasmic waves surround me as angels massage my shoulders as a hundred virgins fondle my balls. Muscles relaxing, every single excited nerve ending sparks and pops into life. Engulfed by the ever-so-familiar warm glow, my mind drifts back to when I'm a boy, a world bathed in soft, orange-brown light with smells of gingerbread and curried goat wafting upstairs from the kitchen below. Tap on, hot water running, I lean back and relax. 'Devon son, don't be using all the hot water now,' Momma yells from the bottom of the stairs as Desmond Decker serenades her from the radio in the kitchen. Head tilting back, the warm water laps across my tense chest and washboard stomach. Super will be round in an hour, I'll get ready and we'll head to the west-end for a night on the tiles. Yeah man, easy now rude boy, we'll have a proper big night out. Meeting up with Shirley and the others, we'll drink dark rum, crack enough jokes then do some dancing and flirting and kissing too. I can't wait to see Shirley later, just thinking about her turns me on. She'll kiss me softly and slowly, cup me and stroke me and she'll take me in her mouth then circle me with her tongue, slow and passionate, making me wait for it.

Yeahhhhh man, yeah.

"Oi, shit for brains," the Interrogator says, awakening me from my heroin induced daydream. *"We've got work to do."*

Ignore him, he's not really here, not in real life anyway, just a figment of my drug-fucked-imagination. Let's get back to my love and my passion.

"Skagg induced wet-dream, more like," the Interrogator says, goading me, wanting to get a rise out of me.

I'm buzzing, it's the heroin talking, of course it is. Once this shits out in the open, he'll have what he needs and can float away, disappear back to when the fuck-ever he's from.

So, hush now man and settle down yeah.

"Settle down? I'm right here, right now, standing over your dirty rancid body with this weapon in my hand," the Interrogator says, menace seeping through his deep cockney tones. *"This piece of heavy artillery is the key to your life, if you can call it a life."*

CLICK.

Anyone can be a big man with a gun.

Gun?

What the fuck?

Eyes spring open, I immediately focus on the black metal barrel pointing right at me. Mortality pours into the room, soaking me, drenching me, drowning me. Struggling for air, my orgasmic skagg-crown dissolves into ice-cold waves running top to bottom through my body, chilling my core, freezing my soul. The dirty stinking dark reality of the room hits me like an iron bar across my head. This is real. I'm drawn to the wooden sideboard with the right-hand door hanging off. Hard to believe this was once clean and shiny and adorned with loving pictures of us all, framed moments of happiness, I see them in my mind's eye. One of my little boy, a toddler with gappy baby-teeth and an innocent smile. Another one of him and her, mother and son, cheek to cheek, hugging, smiling with love in their eyes. The last picture is of all of us, the gang, all together. Me and my queen, Shirley, Paul and super-fit Sammie, (oh my god, she's so fit), and Super with big girl Chantelle. In glorious technicolour, our arms are over each other's shoulders, we're bright-eyed happy with love in our eyes. We all look young and hopeful and full of joy, full of the moment. But, in the dirty cold shit reality of now, the pictures are replaced with shattered brandy bottles and the remains of broken picture frames. A real-life metaphor for my frazzled brain and fucked up half-life.

"Look at what you've achieved, look at your success," the Interrogator says, mocking what I've achieved. *"Hope it was worth it."*

You bastard, you think I'm proud? I'm not proud, not by a long shot. How can I be proud of what I've done, what I've caused, what I've become. Don't have to put up with this crap, I can leave whenever I want, so, matey-boy, buck your ideas up, learn some manners and forget about threatening me.

"A skinny, weak, fucked up addict? Taking me on, having a go?" the Interrogator muses rhetorically.

We both know he's monsteringly strong and can crush me at any time. Got to front it out, can't let me see my fear.

You're nothing more than what I am.

"Apart from I'm the one with the gun, you fucking idiot," the Interrogator says, cradling it with his massive shovel-hands.

Black and shiny, still and quiet, it looks benign, peaceful, non-threatening, like a children's toy. Maybe it is, maybe it's a big made up rouse, tricking me into staying here. Fear is my motivation for maintaining the status-quo while apathy is my friend, keeping me company in my self-imposed purgatory. Maybe I really can leave, the only thing holding me here is me, and my cowardice. It must be a toy or a prop, besides, where would he get a real-life shooter.

I hear myself chuckling.

Hang on, hang-bloody-on, I'm buzzing, not thinking straight. The echo of the skagg still rings around my head, still pumps through my veins into my rotten-to-the-core bloodstream. I'm not thinking straight, the fumes and the head rush and the chemical cock-fuck. Yeah right, as if, a massive bluff, holding me here with a toy, gambling on me thinking it's real, gambling I'll doubt myself?

But, I am full of doubt though. What if it is real, what if I make a break for it and get shot and dead-up, then what?

"Now then," the Interrogator says, calling a halt to proceedings. *"Enough of this mind-fuck banter. Let's crack on."*

Grabbing my hooded top, I pull it over my head and the day-glow yellow smiley-face on the front seems to smile as it straightens out. I shiver as the warmth begins to seep through to my ribs. I'm clucking, shivering, going cold-turkey and I know a few totes on the dreg-ends of the dirty brown heroin won't satisfy my need, my hunger, my yearning. I know I should stop thinking about the sexiness of the skagg and the horrors of the past, I really do. Replaying the memory scrapbook inside my head occupies my mind though, straightens out the brainwaves. The only way I can achieve peace is for me to submit to him, give in to him, open my legs and let him fuck me with the truth. Once I'm done, he'll leave, that's what he said. Once he gets the fuck out, I can get back on track, get Shirley back and re-build my life.

"Okay, family then?" the Interrogator says, reminding me of my regret and sorrow and self-loathing.

SHIRLEY'S PARENTS HOUSE
37, BLUE ANCHOR LANE
BERMONDSEY, LONDON
AUGUST, 1981

Everything's hunky-dory, life's good. Shirley's family seem to like me, surprising really as they hail from Bermondsey, deep-south yeah, and when I say deep, I mean deep. Those people not really into brothers like me, if you know what I mean. We don't go to see them very often, thank god, I wasn't too welcome around them parts so we visit every other Sunday for Sunday dinner. To begin with her old man, Fat Stan, flips his fat lid when she introduces me. 'A darky, in my house, shagging my daughter, my little girl?' he's ranting and raving, veins popping out of his fat neck with steam whistling from his cauliflower ears, all the while Phil Collins is blaring out of the transistor radio in the kitchen. You know what, I am shagging her too, all the time, anywhere and everywhere. And, she's no little girl neither. Heels in the air, legs over my shoulders she loves it, can't get enough of my meaty hard cock. Quivering and shaking with pleasure, her top lip's clammy and her breathing shallow, she'll buck her womanliness into me over and over and over with ah-ha-ha's whispering into my ears. You see, I was wanted once, a long time ago.

Really wanted, really needed, really loved.

Over time though, me and Stan sort of bonded, became sort of mates. Eventually accepting me and Shirley were no short-term thing and I wasn't about to mess her about and piss off. I never told him, but being accepted made me feel valued, like I belonged, like never before. Through him I realise I'm just as good as anyone else, no matter the colour or my skin, the school I went to or the borough where I hail from. While Shirley and her mum get busy cooking us Sunday lunch, Stan takes me to his local, the Lions Head. A typical south-east London pub full of white males boisterously necking pints and getting pissed, then perving over the middle-age barmaid with her tits slung out. Me and Stan usually play some pool while he gets pissed-up, then I'll help him home where our roast beef, yorkshire-pudding and gravy is ready for us. Yeah man, Shirley is a shit cook, she'll burn a poached egg, but her mum's decent and her gravy absolutely top notch. After lunch, Fat Stan will end up having a row with poor old Ethel about something and nothing. His beer induced excuse for him to "say sorry" and take her upstairs, to say sorry properly. Me, Shirley and Lacy, her younger brother, sit there watching Antiques Roadshow listening to Stan "apologising" by shagging poor Ethel senseless. Stifling our giggles, we listen to the headboard banging, him grunting and her yelling, 'oh, oh, oh, ah, ah, ah.' Playing along, she'll try and get him to climax as quickly as possible so that he'll fall asleep and leave her alone. Yeah man, her attempt at pacifying her man. She is, quite literally, scared shitless of him, he must knock her about a fair bit I reckon. His verdict on the Sunday roast is all important, especially with guests in the house. She's anxious and nervous, fidgety and on edge while he shoves a beef, roast potato and yorkshire-pudding combo into his fucking fat mush. Like a high-class wine connoisseur delicately tasting an eighty year old bottle, he chews it slowly, savouring the flavour before passing his all-important verdict. Like saps on tender-hooks, we're on the edge of our seats waiting with bated breath for the Dallas-style end of series cliff hanger. 'Yeah, lovely love,' the fat drunken bastard grunts before shoving another fork-full into his fat lardy face. Sigh of relief, the atmosphere changes, mood lifts and peace on earth restored.

But, if the Sunday dinner wasn't up to scratch, if the beef ever so slightly over done, Yorkshire pudding a bit soggy or gravy lumpy, then we all take a trip down to aggro-city. He'll kick off over any little thing and the argue-apologise-shag-fest begins again. Bless her, on hearing his "yeah, lovely" verdict, Ethel's face softens as the pent-up fear and tension fades away. Human again, she's beaming smiles, curved eyebrows and laughter lines. His happiness makes her feel womanly, no wonder she fakes it in the bedroom. Yeah man, I can see it, she'll make him feel manly and spunky and strong and, in turn, he'll make her feel womanly and leave her the fuck alone.

Just the way it is for their generation, I suppose.

Old-school working-class women will go out of their way

to make their men feel like "real" men, so they don't have to prove they are indeed "real" men by beating the shit out of them or their kids. It's old-school logic, the man has to be a "real" man, the bread winner, the father, king of his castle, master of all he surveys. Real men need to be virile and spunky and strong, with an insatiable urge to fuck, sow their seed and be all-powerful. So, Saturday night, after ten pints down the pub, the old-school "real" men, men like Stan, will be pissed up and ready for their sex, ready to prove to themselves they can still get it up. Failing that, they're ready for a tear up, ready to prove their manliness by beating the shit out of some have-a-go-hero. But, there's a massive problem, they all think the same, they all want to be beasts, they all want to be real men. To be the beast, they got to shag their wives or girlfriends or whores senseless, banging away for ages until the poor old cow fakes an orgasm just to make it stop. If they can't get it up, they'll tear each other apart through a drunken bar-brawl or by picking a fight with the kebab shop owner or bullying a group of kids pissing themselves laughing at the drunken old man giving it large swaying on his way home.

Either way, nobody wins.

After the shagging, the fake orgasms and the fighting, the real men, men like Stan, will sit in their living rooms all alone, supping cans of medium strength lager, wondering how they ended up there, how his life turned out this way and what might have been. Eventually, he'll accept he's no beast, he's never been a beast nor will ever be a beast. After accepting his reality, he'll still go to the pub every weekend, in fact, his loving missus will encourage him to go, get him out of the house and out of her hair. He'll sit in the pub, as he's always done, quiet and on his own other than the occasional nod of recognition between other so called "real men", each accepting their own realities. He'll sit, supping away at his pint, despising himself and loathing who he's become, necking pint after pint, trying to forget. Then, he'll go home feeling dejected and hollow and empty inside.

Quiet and melancholic, he'll sit in front of the telly with his can of lager remembering his youth, when he's strong and carefree, fucking the birds, banter with the boys, enjoying life without a care in the world. Then, he looks across the room at her, his for-better-and-for-worse loving wife. The good looks she once had when they first met are long gone, long forgotten, lost in the tedium of day to day life, surviving and just getting on with it. Twisting himself up, he'll hate himself for thinking like that, then he'll hate her for making him think like that. All of a sudden something will spark it off, something innocent and obvious, a misunderstanding or something.

Then, he'll do it. Lash out.

Petrified, scared of the beast, scared what happened last time is happening again, she'll piss herself and scream, but not too loud. She doesn't want the kids to hear, so she'll hold it down and keep the fear buried deep inside. Regretting it straight away, he'll try and comfort her, hug her, say sorry and try to be a real "real" man, not the beast "real" man. Soft and tender he'll put his arm around her but, she'll shrug him off, scared of what the beast might do, scared of what's coming next. Through the drunken haze of regret, the real man will take the fucking hump and see his arse. Shrug him off? How dare she refute his manliness!

Smack.

Again and again, the never-ending circle.

Tragic and pitiful.

I worked it out watching Stan and Ethel, watching what they say to each other and how they say it, watching their body language and the tone of their voices. Shirley and Lacy haven't got a clue, or, if they do, they never let on. I resist the temptation to tell them, not my place to shatter any illusions they might have of their parents wedded bliss. Nope, we just sit here listening to the Sunday afternoon headboard-banging, lets-make-it-up ritual, laughing our embarrassed laughs.

So anyway, Lacy, her younger brother and a complete

nightmare. From the off, he's on me like a rash, touching me now and again for weed, bugging me constantly, wanting to get his favourite tune on my radio station, (that "hip-hop-be-bop" electro tune). Even though he's nothing more than a bit part player, I could never have known when I first met him, he's the one who inadvertently opened my personal gateway to hell. Yeah, because of him, me and Claude, (mainly Claude), fell into the Millwall-hooligan scene. Even now, after all this time, I still can't believe it, me, a hooligan. That's what does for Ashley too, poor, poor Ashley, breaks my heart to even think about it...

Lacy drops round to Shirley's flat early one Saturday morning after taking a tonne of speed the night before. He hasn't slept and is on one, a right one too, buzzing his tits off talking like a machine gun, rat-a-tat-tat-this, chitta-chatta-that. Giving it large, he's boasting about how he and his mates are going to beat the shit out of some Northerners later on. Says he's heading down to Surrey Quays to meet up with the Millwall crew, neck a few pints, have a scrap and head to the match after that. Panicking, as usual, Shirley's going on and on about me going with him to look out for him and keep him out of trouble. The last thing I wanted is to go with Lacy, especially down to Surrey Quays and especially drinking with a load of Millwall fools. But, she's going on and on at me, Lacy rabbits on and on, speeding his tits off and the baby's crying his heart out, so, I grab my coat and I'm out the door.

Calling in at Claudes for back up in case the Millwall idiots turn on me, he's up for it before Lacy even finishes telling him about it, of course he is, he loves fighting. Heading down to Surrey Quays, Claude's convinced his motor will be cannibalised or torched or maybe somehow tracked back to him, so we jump on a bus. Down through the old dock-yard slums of Deptford, it takes ages even though it's only a couple of miles. Sitting upstairs we keep a low profile by sitting at the front. We sit listening, pissing ourselves laughing as a few younger kids at the back are shouting and screaming, boasting about how many girls fucked, fingered or fancied. Twenty minutes later Lacy gets up and rings the bell and we get off opposite the tube station, outside a pub.

THE SHIP PUB
LOWER ROAD
SURREY QUAYS, LONDON
EARLY SUMMER, 1983

Chock-a-block with Millwall geezers, the entire pub falls silent when they clock us walking in. A couple of hundred half pissed men, primed and ready for smashing heads and kicking shit, sit in complete silence staring at us. Intimidating, feels like we'll be lynched right there and then, tarred and feathered or some other national front crap. Five seconds later though, they return to their pints and resume their general geezerishness and sporadic football chanting. A big greasy foreign looking fella stands in the centre of it, along with the other geezers buzzing around him. He looks every part the boss man and, as it turns out, he is. Pushing our way towards the bar, Lacy shakes hands with loads of different geezers who grab him around his neck, giving it all, "oi-oi-oi-Lacy, you little fucker… how's it going kiddo," and all that south London banterish-bullshit. Taking it in his stride, he introduces us to loads of blokes on the way. Surprisingly, the geezers are known-you-a-million-years friendly, chucking us nods and winks and hard-bastard-grip-you-tight handshakes. I always thought of Lacy as a speed-dabbing, teenage-dickhead, but, turns out, he's connected. You see, the geezers love the "young-wanna-be" little kids, running errands for them, idolising them, making them feel important and significant. The geezer wants to be a mentor, a coach and a father figure because, along with ducking and diving, fighting and fucking, he wants to leave his mark on the world, carve himself a mini Mount-Rushmore in the image of himself. Lacy introduces me as his "brother-in-law Devon, from Brixton." Even though I only went back to the

Frontline a couple of times a month to see Momma, once he mentions Brixton, the Geezers give me a nod of respect.

A few pints later...
The tension's electric and everyone's totally up for it. With the beer and the singing and chanting of football songs, it feels almost tribal. With the handshakes and the knowing nods, the testosterone and adrenaline, to be honest, I'm feeling the vibe. Surrounded by a couple of hundred like-minded geezers makes me feel like I somehow belonged. After a couple of hours and fuck knows how many pints later, the boisterous banter subsides and everyone starts to get serious and more focused. A few geezers, who turn out to be the "top boys", including the big greasy bastard I spotted earlier they call "the Greek", (actually born in Cyprus, moved here where he was five by the way, geography not the hooligans strong point), starts pumping everyone up. Grabbing geezers by the shoulders, he's yelling into their faces before standing on a table on the middle of the pub. As he does, a wave of silence ripples across the pub.

'Right then you cunts,' he yells, snarling like an angry dog. 'Listen up and listen good. Today is our day, and this is our fucking manor. If any dirty cunt comes 'round here giving it large, what we gunna-fucking do?'

The entire pub explodes with screams and yells and cheers, eventually morphing into a long and drawn out Millllllll-waaaalllllllll chant.

Lapping it up, he continues. 'That's right, we're Millwall and fucking no-one likes us, you know why?' he pauses for effect. 'I'll tell you why, 'cause we're dirty horrible cunts. Anyone comes 'rand our manor, looking for aggro, we're gunna fucking give it to them a thousand times over and bite their fucking heads off.'

With that, the entire pub, landlord, tasty-fit barmaids, every single geezer in there goes completely mental, jumping around, grunting and growling. This Greek guy is like a cockney Winston Churchill or something. I'm in awe. This guy's the shit.

'Aw-right, aw-right, calm the fuck down. Nah-listen and listen good. Any-cunt runs, any-fucker slopes off 'rand the back, any-slag disappears, any-mug pisses himself, then be sure of one thing I'll find ya' and cut-ya me-self, right.' He pulls out a huge hunting knife, silver blade on one side and a saw thing on the other. He slices it through the air a few times and jumps down off the table. 'Right then cunts,' he shouts. 'Let's fucking have it!'

I look toward Claude and he's loving it with cartoon ruby-red love-hearts appearing all around him, popping above his head. He's lapping up the manliness and sense of belonging, the sheer aggression. I can see it plain as day, big burly alpha males with arms around his shoulders, treating him like they've known him for years talking of rampaging, punching, kicking, slicing and whacking, he's in his element. Right there, with the boozy adrenalin fuelled headiness blurring his senses, little did we know he's falling deeply and madly in love with Millwall and the hooligan lifestyle.

Following the Greek, we spill out of the pub. Just thinking about it now gives me tingles. Splitting into two groups, I'm behind the Greek while Claude follows a stocky little queer looking fella with crude-cut bleached blonde hair they call "the Albino". Looking around, I can't see Lacy anywhere and a tinge of panic sets in, knowing Shirley will give me grief if anything happens to him. Fuck it though, he's a big boy and I'm not his keeper. Another group of about a hundred or so came from the left, so we total at least a three, maybe four hundred strong. On the edge of crazy, we surround the tube station entrance and bounce on the balls of our feet with our fists clenched, we're ready for anything. 'Oi, oi, they're here, they're here. The fucking scum are here,' a young kid on a BMX bike shouts as he zooms out of the tube station entrance. Then, we spot them, the enemy, the northerners, the dirty scum who are about to be obliterated by a small army of Millwall hooligans. Turns out, they're actually from Brentford, west London, and not northerners at all, (okay, technically north of the river, but not proper northern northerners). As more and more of them spill out, we attack. Running across the road toward them, we collide and have it large, have it bigtime, have it massive. Tearing the place apart with fists, heads and knees flying everywhere, it's utter chaos. Noise, anger, aggression, panic, fight, flight, tribalism, anarchy. I fucking love it. Ten seconds in and the Brentford scum are scattering in all directions. A couple of their main crew stand firm though but get smashed up, heads smashing against walls, skulls stamped under feet, the shit is literally kicked out of them by a swarm of Millwall. Losing sight of Claude, I follow the Greek and a dozen more geezers through the station and down to the platforms. Once there, we see maybe thirty Brentford standing at the end of the platform, huddled together pointing and shouting and goading us. Turning around to face me, the Greek reaches into his inside pocket and pulls out a blue surgical face mask. With a fucked-up demented sadistic smile growing across his lined face, he hooks it around his ears and over his nose and mouth. He scares the shit out of me, and I'm on his side. 'No-one fucking runs or I'll do ya' me-self,' he growls. I believe him, I truly do, in any case I'm not running, no way, these fuckers are asking for it and, after fuck knows how many pints, I'm going to fucking give it to them. A couple of the other geezers pull on surgical face masks while the rest pull out tools, hammers, coshes and knives, while one of them has what turns out to be an ammonia filled Jiff-Lemon squeezy thing. The sight of this hooligan paraphernalia, the dim lighting of the tube station and the roar of both sets of nutters freaks me out, but I'm feeling it. Yeah, I'm shitting myself scared, but can't run, I actually want the tear-up.

Fear fascinates me, it's like a razor blade I suppose. On one side you're falling off the edge of a tower block with the hopeless panic of inevitability wrapped up in dread, darkness and despair. On the other side though, fuck me, is simply amazing. The energy, the passion, the anticipation, the adrenaline rush, the endless possibilities of hope. There's a fine line between both sides, but, on this day and on this platform and in this moment, the fear feels quite exquisite. I'm so fucking on it, I can literally feel the electricity running through me, across my head and down my arms, sparking and crackling between my fingertips. I feel unstoppable, unbeatable, untouchable, like Superman, Spiderman and Santa-fucking-Claus rolled into one. I haven't felt like this in years, I realise I've missed this kind of rush. I thought the hum-drum of family life replaced the need for that particular type of buzz, but, right here, I'm loving it, relishing it, eating it up. 'Millllll-Waaaaaallll…' we chant in perfect unison. Eerie, it sounds intimidating and weird, like a kid's nursery rhyme, innocent yet threatening at the same time.

'Millllllllllllll-WAAAAALLLL.'

After an excruciating couple of seconds, we charge and the carnage begins, pure, unadulterated anarchy. Loving it, I take a few whacks, but feel absolutely nothing. I spot a big bastard lunging toward the Greek with a blade but I'm in there first, he's in slow motion and I'm in Ninja-style double speed. Grabbing his neck with my left hand I smash him maybe five or six times in the face with my right, finishing him off with a beautiful head-butt. Funny, I've never head-butted anyone before but, in the moment, it feels right, feels amazing actually. The feeling of smashing someone in the face, seeing them fall away while their nose erupts is beautiful, in a fucked-up kind of way. Don't get me wrong, it's not like punching a normal every day civilian indiscriminately for no reason, nah. Punching someone who's up for it, someone who knows what's coming in a him-or-me kind of way, someone who know eyes wide open what he's getting into, is simply exhilarating. The whacks I take don't hurt, nah, they make me feel alive, more alive than I've ever felt before. I'm totally lost in the emotion of it all.

But, on the other side of the razor blade…

One of the younger Millwall wanna-be-geezers, a kid really maybe fifteen or sixteen years old, gets cut across the face. Standing statue-still with the hurricane of violence surrounding him, he's holding his cheek as deep red blood seeps through his fingers and dribbles down his arm. The weird thing is he's not crying or screaming, nah, he just stands there in silence. For a brief moment, a thought bounces across my mind about him being my little boy, my precious. How might I feel with him turning up at the front door with his cheek hanging off, or me being called to the hospital just as he's being prepared for surgery? Shit man, it's not right, not by a long shot.

After a few minutes of madness, the Brentford crew get properly fucked up, a few laid out unconscious across the platform. Vampires of South London, we surround our pray, kneel over their lifeless bodies, straddle their semi-deceased cadavers and feast on their souls. A couple of them jump onto the tracks and run-off down the tunnel, preferring to take their chances with a thousand-tonne tube-train than staying and fighting with us. I look around and see the Greek on top of a poor Brentford sucker. Stanley knife in hand, he's grunting away like a prehistoric caveman, hacking and slicing and cutting his face over and over and over with blood spurting literally two feet in the air. I turn away. Too dark, too horrific.

As we chase back up to street level, I catch the eye of an old lady with a couple of bags full of shopping in her hands. Just for a tiny split second, our souls connect as she stares at me with both fear and disgust in her eyes. She looks scared, like she knows I can reach into her chest and rip her heart out right there and then. Judgemental eyes, she stares at me like Momma used to and I shudder. Her head shaking disapprovingly from side to side, I know what she's thinking and I feel bad, guilty-bad, ashamed-bad. She's probably seen the blitz and the horrors of the second-world-war, and now, thirty or forty years later, she's watching us behave like this.

Her husband, her dad and her brother probably fought in the war against the fascists, for us to have the freedoms we have today, and for what? For the next generation to be kicking the living shit out of each other over what football team they support.

It's not right, I know that.

Top of the stairs, we exit the Tube station. Holy fuck, it's chaos. There's Police all over the place fighting with both sets of hooligans while a massive group of Millwall stand at the other side of the, road outside the pub, watching the battle while singing, 'no-one likes us, we don't care.' We hear sirens and bells approaching in the distance so get out of there quick-time, weaving our way through the maze of shit-hole estates, narrow alleyways and railway arches. Eventually, we reach New Cross and Millwalls home ground at Cold Blow Lane. Mingling with the normal every-day spectators, I bump into vaguely familiar known-you-forever faces from earlier on at the pub. Everyone's cheering, hugging and boasting about how many Brentford they'd smashed up. I spot the Greek staring over someone's shoulder straight at me. Maintaining eye contact, he makes his way towards me.

Shit.

'Aw-right, saw what you did with that big fucker,' he nods.

'Yeah?' I say, with a smile. 'Had it coming, the mugs.'

'Too right. Word is you're with young Lacys sister?'

'Er, yeah-yeah, that's right.'

'Nice one, nice,' he nods. 'Tidy bit of skirt that, well done.'

'Yeah, thanks,' I say. What the fuck should I say?

'Anyways, he had a chiv, so you did me a favour,' he smiles, before landing a not so soft punch on my arm. He throws me a wink and a smile before disappearing back into the crowd.

We don't have tickets for the game, so one of the old boys on the turnstiles nod toward the Greek and open it up. As we stream through, the Greek, the Albino and some other heavies make their way behind the goal at the Cold Blow

Lane end while I go with Lacy to grab a pint from the bar just inside the main stand. Just as we're served, Claude appears, draping his arm around my shoulder full of grins and smiles. Says he's heard about what I did with the Greek, and everyone's talking about it. I can't think about it though, I don't want to actually. Adrenalin fading, the reality of the carnage begins to dawn on me. Images of the young lad with the cut face haunts me, even today. Pints downed, the melancholic images of the young lad holding his face fade a little. We follow Lacy out to the middle of the main stand where the young kids, wanna-be-geezers or uninitiated stand. Once they earn it, they stand around the back of the goal with the others, but until then, they are known as "the halfway line." The Greek told me all about it…

The Greek himself was part of the "halfway line" in the seventies, eventually graduating to a hooligan firm known as "F-Troop". These guys, it seems, are a seriously fucked up collection of maybe thirty hardcore villains out to cause nothing but maximum mayhem. F-Troop are the first to wear the iconic surgical face masks you might see on TV, use weapons and focus on hooliganism rather than football. Up until the mid-seventies, most "bovver boys", as hooligans were known as back then, are into fist fights, but, the F-Troop lunatics changed all that. They're into double blade Stanley knives, ammonia, tear-gas and ten-inch metal coshes, in fact, anything and everything to cause maximum damage. Over time the older F-Troop chaps either get locked up, married or just grow out of it, or, in the Greeks words, get "too pussy" about it all. The Greek makes his way up through the ranks, eventually becoming top dog when he and a geezer called Bobby-the-Wolf have a legendary head-to-head after a row in a local pub. The Greek takes a proper hiding, leaving him with his scar across his eyebrow and forehead, but, after a gruelling fight, he comes out on top. Bobby duly retired, or whatever wolves do when they stop wolfing. "Natural selection" and "evolution" the Greek says. He says he knows one day one of the young wanna-be's will do the same to him. "No empire lasts forever," he says.

Back to the match, it's okay as far as football goes, I'm not really into it, not like the Greek or Claude. Millwall win, I think, and avoid relegation, so, after the match, I leave Claude with Lacy and about forty other Millwall hardcore who are heading down the Old Kent Road and a pub-come-club called the Dun Cow to celebrate. Proper Millwall-land down there, no way I'm going, Millwall or not, it's no place for the likes of me. Nah, the Old Kent Road is renowned as the hang-out of old-school villains and, worst of all, wanna-be-out-to-prove-something nearly-villains, who'll start a fight just to earn a better reputation.

Not for me, no thank you.

I get back home at about seven or eight. After hearing about the trouble on local radio, Shirley's pulling her hair out worried so I tell her Lacys with Claude, he'll be fine, no need to worry, but that just makes her even more worried. I take over daddy duties and she goes to bed early to get some sleep, but, we both know she sat on the edge of the bed sulking all night. Later on, I sit looking at my little boy who's asleep in my arms peaceful and quiet. I feel sick and disgusted about what happened earlier in the day. I'm guilty for my part in it, disgusted I revelled in it and actually enjoyed it. I keep seeing the young boy standing there in shock, his cheek cut open and covered in blood. Shed some tears that night, I don't mind saying. What will he say to his Momma when he gets home? Her beautiful, precious, perfect little boy fucked up and scarred for life. Shit, he'll have that scar forever, at job interviews, his wedding day, the day his baby is born, damn, a constant reminder of the fateful day, right up to the day he dies. Imagine, an old aged pensioner picking up his pension with a stripe down his cheek. I bet he didn't even want to go in the first place, didn't really want to get involved in any fighting, probably just tags along with his mates, like what I did with Lacy. His scar a visible reminder of a single bad decision, a go-with-the-flow scar, an unwanted trying-to-fit-in-with-his-mate's medal of honour. It's not right man, not right at all. But, me being me, the next weekend Lacy taps me up for an away fixture. Up North proper, Sheffield I think he said. I'm not up for it so make up some kind of lame excuse, whereas Claude is most definitely up for it. Borrowing a transit van from one of his bouncer mates, he drives himself, Lacy and a small team up there. As the Millwall fans outnumber the home fans four to one, there's no trouble, but, geezers need excitement, don't they? It's simple, all a hooligan wants to do is be a hooligan, stands to reason. Claude says after the match they go into town for drinks, ending up tearing the town apart, running in and out of the pubs and nightclubs, kicking the shit out of the bouncers, punters and anyone else who gets in their way. From then on, Claude commits to the hooligan lifestyle big time. Millwall flags hanging in his front room, replica kit to train in, lion tattoos on his arms, everything. I see less of him after that, allowing me to run the radio station without any of his tinkering and his what-about-this-what-about-that madness.

"Ah, the infamous Radio Station?" the Interrogator says, changing the subject, no doubt as bored as I am talking about this hooligan shite.

Yeah, the radio station…

You're listening to Devious Dee on Dream FM.

Keep it locked.

Even though I mess about on the decks, I'm no deejay. Nah man, I prefer the business side, deal doing side, managerial and organisational side. As soon as I buy the station, we move from wall to wall reggae to soul and funk, then to electro and hip hop and eventually, to House music. House is more "mass market" as Paul would say, which means bigger audiences, which in turn means bigger and better advertisers, and bigger fees. To be fair, whenever he talked about business, I listen. Around that time he wants us to play some new romantics and new wave crap, some sort of urban "top-of-the-pops" bullshit. He's seeing a girl called

Sue, from Bromley or somewhere the fuck, who's the lead singer in a new-wave-punk band and he wants to help her get airtime. Fuck off, I'm not playing no anti-establishment, guitar smashing, yelling and screaming white-boy shit, no way. At the same Marlon is doing well with his music too, deejaying during the night on my station, going to college during the day and working in a record shop in Hackney in the afternoons. Happy and content, he's sorted. Yeah man I'm proud of him. Gets himself a flat and a tidy girlfriend, young blonde thing with perky breasts and a tight little arse.

He's sorted, got it made, made something of his life…

Thoughts drifting, eyes misting and glazing over as my focus zooms out and blurs. I miss him. Memories of happier times surround me but, as ever, are tinged with my sadness, my regret, my remorse of what I've done, what I've caused and what I've become.

"Yep, he had it sorted, until you fucked it up for him," the Interrogator says, judging me and condemning me with one simple sentence.

Don't you DARE.

I've had enough of this, judged and condemned without even a jury to plead to. With this goading and provoking, HE who must be obeyed has this coming, he knows he has.

Jumping to my feet I reach for the stand lamp in the corner of the room. Right motherfucker, you want it, you're going to get it. Swinging baseball bat style, I miss. Shit. Connecting with the wall, it snaps into two. Half a lamp in my hand, I'm standing motionless in the centre of the room, raw emotion pumping through my veins.

"Ha-ha, look at the big man, swinging and missing like a fucking pussy," the Interrogator says, laughing.

I'm ready, you got it coming.

Tense, a Mexican stand-off, right here in south-east London. He refuses to engage first, goading me to step out of line, but I'm cute, I know his game. Stillness surrounds me for god-knows how long, a few minutes, a couple of hours maybe. Eventually, I launch the half-lamp-half-baseball-bat across the room before collapsing to my knees. You god-damn prick, teasing me, taunting me, tempting me with revenge. It's not my fault. It's not my fault.

None of it.

"Boo-fucking-hoo, it is your fault, you know it is," the Interrogator says, truth etching through his nicotine stained croaky voice.

Head in hands, I sway back and forth, groaning and scratching dirty fingernails across my balding scalp. I can't stop thinking about the poor boy with his cheek hanging off. It's not my fault, not my fault. Crawling across the room like a scabby mongrel dog sniffing around the bins at the base of a tower-block, I rummage around the coffee table. Eventually, through my tear-soaked-regret-filled eyes I find my tiny, inch-long paper package of goodness. Spoon in hand with tears rolling, I tap out a few grains of browny-white powder and purse my lips, allowing a dribble of spit to seeps out onto the spoon. I delicately mix the chemical cocktail before I gently caress my lighter under the base of the spoon. The mixture steams as tiny golden bubbles appear. Shivering, a rush of expectant excitement shoots up my spine, sparking across my brain. It's dirty and disgusting, but the yearning is too strong, the need to rid myself of my errors, my mistakes, my deep and utter complete regret. Tearing open a cigarette, I take out the filter and squeeze it until it's wide and thin. Zoning in on the orange syringe, I feel my stomach twist as sour bile juices fill my mouth. Taking the syringe, I pull the mixture through the filter, extracting maximum sweet-sweet goodness. Holding the loaded-pleasure-gun aloft, it's goldenness glistens like a rainbow as a beam of sunlight streaks through the room and hits it like a Pink Floyd-prism. Tap, tap, tap, I gently and ever so slowly push the plunger until a tiny golden pearl hangs to the needle end.

Images of that night, my night of all nights and my baby brother Marlon flash through my mind. I see blue lights and ambulances, oxygen masks and adrenalin injections. I see death and sorrow, regret and remorse. Shaking my head, horrors are replaced with sweet, innocent images of Marlon when he's six years old being picked up from school. We walk home hand in hand with smiles and jokes and happiness. More tears roll. Tears for him, tears for me, tears for the life I once had. The skagg doesn't really help, but it dulls the pain. I must fight it, have to prove "Him" wrong, show some self-control. Breathing deeply, I delicately place the loaded skagg rifle on the edge coffee table. Concentrating, using the Jedi Force, I will it to move, urge it to leap up and fly through the window, out of my reach and out of my life. I don't have a choice then, no evil sadistic life limiting choice. Heart pounding, my eyes lock onto the syringe. Fuck it, I'm no addict, can take it or leave it. Yeah baby, I'm in control. Five minutes will do it, need to build resistance, stamina, a will to survive, five minutes time me and you will dance, bitch. Small steps yeah. I can abstain for at least five minutes, then ten, then before not very long, an hour, a day, a week and then eventually free myself.

I'm in control.

Next season, Millwall are favourites for promotion, farfetched if you ask me, they just about avoided relegation the season before, but, idiot-hope springs eternal in football. Claude's a proper Millwall man now, in with the top dogs, the Greek and the Albino. Those two mother fuckers are crazy, especially the Albino, he's a stark raving psychopath, a raving queen too. Ironic yeah, one of the top dogs in the top firm in England, notorious for smashing heads, is in fact, the campest gay-guy you might ever meet. You can't make this shit up. Both him and the Greek are proper villains though, into everything from armed robbery to cocaine dealing. Buying and selling to other top dogs of rival gangs, their biggest customer happens to be a West Ham geezer called "Jones". The most geezerish geezer of all time. Little did I know back then our destinies are and will forever be intertwined and inextricably inter-linked.

Anyway, with the new season approaching, the Millwall

firm plan a few 'training sessions' at pre-season "friendlies". The first one, and the last one I go to, is Tonbridge United, located in the hot-bed of hooliganism, the garden of England, rural Kent. Claude's hyper, wanting to get a crew of his own together to prove he's on par with the Greek and the Albino. Having his own crew will be a step up, show he's got real clout, a genuine heavyweight who deserves a place at the top table. To be fair to him, he recruits his bouncer mates who work for him, big ugly mugs, hard-as-nails too. They bring their mates and their mates bring their mates as well. I give Paul a call, convince him it'd be a giggle and give him something edgy to talk about with his city-of-London corporate finance chums. He takes some convincing but eventually he's up for it. Meeting outside Claudes flat early in the morning, he turns up with his younger brother, Ashley. A nice lad who used to hang around with Marlon years back, a good footballer recently released by Crystal Palace a few months earlier having completed a youth training scheme. He played in a couple of early round FA cup games but gets loaned out to non-league Crawley Town for most of the season and ultimately deemed not quite good enough to earn a professional contract. With Marlon doing his music and at college in Tottenham, nowadays Ashley's at a loose end. Soon as he heard about what we're doing, he's on at Paul to let him come and, Paul being Paul, (and a massive cunt), he let him. To be honest, I hadn't seen him in a couple of years, so it's nice to see him.

But, I'd have never let Marlon come.

No way, no chance.

Slamming his front door shut, Claude bounces down the stairs. I can tell he's agitated, no smiles, no nods, no 'morning chaps,' only frowns and scowls. Barging me aside, he heads across the road where a few of his bouncer-mates are waiting in a banged-up shit-brown coloured Ford Escort. Big, hairy and mean looking super-hard bastards, they stare daggers at me as they knock back cans of larger and smoke dirty-stinky resin, at ten in the morning by the way. They get out and we all gather around Claude for some nods and winks while he passes round a small plastic coin bag, half-full of glistening white powder, charlie, yo-yay, coke… you know, cocaine in the brain. Tapping it out onto the back of our hands, we snort that shit up before rubbing the residue around our gums. Looking around, everyone's totally up for it, apart from me. As much as I'm buzzing and loving the cocaine-confidence, I've a sick feeling growing in my stomach, a nagging doubt in the back of my mind, a whispering voice of impending doom or something. I glance across at Ashley, although nineteen and joining in with the snorting, his mannerisms suggest he's much younger, a boy in a man's body I suppose. A good-looking lad, he's wide-eyed and naive, giving it large due to the powder and the peer group pressure. I tell Paul as much, but he laughs it off. Being a city-spiv-businessman, he's usually coked up to the eyeballs, and, that morning, he's no different. I'm not happy with young Ashley coming, or, ironic as it sounds, snorting coke. On top of that, I can't get excited about some witless non-league bumpkins from Kent. West Ham or one of the top teams like Liverpool or even Man United, yeah, I can get, but, turnip farmers from the back of beyond?

What on earth are we doing?

Fuck knows.

From Claudes flat, we march double-quick to Deptford train station where we meet thirty or forty more geezers. Respect due, Claude assembled a very tasty team. Twenty minutes later, we board a train heading to Tonbridge via London Bridge. A real eye opener, oh yeah, the journey is placid and pleasant, no yobbish behaviour, no ripping up seats or smashing windows, no chanting or goading, nope, quite the opposite in fact. We sit there quiet and respectful, playing cards and chatting. Yep, the hardcore Millwall hooligan crew travel in a civilised and calm manner, like gentleman, all the while holding down our cocaine-adrenalin induced rushes and spine-tingling shivers. The journey takes about an hour to get to turnip-central, with us stopping at every poxy little station en-route. As soon as the train pulls in, I know we've made a mistake. As far from a hotbed of hardcore hooliganism as you can get, this place is a picture-postcard of middleclass-rural-England. Little wooden walkway with a white picket fence leads from the train station to a wooden bus-stop-come-waiting room thing at the end, everything's painted white, clean and fresh, innocent and respectable.

No way we'll find any trouble around here... as if.

BARDEN ROAD
TONBRIDGE
MIDDLE OF NOWHERE, KENT
PRE-SEASON, 1983

The little village green is teeming with Police, and a surprisingly large amount of Millwall geezers, feels like a Saturday afternoon down at Cold Blow Lane not middle-England. No sign of any country-bumpkin fans though, only bemused local bobbies, more accustom to seeing sheep across country lanes than dealing with several hundred hooligans from south London. Claude's visibly nervous though, chewing the inside of his lip and looking generally vexed, (more vexed than usual anyway). Fuck knows what's wrong with him, but I know he's promised his team a tear-up and a rampage, and, if they don't get their excitement, he'll look like a mug and lose all respect. After a while, we bump into the Greek. I see him before he sees us, strolling around Bumpkin City lording it over his foot soldiers, his pawns and his hooligan plebs. Spotting us, he makes his way over, shaking everyone's hand as he approaches. Claude's on him straight away asking what's going on and when's it going to kick off. The Greek, otherwise known as mister-not-a-care-in-the-world, tells us to chill the fuck out, not to worry, relax and take it easy. He winks, then floats off back into the crowd.

Twenty minutes later…

Two lines of bewildered, totally out of their depth local Police escort us around the back of the village hall towards the football ground. Nothing more than a pitch, no stadium, no stands or anything, just a field with a four-foot-high fence around it. With no sign of any bumpkin fans, my nagging doubt moves into overdrive telling me what a massive waste of time this is. The Greek, still calm and mellow, tells us to be patient, be cool, hold tight on the mic. He's got an air of arrogance about him, like he's connected to the world in some kind of magical voodoo-ray kind of way, knowing what's going to happen before it happens. Freaks me out big time but, at the same time, his persona is alluring and attractive, he's got charisma.

The teams come onto the pitch from the little Portakabins at the far corner, the mighty Millwall in royal blue, Tonbridge United in red and white and both begin their warm-ups. The game eventually kicks off and we make our way around to the back of the goal furthest from the car park where the Police gathered. The confused locals stand mouth open staring at us, no clue what's going on. Still no sign of any aggravation though, which is great by the way, I can't wait to get it all over and done with and get back to London, back to normality. Mid-way through the first half, a large team of rival fans, maybe a hundred or so, make their way through the car park toward us. What the fuck? I can't believe my eyes, or my ears. "Chelsea, Chelllllsea, Chel-Seeeeea," they chant. Chelsea? Nah, this is turnip-united, not Chelsea. I look at the Greek, laughing his sick head off. Makes complete sense now, we're not here to take on a bunch of farmers from Tonbridge, it's always been about the Chelsea. A pre-season rumble on neutral territory, yeah, I get it. The Greek's jumping around, telling everyone to stand firm and not to run. Adrenalin surging, I'm in survival mode, ready to fight, ready to see my missus, see my boy, see a dawn on another day.

Chelsea charge and we charge towards them. Chaos! Fight

or flight urges engulf me, but, right here and now, it's fight. We smash the dirty fucks into pieces, even pussy-boy Paul does well, running in, throwing some punches then retreating. Ashley gets stuck in too while Claude, like a caveman on speed, rampages through the crowd. He and the Greek are side by side, launching punches, kicks and headbutts with bodies flying in all directions. The Chelsea crew stream onto the pitch to get away from us, the fools. The match is stopped when the Police stream on and the players run off then the fighting eases off and the Police make a line across the pitch separating the Millwall from the Chelsea. After some pointing and shouting, Chelsea retreat behind the goal, and we do the same behind the other. A Police chief approaches, with a loud-hailer-megaphone and an official from Millwall with him, suited and booted with a Millwall badge on his breast pocket. They both plead with us to calm down and stop the violence. The Millwall official, an old chap with grey hair, tells us we should grow up, cut it out and be all about football. The fucking decrepit sap, he don't know shit. It's about the tear up, feeling alive. Geezers need excitement. Boring nine to five jobs? Bollocks. Conforming to the status quo? Bollocks. Waiting in line, being good little boys? Absolute bollocks. Nah, we need the razor blade, the fear, the rush of becoming a beast.

After a while, the players come back on, heads down, shoulders up, not wanting any of it wishing they were back at their holiday villas on the Algarve or in Marbella. As the match restarts, we split into two groups and make our way around each side of the pitch toward the Chelsea goal. Grouping together, they seem to shrink in size as we approach, no doubt shitting themselves. To be honest, I'm shitting myself, and I bet the vast majority of the other Millwall geezers are too, other than the hardcore hooligans who live for this bullshit. Got to front it out though and avoid incurring the wrath of the Greek. Jogging around the corner flag and we charge full sprint. The Greek steams into the Chelsea top boy, Tommy McDowell. An absolute legend, he featured as part of a documentary on the BBC about violence on the terraces a few years before. Everyone in the hooligan community knows him, the wider general public too. But, today is his day of reckoning because, like a world championship heavyweight boxer, the Greek lands a flurry of punches to his face before a devastating left hook, flooring him. McDowell stumbles back to his feet and, in super-slow-motion, the Greek grips him by the neck, thumbs probing deep into his throat, he head-butts him in the face, over and over and over, smash, smash, fucking smash. Unconscious, McDowells legs hang from his limp body like a tiny rag doll puppet while the Greek holds him aloft like a gladiator presenting his prize to the baying crowd. Letting him go, he falls into a heap and the Greek stands over the lifeless body, beating his chest King Kong style. The fighting slows then stops as everyone, Millwall, Chelsea and the Police look on in silence, watching the beast feast on his poor lifeless victim. Roaring like a lion, the Greek's in some kind of violent trance, revelling in his evil-ecstasy. Becoming aware of himself and everyone staring, he stops and spins around, lapping up the attention. Police horses gallop in and we scatter in all directions. Ambulances follow, driving onto the pitch to deal with the injured, including McDowell. Players and officials are long gone and the match abandoned ten minutes from full-time. If this isn't bad enough, what happens next is dark and disgusting, truly gruesome shit…

With Police and Police horses on the pitch, together with the ambulances and the injured, we chase the last few remaining hardcore Chelsea into the carpark. Met by more Police, the Chelsea stand behind them goading us. At first, the Police try to split us up, yelling at us to calm down and grow up in their highly trained, highly patronising way. But, the bumpkin Police are pumped-up excited and adrenalin-hyper, they're loving the excitement too, loving the buzz, loving the opportunity for them to be beasts. They want some excitement for themselves, want a proper story to tell the chaps down the pub at the weekend. Stretching across the car park in a line, the Police start kicking out toward us, throwing punches and we do the same, nothing too heavy to begin with. Even though the last remaining Chelsea have just about cleared off, the Police stand firm and carry on fighting with us. Me and Paul get separated from Claude and Ashley, fuck knows where they are, but scanning around I see the Greek. Yeah, rampaging through the crowd of Police, forehead down, fists crunching into heads, boots driving into exploding testicles. An awesome sight, an Olympic standard hooligan, a world class destroyer, a Jedi master of thuggery.

Then, I saw it happen.

It didn't have to happen, it shouldn't have happened.

An innocent, he had no idea what he was letting himself in for, he should never have been there in the first fucking place. I see him out of the corner of my eye, the bit where you think you see something but can't be sure. Poor, innocent, just-a-kid Ashley tussles with a skinny dickhead Police officer who looks about the same age. Barely scrapping, they're throwing handbags and shoving each other, grappling and wrestling. Then, two big burley fat fuck country-bumpkin-farmer Police charge over and look to get involved too. I can't get there in time, can't get by the flying fists and feet of the rampaging crowd.

I just can't help him, can't face what's happening, it's horrific.

I still see it now when I close my eyes.

His scared eyes lock on to mine screaming 'help me' and 'go get my mum,' while inevitability spreads across his face. He see's what's coming, yeah, in that instant, that millisecond where our eyes met, he glimpses into his future.

One of the big burley fat fuck Police raises his standard issue truncheon way above his head, no doubt pausing for a second as doubt ricochets through his mind, then smashes it down towards the back of Ashley's head. Legs gone, eyes roll, poor, delicate, fragile, innocent Ashley falls to the ground. The young skinny officer starts kicking him all over, head, body and legs while the fat bastards nod and smile at their handywork. Dazed and confused, Ashley starts kicking out trying to defend himself, but it's in vein, it's futile, you can't stop the inevitable, you can't dodge your fate.

The two fat fucks eventually pull the young skinny Police away, probably remembered who they were, the Police, sworn to protect us and duty bound not to knock seven shades of shit out of young kids caught up in hooligan madness. I'm trying to get over to him, to help, to stop it, but with every step I take I'm knocked back by geezers mauling, jostling and jousting, tearing and scratching at each other.

Can't reach him, can't save him, can't save me.

Just when I think it's over, the nightmare twists, distorts and turns even more ugly.

Pulling the young skinny officer away, the fat fucks turn back to poor Ashley. Instead of giving him a helping hand to his feet and tending to his wounds, they start swinging their truncheons around his knees and legs while he rolls around on his back trying to cover up. I'm yelling, shouting, screaming for them to stop, stop you mother fucking cunts, stop for fucks sake, but they can't hear, nobody can hear. The fat fucks are loving it, absolutely loving it, living their dreams, taking revenge, bathing in the forbidden waters of manliness. Curled up in a ball, he's trying to protect himself, but, like wolves around a felled baby deer, the fat fucks are whacking, smashing and kicking him, over and over and over. I can't get over to him quick enough, I'm helpless, he's helpless. I'm looking around for Claude or Paul or the Greek or anyone to help, but I'm helpless. Poor Ashley's screaming and pleading and begging them to stop, putting his hand up and shaking his head, but the fat fucks keep on pounding, stamping all over him.

Eventually…

The fat fucks are gone, merged into the anonymous crowd now scattering and dispersing quickly and I reach him.

Rolling around in agony he's groaning hauntingly deep, painful and scared groans from the pit of his stomach. Even today, when the silence takes hold and the voices inside my head subside, I hear echoes of the past, the groans and the pain and the torture. Within seconds, an ambulance reverses through the quickly thinning out crowd as the battling tribes reform into two heaving masses at either end of the car park. Ashley's in the back now, flat out on a stretcher with an oxygen mask over his face and straps over his chest. He's screaming like a wild animal caught in a beartrap, crying for his mum. Pulling his way through the crowd forming at the back doors, peaking in like vampires smelling blood, Paul jumps in and cradles his brothers head. Looking at poor Ashley's twisted up legs, I see him heave to be sick then he looks over to me, blame and sorrow and hate in his eyes. Ashley's pulling at the oxygen mask, panicking, screaming and hallucinating, seeing snakes and shit.

Both legs broken.

Shin bone snapped and a fractured kneecap, all on me.

That's when things changed between me a Paul, when our childhood blood-brother bond was broken, smashed and obliterated. Reading his mind, I can hear his thoughts, blaming me, putting it on me, wishing I'm the one twisted up, not his baby brother. I'm the one who called him, involved him, encouraged him, told him it'll be a laugh. He can fuck off though, the mug. It's definitely not on me, no way, it's on him. He invited Ashley, encouraged him, brought him along, not me. I'd never let my baby brother, my precious Marlon come to this hellish nightmare, no chance. But, contradiction of contradictions, I know who is really to blame, of course I do, I get it. Whether direct or indirect, of course it's on me, I know that now and accept my blame, accept my fate and, and, as a result, accept the consequences. I'll never admit it to him, the fucking snake, but I did that to poor Ashley, I might as well have smashed him with a truncheon myself. My destiny includes Ashley's fate in a twisted tangle of chronologies.

It's all my fault, I accept it, accept all of it.

Blame me.

I'm to blame.

Nowadays, Poor Ashley walks with a limp, every shuffle of his painfully stiff legs feels like a razorblade cut across my soul. Although not a professional footballer, he's done alright for himself, a manager in a fast-food burger joint in, ironically, Kent. He seems positive, optimistic even, says he's happy with his lot, plenty to be grateful for. We both know it's complete and utter bullshit. I see it in his eyes, a sadness, a melancholy, a vagueness and, on top of this, blame and regret and a fierce mistrust, perhaps even hate. Sitting at home messaging his aching legs on a dark night in October, he must wonder what if? What might his life have turned out like if he didn't come with? What if he stayed at home? What if he missed the call from Paul? What if Paul didn't know Devon Walters in the first place?

What-if, what-if, what-if, what-if, what-if, what-if.

I'm so sorry what happened.

I truly and honestly am…

"You expect me to disagree? No way buddy-boy, no fucking way," the Interrogator says unequivocally, giving me no way out.

As the truth washes over me, acid tears stream down my face. Even now, the stark reality of the truth is hard to take, even though I sit here and take it up the arse by him, sodomised by his truth…

Fuck it.

Grabbing the brown leather belt, I loop it around my upper arm, tightening it with my teeth. Spanking the top of my forearm, the vein stands to attention like and erect cock waiting to be consumed by a moist, wet pussy. Reaching over, I grab the needle from the edge of the coffee table and flinch as I gently slide the needle in then out, fucking myself with a microscopic needle of doom. Pressing the plunger slowly and deliberately, I know in a matter of seconds I'll feel nothing and my mind will be free. Watching the dirty-brown golden mixture disappear, I pull the plunger back a

little. As I do, my black, evil, cursed blood surges back into the plastic tube. Staring at the darkness of my soul, it swirls around inside syringe where I can see my whole life contained inside. Dark and poisonous and rancid and trapped, a liquified version of me, me in a bottle. Pushing the plunger back down, the darkness disappears. Heart rate slowing, the belt loosens and the needle slides out of my arm like a post orgasm shrivelled-up cock. Simultaneously, euphoric orgasmic heat emanates from every part of my body. Engulfed by the sofa, I sink into it and the memories of yesterday fade away.
  Ahhhhhhh…
  Gooooodnessss…

5. Changing Times

"As cold as ice, I hope we live to tell the tale. They really ought to know. These are the things we can do without. Come on, I'm talking to you… come on"

Roland Orzabal

17, HAMILTON HOUSE
GREENWICH, LONDON
LATE SUMMER, 1989

Even with the delicious golden sunlight laser-beaming through the window, I'm cold, freezing cold, cold-turkey-cold. The orgasmic rush injected into my bloodstream several hours ago has dissipated, now a long-lost memory of happier, elegant and eminently more sophisticated times. Shivering, teeth chatter while I sit at this god forsaken kitchen table, my gaze drawn through the window west, toward central London. With the sun sinking slowly into the horizon, the dark blanket of night creeps slowly across the sky. Night-time is the worst time, quiet and solemn with more time to think, more time to dwell on my regret, more time to wallow in my self-pity. Hand drifting across my overgrown and unkempt beard down toward my neck, I double-check myself. Skinny, scrawny neck and the once pronounced line separating my round pectorals has all but gone, replaced by a bony pigeon chest of a ten-year-old Ethiopian boy. Raising my deformed hand, I stare into it and see flashes of the night of nights, nightmare memories strobe through my mind.

"What happened to you," the Interrogator probes, knowing exactly what happened.

I know exactly what happened, but can't work out why. "Why" is the question, it's always the question. Elasticity, Paul would say, what goes up must come down. A dickhead and a looser, that's me. Winning for a while though, yeah man, before I fucked it up and pissed it all away…

Thoughts turn sour as coldness fills the room, breath hanging anti-gravity style in the air. Transfixing on the past while I dwell on my future, looking back, then looking forward, I get confused, or do I?

Maybe time isn't a straight-line or one-way street, nah, maybe it's not a "linear construct" as Paul might say. Yeah, maybe time isn't two-dimensional but like a puddle of water where you can move backwards and forwards, up and down, or just splash around in it. Or, maybe it's like a massive plate of spaghetti, looping and winding around itself, back and forth, in and out…

Fuck knows.

Where did I get to?

Ashley, right, poor Ashley…

I had to see what I'd caused, needed to confirm the devastation for myself, so went to visit him in hospital. A sorry sight, a contraption of wires and weights and pullies, and pain, lots of pain, so much pain. The most tragic part is when they tell him he'll have problems walking, and his football career is over. At first, he doesn't believe it, yelling they've made a mistake, got it wrong, mixed him up with some other tragic soul. He gets them to double check, triple check and show him the x-ray pictures. His folks ask for a second opinion, a more senior, better qualified doctor, a world-renowned Harley Street consultant specialist guy and, guess what, he's wrong too. Anyway, Ashley's strong, they know the doctors have under-estimated him, he'll show them, he'll show them all. Ashley's old man, mister self-made-millionaire will pay for specialist surgeons and the best physiotherapy. He'll send him to California or Germany to see the world's best, those that treat world class athletes and professional sportsmen. But, you and I know, eventually, when the harsh reality of the truth sets in, when the emotion has died down and when logic takes over, it'll be easier to accept, but, never easy to deal with. With all the pressure and disappointment, the lost dreams floating down the river of regret, Ashley cracks up with a nervous breakdown. Tragically, he stumbles out of his private room, out of the ward then up the stairs, finding his way to the roof.

Life's not worth living, why bothering trying.

I get that.

Standing on the edge, feet tingling, his eyes wobble and vision blurs. Heart beating fast, he's going to do it. Then, a caring hand touches his shoulder and another around his waist. He bursts into tears and buries his head into the nurses shoulder as they lead him away. Nineteen years old and a nervous breakdown, his whole entire life fucked? White coats and sedatives, he's committed under the mental health act or something, for his own good they say…

Because of me.

Paul came around a few days after, yelling and kicking the door in, blaming me, blaming the world. We end up knocking each other around a bit, nothing too heavy, he's no fighter. Storms off with a bloody nose and we don't speak for ages. Suits me though, means I'm not consistently reminded about poor Ashley, out of sight out of mind and all thank bollocks. Anyway, we'd grown apart way before then, him with his yuppie friends, multi-million-pound business deals, cocaine and Porsches and me, with my Saturday afternoon hooliganism, pirate radio station and my fledgling night club promotions business.

The late nights take a toll on the postman job though. First off, I'm suspended, "persistent lateness" or "non-attendance" or some kind of crap. Shirley, man, she's mad, kicking off big time about me not being a proper dad, not taking my responsibilities seriously. I love her fight, her spunk, her stubbornness but not being a proper dad though, nah, she can fuck off. I'm bringing home more money than ever, I love my boy and, mostly importantly, I'm still around unlike nearly all her friends where their fellas have fucked off before the birth, leaving them as single mothers struggling through life. She knows how to hurt me though, she always did. The beginning of the end starts with arguments at first before we eventually make it up with some make-up sex. Yeah man, we both enjoy the shouting and the inevitable shagging, sometimes we'll fuck during an argument, quick and hard and passionate. Eventually though, the fucking dries up and we only do the shouting and arguing part and, over time, even that dries up too, with us punishing each other by not talking for days on end. A day rolls into a few days, then a week goes by and we'll only start talking again with another argument…

A mug, a stupid dickhead, I never appreciated what I had when I had it. Wish I can rewind time and not do what I did, but, we both know I'm not ready to talk about that.

The love and lust fizzles away, as do the arguments. No heat or warmth, the flame just burned out and we end up living separately in the same house. Not even flat mates, just two random people who happen to live in the same place and share a baby. Too much effort to put things right I suppose, besides, the promotions work is full on with at least two or three promotions per. In a round-about way, Marlon got me involved with the nightclub promotions game. I told you about him going to college, doing electronics or something, well, during the evenings and weekends he helps out in a record shop in Hackney. The pay isn't great, but he blags freebies from promoters and of course the all-important dub-plate exclusives from record producers and distributers. One day, a random bloke walks in and spends a couple of hundred quid on a load of twelve-inch records. They get chatting and he tells Marlon he owns a club in Dalston, asks if he knows anyone who can have a look at his sound-system, something to do with a stereo feed dropping out. Turns out he owns the "Three Hearts" club, well known at the time as a decent soul and funk venue. Bigging himself up, Marlon said he'll have a look at it as he's doing a sound engineering course at college. As promised, he passes through that evening, chats the owner up and somehow gets himself a spot deejaying, warming up on Thursday nights. One thing leads to another and Marlon persuades him to let him put on a party on a Sunday. Why Sunday? Well, Sunday's the worst night, the graveyard shift, hardly any punters venture out on a Sunday and those who do have next to fuck-all cash left over from the weekend. If the owner can get even fifty punters through the door, he'll be laughing. The owner, damn, a fatty named Steve, a greasy haired, unshaven rough-looking guy, as camp as they come. Says he managed a few different clubs in the Soho years ago, reckons he invented the whole New Romantic scene in the late seventies. Yeah man, he romances himself by name-dropping everyone from Boy George to Billy Idol to David Bowie. Marlon doesn't have a clue about any of these guys, or promoting for that matter, so naturally, he calls me and we take it from there. My regulars come, of course they do, they'll come to any of my nights come what may, and they bring a few friends and friends of friends. Steve, the fat-twat owner loves it, trebling his normal Sunday takings, so we end up doing it a couple of more times.

It doesn't last long though...

Why? One word.

Super.

THREE HEARTS CLUB
DALSTON LANE
HACKNEY, LONDON
AUTUM, 1983

I need a doorman I can trust so approach Claude, but he wants a hundred and fifty quid. With only usually a hundred or so punters in, I simply can't afford it. However, Super, on the other hand is skint, (he's always skint), constantly on at me to sort him out with a job and wants only thirty quid. He's big, bad and a complete bastard, and as it turns out, proves to be a great doorman. To be fair to him, he takes it seriously, kits himself out in some nice garments, a decent suit, clean white shirt complete with cufflinks plus a tie and black overcoat. Old-school by todays standards, but he looks the part, and, as it happens, ran the door professionally, turning away the troublemakers, back-street brawlers and pissed-up fanny-chasers.

Until.

A few weeks after our opening night, a couple of pissed-up white boys bowl-up outside. Any other day Super might turn them away and send them packing, but, this particular night, business is slow, so he lets them into the queue. Soon as he does, a couple of fit girls stroll up and, of course, he waves them through the queue and straight in. The pissed-up publonians don't like that one bit, start getting boisterous and rowdy, claiming it's unfair and fit birds or not, they should have been let in first. Unfair? Tough shit I say, my house, my rules. Anyhow, you know about the "Publonians" right? Yeah, of course you do, you've seen them, you probably know them, you might even be one of them. They are the official paid-up residents of the "United States of the Pub", they live for the pub, their whole life revolves around the pub, they spend more time in the pub than out of the pub. Beer and gossip their currency, darts and pool their hobby, final orders their worst nightmare. Anyhow, back outside, the pissed up publonian protests don't last long, nah, Super does what he does best and gives them a quick going over before sending them on their way with a kick up their arses. To be fair, they're lucky not to receive a cutting or "wetting", he's still into his machete back then. Anyway, half hour later the Publonians come back with some mates, tooled up, giving it large and threatening Super with what he's says is a sawn-off shotgun. He gets inside pronto and locks the doors. They start banging and kicking and shoulder-barging, trying to get it. With only me and Marlon to back him up, we're well and truly fucked. Need to think quickly. Stand and fight? Nah, fuck that for a laugh, no way, we call the Police and have it away out of the back window sharpish. Apparently, the publonians did eventually get in, smashing the place up before robbing the till. Safe to say we don't hear nothing from the greasy twat, Steve. My first taste of promoting and I must say I hate the aggravation, but love the cash and, to be honest, absolutely love hosting the night, making sure everyone's having a good time and enjoying themselves.

My regular promotion at Cheeks in Deptford came about by pure chance, which is always the way with me, nothing is ever planned or arranged, shit just happens. Me and Her have a rare night out, one of our attempts at re-igniting our relationship and giving it a go for the sake of our boy. The next-door neighbour, a ginger Irish lady called Carmel looks after the little man once Shirley gets him off to sleep. The lazy fat-bitch sits on the sofa all night watching television feeding her fat face on a carrier-bag full of crisps and sweets while he sleeps peacefully, the easiest tenner she'll ever made. Shirley and I head to the local boozer, a proper old-world kind of place next to the Cutty Sark ship, here in Greenwich. Dark rum for me, white wine spritzer for her before we walk through a deserted Greenwich market to the local curry house. Couple of hours and some tasty dishes later, we take a five-minute taxi ride south to Deptford and Cheeks nightclub, it's usually walkable, but not tonight in Her high-heels. A fairly big place with double entrance doors leading to a wide lobby with some seats on the left and the cloakroom on the right. The club itself is straight through another set of double doors, a basic big room with a stage at the other end and the dance floor in front. The bar runs full length down the left-hand side and a range of seats down the right. Pretty shit to be honest, but, it's open late, not too far from home and plays some decent music too. They play the obvious pop tunes like Tears for Fears and that 'Shout' tune, (what a tune by the way), also rare groove, soul and funk. The club anthem, you know, every club has a certain tune the punters go mad for, is Shannon and "let the music play". Man, it gets everyone rocking, me too.

This particular night, neither of us feel like dancing, so we park ourselves near the bar and set about drinking ourselves out of the nightmare of forced conversation, while, at the same time, desperately seek some common ground. I get chatting to the bloke behind the bar who turns out to be the club manager and nephew of the owner, apparently. Once I mention the Three Hearts Sunday night promotion, and tripling their normal takings, he offers me a Thursday night there and then. Not the big one, a Friday, but Thursday is miles better than a Sunday. Listen, my nights are sweet man, and when I say "sweet", I mean "sweeeeeeeet." Regulars get dressed up neat and tidy, buffed-up and looking good. Yeah man, my nights are sexy nights, strictly rare groove and funk, Curtis Mayfield, Wilson Picket, Earth Wind and Fire. Yeah, I like to think of it as a sex-soundtrack. Cool vibes man, but, I'm desperate to do more than just Cheeks, and more than just a Thursday or Sunday night. Yeah man, I want the big night, a Friday night. Friday is the night all promoters want. Punters work their bollocks off all week long in some dead-end factory job, get their pay packet on Friday afternoon and later in the evening, they're pissed-up, spent-up and hoping to get sexed-up. My first Friday night is at Bonny Boo's in Sydenham, south London, near Crystal Palace. Usually, the place is full of pissed up Publonian fanny-chasers-come-back-street-brawlers, however, my nights are different. Yeah man, I implement a new door policy, strictly tasty birds and tidy blokes, no jeans or trainers and, after what happened at the Three Hearts, definitely no publonians…

BONNY BOO's DISCOTEQUE
NORWOOD ROAD
SYDENHAM, LONDON
EARLY 1984

A friend of a friend tells me the owner's on the look-out for a decent Friday night promoter, so, like a pleb, I get the number from the phone book, call and arrange a meeting. Out of my depth and nervous, I'm suited and booted and looking god-damn slick man, even if I say so myself. Look the part, feel the part, Paul would say, said it gives me confidence, show I mean business, prove I'm no fly-by-night. Looking super-fine, I head down there and meet the owner, Frankie, a huge fat fucker, sweating his tits off with his sleeves rolled up and his shirt hanging out of his trousers exposing his rotund hairy fat mother fucking stomach. I explain my approach from door policy to music selection to advertising and promotions. Impressed, he asks how many

I'll be able to get through the door. How the fuck do I know? A trick question, testing me, one to fuck me up, make me look a prick, but, I'm quick on my feet. I make up some bullshit about doing what they normally would do plus twenty percent, possibly even thirty percent. Shuffling forward in his seat, he grabs his calculator and taps into it furiously while scribbling some notes. I ask for a look around and he waves his hand at me without looking up. A nice place, lots of chrome and smoked mirrors with several different mini-dancefloors surrounding the main deck with multi-coloured flashing squares as floor tiles. The sound system looks okay, a few amplifiers and a pre-amp, plus a dozen or so four-foot-tall speakers, but I want more, I want my punters to feel the music, not just listen to it.

After shaking hands with Frankie on the Friday night, I go to the music store in Catford, (a couple of miles away), that sells guitars and pianos and trumpets, as well as disco and deejay equipment. End up hiring my own three-thousand-watt sound-system, an additional lighting rig, oh, and a smoke machine too. Marlon sorts the music, arranging for a couple of his deejay mates to play a set or two. I get some leaflets done at a printers in New Cross, and hand them out in the local fashionable clothes shops, to attract the super-fit upper-class ladies, and also some record shops across South London to attract the music aficionados who'll appreciate my impeccable style. Yeah man, don't need no every-day pub-going piss-head coming along, I want guys like me, into their music, will appreciate the ladies and refrain from trying to cop a feel at the first opportunity. My nights will be classy and stylish and sexy and sophisticated and avant-garde. Just like me.

The week before the first night is crazy-mad. Everyone I run into has heard about it and is up for it, telling me they'll be there and their mates and their mates-mates will be there too. Gets to Wednesday and Fat-Frankie calls me, rambling on and on and on. The shirt-hanging-out-his-trousers-buttons-popping-off-his-shirt-fat bastard keeps blabbering on about maximum capacity, too many people, losing his license and all this panic driven craziness, says he's thinking of pulling the plug. Pull the plug? No way, not with the amount of interest I've generated, fuck that. I tell him to leave security up to me, I'll be sure we keep the numbers down and make sure there's no trouble. Naturally, I call Super who, unknown to me, takes it upon himself to call on Claude to help-out too which was a good move because the place was packed. Claude, together with Super fit the bill nicely although there's absolutely no trouble, not a peep, no hassle and no damage to the club or the sound system. Twelve midnight, with a good couple of hundred punters inside, I wander around checking everyone's having a good time. Yeah man, sipping dark rum, I'm dancing with the ladies and bumping into old friends I hadn't seen for ages. The vibe's good, really good actually, I'm loving it, loving my creation. At the same time, Marlon's on the turntables reading the crowd like a book, changing the tempo just at the right time, dropping the odd anthem here and there and muting the soundtrack at the pinnacle of the chorus, allow the crowd to sing along. He's good at his job, a natural, my little brother, my little man, my hero, my innocently naïve baby brother…

I hear my own words tail off into the distance as I stare into space. Eyes glazing over, I replay the fading highlights of my childhood, walking him home from primary school at three-thirty in the afternoon. Cheeky, he's teasing me, playing tag and dancing around with a his killer smile, the glint in his eye and his cute little dimples. Turning onto our road, we have a kick around with the other kids who are in the middle of their own world-cup final, right outside Momma's house. Quicker than the other kids, he's agile too, yelling "megs" as he passes the ball between my legs. I'm smiling and I'm proud, so proud my heart swells to nearly bursting…

Squeezing my eyes together, I shake my head and dissolve the memories, too much, too hurtful, too painful. I miss him, of course I do, but, I'm not going there, no matter how much you lead me or coerce me or trick me. Anyway, I'm tired of the shit. I've turned up too many stones, looked for too many worms.

"Bollocks," the Interrogator says, growling under a condemning frown. *"We're not stopping so get the fuck on with it. You talk when I want you to talk, when I want to listen. So, get your lip off the floor and get that tongue wagging."*

CLICK.

Looking up I see it, right there in front of me. The barrel is dark and cold and unforgiving, an eternity of perpetual doom, an infinity of never-ending nightmares.

Don't point that shit at me, I yell, fronting it out, not showing any emotion even though I'm paralysed by crippling fear.

Fuck it, I'll get this over with…

Back at Bonny Boo's, towards the end of the night we count the cash and settle up. Walking into the back office, cash is heaped all over the desk, some counted and bagged-up, the rest just piled up in the middle. Claude and his heavies wait outside while me and Super collect our share. Just as well too, if Claude sees that amount of cash, Frankie will receive a beating, (at best), and the cash will be robbed, my share too no doubt. No way that's happening though, I've worked my nuts off to make the night a success and I deserve that cash, my cash, my hard-earned beautiful cash. Pocketing best part of a thousand as my share, I give Claude a few hundred for him and his geezers, pay Super a hundred quid and give Marlon and his mates fifty quid each. After the equipment hire and leaflet printing, I'm left with best part of six hundred quid. Before promoting, as a postman, I took home just over one hundred a week, so this is good, easy money. Too easy, as it turns out…

Buzzing with the rum and weed and the good vibes, I'm staring out of the window as Super puts his foot down. Four in the morning and we're speeding north towards Greenwich and Shirleys flat. With no traffic about, it's dark and quiet and beautifully still and, just before sunrise, a line of electric blue emerges across the horizon. A new day dawns, in more ways than one. Yeah man, I'm a promoter now, a proper Friday night big time promoter, earning good money, and properly earning it too. Approaching Lewisham, Super suggests we stop off at the Snooker Hall on the High Street for a few frames and a night cap, (even though it's practically the morning). I'm a bit worse of wear but still wide-awake, so fuck it, yeah, why not.

RILEY'S SNOOKER CLUB
LEWISHAM HIGH STREET
LEWISHAM, LONDON
EARLY 1984

Located above a furniture store, this place is quite literally always open and, always full of villains, a veritable who's who of the south-east London underworld. Like a supermarket for crooks, you can get anything in there, so, if you will, please allow me to take you on a tour…

On the pharmacy isle we have a wide selection of uppers, downers, opiates and stimulants, anything and everything to get you high, low and anywhere in between. Or perhaps, on the hardware isle, we might interest you in our wide selection of coshes, knives, pistols, sub-machine-guns, grenades and an assortment of other life reducing equipment. Finally, on the newspaper stand we have a delightful array of rumour, whisper and conjecture, vague details of post office raids and other cash yielding scams along with who's just got banged up and who's banging who's girlfriend and sure to be stabbed up as a result..

Walking in, heads is down, it's surprisingly quiet other than the echoing cracking of balls being potted and an undercurrent of whispering suspicious as the patrons eye each other through slitty untrusting treacherous eyes. Everyone's on edge, ready to kick-off, ready to defend one's honour, ready to boost reputations and not be taken for a mug, but, of course, nobody dares because it's quite literally mad. Yeah man, "mutually assured destruction," do you see? If one person kicks off, everyone does, then it's total and utter carnage so, the only logical response is to hold it down and keep calm. Me and Super agree to mind our own business, get a drink and play some snooker, ten quid a frame. I'm rubbish at snooker, pool's my game, but good news, Super is even worse than I am. Couple of hours later, and a tidy break of thirty-seven under my belt, I've done him for thirty quid, so decide to treat him to a proper English fry-up at a greasy-spoon café near the train station. Down the stairs, just through the door onto the pavement and we hear the unmistakable crack-pop sound of gunfire. Grabbing my shoulder, Super pulls me back into the doorway as panic, confusion and fear whirlwinds around us. Crouching down, we "what-the-fuck" look at each other before edging a peek around the doorway. Holy shit, it's a scene from a Spaghetti Western. The deserted high street has two groups of geezers, one at each end, both cracking off shots at each other as they shout god knows what in Arabic or Turkish or something. With the echoing sound of sirens in the distance, they let off a final flurry of shots then clear off shouting "abba-hala-hallala" or some other gobbledegook. We stand in the doorway stunned, not knowing what the fuck's going on, before pissing ourselves laughing. Adrenalin or fear or something, we literally cry with laughter. Checking the all clear, we stroll down the high street then loop back around the back of the Snooker hall. Within seconds, we're cornered by three Police cars. Quick check Super's clean, which he is, and we're set for a shake-down. Good job too, he's still carrying his blade, yeah man, everywhere he goes, his "baby", or machete to you and me, follows. Just like the old times, the Police deploy the same stop and search tactics, separating us both then asking stupid questions. We instinctively know what to say to complement each-others story, not that we have anything to hide, we're just two chaps coming back from a late night in the snooker-hall.

Taking our names and addresses, they smell our hands for gunpowder before telling us to be on our way. We walk for maybe a half a mile then double back to pick up the car, eventually getting home at seven thirty. Through the door, Shirley's up and steaming mad angry, questioning where I've been until this time, who I'm shagging, what have I been smoking and the normal everyday nagging bullshit. Another argument, another falling out and another cycle of kissing and making up.

From then on, I focus on building my career as a nightclub promoter. My life revolves around finding venues and deejays, collecting then paying out cash, promoting my ass off, smoking my beloved weed, running the radio station, sipping copious amounts of lovely delicious dark rum, pocketing even more cash, and, of course, more arguments with Her. Without really trying, I've a tidy little business with regular nights at Bonny-Boo's and Cheeks and a steady line-up of deejays doing spots at my nights and on the radio station. Each of them has their own style, but they usually throw down a heady mix of soul and funk with a splash of electro thrown in for good measure. Marlon was class and built a reputation as a top line deejay, yeah man, he had a knack of reading the crowd and dropping the tempo just at the right time. Producers and distributors got to know about him too, giving him a constant flow of pre-releases and acetate dub-plates. Claude does the doors for me with occasional help from Super, keeping the dickheads out and controlling who and what goes in, confiscating any weapons or drugs, mainly speed, resin and a few uppers and downers, nothing too heavy. Rather than just confiscating the drugs, Claude starts selling them himself, making a fair penny out of it too. He gained a "monopolistic position", as Paul would say which is code for making an absolute mint. I'm not happy though, nah, no way. Wide-scale dealing might jeopardise my nights if the Police get involved. Yeah man, licenses will be suspended as a minimum, serious time in prison or battles with rival gangs at worst. The problem with

Claude is, well, one of the problems with Claude is, he doesn't know when to stop. If he ruled the world, all my punters, every single one of them, including me, will be jacked up intravenously on smack, sold at a very reasonable price by, you guessed it, the world's best and most successful drug dealer, Claude. But, I figure it's better he controls the dealing than a set of random geezers or rival gangs, who, no doubt, would end up causing major problems with blood and limbs everywhere.

Drugs, drugs, mother-fucking drugs.

It's around that time I venture into chemicals…

Being a roots and culture man, I've always stayed strong with the mother earthiness of the weed, but, working my nuts off all night promoting, now and again I'll share a line of coke with Claude. A proper coke-head, he's pumped-up, fuelled-up, up for anything. His business has diversified, moving from a legitimate security business to wholesale cocaine dealing. Yeah man, he and the Millwall firm shift a lot of coke, in fact, they're more into that than the hooliganism, rumour is they're responsible for up to eighty percent of London's cocaine supply. Inevitably, I become their most loyal customer.

I see that now, now it's too late.

Damn, cocaine and hooliganism.

I can't believe it.

I'm just a simple man from Brixton with a wife and kid and ting, yet, this shit spins around me, engulfs me, takes over and consumes me. I don't know where I start and that shit finishes, I'm becoming it, and it's becoming me.

Anyhow, about my radio station…

Dream FM.

At college, Marlon meets a geeky-kid called David. During the day David's a proper top-of-the-class swat, an unrecognisable non-descript nobody with his head buried deep in a load of text-books. But, by night, he's a super-hero-super-villain making transmitters for the majority of pirate radio stations in London. Fuck knows how, but he builds a biscuit tin full of wires and circuit-boards in exchange for a few hundred quid. He and Marlon become friendly and he introduces Marlon to an old dreadlocked Rasta-man named Skyrocket. What a character, Skyrocket owns a wall-to-wall reggae, roots-and-culture pirate station called "Love-2-Love" operating out of a tower block in Lewisham. Treating it like a hobby rather than a business, he says all he wants to do is educate the eardrums of the south London youth and have enough cash left over for a few pints of light ale on an evening. Playing nothing but reggae-reggae-reggae, all day long, during the night he lets Marlon do a few hours playing Hip-Hop, Electro and eventually House. Skyrocket, or Sky as I end up calling him, says he struggles to get reggae deejays to get out of bed to do the night-shift, and, he has hardly any listeners during the night anyway so he's happy for young Marlon to have a go. Soon as Marlon introduced us, I liked him. An interesting dude, always reminiscing about the old times and his family back in Montego Bay, he reminded me a bit of Pops or Crissy even. Turns out the station is based in a top floor flat of a tower block near the train station in Lewisham. Apparently, he bought the keys and rent-book for five hundred quid from a skagg-head young girl who got herself knocked up at seventeen. She uses the cash to buy a train ticket back up north to settle back with her parents in Newcastle or some other regional shit hole. For an old geezer, Sky's commercially cute and, more importantly, has a decent heart with a good moral compass. I like him, like him a lot.

LOVE-2-LOVE RADIO, WARNER HOUSE
ORCHARD ESTATE
LEWISHAM, LONDON
1984

Twenty-nine floors up, the lift takes forever. Through the door, and I'm in shock, the entire place is a dirty skanky squat, basic and in desperate need of a seriously good clean.

Every room is empty, apart from the living room which doubles up as the studio. Sky carpeted "the studio" wall to ceiling, ceiling too actually, sound-proofing, he said. At one end of the room he's set up turntables and a mixer together with an amplifier with basic speakers, the metal biscuit tin transmitter, a microphone and a tape deck. At the other end of the long thin room is an old dirty brown sofa, (which stinks by the way), and that's it. Man, its basic. The rest of the flat's empty too, literally nothing, no furniture, nothing. Kitchen, empty, not even a cooker just a bit of hose sticking out of the well for the gas supply. Bedrooms, no beds, nothing, only council-grey vinyl lino flooring. Toilet, quite literally, a shit hole, obviously not been cleaned for a million years. David ran some cable from the amplifier into the biscuit tin then out the window up to the roof and into the lift motor room. Inside this, he knocked a hole in the roof and concreted-in a twenty-foot scaffold pole and ran the cable through the middle up to the antenna. How they managed to get that big pole up there to the roof, I'll never know. Anyway, like I say, Sky is an interesting fella with lots of stories about the old days. He knows all the big sound-system operators across London, Saxon, Supercat and Jah Lion, each and every one of them heroes of mine since I was a kid. I'm fascinated listening to his stories and anecdotes.

One night down the local boozer, right near the tower block come studio we get chatting. Pissed up and swaying, he tells me he's too old for the whole pirate-radio thing, that it's more hassle than it's worth. Straight away, I tell him I'll buy it off him, fuck know why. An "impulse purchase" as Paul would say. Now, Sky's a cute old-bugger, tells me he's not sure what it's worth, but, reckons the equipment and keys to the flat are worth at least a couple of thousand, probably more. I offer him a thousand quid, right there and then, but, he's been there and seen it all, hasn't he. After more light-ale for him and dark rum for me, he negotiates his way to three thousand. I don't have that kind of cash hanging around, money's like water to me, flowing through my hands, but I really, really want the station. I go see Claude the very next day, he's loaded with this security business and his cocaine dealing is flying high-high-high. Claude says we should just take the station and the keys, and if Sky complains or utters a single word, he'll wind up in hospital with two broken legs. That's typical of Claude who was quickly morphing into a no-neck, muscle bound freak. I really don't know him no more. Anyway, I can't do that to Sky, no way. So, I put in a thousand, Claude does the same, and I borrow a thousand from Paul, arranging to pay him back twelve-hundred in total, a hundred quid a week.

As soon as I pick up the keys, I switch the music selection and change the name, "re-branding" as Paul would say. Dream FM, yeah man. I can't remember who came up with the name, but I like it. We still play some roots and reggae, but mix it up with rare-groove, hip-hop and electro. Marlon gets his mates involved too, all of them young and ambitious, keen and eager and, crucially, don't expect to be paid, they just happy to be on the radio. The only hard work comes from the DTI, otherwise known as the "Department for Trade and Industry". They raid illegal pirate stations periodically, getting ready for selling off frequencies to new, legal stations. Triangulating our signal, they'll work out where we are, come around mob-handed with the Police, kick the door, arrest everyone and confiscate the kit. After a while, increasingly paranoid about security, Claude screws the front door shut and installs a steel gate in front with two massive stainless-steel padlocks on. The deejays are told to get onto the roof of the block, (only thirty floors up), then hang down onto a rickety old stepladder on the balcony of the flat. Complete and utter madness, not to mention the DTI could do the exact same thing so what's the fucking point. There's no reasoning with him though, any dissent or crossed word results in a beating, anything more than that, then its far-far worse. David, the transmitter-guy, is clever though, bright as a button. He runs the antenna cable up through the dry risers in the internal fabric of the block, making it hard for the DTI to trace where the signal's coming from, and buying us valuable time to launch the kit over the balcony if necessary. Turns into an elaborate game of cat and mouse, them trying to find us, us sneaking around avoiding getting caught. After years of battering us and dozens of other pirates around the head Tom-and-Jerry style, the DTI offer an amnesty, saying we can apply for a "legal" licence as long we go off air, and stay off. Yeah right, like it wasn't sown up from the start. Businessmen and backhanders I bet, a total fix. I'm not about to give it all up in the hope of a remote chance of a "legal" licence, nah, they'll want to control the music selection and adverts and tax the arse out of us. After a year or so, maybe longer, we relocate the studio further into the centre of London to an estate in Surrey Quays and a massive tower block on the banks of the Thames. Closer to central London, we use a microwave signal between the studio in one block and the antenna in another and add more power to boost the signal in order to reach more punters. More punters means more adverts which means more cash in my back pocket which means more of Claudes magical white powder goes up my nose. Sweet. We got two flats down there, both girlfriends of Claude and both with fully functioning ready-to-go studio set-ups. One the main studio, the other fall-back in case we get raided. We give out numbers of the local phone boxes right outside the entrance to the block for punters to ring in and dedicate various tunes to their mates or girlfriends. The most requested tune is "I-O-U" by Freeez, a blinding tune, yeah, punters are requesting it twenty-four-seven and little kids are signing it as they chase around the estate on their bikes. Our deejays and a few wanna-be kids hang around the phone boxes, writing down the shout-outs and dedications then drop them up to the studio every twenty minutes or so.

Yeah man, life is panning out nicely for all of us...

Marlon is an up and coming deejay, at college thing.

I'm promoting my arse off and running Dream FM.

Super's busy with his new life in Tottenham.

Claude has quickly become an urban legend, controlling a fair amount of the doors across South London nightclubs and leading the Millwall army.

Anyway, Paul is wheeler-dealing in the City, making shitloads of cash, mostly at the expenses of all others.

We're all grown up, sorted and happy…

Life is indeed good.

6. Fast Forward to the Past

"If my calculations are correct, when this baby hits eighty-eight… you're going to see some serious shit. A bolt of lightning is going to strike the clock tower and into the flux capacitor, then, it just might work…"

Dr Emmet Brown

THE SOFA
17, HAMILTON HOUSE
GREENWICH, LONDON
LATE SUMMER, 1989

Two hundred and thirty-four. Laid flat out on the sofa, staring at the ceiling counting the polystyrene tiles, I sigh a deep sigh of resignation. How has life come this, counting ceiling tiles like a mental case one-flew-over-the-cuckoo-nest style.

I see you're still here then.

"Where else would I be?" the Interrogator says, knowing I know he has nowhere else to go.

Stone-cold on a mortuary slab, dead in a ditch somewhere, anywhere that's not here? You think this is civilised and consensual, all neat and tidy, a jovial tête-à-tête over tea and scones, like we're business associates, mates or something?

"Mates, nah, not mates, we'll never be mates. You're a disgusting dirty skagg-head loser but, there's more to you than meets the eye," the Interrogator says, seductively, drawing me further into his warped world of mind bending.

Unbelievable, un-fucking-believe-able. Going through this bit by bit is destroying me, taking my brain apart piece by piece. You're bugging me like a dirty wet fart, lingering and stinking up my mind up, distorting my reality and eating away at my soul.

"Forgotten who you're speaking to?" the Interrogator says, knowing for sure I haven't forgotten. *"Forgotten what I can do?"*

Oh yeah, big man with a shooter, a real hard man with his military grade hardware. Listen, it's the only reason I'm still here, why I choose to be here anyway. I understand threats and fear, pistols and pressure, I get it, I fucking invented it mate. But, you got the power, you've got the gun while I've got fuck all. You're playing this situation, taking advantage, leveraging my mind, exploiting my intellect because you're fucking vacant man, nothing but an empty hologram with no substance, no real heart.

CLICK.

As the safety catch moves into the armed position, my eyes are drawn to the opening of the barrel. Nineteen-sixties Batman-style cartoon words float from the opening spelling 'DOOM.' Hallucinating, I shut my eyes, blocking out the multi-coloured day-glow swirls vortexing around the barrel. I squeeze my eyes together until the madness subsides. Cartoon words? Shit man, all this thinking, all this dwelling, all this regurgitating and regretting the past makes me cluck. Need some goodness, you know what I mean? Yeah man, a pick-me-up, columbian, china-white, charlie, powder, toot, coke, coca, yo-yay. Need to get on one, get sorted, get high as the sky, helps me remember, helps me talk. Hmm, yeah man, thinking about it, if you want anything more out of me you got to get me something, anything, whatever the fuck you can get.

"You think I'm leaving you here, on your own?" the Interrogator asks, not really asking, more like telling. *"Even worse, you think I'm getting you, a skagg-head, any type of drugs, being your skivvy?"*

Why, where the fuck will I go?

Anyway, I'm tired of running, don't have the energy to run. So, listen up and hear me now, there's no negotiation here. Shooter or not, you get me some chemicals or I'm out the window and you'll get fuck all…

Leaning back, arms behind my head, a broad smile stretches across my glowing face. I feel the sexy surge of power, like what I used to feel and, god-damn, it feels good. Haven't felt like that since, well, since before this craziness. Yeah man, I've got the power now. I've nothing to lose, we both know I'm already dead, dread, just a walking duppy-ghost, hollow, a mere shell of a man. So, stop dicking around, get on your heels double-quick time, and get me some shit.

"Who do you think you are?" the Interrogator says, not believing what he's hearing, tapping the gun onto the table.

Good, he's listening. I got his attention.

I said.

I want SHIT.

Energy pulsing, I'm excited, maybe I'm on the turn, maybe things are looking up, maybe I'm on my way to getting better and getting out of here. Yeah man, get some cereal or bread or something, chocolate too, plus some crisps, chocolate and a drink as well, Rola-Cola or Lilt or something. Oh, and some pens, a couple of biro's yeah, and a writing pad or something.

"Make a list, shall I? Fuck off. You should eat something though, you look like shit," the Interrogator says, an almost caring tone to his voice. *"A wash wouldn't go a miss, you stink of shit you dirty tramp."*

He's right, I do look and smell like shit.

I'll jump in the bath while he's out, scrub this shit off me. Refresh and renewal, like a wormy-pre-butterfly thing, got to break out of my cocoon, spread my wings and flutter a little.

Right then, here we go.

I head across the hallway towards the bathroom and see the bedroom door out of the corner of my eye. Echoing screams of terror reverberate around me before fading into the distance as I look away. It's like an anchor pulling me back to the monster-me and what I did. Stronger now, I can take it or leave it, don't have to be dragged back.

Fuck the bedroom, fuck him.

I'm in control.

Edging the bathroom door open, I enter slowly. Nostrils flaring, the rancid stink hangs heavy in the air. Looking around at the dirty shit hole, a wave of despair flows through me, how long has this been this way. Leaning over the bath, my back aches and I feel like an old man, damn, I am an old man, I've lived multiple lives in this fucked up and twisted body. Pushing the plug in, I twist the tap and hear a gurgle-gurgle before light brown water trickles out. A few seconds later, the dirty-badness fades to a steady flow of clear fresh water. Stripping off, I look through the mottled-grey-smeared-with-shit mirror and catch sight of this emaciated body. That's me, really me? Damn. Head shaking, I shut my eyes, I can't look. Ugly, disgusting images flash through my mind, like those Ethiopian kids from Band Aid. Feed the fucking world, nah man, nah, feed fucking poor Devon more like. Stepping in, I inhale sharply as the ice-cold water stings my ankles. I gently lower myself into the half-full bath, arse cheeks first, then pelvis then, oh-my-god, the balls!

Feels hot it's so cold.

Slam, click-click.

Ears prick as the front door slams, and the locks click. He's gone, left me, done what I asked? Shit, it's working, I'm in control, the worm is indeed turning. You know what, I can do one right now, run off, vanish into the urban mass of inner-city London before he realises I've gone. Balcony maybe? Three floors up, but doable. Might snap a leg though, break my neck probably and then what, a cripple and in pain and he'll still have me. Reminds me of Marlon's little muggy friend, Kingy, who, aged ten or eleven jumps off the top of the garages at the Loughborough Estate. He's maybe three floors up too, knees himself in the mouth and bites his tongue off.

Funny.

Anyway, even if I do successfully jump without breaking a leg or my neck, where do I go? Momma don't want to know anymore, slag-bag Shirley can fuck off and Super's doing time at Her Majesty's pleasure. Marlon? Paul? Damn, I don't have anyone, not a soul. Poor lonely me, poor lonely crazy old Devon. Still, at least he-who-must-be-obeyed has left me alone, gone to get me some shit. Yeah man, shits on it's way, good times ahead. God-damn, I'm so cold, my legs are numb and my jaw aches. I must get clean though, must refresh, must cleanse. I hear my teeth chattering together, clickity-click like a tube-train. Mother fucker it's cold, but, at the same time, weirdly, I feel at ease, relaxed and mellow, I've not felt this way for can't remember how long. Even though pain sears through my ugly, deformed hand as the red-hot-ice-cold water laps over it, I close my eyes and the pain eases. Calm and at ease, the water cleanses my thoughts. I'm thinking clearly now, no crazy painful memories, no questioning, no probing and no digging shit up. It's been weeks or even months since I've been here alone, without him. I've been talking shit forever, recalling this crap from time and realise I haven't thought about how I'm actually feeling. Instead, I just tell stories about how I used to feel, once, way back when. Reminiscing about the past, I've forgotten where I am in the present, or where I might be in the future.

Quite literally, I'm lost in the mist of time.

Until now, that is.

Don't quite know what's happening, but I feel weird, different somehow. I can't hear anything in my mind, all the screaming, confusion, regret, remorse and the teasing, goading, judgemental voices too. Wrestling with heavy eyelids, the ice-cold water feels warmer more, more bearable, comfortable even. Relaxing, I feel myself drift a bit.

Deep breaths, in and out, eyes closed…

NO.

Can't sleep in the bath.

Might drown, for fucks sake.

Eyes open, wide open.

Up and out, I grab the once light brown but now mouldy grey, crispy towel. Clothes back on, ignoring THAT bedroom door and the dark secrets behind, I head to the kitchen. Balcony door? Fuck, it's locked. Smash through, but then what? Nah man, I'm trapped, and not just in this shithole. Trapped by circumstance, trapped in this body, this mind, this life. Some people are just born trapped, can't escape your destiny, can't get off your train, can't change direction. God knows I've tried, the scrapyard, the postman, the going steady with the promotions and radio. It's all beginning to make sense now. I need a smoke, need to feel the motherly love of the herb, my comfort, my soul.

Reaching into the coffee table, I pull the small plastic bag of weed out of the cigarette packet. As I do, an inch-long paper wrap falls out. Nostrils flaring, rushes run up and down my spine and my stomach pangs. Beautiful, invigorating, sexy, but, I get it now. At last, clarity. I get that heroin's for losers, no-hopers and scum-of-the-earth-weak-willed-dirty-skagg-heads, so, with my new-found power, I speak out loud and tell it "not now." That's right bitch, I'm in control, I run tings… you know the rest. There's plenty of time for you, my powdery friend. I'm in control now and will do you when I want to, not you. Besides, now-time is spliff-time. Tasty five-skin rolled, sparked and inhaled. The goodness seeps into me and a wide grin spreads across my face. Yeah, a white blanket of warmth gently kisses my throat, hugs my lungs and tingles through my body. Sitting back, the sofa surrounds me and I feel comforted and safe. Blowing a perfect smoke ring high into the air, it hovers above my head like a halo.

Saint Devon, repenting for his sins.

Yeah man.

Relaxing, I feel at peace and allow my eyes to hang heavy.

Breathing deep and slow, my eyes close…

Glancing across at the dirty rug in front of the balcony door, I see it move, then do a kind of wave before shimmering like is diamond encrusted. What the fuck? A wave of golden glow surrounds it and it glistens like it's magic beans or Aladdins-magic-carpet. Another wave motion and it rises at one end. What. The. Fuck? It's alive, like a snake slivering across the floor toward me. I'm not scared though, nah, this feels familiar, comfortable, safe. I'm drawn to it, it's pulling me in, and I yearn for it. Getting up, I step towards it and it shines even more brightly. Hopping aboard, I put my arms out to steady myself as it hovers for a few seconds then moves slowly around the room before picking up speed. It's whizzing around the room, just like me, whizzing my tits of on this awesome magic carpet ride. The speed increases quicker and quicker, before a gigantic flash-shazzzzzam explodes around me and I'm vortexing through time. Travelling at the speed of light now, I'm surrounded by multicoloured beams of light like when the Millennium Falcon jumps into hyperspace. Holding on tight I'm not scared, far from it in fact, this shits cool, and I'm loving it. A warm summer wind rushes through me and I loosen my grip before stretching my arms out. I'm flying through space and time on a magic carpet, tripping my tits off, but it's lucid and real, and I'm controlling it, sort of. I lean to the right and feel the g-force push me to the left, I lean back and we zoom upward anti-gravity style. I weave left then right while the rainbow of dayglow colour engulfs me. Pulling my arms down to my sides, I slow down and the colours spin more slowly. Inertia taking hold, I make out familiar shapes. Slowing down even more, I'm on a high-street somewhere, shopfronts and cars and people walking around. Yeah, I'm on the Frontline at Railton Road, near the railway bridge. Eventually my magic carpet slows down to a subtle gliding pace, hovering eight inches above the pavement. The people look odd, dressed funny and the cars too, they're old-school and quaint. Ah, I get it, I'm back in Brixton, it's the sixties and I'm a kid. Beautifully golden ginger-bread-curried-goat smells hang heavy in the air while Desmond Decker echoes in the background. I've time-travelled back to before the madness, before Paul, before he became a cunt, before Shirley, before the craziness, before I became a monster.

SWITCH.

The colour drains from the old-school images, they fade and eventually go dark. Magic carpet gone, I'm walking now and see silhouettes heading towards me, jostling into me and bumping me out of the way. I see coloured lights in the distance and feel the hum of a rude-boy bassline in my stomach. Oh, I get it, I'm in a dark and moody nightclub now and the deejay is dropping some serious beats. Looking super-fine, I drift across the swaying dancefloor and see the punters looking at me, their smiling faces illuminated with the sexy up-lighting. I spot three girls staring, whispering to each other and giggling. Yeah man, they like what they see, of course they do, what's not to like, Devious Dee in the house baby! Then, I see her, my princess, my queen, my beautiful everything and her gorgeous pretty face. She's happy and beautiful and young and naive and care-free and staring at me. Glancing into her vodka and orange, prodding the ice with her straw, she looks up and catches my gaze, a two second connection, then she looks away, all coy and sweet and innocent. A smile forms at the corner of her mouth, her cheek rises and her cute dimples form. Looking up again, she knows I haven't taken my eyes off her. Earth shaking, my vision wobbles and I feel a pang in the pit of my stomach. That's THE exact moment, the alignment of planets and stars and galaxies as voodoo-ray magic casts it's spell and violins and orchestras chime out with angels singing in perfect harmony. I understand it now, I get it. I could never articulate it before, couldn't pinpoint the emotion, but I'm feeling blinding, euphoric, exhilarating, breath-taking, unadulterated and untainted love. No doubt about it. Something as simple as love, and I couldn't explain it. Even though we chat for hours about our dreams and fears, sharing things I've never shared with anyone before, not even myself, I never properly told her. I said the words, of course, but never really explained it to her, never told anyone else either. Blokes like me don't talk about that, scared of coming across like loved-up saps, petrified by letting our guard down and getting hurt. We create a social shield of geezerism to protect us and to hide our vulnerability. I never found the courage to drop my guard, dispose of the protective outer-layer, lose the south London suit of armour we use to protect the real us. I never cried in front of a girl, until her...

"Twinkle? Twin... kle?" the Interrogator whispers. *"Little Star?"* he says, softly, like I'm five years old and it's early

Christmas morning. *"Wakey, wakey."*

No, no, please. Don't wake me, don't drag me from my perfect reality to this fucking nightmare. Take me back man, reverse this shit, bring me back to her and the love, the wanting and the yearning.

'You're dreaming brother, you've been a'kip yeah, asleep on the job,' the Interrogator says, crushing my dreams like an emotion vacuum.

But, what the fuck, I've slept? During the day, like when I'd bunk off school and throw a sickie and stay in bed all day?

"Must be all that weed you've been smoking dred," the Interrogator says, diagnosing my illness. *"Got you some goodness, just like you asked. Whizz, herbs, crisps and chocolate."*

Saliva builds in my mouth.

Chocolate, a wide selection too, Kitkat, Mars, Marathon. Looks good man, really good, well done, bravo!

"Bravo? Fuck off. I ain't got this for you, right," the Interrogator says, taking charge. *"So, sort yourself out and get some chocolate down you because time is pushing on, and time is money, yeah."*

God damn, he's relentless. No point in arguing or delaying the inevitable, let's just get this shit over and done with.

Where did I get to?

Yeah, Bad-Boy-Cee. Claude, in the place to be…

Still into the whole hooligan thing with the Millwall crew as well as running his doors business, his main occupation is crime. Cocaine, guns, gangsters and, of course, steroids. Him and the Greek are really tight now, so I see a lot of them two along with the Greeks partner in crime too, the Albino. Unlike the Greek, who's mainly into cocaine, the Albino is into full-on mayhem. Claude tells me steer clear of them both, especially the Albino because he's a proper head case, a fucked-up psycho. Born evil, the Albino isn't just a normal bloke doing bad things, nah, he's malicious, vindictive and a down-right dirty evil bastard. Claude tells me he initiates the newbies into the hooligan firm with a Stanley knife across the forearm and at away games, he'll go out of his way to get split off from the pack, deliberately getting himself cornered just to ensure he has a fight. He'd often say he only ever feels alive, when he's close to death. Part of Millwall folk law, everyone knows of him but, at the same time, everyone steers clear. Yeah, everyone nods and smiles to his face and he's everyone's his best mate but, soon as he turns his back they cow away and whisper about him. Claude tells me about an away fixture in Birmingham, might have been Stoke, up north anyway…

RANDOM FOOTBALL LEAGUE TEAM
RANDOM DIRTY NORTHERN CITY
MID 1980's

Hours before the match, the Millwall crew arrange a fight at a back-street pub with the local firm. Yeah, any violence at the ground is usually wanna-be kids out to make a name for themselves, or over enthusiastic pissed-up pent-up-with-anger middle aged slobs out to prove they can still get it up. The real violence always happens far away from the ground to avoid anyone getting life bans or banged up in prison. Anyway, as normal, the Millwall firm smash a few heads and have a right laugh. Problem is, a Millwall youngster gets himself cut across his face, from his ear to his mouth. Turns out he's the son or nephew or something of an old time Millwall hard nut, Mad Mikey McCrudden. They always have shit names like. "Stab-you-up-Steve" or "Kick-your-head-in-Kevin". Get a life, you utter fools. The Albino gets possessive over the youngster, all angry and twisted. 'How dare they, how fucking dare they,' he's screaming and ranting and raving before gathering a couple of the hardcore faithful together and go looking for whoever did it. Turns out, they march round to house of the northerners top boy, kick the door in and tear the place apart and sit in the dark waiting for him to get home. A few hours after the match, he makes his way home and is promptly bound and gagged and has the living shit kicked out of him. Meanwhile, the

Albino get busy in the kitchen, boiling up a chip pan full of oil. Yep, a million degrees of hotness gets tipped over his head, literally melting the skin from his skull. Ten weeks in intensive care and a shit load of plastic surgery, he nearly dies. Damn, both him and the cut-up youngster are fucked for the rest of their lives, all over a stupid game of football.

DISGUSTING.

Claude becomes part of Millwall folk law too, not bad for a dreadlocked brother from Brixton who supported Crystal Palace as a boy. He made his name at an away game at Luton. I'm not into away matches, (or home matches to be honest), but I go down to Cold Blow Lane now and again just to show my face. I'm ashamed to admit it, but the buzz is indeed exciting, I get off on the adrenaline, the camaraderie and the thrill of it all. But, after doing the same thing week after week, when you're smashing up the same geezers you smashed a couple of months before, it becomes repetitive and boring and pointless. It's less about the buzz and more about a sort of made-up-shallow-pride, we create reasons to fight, pretending we're standing for something, defending a principle rather than just mindless shit-kicking. We, the hooligans, create different levels of pride, our manner, our pub, our bird, our young-un, our tube station, our side of the river, anything to provide purpose, legitimising it in some way. Even more puzzling is that after a Saturday afternoon kicking the shit out of each other, all the top-table gangs in London, Millwall, Chelsea and West Ham will be doing high value drug deals together on the Monday morning. Crazy.

So, Luton.

All the gangs in London plan a massive straightener in Luton, (don't know why they chose Luton, it's a shit-hole). A kind of multi-sided war to end all wars and prove who is the best, the most mental, the most savage, the most fearsome. The Police know about it too, apparently, Claude says the place is teeming with Police with cameras as well as undercover Police who'd infiltrated the gangs, posing as hooligans. As planned, fifteen minutes after kick-off the violence kicks off. Seats ripped up and flung onto the pitch, fighting breaks out all over the place. Expecting the fight to be outside the ground or in the city centre, the Police are caught out and it's anarchy and chaos and the players run off the pitch, followed by the stewards too. Along with the Greek, Claude finds himself in the middle of the pitch kicking the shit out of anyone unlucky enough to get in the way. His craziness makes it's way onto the television too, adding to his legend. Later in the evening Match of the Day shows a few shots of the trouble along with some condemning words from the presenters about how the beautiful game is being ruined by these mindless thugs. As the camera zooms in, there Claude is, proud as punch, wrecking an idiot fool who chances his luck with a peach of a right cross. The Albino, so Claude says, attacks a Police officer, smashing him around the head with half a toilet seat he's ripped out of the toilets with his bare hands. Puts the officer in a coma and nearly kills him. After a couple of minutes of chaos, hundreds are left injured, knocked out cold or running for cover. Moments later, the Police make a guest appearance in vast numbers, tooled up with shields and truncheons. Eventually the trouble subsides, but the stadium has been fucked-up, seats ripped out, toilets smashed up, small fires dotted around the place. A whole host of the Millwall crew get arrested and locked up, including Claude, but the Greek and Albino get away. No beatings, no fitting up or any of the old-school shit, nah, straight to court the next day. Sentenced to three months in prison for drunk and disorderly or affray or something. To be fair to him, he puts his head down, does his time and, impossible to believe, gets released a few weeks early for "good behaviour". Once released, he's treated like an old-school war hero and the Millwall firm arrange a big welcome home party for him in a pub in New Cross called the Penguin. He's a top dog now, part of the elite, part of what they call the 'management team'. Yeah, these are twenty or so seriously heavy geezers, proper villains, thieves, fences, armed robbers, drug dealers, money lenders and down-right wrong-uns. Each one of the "management team" has their own gang or team, which collectively make up the Millwall firm known as the "Bushwackers". Claude has maybe a dozen geezers of his own from his security business, each of them have mates, and mates of mates. All in all, I reckon they have five-hundred geezers ready and willing to fight, and maybe another five hundred who'll join in and go with the flow when needed, that's more than most army battalions. Even more concerning, add up all the firms from all of the clubs in England, and you'll have a small army. Add up all the countries who love the fighting, Holland, France, Russia, Italy, Argentina, nearly all of Eastern Europe and loads of others, and you have a small country of hooligans.

The United States of Stupid!

Claude is drawn further and further into this world, meaning I see less and less of him, which is no bad thing. He builds himself a weights gym in his front room, training like a dog every day for hours on end for a couple of weeks then rests up for another couple of weeks before starting over again. Pumping iron till all hours in the morning, he tears his body apart. When he's "on", he only ever eats eggs and meat. Six eggs for breakfast, raw, down in one, then two steaks for dinner and bits of chicken throughout the day. At the same time, he's injecting himself with all manner of shit, something about two different chemicals, one a growth hormone given to cows to fatten them up before slaughter and the other a stabiliser, probably to stop him growing udders or tits. On top of that, he dabs a speed kind of powder before bed to burn fat while he sleeps, and then takes laxatives to help him have a shit. To begin with he looks good, great even, toned and muscular and athletic. After a while though, he grows muscles on muscles, and muscles where muscles shouldn't be, more monster than man. He's obsessed by weight training, I think to keep his mind busy so that he doesn't have to think about his missus and his kid, or the business with Snakehead. With all the training, eating and injecting, he looks like Mr Universe, with no neck, veins popping out of everywhere. Shit, his biceps are as big as my head. The Greek's the same, pumped up and fucked up, he looks like the Incredible Hulk. An intimidating twosome, they become big buddies, body building, hooliganising and drug dealing all over London. Plus, they're in partnership with the West Ham crew, who actually hail from a posh part of Essex, not the deepest darkest hell-holes of East London. Collectively, they take villainy to a whole new level, shotguns, Range Rovers and wanna-be-scarface gangsters. As soon as all the serious shit starts coming on top, I should have done one and got out, gone steady and been happy with my lot but me being me, I'm never going to do that...

CLAUDES FLAT
MAPLE HOUSE, ADOLPHUS STREET
DEPTFORD, LONDON
1986 OR 1987

She's hormonal and argumentative, as usual, so I do a quick one and head around to Claudes flat. Pumping iron, he's sweating and grunting and listening to "I Can't Wait" by Nu Shooz, so I skin up and get mellow while watching his veins bulge and muscle tissue rip apart. Nicely buzzing, bang-bang-bang, there's a knock at the front door. Head spinning around, Claude questions me with his laser beam eyes, 'who-the-fucks-that' and 'did-you-bring-them-here?' Grabbing his pistol, an old six-shooter revolver thing from the Second World War, he shimmies slowly down the hallway. Ninja-like he rests an ear behind the front door. Door unlocking, I hear raised voices from the hallway but can't quite make out what's being said, I can tell it's on the verge of an argument though. Shit, who the fuck will argue with a pumped-up monster like Claude? Twenty seconds later the voices soften before turning into laughs. Steadying myself, the voices get closer and my heartbeat rises. Adrenalin pumping the door swings open. Dipping his head, Claude walks in followed by an equally pumped-up looking white boy. I hear the Darth-Vadar theme from Star-Wars in the background and know something terrible is about to happen. Forehead down, eyebrows veeing in the middle, the white boy stares at me like he wants to rip my head off, break my back and piss on my remains. Taller than Claude, he's maybe six-foot-six, sort of handsome with a strong jawline and a boxers nose. His hair is weird, jet black, sort of shaved around the sides and slicked back on the top with a widows peak dipping into his lined forehead in the middle. Turns out his name is "Jones," from the West Ham Crew. Looking everywhere other than in his direction, I can tell he hasn't stopped staring at me, killing me with his glare. I must look at him eventually, can't blank the guy, he'll take offence and give me a hiding. I look up and give him a I'm-not-a-threat smile. That's when I saw it, just for a millisecond, a tiny pause, a glint of recognition, a moment of don't-I-know-you-from-somewhere?

'Aw-right mate,' he says in a steroid-enhanced gravelly broad cockney accent, so broad he sounds almost gypsy, you know, cockney with a twang of Irish, a hint of West-Country with a flavour of inbred-Norfolk. 'So, you're the famous Devon, yaah. Devon, from Brixton?' I nod. 'Railton Road, Coldharbour Lane, Angel Town, yaah?' Something about his words, always a hidden meaning, an undercurrent of hurt, a subtext of fuck-you.

'Um, yeah-yeah,' I say, not knowing whether he's being friendly or lining me up. In any case, he knows his geography of Brixton. Then, his deeply lined forehead and chiselled scowl lines morph into a smile. Steroid mentalists like these are prone to dramatic emotional outbursts and mood-swings, so I have to be careful. Yeah man, I've seen Claude down at Millwall being as nice as pie one minute, hugging and kissing and joking then switch, he's smashing some poor fucker in the face.

'We were wondering if you were actually real, or just Claudes wet dream.'

'Eh?' This monster's a gay?

'Yaah, Big-Cee's always going on about his mate Devon. Devon this, Devon that, Devon, Devon, Devon, thought he was shirt-lifter to begin with but he's alright though, aren't ya Cee. One of us, yaah.'

Ah, definitely not gay! They smile at each other, in silence, both seemingly agreeing with the mutual admiration.

Jones sits down on the end of the weights bench, leans over and looks right into my eyes like he's looking through a window into my mind. Sitting and staring, he's weird and off-putting and making me feel uncomfortable, and he knows it too, the wanker. Out of the corner of my eye, I see Claude steadying himself, shit, I tense up, ready for what's coming.

'Yaaahhh,' Jones sings, breaking the silence, 'I know you-you know, never forget a face me.' Solemnly slow, his words are deep and serious. Head buzzing, thoughts flicker and crack through my mind. Where's this going? What's next? When's it coming? What does he mean, "he knows me?" He thinks I'm a gay? What's with all this gay talk? Clocking the confusion in my face, he smiles a "yeah-I-know" smile.

'You got a brother, yaah, what's his name now, Brenton, Leon or something?'

My eyes are locked on his.

'Nah, nah, nah, hang-on. Fucking cracked it. Marlon... yaah?'

He's waiting for a sign of confirmation but he's not getting it though, no chance, poker face Devon in the house. He's sitting there smiling like a big green incredible-cheshire-cat-hulk monster with all the knowledge, all the cards, all the power. He's revelling in it. Yeah man, I can see it in his face, loving my confusion, aroused by the conundrum he's created, he's washing his cock in the waters of my puzzlement.

'Yaah,' he continues. 'I know you, your brother and your

mate too, Winston yeah? Win-stone, the super-man? And then there's the other one, yaah, the white boy, what's his name now?'

What. The. Fuck.

And what's with these "yaah's" like he's a posh Oxbridge boy or something. So he's heard of Marlon, Super and Paul, so what. Claude's probably been talking about them, like he has me. Must play it cool, can't give myself to him, can't qualify his power, can't give him the satisfaction, the big ugly know it all bastard. But, he knows about Super, and that bugs me. Nobody ever refers to Super as Winston, apart from his Momma and me when I wanted to get a rise out of him. Nagging my brain, the voices inside my head are shouting at me not to mess with this mysterious guy, I know if I don't front it up, he'll see me as weak and do for me.

'You know all about me man, you sure Claude's the fairy?' I smile, playing Russian roulette with his emotions.

Staring deep into me, I realise I've made a mistake. I've suggested he's a gay and that's offended him. Still staring, not emotion, no response, the silence kills me. Just bring the pain and get it over with.

Then, he bursts out laughing. 'Ha-ha-ha, yaah, yaah.'

I'm laughing too, in a play-along-don't-get-hurt way.

'Fucking diamond, yaah, diamond geezer,' he shouts, arms wide open, eyebrows up, laughter lines growing and face beaming. Claude smiles a nervous smile.

'Right then Millwall, let's get this sorted,' he says, standing and clapping his massive hands together, rubbing them furiously as he follows Claude go through to the kitchen.

I sit in a complete daze, replaying what's just happened.

'Right then, I'm off then my man, catch ya' later sweetheart,' the white boy yells from the hallway in a mock-Jamaican accent.

Claude comes back in, pleased as punch with himself. 'Another five-grand banked, easy money,' he says.

'Who the fuck?' I ask, not acknowledging his triumph.

Nodding, he smiles and sits down next to me. Tells me his

name is "Jones" or the "Guv-nah" as he's otherwise known is the top boy in the West Ham firm. On the terraces since he's a young kid with his old man, his uncle and cousin, who are all major league villains too by all accounts, nowadays, he runs the West Ham "Inter City" firm. No surprises there then, villains, gangsters and hooligans, but, here's the mind-fuck. Claude goes on to say he used to be a Police officer based in Brixton at the time of the riots in eighty-one. Shortly afterwards, he moves into the vice squad and, six months later, gets caught with his pants down being sucked off by a prostitute. Gets himself suspended on full pay for a year then eventually sacked. Classic bad-boy-made-good, now-turned-bad, him and his wife split up and he moves back in with his parents in the East End. After weeks of sulking and feeling sorry for himself, he falls back in with his villain mates from school, and, before long, he's running with the West Ham crew.

I can't move, can't even blink.

A villain who becomes Police, then turns villain, and, who was around at the time of the Brixton riots? Can't let Claude see my puzzlement, must hide it, must be the big man in control, cool as a cucumber. But then, more mind-fucking. Claude goes on to say Jones constantly boasts he's the one who arrested Super on the day of the riots, and actually started the riot, it's his claim to fame. I can't believe it, even now, after all that's happened.

My life's always been splattered with coincidence and fatalism, but supposing it's true. God damn, that's too much to handle. For sure, I remember Super being arrested and the carnage that followed but Jones happens to be the Policeman, that Policeman? No way, no fucking way. Claudes words hang mid-air cartoon like in those shitty Batman shows with the "blam" and "caboom" special effects. The special effects slowly grow larger and surround my fucked-up head before spinning around and around. Even now, when I close my eyes, I remember...
BRIXTON, 1981.

Heat hazily shimmers against the pavement as Prince Buster thumps through the stereo of Pauls stinking gold Triumph Dolomite, the one with the leaking black-vinyl sunroof. Finishing his second spicy meat patty, Super necks the last of his ginger beer meanwhile Paul tuts through the rear-view mirror, pleading with Super not to drop any more crumbs. Climbing out, Super heads into the ABC Taxi-cab office with a large bag of weed in his inside pocket, while Paul complains about the mess on the back seat. A minute later, Super reappears and throws us a I've-got-the-cash-no-worries wink and wry smile before shoving a roll of cash into his sock. As he rises two plain clothes officers are on him, pushing, shoving and attempting to get handcuffs on him. Leaning back, Super flings his head forward, smashing into one of the officers. God damn, blood spurts everywhere. Dazed, the officer wipes his nose with the sleeve of his jacket, seems to smile and yanks Super toward him, as he does lands a Henry Cooper right hook. Holy shit, clash of the titans. As Super drops to his knee, panic rushes through me, I'd never seen him hurt before, literally ever. Loads of youths run over to see what's happening, Police too and very quickly everyone's wrestling and fighting which leads to chucking bricks and, eventually, flinging petrol bombs. Swarms of Police charge us with plastic riot shields and truncheons, while bells and whistles and football terrace roaring sounds surround us. Suddenly, we're in the middle of an urban disturbance, a full on, fuck off, rip the place apart riot. Later on in the evening we get separated and, after searching for Marlon, we head for the town centre and rob the place clean. In and out of shops, we take whatever the fuck we want, yeah man, I rob a bright white nineteen seventies flared suit, and Paul robs a couple of bottles of brandy. Eventually, we catch up with Marlon, who, turns out, stayed on the Frontline all day, rioting, fighting and just surviving. When we spot him, he's messed up, dirty, tired and fatigued, and squaring up to a van full of Police who quickly fuck off when they see us approaching. Brave like a lion. Damn, it's so long-ago man, enough water under the bridge since then...

So, Jones is the one who arrested then kicked the shit out of Super? Nah, no fucking way. Claude continues with stories of Jones, Jones this, Jones that, Jones-Jones-Jones, but I don't hear a word. All I hear is the urban soundtrack of the riot, the venomous hum, the baying crowd, the Police bells in the distance and the wall of non-specific sound. The noise of urban warfare surrounds me as I see cars on fire, smashed windows and faces of the young Police officers who don't know what the fuck's happening. I remember it so vividly it feels almost real.

Claude picks up his dumb-bells and starts pumping again, like the Jones coincidence is completely normal whereas my brain hurts as I try to understand it fully. Don't know how long I'm there but I remember smiling and chuckling to myself as I work it out. Yeah, Claude, the fool, is messing with me, he's set this up as an elaborate piss-take. I bet him and Jones, if that's even his name, are both bent doubled over crying with laughter planning this one. Claude will have thrown a few names at him, "remember to mention Angel Town, remember to mention Winston too," then Jones will wind me up proper.

Ex-police who arrested Super, and started the riots?

Ex-police who's now a drug dealing hooligan?

Nah, no way.

I worked it all out.

Worked him out, the mug.

Claude's on the weights bench now, pressing away, grunting and moaning like he's shagging his bird while I'm like Einstein, thinking it through, over and over. Then it struck me, what if, in a mad world, I'm wrong and Jones is in fact Police, and this shits real shit and not a massive piss-take. Supposing what Claude said is true, and not just true, but double-true, swear on the bible true, the whole truth and nothing but the truth-true? Shit, supposing Jones isn't just "ex" Police but actually "now" Police, maybe he's undercover-police, deep-undercover, a sleeper cell or something? I've heard rumours about a special Police unit that plants undercover officers in hooligan gangs for years and years to get information and intelligence. Jones is one of these? Fucking hell, that's more like it, that's how he knows all about me, about Marlon and about Super. God damn, with what he knows, he can finger the Essex gangsters, nail most of the cocaine supply into London and deal with the two main football hooligan firms at the same time.

A massive sting operation or something, the sting of all stings, sting of the century.

Shit.

Double shit.

Panic.

On top of this, a wholesale amount of cocaine has just changed hands in this very flat and I'm here, named, seen and probably caught on tape. Fuck, I'm directly implicated, completely exposed and at risk. Vulnerable, I got to get out of here, but, at the same time, got to act normal, stay calm, breathe deeply, dare not alert Claude. Man, if he suspects I know the truth, he'll fuck me up, get me to take the blame, make me his Lee-Harvey Oswald. Nah man, right now, calmness is required.

But, hang the fuck on.

By all accounts, Jones is a proper villain, a monster. How deep is deep under-cover? The Police have rules about how far he can go, what he can do and not do. Yeah, they can't compromise future arrests by him breaking more laws than the crooks he's trying to catch. Entrapment or something, the defence lawyers will have a field-day and the villains will get away scotch-free.

True say man, true.

Smiling again, I safely conclude Claude is indeed messing with my mind and definitely pranking me, the pair of jokers. Still pumping away, Claude must be belly-laughing inside, watching me flip between the truth and reality then back again. But, ha-ha-ha, I'm the one belly laughing now, I worked it out, solved his little scam, undone his joke at my expense. Still, something isn't right, can't put my finger on it but it's there, right in front of me.

Up off the bench, Claude stands in front of me pissing himself laughing. I'm a confused, a frightened little kid who's seen a ghost, all the while he's perfectly fine and calm and laughing like an overgrown ugly as fuck chesire cat. If all this about Jones is indeed true, he must have accepted it as perfectly normal, a quirky coincidence of life, just one of those things. He is convincing, that's for sure, like he genuinely believes what he's saying. I'll play along and quiz him about the ex-police bit…

Claude says, soon after the riots, the Government holds an enquiry to find out the root causes, deflect their complicity, pin the blame on someone. Afterwards, the Police have a big shake up, moving the meatheads out of the highly volatile inner-city areas such as Brixton. Jones, apparently, is recruited into the vice squad in Londons west-end. After the pants down incident, where the prostitutes pimp receives a fractured skull, Jones is suspended and, six months later, sacked. His wife, embarrassed and disgusted, moves out along with his little boy. Jobless and family obliterated, he sets about drinking himself to oblivion. Can't afford the mortgage repayments so, after a few months, loses the house and, swallowing his pride, moves back in with his parents in Dagenham. Before long, he falls back in with his boyhood mates in the East End, sorts himself out, drops the drink in favour of pumping iron and ends up at Upton Park watching West Ham. Sounds far-fetched, but, kind of plausible in a tragic way, but, for all I know, all of it might be true right up to him getting sacked. From then on, the Police might have created the back-story, making it appear he's been sacked but, in reality, placing him deep undercover, a sleeper-cell gathering information and intelligence, ready for the biggest arrest of villains in history.

Yeah man.

Starts to make sense now, starts to come together.

All of us are tearing London up with hooliganism, drugs, clubs and pirate radio and, up till now, nobody of any note is arrested and nobody does any serious time. Okay, Claude does a few months for the Luton thing and Super's doing his stretch for the Deep River monstrosity, but still, you got to wonder. We're either really lucky, or really fucked. …

7. The Beast

"You don't want to be trapped inside with me sunshine. Inside, I'm somebody nobody wants to fuck with…"

Michael Gordon Patterson

17, HAMILTON HOUSE
GREENWICH, LONDON
LATE SUMMER, 1989

Head in hands I concentrate hard, waiting for something to happen. It's impossible though, especially when my ass is this cold and all I can smell is disgusting shit. Thoughts turn to Paul, the mother fucking shithead and THAT night. The cinema of my mind shows it again and again and again, always in glorious super slow-motion technicolour…

Ravers raving, lasers scanning, big wheel turning, and me, locked in THAT room with the snow-globe of cash floating around me. The screen fades to black and the silence is broken by off screen echoes of pain and torture and death…

"Thinking about what happened, about your role in it, the part you played in everyone's demise?" the Interrogator asks, knowing for sure I am, as I always do.

What the fuck you doing in here, you dirty fuck. Get out, get out and leave me alone. In any case, fuck you, you're involved as much as me, you're the jinx around here, you're the Jonah. I should be holding the shooter, not you. Man, if I was, you'd be done big time, gone once and for all.

CLICK.

Looking up, I'm confronted by the end of the barrel and a mass of blurriness all around it. Heart rate jumps. Right here, right now, this is it, in this god-forsaken shit-hole, man, the indignity of it. I hear the get-away-car downstairs in the car park rev it's engine, ready to speed off. I get it, it's my taxi for when Elvis eventually leaves the building. He'll get what he wants, have his dirty hands up my skirt and have his way with me, so now it's time. Staring into the spiralling darkness of doom, I see the chapters of my sorry life slipping away. One by one they meet the tip of the bullet deep inside and melt into oblivion. Shit man, it's coming on strong. Head fuzzy and dizzy and nauseous, trippy almost, my guts ache and pang, turning inside out.

Must front it out, must not let him see my fear. Put that

thing down man, you'll have my head off.

"That's the point, dickhead. You got it coming," the Interrogator says, threateningly scary.

Got it coming for sure, but now isn't my time. So, put that thing down and be serious, you'll get nothing more, ever.

Must get him to focus.

Slowly, he lowers the gun, thank fuck. Heart rate slowing, calmness ripples through the room.

Yeah man, calmnessssssssss…

Now, where was I?

I always thought something great will happen, that I'll be someone, make something of myself. Before what happened, I really and truly believed I was destined for something great, something monumental, something meaningful and significant. No matter whatever shit gets thrown my way, getting shot at, the riots, the beatings and the Frontline bullshit, I always thought I was untouchable. Just unlucky I suppose, fate maybe, not sure what you call it, but shit just happens. So, in between living and dying I just sit here, on this dirty stinking shitter, feeling like shit while trying to have a shit. Constipation though, bunged up and blocked, an unfortunate side effect of the browny loveliness that is heroin. Oh, the irony of it.

"Life's what you make it for fucks sake, anything is possible," the Interrogator suggests, like a walking-talking fortune cookie.

Oh, fuck off. I've spilt the beans, scratched the itch, picked the scab. What are you still doing here anyway? You're just as messed up as me, just as much to blame. The only difference is you have the gun.

"Shut the fuck up," the Interrogator says, spit flying from his angry mouth. *"Do your shit, wipe your arse and let's get it over with."*

Okay-alright. Super.

Always the wrong side of crazy, always rampaging and fighting the world, always angry, always a chip on his shoulder, always against something. The other kids tease him about his picky hair or his clothes or his Momma being a big fatty-boom-batty. That, my friend, is always a big mistake. He'll front up to anyone, no matter their size. Ten, maybe eleven years old and we're walking home from school, just chatting and walking and taking the piss out of each other when four or five kids, maybe fourteen or fifteen years old stop us and try and tax us, or, in other words, demand money from us. Nothing too heavy, normal everyday inner-city stuff, pushing and shoving, just everyday dog-eat-dog back street jostling. But, tax us? Nah, no way. Super swings his school bag above his head, screaming like a crazy. A couple of them back off and walk away, but three of them stand firm. The biggest one, by the look of him from Nigerian decent, charges forward. Man, he can fight and promptly gives Super a proper going over, grabbing him by the ears and kneeing him in his head. Struggling free, Super flings some punches but it's no good, the Nigerian is caveman strong. I run in to help, but the other two kids hold me back and after a while, we just stand and watch them battle, neither of them will stop, both as stubborn as each other. Eventually, exhausted and on all fours, Super looks up at the Nigerian who's standing over him, all African and caveman looking. 'You good man, but not good enough,' the Nigerian says before snorting up a massive mouthful of green phlegm and spitting it over Super. He stares for a few seconds before hi-fiving his buddies and walking off. Standing up, Super wipes his face and stretches out his chest. Scanning around he spots two empty milk bottles on the steps of house over the road. He jogs over, grabs one in each hand and smashes one against the wall before launching the other towards the Nigerian. Flying through the air in slow motion, it smashes just behind him. The Nigerian spins around and sees Super looking bruised, his nose bleeding and half a broken bottle in his hand. 'I'm still here, we're not finished,' Super shouts. The Nigerian stares for what seems like ages. 'You're crazy,' he shouts, circling his finger around the side of his head before turning and walking off quick-time. Super waits, watching them disappear into the distance before turning to me. 'Fucking pussy, we just getting going,' he says, genuine disappointment in his voice.

So, that's Super.

Heart as big as a lion, brain the size of an ant.

But still, he's like a brother to me, known him literally all my life. My Momma and his Momma went to the same kindergarten back in Golden Springs, Jamaica, and travelled her on the same boat in nineteen-fifty. I love him, and don't mind admitting it…

Leaving school, I've no clue what I want to do with my life, never even considered it to be honest. No exams, or a job lined up, Pops is going on and on about me getting a trade, like a plumber, electrician or joiner, which, of course, is sound advice. Momma picks up an application form for an apprentice job with the Gas board, fills it out and sends it off without me even getting the chance to say no. I'm raging, even though I don't know what I want to do, I know I don't want no boring nine-to-five job. Nobody I know has a job, apart from Paul. Everyone else, Super, Claude, Crissy, all the rude-boys I left school with, in fact, everyone around the Frontline, don't have jobs, unless you class juggling, dealing, ducking and diving as a job. Twenty quid a week as an apprentice on a youth training scheme?

Nah, no way.

Anyway, this particular morning, I'm in bed half-awake-half-asleep contemplating knocking one out when Momma storms in. Hands in the air, she's waving a letter around rabbiting on about an interview or something. Face beaming, she's smiling and happy and proud. Faithfully high hopes, she'd say I'd be a lawyer or a doctor or something respectable, something to be proud of. I know I've let her down badly, Pops too. Shit man, poor old Pops, working his entire life on the London Underground, nose to the grindstone, doing overtime in the dust and the grime, just to make ends meet. He doesn't complain though, never, not once. He's a proper man, a real man, he put his family before himself, before his own hopes and dreams. I used to resent his lack of ambition and his boring life, work, dinner, pint of light ale and game of backgammon with the old boys down the pub, then bed. Now though, after what's happened, I totally get what he's about, envy it almost. I'm so proud of him, I wish I told him. That's what Super misses you know, a daddy, compensating for being the only man in the house by being overly manly, Super-manly, if you catch my drift. He never knew his father, just fucked his Momma then does the off's quick time. Super romances himself by telling everyone his old man's from East Africa somewhere, accounting for his dark skin, narrow nose and slitty oval eyes. He'll make up all manner of shit about his daddy, all of it total and utter crap. Famous boxer, footballer, cricketer, rich with loads of cars, in the British army coming back sometime soon, all of it complete and utter bullshit. Over time he eventually accepts the way things are, but, he'd say all the time he hates his daddy, whoever the fuck he is, and if he ever meets him, he'll cut his head off, set him on fire and murder his stinking arse. I feel for his Momma, his poor, old, demented mad bitch Momma. Fierce, angry and always frowning, she makes up for his daddy not being there by giving him enough claps around the head in a vain attempt at controlling him. That will never work, he's born bad and she knows it too. Behind all the fierceness, all the anger and all the front, she's sad and lonely. She'll come around to Mommas, sit in the kitchen all night and weep tears of sorrow and pain. Sitting a few steps from the top of the stairs listening to them talk, I can't really make out what they're saying, but I know she's crying. I used to think she cried about Super and him being out of control, but now I know she's crying about being alone and lonely... just like me. I know the feeling, all alone in the world with absolutely nobody to talk to, nobody to hug or kiss, nobody to check you're still alive, nobody to care, nobody to give a shit...

Where was I? Gas board, yeah.

A couple of weeks later I get a letter inviting me to an

interview for the gas board job Momma applied for. Instructions say report to their offices zero-nine hundred hours Monday morning in Croydon. Damn. Nine, in the morning, in Croydon? The weekend before, we head to an all-night blues-party in Stockwell at some flats opposite the Oval Cricket Ground.

BLUES PARTY AT SOME RANDOM FLAT
ASHMOLE ESTATE
STOCKWELL, LONDON
AUTUM 1971

Huge sound system, plenty of fit girls, lots of dark rum, even more herbs, the flat is rammed-full and the party is sweet. The whole estate is involved with folk dancing outside on the balcony, in the car park and down the road…

Looking back, these are just like the raves we have nowadays, just like my rave, the big one. Shit man, those memories are too deep, too buried, too hidden away. Can't go there yet, no way.

Back to the blues party at the Oval.

Inside, it's baking hot with everyone bouncing and dancing and loving the vibe. So hot, the ceiling literally drips with sweet sexy sweat. Good tunes with a serious bassline, a young guy in an army uniform is toasting over the top about being sus-stopped while we sip some rum, chat to some girls and are loving the vibe. Later on, a fool of a rude boy from fuck knows where bounces into me.

'What'am bwai, what da fook ya'ah do?' he says with a side look and a screwed-up face.

'No problem man, cool yeah, no worries,' I say, shit happens right, it's mad busy and rammed, he can't help it.

Rather than a graceful nod, he bigs himself up and starts testing. 'Ya Devon, right. Devon from Railton?'

Uh-oh, he knows me, that can't be good. 'Yeah-man, that's me, who the fuck wants to know?' I say, can't back down, he and everyone else in the dance would think me a fool.

'Ya nah-remember me, nah. Ya fooking shank me-gal from time, dred, you dis-res-peck dis broddah,' he says, pushing me in the shoulder. I haven't got a fucking clue what he's on about, and definitely can't remember fucking his girl.

The crowd around us parts a little as the music drops and the dance-hall-hum fades. Suddenly we're in the middle of a cheap spaghetti western, both of us facing each other like a pair of Clint Eastwood cowboys, I'm the sheriff and he's the outlaw. Then smash, the outlaw stumbles to right and the crowd lets out a collective, "ohhhhhhhhhhhh-shhhhhhhitttttt." Magnificently manly and absolutely awesome, Super stands there proud as punch, my hero. Face screwing up with a fuck-you-up-in-a-split-second look about him, he's landed a peach of a right hook on the side of the outlaw's head. The fool's falling about the place trying to scramble to his feet but Super stands there like the bad-man George Foreman looking mother-fucking super-cool. 'My man got an important business meeting on Monday, can't be turning up with bumps and ting,' he says, calm and matter of fact, nodding towards me. He steps forward with fire in his eyes and the crowd steps back in awe.

The outlaw stares, silent and tense as everyone watches on, yearning for carnage. The tension is excruciating. Realising he's made a monumental mistake, the outlaw shakes his head and looks away, 'ya-ah dead-man-walking Devon, me know where ya-ah yard at yeah,' he says, exiting through the crowd, head dipped, shoulders up and tail between his legs.

Bassline resumes, crowd comes together again and we're back in the grove. Super turns to me. 'So anyway, you were saying,' he says, like it's nothing.

The lion-heart of Brixton, a true brother and I miss him. Don't get me wrong, he's truly bad and has done some seriously fucked up things. Yeah man, it pains me to say, but he's done hideous things, things I'm not proud of, disgusting things, things he should be disgusted with, but I know for sure he's not. Nowadays, he uses his warped paranoia to justify everything and I mean everything, every dark evil thing that goes on in his fucked-up head.

UPPER CLASS BAR
KINGS ROAD
CHELSEA, LONDON
NEW YEARS EVE, 1975 or 6 or SOMETHING

New Year's Eve and Paul suggests a pub in Chelsea, said the place will be full of Sloane Square posh girls looking for a bit of rough, (and god-damn, we are indeed rough). Through the swing doors I instantly feel completely conspicuous, but there's a nice vibe, everyone's happy, celebrating and having fun. Downing some drinks, pretty soon we too are having a good time, drinking, chatting to girls and having a laugh. Everything's tidy and we're loving the New Year feeling. When I say "we", I of course mean me and Paul because all night long Super sits chewing a wasp, vexed and moody, says he hates being north of the river and this place is full of villains and gangster types. It's not, of course it's not, it's just his paranoid and freaked out mind playing tricks on him. Nevertheless, he's going on and on and on, hate this, hate that, hate the music selection, hate the rum, hate the colour of the wallpaper blah-blah-blah, all night long. He can moan for England, but, when he's in a hating mood, we know to steer clear. Once he gets something into his head, the only way it's coming out is when his blood or, more often or not, someone else's blood is spilt on the floor. The night goes on and me and Paul get more and more pissed-up drunk while Super gets super-drunk, triple-pissed-drunk, nasty-drunk, evil-drunk, self-destruct-drunk. Rather than pacifying and mellowing, the rum and coke he pours down his throat just magnifies his hate, fuels his vexation, builds his anger. He argues with himself at times, yeah man, I'll catch him having a full-blown conversation with himself and when he catches me watching, he tells me to 'fawk-arf batty-bway.' Anyway, this particular night I see him mumbling away to himself, now and again smiling and chuckling before bobbing his head away to whatever tune he can't get out of his mind. I decide right there to ignore him, it's New Year's Eve for fuck sake and I'm feeling good and not letting him bring me down. Me and Paul get chatting to a couple of tidy girls from Buckinghamshire or some other wherever-the-fuck-shire. Close to midnight, we're smooching with the shire girls getting ready for some Big-Ben-striking-twelve tongue action when a skinny white boy edges by. Proper mister-unlucky-wrong-place-wrong-time kind of bloke, he nudges Super's arm. It's not his fault, the place is packed, doesn't mean anything by it, probably doesn't even realise he's done it. Super grabs his arm, drags him back and warns him to be careful or else. Mister unlucky apologises, 'sorry mate, no offence, happy new year,' he smiles before returning to his girlfriend or wife or whoever. Loved up, they're kissing and drinking, smiling and joking, loving life, loving each other. I spot Super screwing him through the crowd, melting the skin from his skull and burning a hole through his brain with his laser-beam eyes. Me and Paul tell him to relax, enjoy the night, it's New Year's Eve for fucks sake. Doesn't work. Twenty minutes later, I see Mister-unlucky head toward us. Five-pound note in his hand, he's probably going to the bar or the cigarette machine maybe. 'I'll take that,' Super yells, grabbing the cash. 'Dry cleaning tax yeah,' he says. Mister-unlucky starts laughing, thinking Super's having a laugh. Big mistake. Split second later, forehead and nose collide, blood spurting, the pub erupts with screams of shock and wails of horror, Super's soundtrack, his signature tune. Super doesn't hear nothing, he's tripping on his instant adrenalin rush, his fix of life, his wave of energy. Mister-unlucky stumbles around holding his face when he's caught by a lightening left upper-cut which literally takes him off his feet. Time stands still and the pub falls silent as he arcs through the air. Mid-air, Super follows up with a right hook, forcing mister-unlucky to do an almost backward summersault. Landing in a heap of arms and legs, the pub circles around him. Slowly, eyes move from the carnage on the floor to the monster in the corner. Standing there, a mountain of angry on an island named "fuck-you", Super's grinning, proud as punch, absolutely loving what he sees as adulation, but everyone else sees as disgust and fear.

The screams fade into an eerie silence apart from the echo of "don't let the sun go down" by Elton John on the jukebox. A dark, surreal scene for sure, and about to get even darker. Super's eyes are wild and demented, yet he's grinning like a Cheshire cat. Yeah, it's in the eyes, always, you can see a lot in the eyes, every emotion, every feeling, every freeze frame of history right there, in the eyes. Mister-unlucky writhes around on the floor with blood everywhere. His girlfriend kneels beside him screaming, crying and covered in blood too, the poor cow. Then, I see it, the broken pint glass in Super's hand. Fuck. Grabbing Super, I pull him through the crowd who, no doubt spotting the broken glass too start shouting, screaming and pawing at us. Even now, I can remember their faces, horrified, disgusted and distorted, they're scared and repulsed at the same time. Can't blame them, I feel the same. Right there Super scarred their entire lives forever, quite literally. Damn, from then on, they'll always remember "that" News Year's Eve when that poor bloke gets glassed in the face...

Outside, we have it lively back to Paul's car then straight back home. Super sits in the back sucking on his cut-up hand, staring out of the window as if nothing has happened. He just sits there, cool, calm and collected, watching as the scenery zoom by.

That's the real Super, the real darkness, the real monster. Big, brave and loyal, but stupid as fuck and mentally deranged.

One time, after a long night out, we're sitting beside each other in my room, getting mellow and serious and philosophical with Marlon sleeping soundly in the bed opposite, when he tells me he thinks he's mad, a proper crazy. Says he hears voices in his head, with music in the background, telling him what to do and how to do it. I tell him he's smoking too much weed and needs to calm it down, but he just shakes his head and laughs it off as something and nothing.

Damn, even with his faults, I miss him, wish he was here right now, with me, helping me, saving me…

After the arrest on the day of the uprising in eighty-one, where Claude reckons Jones was the Policeman who arrested him, he gets charged with affray and, after two months on remand, he's sentenced to six months. Might have been longer but they arrested so many the prisons will probably have been full. We go see him a few times at the Scrubs before he's transferred to a smaller prison in the countryside.

I hate it there, full of scum visiting scum.

HMP WORMWOOD SCRUBS
DU CANE ROAD
SHEPPARDS BUSH
LONDON, 1981

The "Scrubs", a perfect name. As soon as you go through the main gate it's dog-eat-dog-eye-for-an-eye-watch-your-back city. Some how you're made to feel like a criminal, just for visiting. Yeah man, visitors, inmates and guards alike are looking for angles. Heads down, slitty-evil criminal eyes are eying you up, assessing the threat, looking for an opportunity. Tentatively through to the visiting hall, I see mums and dads with their heads in hands, weeping and sobbing, thinking how on earth their son has turned out like this and where-did-it-all-go-wrong. Heart-broken mums and gutted dads are distraught, their lad was meant to play for England, be a doctor, an architect or lawyer, something respectable, something to be proud of, not robbing cars, holding up banks or burgling old-grannies flats for a twenty-quid fix. I look around and see wives and girlfriends, short skirts, big hair and way too much lipstick. Draping themselves over the screwed-to-the-floor tables, they're tongue-kissing their blokes, trying to convince them they're not having it off with the milkman or the next-door neighbour while he's locked away. Kids are there too, crying their eyes out because they miss their daddy and can't work out why he's holidaying in a place like this. Then, there's the guards standing with their backs to the wall, looking at nothing while seeing everything. Scorn in the eyes, looking down their noses at everyone, they hate their lives, hate their predicament and hate their how-did-I-end-up-here reality. Yeah man, they locked up too, more locked up than the inmates because, unlike the inmates, the guards are there by choice. They'll do their eight-hour shift, dealing with the scum, the shouting from the cells, the fighting on the landings, the bumming in the showers, the hanging from the window bars and the overdoses on the bottom bunks, then go back to their loving families in the suburbs. Kissing their wives and hugging their children, they never talk about the horrors, the incessant noise, the indiscriminate abuse or the scum-of-the-earth real-life nightmare they've been through.

Thought provoking.

Walking into the visiting hall, I see Super before he sees me. An injured puppy-dog, head down and shoulders up, he's staring into the table casting a sorry sight. When he spots me though his face lights up with smiles and wide brows. Says he loves the place, like a holiday camp with three square meals per day, time to work out, play pool or table tennis and catching up with old friends. Says he's learning to read too. I see sadness even fear in his eyes, he's obviously lying, trying to convince himself otherwise. Life on the inside changed him. Less anger, more sour, full of spite and hate. Hating the Police, hating politicians, hating the guards, hating the other inmates, hating everyone, hate, hate-hate and more hate. I can't face going see him often, no way, I simply can't face seeing him like that.

When he gets out, after the Claude versus Snakehead war, as part of his rehabilitation, he moves from South London to Tottenham, near Marlon, actually. As part of his parole arrangements, he's given a flat on a sprawling shit-hole estate which makes the estates in Brixton, like Angel Town or Sommerleyton, look small and decidedly desirable. Locals call it "The Farm", a jumbled mass of grey concrete blocks connected by high rise walkways with shops on the ground level and car parks beneath. I don't like it up there, nah man, that particular maze of madness isn't for me, the vibe's cold and off-key. Living so close together, everyone in and out of each other's pockets, living literally on top of each other can't be good for the soul. But, here's the rub. Even though everyone's so close, they're massively suspicious of each other and ironically, completely distant and discordant. They walk around saying 'morning' to each other in a cheery happy go lucky way, but, in reality they're thinking 'fuck you', wishing they're a million miles away. Although I miss having Super around, secretly I'm happy he moved away. He's close, but not too close, and out of my hair, plus, being in Tottenham, he can look out for Marlon too. Things are tidy for a while, life's working out well for him. Since prison, he's calmer and more mellow, godfather to my boy and uncle to Marlon, both jobs he takes seriously.

Although his life up till then was pretty god damn shit, his real problems start a few years later when an old man is killed during a Police raid on his flat, just around the corner from The Farm. Story goes the Police are looking for his suspected drug dealing son, and his sons guns or drugs or cash and things go terribly wrong. You see, the Police, just like the rest of society, are full of prejudice, of course they are, they're not immune just because of their career choice. They must think if the son's a scum-bag drug dealer villain, the father must be scum too, blaming him for fucking up the raising of his boy. They don't think for a minute he might have wanted the best for his boy or that he might be disgusted, ashamed or even embarrassed by him.

This particular morning, they kick his door, don't find the son so rough the dad up, treat him like a suspect. Tragically, he has a heart attack or stroke or something and drops down dead. Normal everyday folk, as well as the local council leaders, are up in arms complaining, protesting and marching down to the Police Station and Town Hall. It's all over the evening news reports, tension brewing, I remember thinking this is way worse than the original Brixton uprising in nineteen-eighty-one. This was less a release of anger and more like a proper political movement. Paul says we're on the brink of a revolution, the inner cities are fighting back and are about to take control. Brixton, Tottenham, Birmingham, Liverpool, Bristol, Leeds, everywhere and anywhere, citizens are revolting and rioting, and absolutely loving it. Anarchy, yeah man.

DEEP RIVER ESTATE
TOTTENHAM, LONDON
OCTOBER 1985

The newspapers and television news stir it all up with reporters and journalists roaming around, asking all and sundry leading questions about how disgusted and how scared they are. Interestingly, not "if" but "how" scared they are. The media love conflict, tension, friction, they love the headlines, the readership, the advertisers and of course the money. Actually, it's not even the money, they love what this brings, cars, boats, girls, orgasms, power, control, anything to reinforce their personal narcissism. Fuelling every little discord, they want it to go dark and dirty, allowing them to be judgemental and condescending, in turn allowing the majority to look down their noses at the minority, making them feel safe and secure and on the right side of society. The more threatened everyday folk feel, the more they cling to what they know. The reporters and owners of the newspapers don't want citizens to think or see the truth, nah man, they want them to shut the fuck up and do what they've always done, and buy what you've always bought. Yeah man, I worked it out years ago, the "commercialisation of pain", as Paul would say or the "prolongation of inertia", whatever the fuck that means.

Deep though.

After the death of the old man, throughout the following week tension builds day by day and, once the weekend arrives, the locals march on the Police Station and Town Hall. Super, man, he's right in the middle of it, (of course), militant and angry, out to prove a point and finish what he started years before in Brixton. Marlon calls me to say he's seen him leading a march toward the Town Hall, and when he tries to have a word with him Super tells him to 'fawk-off.' He loves Marlon like a little brother or even the son he never had, so dealing with him like that wasn't like him, not the Super I knew and loved and grew up with. Later that evening, it kicks off big time. The formula for chaos? Rioting plus petrol bombs plus violence plus mass-demonstration plus conspiracy theories equals, yes, you guessed it, Super.

Simple, fool-proof.

Super tells the same story every time we talk, like he's reading it from a book, like he's observing it in the third person or like he's tripping and having an out-of-body experience. Apparently, according to him, the march on the Town Hall went tits up, or exactly to plan, depending how you look at it. Stones and rocks are flung, windows smashed and total madness kicks off. The Police chase the trouble-makers, (aka, Super plus a couple of dozen other rude-boys and hanger-oners), back into the estate then block off all the entrances and exits, locking it down like Belfast or something. Then, they set about rounding up not just those involved at the Town Hall trouble, but all the rude-boys and troublesome kids from the neighbourhood. Firing off some tear-gas to hype up the fear, they're ready to clear out the shit, sweep up the crap and lock away the crusty edge of society. According to Super, he tries to calm it down, reason with the rude-boys while pleading with the Police, but, as the night goes on, everything gets out of hand. Super says a local bad-boy set's up in one of the tower-blocks with a high-power air-rifle, taking pot-shots at the Police. Soon as the shooting starts, Super says he heads back to his flat, sits on his balcony spliff in hand and watches the madness unfold, before eventually falling asleep. Four in the morning, he's woken by a room full of machine gun toting Police standing over him screaming get-on-the-floor-get-on-the-floor-don't-fucking-move screams. He's questioned for eighteen hours straight before being charged with murder.

Murder of a Policeman.

Damn, it's serious, the most serious shit or all shit I reckon.

Story goes a local bobby, not one of the door-kicking-in crew, just a normal Joe gets separated from his buddies and is chased through the estate by a mob of villainous scumbags, true dark-man life takers. Shit, just recalling this makes me sick, it's evil, born-bad darkness, difficult to repeat.

I tell this story out of respect, so we never forget the darkness.

Never repeat the mistakes…

After a ten-minute chase, he's cornered. The dark-man beat the living shit out of him then drag him down to the underground car park beneath the estate. Then, it gets seriously dark. They take a machete to his neck. Even by Super's fucked-up standards, it's seriously deranged, fucked-up shit.

Disgusting. Despicable.

Not right, not by a long way.

Something Super might have done? Man, I really don't know. He loves his machete, his twelve-inch steel "baby" as he calls it. Yeah, even though he'll fantasise about using it in that exact way, he swears he's innocent. Even whispering, when nobody else can hear apart from me, his best mate forever, he denies it. If he did do it, he's convinced himself he didn't. Always bitter and negative and suspicious, but could he have done that, man, I just don't know. Either way, nobody deserves what that Policeman suffered, nobody apart from rapists and kiddie-fiddlers. Yeah, fuck them, hack their heads off and torch the remains for sure, but, a simple bloke doing his bit for the community, trying to Police the bad boys on the estate?

Nah, no way, it's not right man.

It's sick… sick, sick, sick.

Marlon reckons everyone on the estate suspected Super, but, of course, nobody saw him do it, no eyewitnesses, nothing. Guilty or not, he's convicted with no witnesses, no weapon, no motive, nothing. How they got away with that, I'll never know. Someone has to pay the price though, justice has to be seen to be done, the authority of the state must be apparent, otherwise it's chaos, anarchy and madness. A swift arrest followed by a decisive conviction will settle everyone down, give everyone confidence the baddies are locked up. Yeah, this allows Joe-public to go about his business, pay his taxes and comply with the law with no fear, allowing the establishment to continue to get rich. Yeah man, the conspiracy allows the "minority" to rule the "majority", with no threat to the inherited privilege given to them by their grandfathers through dodgy handshakes at private clubs in Ascot or Mayfair or somewhere. Yeah man, Paul told me these are the very same mother-fuckers who created the British Empire, enslaving whole nations around the world to plunder their resources…

Wow, I fucking get it. At last, through my haze of urban shit, I can see the world for what it really is.

Look at me ranting and raving, giving my political and societal views on the world. Want to know what really scares the living shit of me, what really fills me with dread? Police with heads cut off, nah. Miscarriages of justice, nah. What really scares me is if Super is innocent, then whoever did it walks free amongst us right now. Yeah, sitting on the bus or the train or whatever, minding your own business, listening to your Walkman, reading the paper or your book and right next to you sits a stone-cold-devil-in-disguise-head-hacking-cop-killer-dark-man. You might share a glance, might even share a smile and pass the time of day together. It'll seem pleasant and mellow, normal almost. But, deep inside, he's got a secret, a dark, fucked up secret, a proper skeleton in his closet. He'll play back the moment over and over in his head, seeing it in his minds-eye while looking at you. At first, he'll see it in glorious technicolor, he'll be the hero in his own Hollywood blockbuster, but, when the adrenaline fades, when his accomplices start to wonder if they might be next, he'll dwell on it. Yeah man, he'll see his victims wife and kids on the news, see their grief, their tears and their sadness. Sure, at first, he'll dismiss it with a "fuck them" and try to justify it, creating elaborate arguments to justify why it's right, why he deserved it, him or me and all that bullshit. Then, weeks or months later, just before he goes to sleep, he'll feel it. He'll feel the same as I feel about what I've done. The weight of regret hanging heavy on his soul, it'll be the noose around his neck, the razor-sharp steel on his personal guillotine of guilt. He'll be thinking about what might have been, what if he didn't do it, what is life might have been like, what if he just went down the pub, went home or went to his mums? What if, what if, what if? He'll be fucked with regret, crucified by guilt, buried by melancholy. Then, back on the bus or the train, he'll sit next to you and smile, wondering if somehow you know his deep dark secret, if you've worked him out, if he's given himself away some how. He'll be sitting there thinking about it, playing it back, over and over in his warped head, right there, next to you, right now.

Scary.

Super should have kept his head down, remained in the shadows and steered clear of the attention. Instead, he's doing a life sentence at Her Majesties pleasure, no release date, just "life". I know he'll never get out and I think deep down he knows that too. Prison nowadays isn't like before, when locked away in nineteen-eighty-one, after the uprising. Nah, he's big league now, in with proper lifers, killers and rapists and the diabolical scum of the underworld. He goes downhill quickly once he's sentenced, his spirit broken. With no evidence, no witnesses, no nothing, he's sour and vile, consumed by conspiracy and grand plans of invisible hands. His Momma tries to get a campaign going, petitioning the Home Secretary to review his case, but, no matter how much pressure, he's found guilty, sent down and the establishment can never release him. If they did, they'll never live it down, never admit they have it wrong and couldn't stomach the general public fearing the real killer is still on the loose. I've not been to see him in months, can't face it, can't see him like that.

Damn, it makes me so sad.

So, that then is the tale of poor fucked up, locked up Super…

"Listen to you, all melancholy and regretful and tearful. What about you, what about what you've done, what you've caused," the Interrogator says, seeing through my attempt to side-step my reality.

I know what I've caused, and I know He's right, but, I can't let him win. If he wins, I lose, and no matter what I've lost, I'm too pussy to lose this particular game. We both know what happens when you lose.

So, fuck you.

"Fuck me? Give it a rest. You can't dodge this one buddy," the Interrogator says, reading me like a book.

Dodge it I will.

Change the subject.

So, anyway, Paul…

Shortly after Super get's sent down, Paul is back in touch. We drifted apart ever since young Ashley's life changed in Kent, at the not-so-friendly football match-tear-up against Chelsea. Super being in prison breaks the ice, sort of re-bonds us a bit. Truth be told, it feels good having Paul back on side. He's still working in the City at his old man's firm, buying and selling companies or "asset stripping" as he calls it. The city slicker shit is massive, so cash falls out of his arse, birds leap into his cock and cocaine shoots up his nose.

Yeah man, a proper son-of-Thatcher success story, banking his first million aged thirty-two he lives up to the stereotype and promptly buys himself a Porsche. Gleaming white with silver wheels, custom made red leather interior and a massive kitchen-table wing on the back, it was a work of art. He likes Porsches, watches too, Rolex, only ever Rolex, big, gold and ostentatious, just like him. He likes suits as well, actually, he's obsessed about suits, only ever Graves and Sparrow from Saville Row, suit maker for the royal family, so he said. In fact, anything that cost money he liked, the more expensive the better. Looking the part though, he's suited and booted with his hair slicked back and a constant all over sun-bed-tan. Yeah, he loves the fact he's every inch the city slicker yuppie. After getting back in touch, he starts coming down to a few of my club nights with some of his business associates for what he calls "a special night out". Other corporate finance executives might take their associates to the opera or the theatre maybe, whereas Paul takes his to back-street south London nightclubs. Exact same format all the time, edgy nightclub plus cocaine multiplied by sex equals big business deals. I start snorting on a regular basis around that time too, before that, I'd do the odd line at a weekend to help keep me awake. I'm careful never to do too much, to control it, taking just enough to see me through the night because that shit is moreish. But, when me and Paul are together, man, we're quite literally cocaine snorting-machines. Line after line after line after line after line, snort-snort-snort, coke-coke-coke, helps me forget about Super, at least put him out of my mind anyway, (that's the excuse I'll use for now). But, reality is, I just fucking love coke, and at the time, coke loved me in more ways that one. Coke is the worlds best sex aid, coke and sex go together like strawberries and cream, pina and colada's or Porsche and Rolex, plus, Paul is an utter fanny magnet. Yeah, everywhere he goes women drop their knickers. I reckon it's the money or the power or something, but he swears it's all about confidence, girls love a confident man, a man who'll take charge and show them who's the boss. He's right, I can see it, feel it almost, his confidence sort of rubbed off on me. A few lines of coke and I'm the life and soul of the party, pulling girls left right and centre. Paul's all about the girls, he likes them dirty and he likes his sex to be even dirtier. Yeah-man, he loves prostitutes, lots of them too, the dirtier and skankier the better. He'll say it's the "perfect transaction", money for pleasure, plus, he reckons the girls love cock and cocaine too, so it's a "win-win" as he calls it. As for Paul's so-called associates, or "guests", all of them wide-boy city types just like him, and, just like him, full of complete shit and caricatures of themselves. I fucking hate them, and hate having to even speak to them when he brings them to my nights. Shallow and hollow and living a lie, they'll be all best mate forever 'lets-do-lunch-yeah' but I'd never hear from them again. It's all about what's in it for them, how they can gain an advantage, how they can increase their power. All about the greed, and, although I'm cool with the "greed is good thing," blind greed, greed at any costs, is not cool.

Look what it cost me.

If anyone appreciates that.

It's me…

8. The Lost Boy

"Look at your reflection in the mirror. You're a creature of the night, like in a comic book. You're a vampire, a god damn, shit-sucking vampire. But this is no comic book… these guys are brutal killers"

Corey Haim

17, HAMILTON HOUSE
GREENWICH, LONDON
LATE SUMMER, 1989

Through the blurry reflection I see him, and he sees me. We both half-recognise the stranger staring back. Pupils wide, I gaze through the window and the transparent self-portrait and see the jet-black silhouette of the City of London skyline in front of the orangey-pink redness of the setting sun. Tower Bridge and the dome of the Saint Pauls peek through the clouds, as too the Nat-West Tower, scraping tall into the sky. Yeah man, this is my city, I'm London and London's me, it made me who I am.

"And, who exactly are you?" the Interrogator says, existentially messing with my mind, like he always does.

Who am I, fuck off, who are you, and what are "you" still doing here? Don't you get it, I don't want you here, forcing me to go over and over this shit, regurgitating the bile of my life. Some memories should stay buried, stay deep inside. I just want to sit here and dissolve into my own regret without you rabbiting on and on, prodding and probing. You know what, you should use the hardware and put me out of my misery, we both know it's coming so let's just fucking get it over with. You must know by now, this life, right here right now, isn't worth living. I've nothing left, not even any brown…

Maybe?

"Maybe… get you some heroin? Fuck off, no more shit for you my friend," the Interrogator says, cutting me off, decapitating me. *"You'll have to cluck until it's time."*

Fuck it, I'll go myself.

"Don't make me laugh," the Interrogator says, theatrically singing every syllable. *"You've don't have arsehole for it."*

Arsehole my arse, I can leave this shit-hole any time I want.

Grabbing my dirty white Reebok Classics, I push my heels in and stand up.

Right then, I'm off.

"No. You. Are. Not," the Interrogator seethes, terror scratching through his voice with evil in his eyes. *"Sit your ugly bom-ba-clat arse down."*

I've seen that look before my friend. I know what it means.

KerrrRRR-LICK.

Can't show him my fear, must big up my chest.

Big man with his tool, you're nothing without the gun, not even real man. The only thing that's real is that thing, so shoot me big man, end it now, put us both out of our misery.

"Sit down, or I'll put you down," the Interrogator threatens, stepping back and raising the gun toward my head.

It's coming, I know it is, He knows it too. Must front it out though, can never let Him see my fear, my cowardice. The weaker I become, the stronger He gets so I must be strong, fight against it, fight against Him and all that He stands for. You know what, I'll get Him out of here myself, get Him out of my head, stop Him messing with my mind.

Pushing the chair back as I stand, I square up and clench my fists. Deep breath, chest big and broad, I'm in control and ready, ready for anything. Adrenaline surges and pure unadulterated life force surrounds me as energy pulses through me. "Come on," I scream, roaring like a lion as violence fills the room. Shuffling my feet, I duck to the left then swing an Apollo-Creed style overhead windmill with my right. Head smashes against the wall, fingers push into eye sockets, teeth rip into flesh.

I'm like a bare-knuckle gypsy fighter and I'm loving it.

Left jab, right cross, left hook body, left hook head, I'm on fire, like Cassius Clay in his hay-day. Kick to the balls, knees bent, upper cut to the head, yeah, bring the pain!

Shit, hang on, fuck.

The pain is in me.

I'm being done.

The blows are landing on me and I'm watching it on the

telly, giving a running commentary of me being royally fucked up.

Flying through the air across the coffee table, red-hot pain sears through my shoulder as a blinding nuclear mushroom cloud burns through my retina. Collar-bone snapping, teeth grinding, eyelids squeeze together. No time to think, no time to breath. Grabbed to my knees, I brace for impact.

CRACK.

Sideboard, sideboard, sideboard, I hear him grunt like an animal with every impact. Head smashes into the once polished wood which cracks and splinters exploding around me. Pain shoots through my forehead as a lightning bolt pierces my brain, entering my spinal cord.

I'VE MADE A MISTAKE.

Please STOP.

Every nerve ending screams out in unison as pain sparks through my entire body. Stumbling about the room, my throbbing forehead feels the size of a watermelon as blood drips down my face. I feel it's warmth, taste it's sour metallic flavour, turning my stomach, it's disgustingly moreish. Head spinning, my eyes blur then immediately focus as the adrenalin surges. Look left, shit. The brass lamp from behind the sofa arches through the air.

Duck?

Too late.

Five years ago, maybe.

Now, way too slow.

DING DONG.

Big Ben strikes, then…

Darkness.

Stillness.

Silence.

"Open your eyes, shit for brains," the Interrogator shouts, kicking the soles of my feet.

Squinting, beams of ultra-bright sunlight slice across my

pupils like razor blades.

You're still here then.

"Where else would I be?" the Interrogator asks, rhetorically, incredulity straining through his voice.

Scanning the devastation I get to my knees. Sideboard smashed, one door completely missing, the other hanging on by a single hinge with a massive head shaped hole in the middle. My forehead throbs. Photograph albums and random official looking letters and utility bills lay strewn across the room, covered in dark red blood, my blood, the blood of a pussy. Beside me on the floor, in two halves, are what remains of the brass lamp.

What the fuck happened?

"What had to happen, that's what happened," the Interrogator says, absolutely, one-hundred percent right. *"You got a bit facety, a bit naughty, a bit larey, so I sorted you out, put you in your place, showed you who's boss."*

He did indeed put me in my place and show me who's boss. Pressing play on my cranial video player I see looney-tunes cartoon images of me smashing into the sideboard and the brass lamp crashing into my head. Trying to move my arm I hear a scream then feel a crunch as pain surges through me.

"It's broken, dickhead," the Interrogator says, diagnosing my injury perfectly. *"Give it a couple of weeks, it'll set itself."*

Right, right, I nod, not letting him see my pain while I shake uncontrollably. Shock or adrenalin or something.

"You calmer now?" the Interrogator asks, serenity in his voice. He's mister ice-cold-cool-as-a-cucumber and I'm mister dickhead.

Using my hooded sweatshirt, I pull it around my injured shoulder then around my neck and, then, using my mouth and good arm, tie the arms together to make a make-shift sling. I'm in pain, but I'll be okay. This pain will heal, unlike my broken heart which will never ever get better, or my damaged soul that I know is beyond redemption.

What time is it?

"Morning, not that it matters. Learnt your lesson?" the Interrogator asks, like I'm a snotty nose five-year-old kid who's just spent a long twenty minutes on the naughty step.

Fuck off, patronising prick.

Let's get this shit over with.

"Good, good. That's better, much better," the Interrogator says, verbally patting me on the head. *"Tell me about Shirley."*

I sit cradling my arm on the edge of the sofa, almost lying down but not quite. The more I tell him, the quicker this ends.

DEAN STREET
SOHO, LONDON
LATE 1980

We met in the winter, the year before the riots, I think. Me, Paul and Super enjoyed touring around Londons west-end on a Saturday night, visiting the best bars and clubs seeking out the fine west-end-girls. Much better up west rather than Brixton. No aggravation from the Police sus-stops, no tribulation with no rude-boys wanting to make a name for themselves or hassle from pissed-up-fuck-head Publonians wanting to fight the world. Anyway, this particular night, we stroll around Soho smoking our weed and eventually stopping off at this pretty cool wine bar. Paul gets some rum in and we spot three tidy looking girls having a drink by the bar. Stunning blonde Sammie, Chantelle, who's a heavy sister with a massive seventies throwback afro, and, of course, the pretty, dark-haired one who turns out to be Shirley. Paul wanders over and gets chatting and soon after, me and Super join and we're chatting and flirting and drinking and laughing and smiling and winking. Damn, it's good. We stay at the wine bar for ages before heading to the club underneath Charing Cross train station for some dancing. A new romantics place, Paul knows a friend of a friend and gets us on the guest list. I fancy her straight away, with her pretty face and honest eyes. Yeah man, those kind, truthful, beautiful eyes grabbed me straight away. Although younger than me, she seems older, wiser, more mature and more together and confident. We stay at the club for a couple of hours before heading to an after-hours dance in Deptford.

Driving a little white VW Golf, I jump in with her while Paul, Super and the two girls go in his car. We get sus-stopped on the way, yeah man, shit, I remember it now, the whole area's in lock-down. It's the night of the New Cross fires, where a load of youngsters died at a house party. Dark times man, dark times. Maybe it was a warning, a hint of fate, a drop of destiny. The after-hours dance is cancelled, so we come back here, to her flat, this flat. We sit drinking tea, dipping custard-cream biscuits, chatting about everything and nothing. You know what, I'd never chatted like that before, nah. Before her, I'm into cheap one liners, banterish-banter and comic book come-ons. Meanwhile, classy as ever, Paul's getting sexy with sexy Sammie out on the balcony while Super has his hands full with big girl, Chantelle, who's falling about the place pissed-drunk before eventually passing out on the other end of the sofa. With no sex on the cards, Super rummages through Shirley's collection of records and tapes while me and her just talk and chat and connect all night long. After a while, Paul and Super fade into the background and all I can see is her, her eyes and my future. Intense man, I've never felt anything like this before, or since. Mesmerised and bewitched, I'm quickly falling into a loved-up-trance. She's actually interested in me, asking me loads of deep questions about me, my family, my friends and why I am the way I am. Thought provoking for sure, I question myself, considering who I really am and, more importantly, who I really want to be. At twenty-five years old, it's the most grown up conversation I've ever had. She helps me become a man, a real man too. I feel cared for, cherished and special. She just listens and gets me, understands me, empathises with me. After a while, we start kissing, gentle and slow, no skirt-up-knickers-down rushing, none of that, it's calm and gentle and loving and grown-up. Straight away, I feel like I belong, feels warm and comfortable and safe. I'm crazily in love with her from the very start and I'm sure she feels the same, but we don't tell each other, nah, we play the game of telling each other we "really like each other" or "really like spending time with each other". We both know what we really mean though. Start seeing each other every weekend, yeah man, misty-eyed and loved up. I'm thinking about her all day every day, wondering what she's doing, what she's thinking, whether she's thinking about me like I am about her. Paul and Super tease me I'm like a loved-up-puppy-dog, and, you know what, I am. Can't help it, and don't care.

A few months after the riots, I'm still getting sus-stopped all the time back at home so decide it's best to spend a few nights each week with her, over here in Greenwich, weekends too. Couple of months later, I decide to go steady, leave the scrap yard job and move over here full-time. Get myself a job as a casual in the Post Office sorting the letters at six in the morning. Man the early mornings kill me, I love my bed, but it don't matter, I want her so badly, want us so much, I'm prepared to do anything. You know what, just being a regular Joe, a normal bloke and an everyday citizen is cool, mellow and steady. Looking back, not standing out from the crowd and not looking over my shoulder every ten minutes, waiting for hassle from the Police or trouble with rude-boys is pretty much perfect, I should have been content with just that. I'd become exactly what Paul and Super teased, a puppy-dog-goggle-eyed-loved-up sap, and, I don't care, I love it, love being normal. All I can think about is Her and how great she makes me feel. Yeah man, we do the normal things normal couples do, things I've never done before but are completely normal for most people. Stroll along the river hand in hand, picnic in the park, movies with popcorn.

Seeing each other for best part of a year and kaboom, nuclear bomb detonation, she falls pregnant. All of a sudden, without realising it, we're proper grown-ups. Sharing a flat, matching his and her toothbrushes, going steady, proper job, lead in the pencil, bun in the oven, damn, everything's good.

Beyond good actually.

Fuck it, life is great!

When she eventually gives birth, I'm in absolute awe. Feel like a man, a real man, a proper man, for the first time in my life I feel whole. I cry the day we bring my little baby boy home. I love him, of course, but I know now I'm crying for me, sad my childhood's over, mourning the past, scared of the future, fearful of expectations now I'm a dad. The enormous weight of responsibility is overwhelming and exhilarating and breath-taking and unbelievable and inspiring, all at the same time. I have a son and heir, a lasting legacy, something to be proud of and leave to the world. I can literally live for ever, through him. It's what mankind strives for, I think, it has to be the point yeah, survival. Fuck knows what we're surviving for, but creating life must be the purpose of life. The birth came after a hard forty-hours in labour. Needing a blood transfusion, they keep her and my boy in hospital for a week after that. Arriving home, she suffers big-time baby blues, can't even want to hold him. He doesn't take to her milk so I'm up at all hours making bottles of powdered formula. I think she feels less of a woman because of that, some how deficient or abnormal, but, reality is and I wish I told her this at the time, she's even more womanly because of that. Yeah man, fighting the natural instincts while still managing to provide for her baby is the essence of a real woman, a womanly woman, my woman, my princess. Every now and again I catch her weeping for no reason, just having a cry. God damn, it's hard to see her like that, especially when we have him, something so small and beautiful and fragile and perfect. Something we made together, belongs to us, the living embodiment of our love for each other. I sit watching them both sleep, both smiling content, happy, peaceful, comforting and safe smiles. Beautiful, my heart literally swells and I feel it in my chest. When she's awake though, we argue all the god-damn time. I want us to be normal, back to the way things were but all we have between us now are arguments. Sex? Out the question, we don't even hug, we live more like brother and sister, I'm fetching, carrying, working, sleeping while she sleeps and cries and moans and mothers our boy. We drift on like this for a few years, both lazy I guess, both in a state of contentment where we weren't happy, but not so unhappy we want to do anything about it. I don't want to lose her, of course I don't, I just want what we used to have.

I'm sure she feels the same, even now.

Is that love?

I don't know.

I hope so.

HER FLAT
17, HAMILTON HOUSE
GREENWICH, LONDON
SPRING, 1988

The owner of Bonny Boo's, Frankie, calls me out of the blue. I hadn't seen or heard from him since my first proper night all those years before. After some bland, non-descript yeah-yeah-yeah chit-chat, he tells me he's bought himself a nightclub in Spain, near Malaga, and wants me to go out there do some promotions, help get it established. He'll pay for the flight, a nice villa, plus two-thousand quid for two weeks work. A thousand up front, then a thousand when I get back. Sounds good, sounds great actually. I've never been on a plane before, in fact, I've never really been out of London to be honest. As kids, we never went away on holiday or anything like that, nah, best we manage is a picnic at Brockwell Park with Momma and Pops, and the other folk from Mommas church. Thinking Frankie's offer through, I'm daydreaming about us all going, Shirley, me and my boy. Yeah man, a nice break, change of scenery, sun on our backs, maybe find ourselves again, find us again. She'll love it, even more if I make it a surprise. If I tell her up front, she'll pooh-pooh it and find a reason not to go. I go see her old man to get her passport, she'd been to Germany on a school exchange when she was fourteen, apparently. I don't have a passport so go to get one from a Government place in Victoria, central London. Day off work, I head up there early doors and they keep me waiting around all day, form filling in and picture taking, I have an interview with some government no-mark civil servant lady. Seventy quid and several hours later, I eventually get it. Arriving home an hour later at six pm, I find my boy is being cheeky, throwing his dinner around and having a whale of a time, while she sits on the edge of the sofa, head in hands, crying her eyes out. Excellent, perfect, she'll love my surprise and be super-happy, see me for the fantastic partner I am, maybe even suck me off if I'm lucky…

Wrong!

Soon as I tell her, she flips her fucking lid, completely going off on one, yelling all I ever think about is my promotions business, never her and never my boy. The arguing continues all night, only pausing when I put the little man to bed. As soon as he's fast asleep and I get back into the kitchen she's on me again, on and on and on and on, yelling I'm not a real man, selfish, self-centred, never think about anyone but me. Then, all this really negative shit comes out that she's not happy and hasn't been happy for years.

Shock, annoyed and upset, where the fuck has this come from? I've spent the whole day in a sweat-box-Government-shit-hole sorting a passport out so we, not just me, can go on holiday and then, I get this crap. I'm tired and emotional and frustrated and hurt. I've done this for her, not me. All this "unhappy for years" talk rips into my heart, man.

She's crazy, a raving looney.

That's when I did it…

Trailing off, I hear my own words echo down the dark alleyways of my mind as I stare a condemned-man stare at the floor. Eye lids slip slowly over my blood-shot-tear-welling eyes as I breathe deeply.

I did something I regret…

I'm so tired, stupidly tired, crazy tired, the most tired I've ever been. It's not an excuse, of course not, but, I'd spent the whole day in the government hell-hole waiting and waiting and waiting, bored shitless with a load of immigrants arguing and screaming and crying, the noise is unbearable. Then, soon as I get home, she's giving ranting and raving and screaming and crying and balling me out. I'm sad and gutted and disappointed and fucking hurt. I know I've got to get out, defuse the tension and stop the madness, but, she's standing in the doorway refusing to let me out like I'm a little kid being grounded. She's yelling and screaming, going on and on and on and on and the Irish bitch next-door neighbour bangs on the wall, shouting for us to shut the fuck up, all the while she's making way more noise herself, the fat fuck. I'm tired, not thinking straight, she's shouting, next door are shouting and the whole world shouts and screams at me. With the noise and confusion and sadness and shock, I can't think straight, I got to get out but I'm trapped. I sorted this out for her, for us, not me, us. I'm fucking gutted and hurt and sad and upset and regretful and mournful and mad.

How can I be so wrong?

How can she be so ungrateful?

On and on and on and on, she's screaming at me about how I can't run away from my responsibilities, that I should be a real man and I need to be a real father. Who the fuck's running, and who's not a real man? All I want is a nice family holiday and for us to get back on track, back to the way things used to be, when we were happy. How can I be running away, quite the fucking opposite in fact. There's me, a mug, doing these nice things and she's going on and on and on while the fat fuck next door's yelling and yelling and yelling. Confusion and rage wells up inside. I've had enough of this shit. I hear a car engine downstairs in the car-park revving louder and louder with more and more revs, the noise is deafening. The more they yell, the louder the revving gets. Ten thousand revs and it's screaming it's two-litre engine heart out.

I can't think straight.

She's right in front of me now, not letting me escape, with hate in her eyes and spit flying from her lips as she screams into my face. Ugly and distorted and disgusting, she's not the women I fell in love with.

Something deep inside my head snaps.

The revving engine, the shouting, the yelling.

Eyes wobble, my vision forms into a long dark tunnel.

Fear, panic, sadness, disappointment, guilt, despair, frustration, regret, hate, anger and disgust strike through me.

Every emotion consumes me.

That's when I did it.

Both hands around her neck, I squeeze.

Shut the fuck up, bitch.

It's easy. She's delicate and weak and fragile and beautiful.

She stops her shouting and sees sense.

Next door pipes down too.

It's all calm now.

That's better, much better.

Slamming against the kitchen door, the back of her head bounces off and back into mine. Nose throbbing, it stings, but not half as much as her poisonous words burning through my flesh into my soul.

Right then, fear bursts through her pupils as I squeeze tighter. The ungrateful cow. I'm working like a dog, up at the crack of dawn every day, taking shit from dickheads, not to mention my promotions business, fathering and mothering for the boy and I'm selfish?

Struggling, panic dances in her eyes as she tries to get away. She can't though, I'm way too strong and she's way too weak.

I want to shut her moaning up, once and for all.

I want her to love me.

I'm so sorry I did what I did.

You must believe me.

Our foreheads collide fuck knows how many times.

I need her to feel the pain I'm feeling, feel as bad as I'm feeling, feel how awful she's making me feel. I'm possessed, body snatched, taken over by aliens or something. It just isn't me, the vampire monster, usually buried deep down inside my soul, has surfaced and feeds at his demonic last supper. Even though I can't admit it, even to myself, I've always known I've a symbiotic demon living within me. Until now, I'd managed to supress him, keep a lid on his ambition, control his murderous intentions, but, once he's commenced his reign of terror, breathed his first breath of human air, tasted human blood, he can't be stopped.

My poor defenceless princess.

After god knows how long, the madness stops.

Sweat dripping from my forehead, silence and peace surround me. The revving motorcar of rage inside my mind has disappeared, her shouting has ceased and the fat motherfucker next door has stopped her yap-yap-yapping. Finishing my demonic act and releasing my grip, my head rests onto hers. Our foreheads and noses touching, I feel her shaking and quivering and panting short breaths, just like when we'd orgasm after our legendary all-night sex sessions. But, right there and then, she's not feeling the euphoric rush of cortisol pulsing through her pleasure engulfed vulva. Nah, I know now she feels nothing but complete fear and utter disgust. Blood everywhere, tears fill the room, hers and mine. Confusion fills my heart as loathing fills my soul. Even now, when I close my eyes, I see the fear in her eyes, proper scared-for-her-life-she's-seen-the-devil fear. Gutting me to the core, I can't get her eyes out of my head, my beautiful, kind and gorgeous and perfect, all I ever wanted princess. Can't look at her, can't face what I've done, so we both stand there perfectly still, not saying a thing. Time slows down as reality rips through my mind.

What have I done?

What am I doing?

Hands open, she slides down the door cowering on the floor, a picture of tears and blood and sadness and heartbreak.

Hating myself, I have to run, escape.

But, the disgustingly horrible sick cunt I am, I stand there with my hands pushing against the door while she cowers beneath.

What have I done?

I crouch down to say sorry.

Please believe me, I am sorry too, really, deeply, truthfully sorry, turn back time sorry but she starts screaming get-out-get-out-get-out-get-out screams. Hysterical now, she's yelling and hollering incoherently about calling the Police and getting me locked up. She's right, of course she is, too right. She should have called them, got me carted off to a padded cell to be gang-raped by a shaven headed neo-Nazi paedophile mother-fucker, that's exactly what I deserve. Gypping, bile flows into my mouth and I feel sick, sick of me, sick of what I've done to my princess, sick of what I've become. I'm a monster, a disgusting, despicable, degenerate demon and a crazy wife beating bastard. The single most precious, pure and beautiful thing in my life and I destroy it.

Obliterate it.

Ruin it.

Unable to breathe. Must leave.

Run, run, run.

Run away, away from what I'd done.

Away from what I've become.

Hurry-hurry-hurry into the bedroom…

Grabbing the holdall from the top of the wardrobe, I rifle through the draws, indiscriminately stuffing clothes inside before heading for the front door. Passing the kitchen, I catch a glimpse of the worst sight of my entire worthless life. Our eyes meet and my heart literally breaks and shatters and dissolves. I see utter sadness, not anger or even disgust, just sadness and man, that destroys me.

Front door slamming shut I'm outside on the open walkway, everything looks odd and unreal, bathed in a hazy golden sunlight. The edges of the buildings warp and shape shift while the sky above me is on fire with neon blue flashes of fork-lightening. As soon as the ice-cold air hits me, I shiver a shiver I've never felt before, or since. Someone not only walks over my grave, they piss on it, drive a bulldozer over it and napalm the fuck out of it. Crying sick-to-the-pit-of-my-stomach tears, I trundle down the piss-stained stairwell knowing I'll never see her again. She's my princess, my beautiful, precious flower, but, in a single moment of madness, my sunshine vaporised. Consumed by internal darkness, I replay the sickness over and over, step by step. I realise now I died, in that very moment. I know it sounds over-dramatic but the person who was once Devon Walters, the caring father, loving husband, doting son to Doris and Patrick Walters and big-brother to Marlon died. Simultaneously, the dirty evil vampire-monster me, the bastard prince of darkness me is delivered to the world. Tears streaming down my face, I find myself near Greenwich market, on the one-way system. What the fuck am I doing? Spinning round and around, unable to catch my bearings, the brightly lit shop fronts and cars and buses orbit around me while normal every day non-monster citizens avoid me.

What do I do, where do I go, what next?

Can't go back to Momma's, how will I face her? Marlon's maybe? Nah, cant face being judged by my little brother. Claude? Fuck no, he hates women beaters, so will smash me up there and then, cut me up and set my dying body on fire.

Plane tickets, cash in my pocket, passports too?

Spinning around, I see a taxi.

Arm out, I flag it down.

'Gatwick,' I blurt out, climbing in.

'Gatwick?' the rosy-cheeked-twat of a driver queries.

'Yes Gatwick, you cunt, and fucking quick-time too,' I growl through the rear-view mirror.

This is me now, a monster. I don't give a fuck.

Scared shitless, looking straight ahead he puts the car into gear and sets off. I spot a Polaroid photo of him and what must have been his missus and his two little daughters jammed into the air-vent on the dashboard. Smiling and happy, they're on holiday or something with the sun setting over their shoulders, each of them with a pinky flush of a tan and giant smiles. Fuck him and fuck them, I don't care about any of the shit now, I'll scare and bully and fuck my way through whatever life this is. It's easy to hate, easy to destroy, easy not to think, easy to be ignorant, easy to believe your own hype, easy to be closed minded, easy to re-affirm your own point of view at every opportunity and easy to prove yourself right.

It's hard to love.

So, fuck it. If this guy gives me any lip, any problem whatsoever, I'll strangle the fucking life out of him, lock him in the trunk and torch this shit hole of a taxi.

This is me now, my life as a demon.

Face as white as a sheet, he sets off nice and gently without saying a word. He'll never know, but right there and then, he saved his own life and ensured those two precious little girls weren't prematurely orphaned. Sitting in the back, I watch the rain sodden scenery of South East London fade into the greyness of the suburbs before eventually morphing into the green fields of Sussex. Replaying what happened over and over, it doesn't feel real, more like watching a dirty wife-beating-bastard on television or in a cheap B-movie. However much my subconscious-mind tries to convince my conscious-self it's not me, and I didn't really do what I did, deep down inside, I know. Yeah, the sad realisation soaks over me that I know exactly what I've done, and I know the consequences too.

I hate myself.

Passing the signs for the airport, thoughts morph and drift

and I wonder about my place in the world. I know I don't deserve to be here and I can end it all, bring the sorry saga of Devon from Brixton to an end, once and for all, if I want. Yeah man, hanging from a tree, gun to the head, fist-full of tablets, under a bus, leap off a tower-block. Maybe I can right some wrongs beforehand, somehow gain redemption or at least forgiveness for all the hurt I've caused. Yeah, I'm warming to the idea, I like it. Maybe seek out a kiddie fiddler and slit his mother-fucking throat or go on a rampage with a shotgun and take some villains out before doing myself in.

Might make Her proud, make Her forget about the vampire-monster me and see the hero-me, the real me.

Pulling off the motorway we glide into the airport car park drop off area. I bung the lucky-to-be-alive-taxi-driver fifty quid which he accepts without making eye contact. Grabbing my bag, I follow the signs for "departures" and find the check-in desk. The lady behind the desk tilts her head and looks at me with a puzzled frown, before telling me check-in doesn't start until early morning, way after midnight. I see a long row of hard-plastic seats at the far side of the hall and plonk myself down. Struggling to get comfy, I wait there all night until the flight's called at four-thirty in the morning. I think I slept a bit, dosing on and off, but I'm shivering and shaking like a dirty skagg-head clucking for my next fix. Soon as I wake-up, I ring Paul, getting the dirty bastard out of bed and tell him whats happened and where I'm going. He goes off on one, telling me I don't appreciate what I've got, telling me I'm a villain and a wrong-un, and he doesn't know what's happening to me.

Fuck off.

Phone down.

Cunt.

The last thing I need right now is this shit, especially from him going on like Momma or Mother fucking Teresa. I call Marlon too, he's just got home from deejaying at a club in the west-end. I ask him to look after the radio station, and to look out for my boy too. Although he doesn't ask questions or judge me, I hear devastating disappointment in his voice. I've let him down, I'm mortal to him now, not the superhero older brother he worshipped when he was a boy. I tell him I love him, that I'm sorry, that I don't know when or even if I'll be back.

Through check-in and then security in a trance, I board the plane and find my seat without saying a word or making eye contact with anyone. Never been on a plane before, I thought I might be scared, but the take-off is fine, in fact, my thoughts are dark. Maybe we'll run out of runway and crash, hit a flock of birds on our assent and our engines will blow-up or the navigation system goes haywire and we collide with another plane. Not sure why, but the thought of dying with hundreds of other people is kind of comforting. Watching the land fade away as we bump through the clouds into the deep blue early morning sky I'm misty-eyed and melancholic. Crying for my previous life, I watch it fade away into the distance and the fluffy white nothingness of the clouds below. Way up high, I feel small and distant and insignificant, completely detached from reality. I like it. Maybe I'm bad-dreaming or night-maring, maybe I killed myself in the kitchen and I'm in some kind of limbo reality, maybe even hell.

It isn't any of those things, I know that now.

I'm exhausted and tired so, leaning back in my seat, close my eyes and allow regret and sorrow to flow through me. Nothing seems real, it all feels like a fucked up nightmare. I've ruined everything and hate myself for it…

AEROPUERTO DE MALAGA
MALAGA
SPAIN
LATE SPRING, 1988

Engines roaring, panic rushes through me. My whole-body shudders and shakes as my fingertips push hard into the arm-rests. We're crashing, we're dead, we're doomed. The

Devil has come to rescue me from my torturous limbo and intends on crashing the entire plane, killing two or three hundred innocent souls, just to get me. Thoughts of facing my destiny are petrifying so I force my eyes open as I'm thrown about anti-gravity style, seatbelt saving me from smashing into the seat in front. The engines roar again, and I know the end is nigh, he's come to take me back to hell to serve him for eternity. Suddenly, the so-cool-I-can-lick-myself Captain comes over the intercom thing, "welcome to Spain," he says in a soothing, professional tone. "Thank you for choosing to fly with whoever-the-fuck-nobody-cares airways."

Twenty minutes later…
Still early, the sun's up and it's hot-hot-hot.
Picking my bag up from the carousel collection thing, I head outside the terminal and towards the line of Taxi's. No clue where I'm going, I've got the address of the villa on a torn off bit of a brown envelop in my back pocket. Unravelling it, I show it to the taxi drivers, each of them shake their heads and give me a 'no-no-no' gesture, pointing me further down the never-ending line. I get to the last taxi, I kid you not, the very last taxi in the queue of maybe twenty or so and I find Juan-the-Robot. Twenty year old black shoes, scuffed grey around the toes and the heel practically worn away, he's wearing blue chinos, short sleeve pink and white shirt with two or three buttons undone and jet-black hair in a basin haircut. No emotion, steel-like poker face, he grabs my bag and nonchalantly chucks it in the boot before motioning to the back door. We drive for about an hour on a winding coastal road with deep blue sea on the left and mountains on the right before pulling into a town called Fuengirola. We drive around for a few minutes before getting to a small, narrow street a few streets back from the beach, only wide enough for a single car. Juan-the-Robot points with his finger. 'A-key, a-key,' he says over-

enthusiastically verging on aggressive. I get out and he's shouting 'blah-blah-blah-potatoes,' so stuff a few English quid into his hand. Shuffling quickly back into motor, he sets off no doubt laughing his tits off having mugged me off. Me and my bag stand there on the deserted street with not a soul anywhere. Damn, its fucking hot. Looking left then right, I creak my neck to look up to the top of the three-story townhouse.

NO. 6, CALLE TOLEDO
FUENGIROLA
COSTA DEL SOL, SPAIN
LATE SPRING, 1988

Knock, knock-knock, knock.

Friendly knock will do it.

Immediately, I'm transported back to being eleven years old, running errands for Crissy, knocking the door and waiting for little-miss-micro-shorts to play the secret-code game before opening up.

After an age, I see movement behind the mottled glass door, a small creature crouched over, fiddling with the lock. Door swings open and an old woman stares at me, complete doppelganger for Mother Teresa with a turquoise nylon tabard and net scarf around her head. 'Erm, Frankie sent me,' I smile. Eyes narrowing, she probes me with a death stare. 'Fran-kie, in Eng-er-land?' I say slowly and over pronounced. Giving me the once over, her left eye squints as she looks me up and down before turning and hobbling slowly up the stairs. After a five-second-per-stair age, we stand in the doorway at the top. Opening the door, she nods me in. The smell hits me first, musty, like an old man who's pissed himself or something. Scanning around I see terracotta tiled floor with white walls and to the left, a picture of a beach hangs above a bamboo headboard and a single bed that's seen better days. Straight ahead, a dirty net curtain sways in front of a half-open window. On the other side of the room, a bathroom with a rubber shower thing attached to the taps. Basic, proper old-school and most definitely not the "luxury villa" Frankie promised. Old Mother-Teresa rattles on for a while in Spanish with her arms gesturing everywhere. Fuck knows what she's saying, but I smile and nod away in agreement. After god knows how long, she hands me a key and heads back down the stairs waving her hands above her head. Springs pinging all over the place, I lay down on the bed which, although lop-sided and fucked, is surprisingly comfy. Closing my eyes, I can't stop thinking about Her, what she's doing right now, probably getting little man ready for nursery and giving him breakfast. Horrible pictures of what I've done flash through my mind and I retch to be sick. Then, practicalities spring to mind, did she go to the hospital or call the doctor or something. There's bound to be lumps and bumps, bruising and swelling, cuts even. The Police were probably called, yeah, I bet the Irish bitch next door rang them. They'll be round mob-handed, ready to give the wife-beater a kicking. One look at her, a sexy, good-looking girl with sweet-sweet breasts giving it the Princess-Diana coy-look, they'll take down my description in preparation of a grievous bodily harm charge, maybe even attempted murder. Shit. How will she drop the little-man off at nursery with her face the way it is? How will she explain it to the other mums at nursery, the teachers, to her mum and dad, to her friends? They'd hate me, even more than they do already, especially fat-Stan, he'll be after blood. Lacy and the rest of the Millwall crew too, they'll be after me, attacking one of their own and all that.

Yep, public enemy number one.
Everyone hates me, I hate me.
It's easy to do.
Knock, knock.
Eyes wide open.
It's dark outside.
What the fuck?
Asleep, all day?

Disorientated.

Where the fuck am I?

Knock. Knock. Knock.

Old Mother Teresa?

Nah too heavy, too spritely. Shit, it's a mans knock.

Looking around, no tools to speak of, just a heavy ashtray made of chiselled dark brown marble. Fuck it, better than nothing. Ear to the door, no sign of any 'you grab him, I'll chiv him,' type words. Door knocks again. This time a cheery knock, knock-knock, knock, knock-knock. Hand on the handle with my foot a few inches behind the door, I twist it open.

I see a young white guy grinning and nodding his head, a tall, lanky streak of piss with a tidy looking spliff hanging out of his mouth. Good-looking chap with a good tan, blue eyes and long curly beach-bum hair. Looks friendly.

'Dev, Devon, Deeeevon?' he says in a chirpy London accent. Doesn't sound like a geezer, or look like one.

Glancing over his shoulder, I eye down the stairs.

He's on his own, good.

'It is Devon, yeah? You are Devon?' he smiles as his eyebrows arch. 'Habla' English,' he says slowly with a smile.

Narrowing eyes, I stare at him. Police maybe?

'You Devon, from Londres, yes?' He's a joker, it seems.

Turns out his name's Matt and works for Frankie's brother Geoff, who runs the club. Enthusiastic and eager, he suggests I grab a shower before we get down to the harbour area to have a look around. A minute later I'm standing in the bath behind this flimsy plastic curtain while he's sitting on the bed skinning up a couple of joints. Ten minutes later we ignite our spliffs, (good shit by the way, Moroccan apparently), and stroll about half a mile into the town centre. Not sure what I expect, having never been abroad, but I can't believe it. The long stretch along the seafront leading to the harbour is door to door with bars, neon lights and loads and hordes of semi-drunk lads and lots fit girls wearing bikinis partying in and out of the many bars, each and every one of them having a good time. No aggravation, no moodiness, no trouble, no tribulation, everyone's having a good time, laughing, joking and enjoying themselves. Back in England, it's usual to see lads like these smashing ten tonnes of shit out of each other on a Saturday night but people on holiday, it turns out, are different, chilled and happy and mellow. Like a tour guide, Matt tells me all about the place, the best bars to meet girls and where to get weed from, which turns out to be a group of North Africans hanging around the main square selling moody watches and baseball caps. He also shows me the best place to get a proper English fry-up, the Hat-Trick Bar near the harbour, a life saver! Strolling along, he tells me his story. Turns out he came to Spain with his mum and sister a couple of years ago. They arrive on holiday for two weeks, fall in love with the place, and, with not a lot to go back to London for, they end up sticking around. Mum plonks him in a Spanish school the Monday after they're due to go home and he learns Spanish almost fluently within a month. His mum gets a job cleaning and his sister as a waitress in a small family run restaurant called La Luna. Poorly with her lungs or something, a couple of years back his mum moves back to blighty and his sister's shacked up with a wanna-be actor living in Marbella. Nowadays, Matt lives day by day, just happy to be here I reckon, earning a few quid as a "go-for" for Geoff.

LONDON PUB
FUENGIROLA
COSTA DEL SOL, SPAIN
LATE SPRING, 1988

Talking and chatting, we eventually stop outside a place called the "London Pub". Let me tell you, this is no "pub" as I know a pub, no way, this is a nice bar with a large nightclub in the basement. Decked out with mini London landmarks, which to be honest look as tacky as hell, the rest of it looks pretty cool with mirrored walls and a decent lighting rig. Problem is, it's empty, certainly not as many punters as the other bars we went by earlier. As we walk in, a big fat bloke rolls towards us, all smiles and sweat and massive handshakes. 'You must be Devon then,' he snorts, like a pig. 'I'm Big Geoff.'

Big-Geoff?

God-damn-enormous-Geoff more like, what an understatement, this mother-fucker is a twenty-five-stone mountain of Frankie-look-a-like whale blubber. Grabbing my hand hard, he shakes it furiously, too much for my liking before sitting down where he tells me about the club. Him and Frankie bought it three or four months ago at an auction in London, but, with so many bars and clubs in such a small town, the competition's fierce. Plus, there's an Algerian crew headed by a Turkish/English guy who operate what sounds to be an elaborate protection racket, meaning everything is pretty much stitched up. He goes on to say they are living on their savings and are basically on their knees, so must turn this sinking ship around. Sounding dodgy, my spider-sense tingles, thirty-foot neon warning signs flash above my head and the golden sunset floating around my weed-soaked brain fades into dark storm clouds. I should have made my apologies and fucked off right there and then, but, of course, I didn't. Geoff goes on to say we can't get into anything too dodgy and got to be subtle and low key, otherwise the Algerians will pay him and us a visit. Low key? Me? Low key isn't me, Devon-heaven is all about the glam-baby, but, to be honest, right now, subtlety suits me fine. Yeah, I don't need no gangster shit, especially not over here, a million miles from England. I decide to put the vampire monster-me, the dirty evil bastard-me, the nightmare-shadow that always follows me to the back of my mind, have a holiday, spunk some of the cash Frankie gave me up the wall and get it all out of my system. Yeah, I'll go home and make it up with Her, properly make it up, go steady, treat her so well, be a better daddy, might even marry her. Yeah man, the more I think about it, marriage is the answer, prove to her how much I love her, need her, want her.

That, my friend, is a plan.

The next few days are nicely normal, beautifully boring and ploddingly mundane. I drop into a lovely routine of sleeping during the day, having a spot of dinner then, along with Matt, visiting most of the other bars and clubs to see what goes down well. We visit an ultra-modern place called "The Olympic", right on the edge of the harbour wall. We queue for a while watching a few younger kids who are turned away before eventually paying a "mill" to get in, (about a fiver, Matt says). Inside, it's very cool, not like the other places we visit, mostly cheap disco-dives, nah man, this place is a cross between a wine bar and a nightclub, with white marble and smoked glass everywhere. Dimly lit with the odd ultraviolet light dotted around, it's got a decent sound system pumping out a new kind of almost disco music, stripped down and metronomic. I remember this "move your body" tune the punters seem to love, repeating the "move your body, rock your body," line over and over with a killer piano riff. Responding straight away with arms in the air and cheers, the crowd is different to the crowds back home who are more into necking beers, chasing fanny and back street brawling. The Olympic crowd are super cool and all about the stripped down, rhythmic, melodic and sexy music. With the thud-thud-thud of the bass-drum, a simple snare and a high-hat riding over the top, and of course, the "move your body" vocals echoing around me, I fall for it straight away. Might be the weather, the change in water or whatever, but the Olympic set-up seems to work perfectly. No downing of pint after pint getting drunk as quickly as possible to drown out the boringness of their lives, oh no, this crowd is into sex-on-the-beech-pina-colada cocktails and tall-thin glasses of champagne. With an almost exclusive vibe, it's superb, easily the best club I've ever been to and way too good for a shitty little bar in a Costa-Del-Fanny resort. Big Geoff needs is this type of place, but, as Paul says, on a "mass market" scale, available to all, not just the privileged few. Yeah, offering the run-of-the-mill-shit-for-brains-happy-holiday punter a taste of exclusive glamour, an avant-garde experience or just something new to tell their mates about back home, is the key. I'm on a roll here, make them feel special, extravagant and ostentatious for just one night, and give them a memory that'll last forever has to be a winner. You can't put a price on memories, nah, of course you can't, so they'll pay us for the memory, the feeling, the self-gratification that they have experienced something unique and special.

Next day, back at the London Pub, I arrange a meeting with Big Geoff and his deejay, a decent but not too bright fella called Toby, from Birmingham. Pitching them my idea, they don't really get it but go with it anyway, I could have told them any old shit and they'd still have gone for it. Right, let's get to work. First job is to sort the music, I want the same music I heard at the Olympic, no question about it, and definitely no chart music. Toby manages to get hold of some vinyl from somewhere, a compilation album and a few singles. After that, sound-system. It was already at maximum capacity and any more power might have shorted the amps, and Geoff didn't have any money to hire-in an additional rig, so we spend an hour or so messing with an equaliser to boost the bass and mid-range, then we turn all the speakers inward to face into the dancefloor. Next job, lighting. We decide to turn off all the old-school disco lights and just keep the lights behind the bar and a few moving spotlights over the dancefloor, to keep the vibe subtle and cool. Next, promotions. Matt gets some of his attractive girl mates, all scantily clad, (and well fit by the way), strutting up and down the seafront all evening with a load of balloons telling everyone about it. Then, I get the resident bouncer-handyman guy, an eastern European fella called "Marv" to stand on the door and get a queue going, and to only let someone in once the queue gets ten-people deep. Final thing to sort, boosting revenue. Takes some arm twisting but, on the opening night, for the first time ever, Big Geoff agrees to charge punters to get in. He's sure this'll result in absolute desolation and an empty pub, but admitted he was desperate and was willing to give anything a go. I reckon charging a couple of pounds to get in attaches a value to the night over and above a normal run-of-the-mill place.

On the night, it's pretty full, not totally rammed, but full enough to ensure the night's a resounding success. The biggest tune of the night is this, "love can't turn around," track, beautiful vocals and a killer baseline, deejay Toby spins that maybe ten times. The night's a turning point for sure, yeah man, pissed-up-publonians dancing to what are essentially disco tunes, singing about love? I bet they can't believe it and, if I'm honest, I can't believe it either. Only a couple of years back I'm with the Millwall crew in the back streets of South East London kicking the shit out of fellow hooligans. Pleased as punch, Big Geoff, the greedy fat bastard is up for doing it again the very next day and the day after that too, but I persuade him otherwise. We need to keep it special, keep it exclusive and illusive. With most punters on a two-week package holiday, we can't over-do it, so we agree twice a week maximum as a rule. Next time we do it a few days later, it goes down just as well, better actually. Bigger queues outside while inside, the crowd are more chilled-out-cool-clubber-wanna-bee's than piss-head-natives-of-publonia.

After a long night, we usher the final punters out just as the sun's coming up. Leaving Matt to finish clearing up, I head through to the back office to see Big Geoff. Sitting opposite, I skin up while he counts shit-loads of cash. We chit-chat about him and his missus and the taxi-cab firm he used to run back in London. Then, knock, knock. We look at each other, then toward the door. Matt knows not to disturb us counting, so who the fuck? Handle twisting, the door swings opens. Tanned, gelled-back jet-black hair with super cool ray-ban shades on, in walks the epitome of cool. Cooler than cucumber cool, he's a white linen suit and looks like he's just stepped off the set of Miami fucking Vice. Six feet tall and seventeen stone, he has a face of a boxer, you know, nose slightly flat and bent to the side, deeply lined forehead, scar across his left eyebrow. 'Alright chaps, blinding night eh?' he smiles with gleaming white teeth, shaking hands with Big Geoff, and then me.

'Alright Turkish, how-how-how's it going?' Big Geoff stutters, smiling a little boy smile.

'Didn't catch ya' name,' Turkish says, nodding towards me with a broad east end accent, ignoring Big Geoff.

'Devon,' I say. 'From Brixton.' I always mention Brixton, seems to carry a bit of weight with geezers.

He nods and smiles. 'Frontline, yeah, nice one,' he says before telling me he runs most of the bars and clubs across the Costa-del-Sol, three in Malaga, two in Torremolinos, one in Benalmedina, one in Marbella and is just about to open one in Puerto Banus. He's not lording it over us, proving his manliness or anything like that, nah, he isn't flash, just matter of fact. Goes on to say he wanted to buy this place, but, fair play to Geoff for out bidding him. Seems a reasonable guy, respectful even, but, dangerous for sure. Yeah man, walking into the back office of a club not knowing what to expect, on his own too? That's stupid or dangerous, and this guy aint no stupid. Nah, I can tell straight away he's someone who trusts himself, has supreme confidence in what he can achieve, is the master of the universe and king kong wrapped up into one. He scares me, and I think he knows he does too. He asks if we're interested in what he calls "franchising" the night across his other clubs along the Costa. Managing the promotions, but for a fee, rather than a share of the takings. I tell him the night only works if it feels exclusive, not available at every tom-dick-or-harry pub, club or bar, and, in any case, I'm due back in England in less than a week. Surprisingly diplomatic and delicate with his language, Big Geoff says he wants to focus on his place, doesn't want to over stretch himself. Turkish stares at Geoff, thinking things through, considering what he's just heard. 'Fair play, I respect that,' he eventually smiles before shaking our hands and turning for the door. 'Pop around for a glass of wine later if you like,' he says, throwing me a wink. 'Geoff knows where I'll be.'

As soon as he leaves, Geoff slams the safe shut, spins the dial mechanism and locks the office door. Hyper, he's breathing heavy and quickly, panting almost and sweat literally pumps out of him. He's bumbling all manner of crap, all fast and quick, telling me stories about Turkish and his gang, "the Algerians". They take their victims up to the "campo" which I learn is the countryside up in the hills overlooking the Costa, strip them naked, fuck them up the arse then torture the life out of them, all before slitting their throats. He says they get away with it because the wolves and vultures eat the victims remains, bones and all.

Hold. Fucking. On.

Algerians? Bumming? Throat-slitting? Vultures?

Nah man, nah, that's not my scene at all. I can most definitely see Turkish operating this way, he's exactly the type for spot of sadism, calm and professional on the exterior but a fucking monster on the inside. Out of my depth, the last thing I want is any gangland shit over here. My thoughts immediately turn to the airport and getting home, seeing Shirley and not getting gang-raped by a bunch of north Africans before being eaten alive by motherfucking vultures.

Vultures, for fuck sake!

I leave Geoff at the club at about six-thirty, with Matt in tow. Setting off towards my digs, a white 3 Series BMW convertible pulls up at the curb. Roof dropped with red leather interior, man, it's a sweet-sweet car. Turkish sits there smiling, eyebrows arching while he nods to himself Sonny Crockett style cruising on Miami Boulevard. 'Breakfast chaps?' he smiles.

'Breakfast, sweet,' Matt says before I can get a word in.

'Right-right,' Turkish smiles his Colgate-white toothy grin. 'Get in then,' he says, in a what-you-waiting-for tone.

Matt smiles, nods and climbs into the back seats like an excitable little kid on Christmas morning, diving into his pile of gift-wrapped toys. Getting in the car with mister-miami-vice is the last thing I want to do, but, being a pussy, I don't want to offend him so climb in. Wheels spinning, we set off and drive for twenty minutes along the coast road, not, thank god, up to the campo. With the sea to my left, a perfect deep blue set against the light blue horizon and brightening sun-coming-up sky, and the cool wind swirling around me, I'm taken by it. Closing my eyes, I hear the gliding guitar riff from that "how soon is now" tune by The Smiths in my head. Yeah man, I imagine myself doing this in my own flash motor, with my Shirley sitting next to me and my little boy in the back.

This is the life I've always dreamed of.

VILLA CARNATION
LA CALA DE MIJAS
COSTA DEL SOL, SPAIN
LATE SPRING, 1988

Eventually, we pull into a small fishing village called La Cala and stop outside a white-washed-high-walled villa, with big imposing dark wooden gates across the drive. Turkish presses a button on his keys and the gates slide open. Now that's cool. Pulling in slowly, he parks up under a wooden car-port, he gets out and we follow him inside. Through to the kitchen, as big as this flat, we tuck into coffee, orange juice, croissants and this tasty chocolate bread thing. Then, oh-my-god-amazing, in walks a tall, blonde, super-fit Scandinavian super-model wearing a long white flowy dress with a drop-neckline down to the top of her breasts and a long split up the back, finishing just below her very shapely arse. Beautifully long, tanned, sexy legs and a scornful smile, she looks at us with nothing but distain in her eyes. She is most probably the most beautiful women I've ever seen, and god damn, she knows it too.

'Morning dear,' Turkish smiles sarcastically.

Not saying a word, she pours herself a coffee, throws Turkish a dirty look then struts towards the pool swinging her arse from side to side like she's on a cat-walk, knowing full well we're all staring with our dicks hanging out.

'Charming,' Turkish tuts. 'Put some clothes on, for fucks sake,' he yells after her. Turning to us, he shakes his head. 'Put your tongue away son,' he laughs, jerking Matt out of his wet-dream fantasy.

Turkish spends the next twenty-five minutes going on about us doing promotions at his clubs, telling us we're wasted with Big Geoff. Goes on to say he'll look after us, sort us out with a villa, a car and some decent clothes, (the cheeky bastard). Looking around the villa, at Turkish and his missus, (especially her), life looks good, really good, fucking sweet-as-a-nut good to be honest. Sun, sea and sex with a fit Scandinavian will be very, very nice. Yeah, his pitch of a new life is ultra-appealing, especially after my demonic bastard nightmare with Shirley. Maybe we can start again, maybe she can forgive me, maybe I can get her and my boy out here with me and do things right, build a better life for us. Man it's tempting for sure. A lot to think about.

Turkish drops Matt off first, then drops me back at my digs at around ten, thank god. No torture, no pain, no campo, no throat slitting, no bumming and no vultures feasting on our dead-as-a-door-nail cadavers, none of that madness. Laying on the lop-sided bed as the cool sea breeze wafts gently over my sweating body I wonder if I can actually give this a go. With a totally fresh start, I can be who I really want to be, bury the London-bomb-ba-clat-demonic-vampire-Devon and re-create myself a new life as a chilled-out club promoter, right here in the land of sun, sangria, sand and sexy Scandinavians. The idea grows on me, the more I think about it, the more I think I can actually give this a go. Yeah man, Turkish doesn't seem that crazy, obviously a serious man not to be crossed, but crazy? Yeah, okay, probably a bit crazy, but not as bad as Geoff makes out.

Later in the week, I visit Big Geoff to check everything's sorted for our third special night. I'm due to go back to London the day after the next, so this will be the last night I host. When I get there though, Big Geoff's in a right state, sweating, panicking, worried and on edge. Says he hasn't seen Matt for a couple of days, reckons one of his girlfriends who works behind the bar saw him getting into a fight with a North African type down near the beach. Matt, fighting on the beaches Churchill style? Nah, not the type. Then, time slows down as Geoff's words echo around me. Tunnel vision forms with the Turk's fat face smiling at the end, kaleidoscoping slowly round and around. Light-headed, my knees wobble beneath me like I'm standing on the roof of a massive tower block, looking over the edge as my eyes zone in and out of focus. Half on, half off, I balance three hundred feet up as the soles of my feet tingle and arsehole twitches. Reality hits me. Turkish must have grabbed him, fuck knows why, maybe staring at his bird or for us rejecting his offer. Damn, he must have taken poor Matt up to the campo and sorted him out Algerian style. Closing my eyes, I can see a half-eaten torso decaying in the shimmering heat of the Spanish countryside and heave to be sick. Maybe Matt went back to see Turkish, offer his services, tell him he wants the villa and car and fit Scandinavian bird and everything. Poor, young, naive Matt chased the dream, which turns out to be a nightmare. Panic surges through me, an adrenaline-rush like never before, fight or flight instinct or whatever they call it. Maybe I go see Turkish, try and figure things out, play this to my advantage and start over, or, I maybe I get the fuck out of this Costa-del-crime madness. Easy choice.

'Geoff, mate, don't worry,' I laugh, putting on my academy award winning poker face. 'Saw him last night with a couple of fit birds. T'cha, he's probably just nursing a hang-over or having his cock sucked.'

We both smile a you-know-I-know-that's-bullshit smile.

'Yeah, right. What's he like, eh,' Geoff snorts.

'Lucky bastard,' I tut. 'Listen, if I see him, I'll get him to pop round yeah.' I edge around him and squeeze his arm. His I've-seen-the-future-eyes tell me he knows he'll never see me again.

Super-cool, not a worry in the world, casually walking back to my digs, I'm careful not to attract any un-wanted attention. No sign of old Mother Teresa, just as well I guess, but I leave her a few quid on the pillow, she's alright really. Thirty seconds later, bag packed, passport and tickets in the back pocket, I'm up and out of there. Zigzagging my way to the local bus station, I catch a bus to the Airport. That's smart, I'm not about to leave any trail, I don't need no Taxi driver spilling the beans, nah man, anonymous joe-public transport is far better. At the airport, my flight's not for a couple of days, but I manage to get my ticket changed to a flight later that evening, hundred and twenty quid, but well worth it.

Back at Gatwick, soon as we touch down, I thank God I'm out of all that surreal madness. I haven't heard from Frankie since, or managed to get the rest of the cash he owes me. Don't care though, just glad I'm not caught up with the Algerian and vulture bullshit. After Spain, I feel refreshed and different, I seem to have gained a brand-new profound perspective on life. Yeah man, I'm truly thankful for what I've got. Most importantly though, I know now, above all else, all I want is Her.

HER FLAT
17, HAMILTON HOUSE
GREENWICH, LONDON
LATE SPRING, 1988

The journey back from the airport seems way longer than the journey to the airport, what itself seems a thousand years ago. I get out outside the pub on the corner of the estate, and grab a swift livener, a tasty little dark rum nerve calmer before walking the two minutes back here. Turning into the car park I spot a bright red Porsche, Paul's Porsche. Even though I'm a wife-beating bastard, I'm also his best mate and he's popped round to see how she's doing, check how the little man. Climbing the stairs, I nervously fumble the key, just about managing to find the lock. Fucking hell, I can't believe it, marriage, tie-the-knot, lock-down, get-wed, double-up, get-hitched, splice-life, settle-the-fuck-down. It's happening, contentment at last.

Twist of the wrist, but it's jammed or locked.

Or, she's changed the locks.

Damn.

Understandable really.

But still, I'm excluded, left out, locked out, not just locked out my flat, locked out of my life, her life, our life. I get it though, after my monstering she's scared, petrified, angry too no doubt. No problem, play it cool, keep it real. Knock-knock. No answer. Maybe she's taken my boy up to the Park, breath of fresh air, play on the swings and all that. Maybe uncle Paul will treat them to an ice-cream or a can of pop. Yeah, I'll go up to the park, have a look around for them, surprise them. Neutral ground too, that's good, that's steady, that's clever. Things are falling into place, it's meant to be, yet again fate is showing me the path. Smiling to myself I turn and, just before the top of the stairs, hear a 'hell-o, hell-ooo.' Turning back, I see her head half poking out around the door and feel a pang in my stomach, she looks good, really good, hardly any signs of my viciousness, just a bit swollen, puffy around the eyes and nose. Her cheeks are a bit pink, she doesn't look as bad as I thought she might, in fact, she looks pretty damn good. Make-up and lipstick, making an effort to cover it up I suppose. A wave of relief splashes over me, maybe my heinous act wasn't as bad as I think I remember, maybe I've exaggerated it and blew it up in my fucked-up mind. Something's not right though, a tiny glint in her eye or something. Doubt, confusion and fear zaps through my mind.

Dressing gown, lipstick, middle of the day?
Yeah, we both know what's going on.
I'm no mug.
It gets out of hand.
Really out of hand.
I'm not proud. Not proud at all.

Her eyes flicker when she sees me, just like they did when I held her up against the kitchen door. I sprint toward her and she slams the door shut. I shout for her to open up, open the fuck up, right now, the slag. I know what's going on, I'm no mug. Hands either side of the door, a moment of eye-of-the-storm calm surrounds me. I look at the letter box and then the floor. I don't want this, I want the opposite in fact, I want to marry the slag-bitch-whore. The get-away car inside my mind begins revving it's engine. Blood pumping, adrenalin surging, the engine morphs into a lion, roaring it's heart out. A thousand lions roar, yeah man, every lion on earth roars me on. I'm the lion, king of the jungle, a proud lion protecting his pride. She's my pride, my pride and joy.

And, mother fucker, I'm no mug and not being mugged off, no fucking way, not by these cunts.

Crashing my foot against the lock, the door smashes open and the bottom hinge goes flying. I'm in the doorway now, fire in my eyes as the door hangs there in two pieces. I'm deranged, pumped up, ready to rip some mother fuckers head off, rip tear entire shitty tower block apart. Electricity sparks across my fingertips as my energy charges. I'm no mug and will not be mugged-off. She pushes my boy into his bedroom and slams the door behind them. Paul, the wanker, rushes out of the kitchen, spots me and freezes. Standing there in his ball-hugging Italian Speedo underpants with his toucan-beak shaped cock, the shit-cunt's staring at me like he's seen a ghost. I'm no mug and I'm not about to be mugged off, especially by him, the cunt. No fucking way on earth that's happening. Flying forward like Superman, I chin him with a great right cross. Stumbling about the hallway, he's grabbing onto everything and anything to stop himself falling. Struggling, he's shouting my name, pleading for me to stop and listen.

Stop?

Listen?

No fucking way buddy-boy, I'm not stopping, I'm winning.

Cowering down like a bitch crawling back into the kitchen he's screaming my name while I'm kicking him in his skinny white arse. Then, she leaps out of the bedroom and starts slapping and grabbing me, screaming at me to stop-stop-stop.

Stop?

I fucking love her, want to marry her, the dirty slag.

Flinging a backhand, her head bounces off the wall as she reaches out in all directions. There's me walking around in Spain like a loved-up sap thinking of marriage, while she's here getting lunchtime-fucked by him, the dirty cunt, my supposedly best mate, and while my boy's in the flat babysitting himself in front of the television.

FUCK.

THAT.

Penalty kicking him in the stomach, he spins one-eighty and lands on his back. I'm on him now, hands around his throat smashing my forehead into his face. Nose explodes and blood spurts everywhere. Grabbing his throat with my left, I'm punching him around the head with my right while his arms are all over the place trying to stop me. Deep red purple blood smears over his ugly face, mine too, and I'm loving it, I'm on top and I'm winning. But, the truth is, inside, I'm dying. With every grunt of aggression, every whack, every head-butt and every smash, every drop of blood my heart's being broken into a thousand tiny pieces. Tiny fragments of me explode throughout the flat as my humanity bleeds out into the soulless concrete blocks. As each moment passes, the Devon I once was decays and dies bit by bit. All the while, she's yelling and screaming and my little boy's in the background balling his eyes out, listening to his daddy attempting to murder his mum and his uncle Paul. I'm screaming as car-crash tears flood out and my whole world crumbles around me, a vast abyss opens up beneath my feet and fear fills me. I don't know how I know, but I know it's the gateway to hell and my past, present and future are spiralling towards it. Satan, Beelzebub, Mammon, Ababddon, Belphegor, Asmosdeus, Lucifer, the Devil himself and the seven princes of hell call me toward it. Fallen angel voices merge with the lions roar and the howls of the werewolf deep inside me. Calling, they urge me to join them, plead with me to become one with them, invite me to be fucked by them for an eternity of orgasms. I can't stop, it's meant to be this way, it's my fate, my destiny, I've always known this is my future.

Devvvvooooonnnnn…

Fuck my missus?

Fuck her while my boy's in the next room?

The fucking cunt.

Kneeling over him now, I know what needs to be done. I feel the awesomeness of inevitability, the weight of expectation, the magnitude of my destiny. Gripping his neck with both hands, I squeeze the life out of him. As my thumbs plunge into his adams apple, his eyes bulge and his face turns red, then purple. Free falling, we're both spinning and tumbling through the air, through the gates of hell. Fuck the inevitability of my fate, all I can see is him and her together in a tangle of sweat and white flesh. Grinding into her, pelvis to pelvis, she's impaled by his giant cock as she kneads her own breasts and he flicks her erect nipples with his tongue. It's horny as fuck, if it wasn't as disgusting as hell. Her breasts brush against his skinny white-boy body while she flings her head back as ecstasy consumes her. Squeezing my eyes together, it's too hard to see, too hard to imagine, too impossible to comprehend. On top now, she slowly gyrates as he pushes deeper into her while his dirty oily hands are all over her, in her mouth, circling her engorged vulva.

She stares deep into him and mouths "I love you".

The pair of utter shit cunts.

She loved me, once.

Rose-tinted memories flash through my mind, our first day in school together, smoking our first spliff, me meeting Shirley and him meeting sexy Sammie in the Soho wine bar. We've twelve years old again and I see his face smiling and us laughing and joking. He was my best friend. Disappointment guts me. Fists clenching around his neck, his eyes roll back. All my hate and strength and emotion poor out of me into him. I squeeze my eyes tight shut and grit my teeth and, eventually, his body comes to a silent, peaceful rest. No more struggling, no more resistance, no more violence, no more tension, no more trauma. The most intense high washes over me and I feel pure, unadulterated evil pulse through my veins, it's delicious. More alive than ever before, I love it, relish it, savour it and, embrace it, wholly and fully. Circling my head, demons surround me with greed and lust and envy and gluttony and hatred and lust in their eyes. Neither male nor female, I feel them singing, 'Devvvoonnnnn…' Right there, at that specific moment in time, I'm crowned the Prince of Darkness as a razor-sharp crown of thorns is placed onto my head. Piercing my skull, toxic black-blood trickles across the thorns and down my face as the demons take it in turn to zoom in and lick it up, sucking at my wounds as they do. I feel their excitement, their wanting, their lust, their yearning for my soul.

I stare down at him.

I've killed this mother-fucker, ended him, destroyed him and wiped his memory from the face of this fallen world. He fucked my missus, ruined my life so I've ended his. I've committed the cardinal sin, the worst sin, the sin of all sins. I've killed. Roaring, the demons circle quicker and quicker, creating a vortex around me, urging me on, physically moving me. Their demonic screams scratch through my mind as I squeeze the remaining life-force out of him.

Vision wobbling, his smug smiling face zooms away from me at the speed of light down a lengthening long dark tunnel. 'Devvvvoooonnnnnnnnn.'

They want me so bad, I feel their love, their lust, their wanting. Do it, do it, do it, I'm squeezing harder now and the screams and yells and roars increase and intensify, engulf me, overtake my mind and consume me.

Why?

Why did he do it?

Why do her?

Why Shirley?

Why me?

He can have any woman he wants.

He's got the looks, the money, the confidence, the money, the cars, the money, the looks, the watches, the confidence.

He's got everything.

Why her, why me?

All still now, I'm floating in outer space. Closing my eyes, the demons are gone and the white noise echoes into the distance. I hear my heart beating as I look back towards earth and marvel at the thin electric blue haze protecting humanity. I feel earths gravity, it's pull, it's warmth, it's tenderness. My orbit picks up pace and I begin to fall. Gathering speed, I can feel the wind rushing through me, taking my breath away as I struggle for air. Five miles up, I can just about make out the outline of England and the boot of Italy. The whole of Europe can fit into the palm of my hand. Supersonic now, the clouds race through me as the ground approaches at pace, I see the massive u-shape of the river Thames, blue and majestic, I've never appreciated it's beauty before. Squinting, I know what's coming. Crunching head-first into the ice-cold pavement, time stands still as my entire body reacts and every muscle tenses.

I'm surrounded by darkness.

Eyes opening, I release the lifeless corpse from my grip. Looking around, I see her standing in the doorway, like she was before I left for Spain, after I did what I did. Crying, her lip's swollen and bloody and her tear filled eyes slowly pan up from Him, toward me. Then, she does it, jooks a dirty broken bottle into my jugular, drives a stake through the heart. 'I never loved you,' she whispers, her slow, deliberate and meaningful words echo into forever. 'You've ruined me, I wish I'd never met you.'

Ruined?

Worse than any other pain, it properly guts me. In two sentences, she slices me open, pushes her hands deep inside and rips my guts clean out.

Never loved me?

Never?

I loved her, still love her, the slag.

'Shut up.' she screams, turning to my boy who's standing there in the doorway to his bedroom, all little and lonely, scared and confused, crying his little eyes out. She looks back at me with hate in her eyes, proper pit of your stomach hate. 'He's a mistake, just like us. Every time I look at him, I see you.'

He darts into his room and slams the door shut. Deliciously sour and disgusting bile flows into my mouth. A Mistake? She said that, in front of him, in front of my boy, my son and heir? I feel dizzy, sick. The roaring starts again, this time unbearably loud. Fists clenched, the whole building wobbles and shakes as the power surges through me, I'm Krishna, Buddha, Jehovah, Allah, Zeus and Jesus rolled into one omni-god, I'm King-Arthur, King-Kong and master of the mother fucking universe.

I fly toward her at the speed of sound.

Fuck my best mate?

Cuss my boy?

Never loved me?

The whore-slag-bitch!

Screaming, I drag her by the hair into the hallway. She's

struggling and I stumble back through the door into our bedroom. I see the bed, still messed up with duvet piled up in the middle and my nostrils flare with the smell of dirty, sweaty, snake-in-the-grass pornographic sex. Him and her were at it right there in my bed, with my boy in the next room. The door slams shut and it's just me and her now, just us, just like old times. Me, the loved-up sap. Her, the dirty, best-mate-fucking, son-hating slag. I regret what happened next.

I took back what's mine…

I catch the reflection of myself in the picture frame on the bedside table, the picture of the two of us hugging with our little boy in-between. Family happiness in a frame, pure unadulterated contentment frozen in time. I look at her laying there out cold, her face bruised and battered and swollen with a cut across her left eyebrow.
An icy coldness washes over me.
What have I done?
What have I become?
I have to leave.
Closing the bedroom door slowly and quietly, refusing to look at the cadaver in the kitchen, I edge around the remains of the front door out to the balcony. The fresh air stings as it enters my bad-to-the-core lungs. What have I done? Where now, what now? Can't go home, how can I look Momma in the face after what I've done. Down the urine stained stair-well, I walk and walk and walk, walk my arse off. Replaying it over and over, tears roll down my cheeks. What have I done? As they flow, the final remains of my humanity seep out while inside, the evil badness grows and multiplies like a cancer. Eventually, I find myself near Claudes flat. Solid, old-school, non judgemental friend, Claude. He'll never let me down, after all, I was there for him when he needed me. Ten minutes and a spliff later, he

says I've done the right thing, says Paul took an absolute liberty and definitely, one-hundred percent deserves what he got.

Haven't been back in that room since, just can't do it, can't face it. Guilt, I suppose, and I am guilty, I know that now. I wish I could turn the clock back and re-live that moment, do things differently. I wish I can magic up an alternative reality where the taxi back from the airport gets caught in traffic, or where I don't knock and she don't see me and I carry on down the stairs, living on in ignorant bliss. I wish I respected her privacy, respected her, left it for another day when there's no red Porsche outside, no dirty sex, no violence, no killing, no pain and no regrets.

Ignorance is bliss.

I just wish…

9. Dance with the Devil

"Pleased to meet you, hope you guess my name. What's puzzling you is the nature of my game. Just as every cop is a criminal and sinners are saints... you can call me Lucifer."

Jagger & Richards

THE KITCHEN
17, HAMILTON HOUSE
GREENWICH, LONDON
LATE SUMMER, 1989

Early morning sun casts beautifully golden rays through the dirty net curtains as warmness caresses my face, kissing me good morning. Refreshed, I haven't slept like that for ages, longer than I can remember anyway. Throat dry, need a piss and pang, stomach's rumbling too, I'm hungry, that's a good sign. I yawn a goodbye-great-sleep-hello-world yawn, then swing my feet around, stand and stretch out.

"You should clean this place up, it's a shit-hole," the Interrogator says, stating the obvious, like he always does.

Probably should sort it out, straighten it up, make it at least habitable. Yeah man, pull myself together, try living again. Stopping in the hallway, my eyes are drawn the bedroom. The screams usually emanating from inside don't seem as loud as usual. I know I have to go in, eventually, one day. I know I can't put it off forever.

"You sure you're ready for this?" the Interrogator shouts through from the Kitchen, reading my hesitation like a book.

Turning, I face the door square on. Deep breath, I must face the fear, face the past, face the future. Staring deeply, I try to compose myself. Leg shaking, my vision blurs and the white gloss paint ripples and bubbles before charring around the edges. Melting away, it reveals the raw wood-veneer beneath. Scorched black and smouldering, it bends and warps and glows super bright before fading into opaqueness. Squinting, I can just about make out what's on the other side. The walls have gone black and are pulsing and shapeshifting. Feasting on the decaying body, maggots are literally falling out of the wall and I somehow know a palpable stench of deceit hangs heavy in the air, infecting every part of the room. Bile flows into my mouth when I see the horrific decomposing body laying across the bed, dark grey, blackening and decaying and utterly disgusting. I retch as the body looks to be moving as maggots and cockroaches emerge from every orifice and deep rips in the grey-black flesh.

It's disgusting.

I'm disgusting.

Opening my eyes, reality stuns me back into this world. I feel numb, not sick as I usually do, just numb. I don't feel remorse or guilt or anything, just a vacant numbness. Time to go in, go in for real, not just through the splinter in my mind's eye and skagg-warped imagination. Two steps forward, heart rate jumping, beads of sweat form across my forehead. Breathing deeply, I fill my lungs. Clasping the handle, it shakes and vibrates and feels warm. Gripping tightly, I push down, slowly. Eyes closed, deep breath. Must try to control it, con-fucking-trol it, man. Twist my wrist, push forward and the door opens. The bed remains unmade but the stripe of blood across the wall's hardly visible, not quite the deathly black I imagined it might be. There's no dead body either, no maggots emerging from dead eye sockets, dead mouths or dead ears, just a feint indentation of where their heaving-sexing-disgusting bodies once laid. Feet nailed to the floor, my eyes scan around while I replay what happened over and over and over. I spot the picture-frame on the bedside table, me, her and our baby boy smiling content smiles of love and joy. Tears well in my eyes. Releasing the door handle, I sit on the edge of the bed, head in hands. I never imagined I'd be capable of this, didn't think it was in me. I thought I'd killed her, I thought my brute force, my manic beasting and shear caveman aggression took her privacy and her life. Maybe I'm not a killer after all, maybe I've been mentally crucifying myself for no god damn reason. But, I did violate and defrock her. So close to the dream, so god-damn close, I had everything, all I ever wanted but didn't realise it until too late, way-way too late.

"Oi, old China," the Interrogator yells from the other room.

"Ready when you are buddy."

Just leave me alone, leave me in here to dwell on my sorrow. Why torture me, nah, this is worse than torture. A good beating, a broken arm, even fingers cut off I can take, but having my head messed with, my brain dissected and disassembled bit by bit is something else.

Getting up from the bed, I take a mental picture to replace my minds-eye video-nasty image I've been carrying around for fuck knows how long. Nodding to myself, I gently close the door and head back through to the kitchen.

"Oi-oi, what-g-wan rude boy? Feeling better?" the Interrogator says, not really asking, not really caring. *"Where were we?"* the Interrogator says, getting right on my nerves.

I'll move it on though, I'm in control yeah.

So Spain, España, La Vida. Yeah man, I learned a lot in Spain about myself, about fear, about the unknown and about temptation, but mainly that the club scene is changing, big-time. What I saw at the Olympic was super cool and sort of unique, hardly any clubs in London are doing stuff like that, certainly none are playing that type of music. A place in Vauxhall is doing what they call "Ibiza Beach Parties", but it's small-time, cliquey and a bit self-aware for my liking. It's not as cool as the Olympic, nah, a bit gimmicky, with a few blow-up paddling pools and a foam-cannon thing, spunking out masses of foam over everyone like a massive cock ejaculating. Even though covering punters with pseudo-spunk isn't for me, the music selection's spot on and their deejay an absolute genius. I tell Marlon about the Olympic who tells me he's been playing House music wall to wall on Dream FM for months now. News to me I must say, but, I'd stopped listening ages ago, it's just business to me now. I prefer my old-school dancehall dub-style cassette tapes anyway, yeah man, that's real music, played with real instruments by real people, not like the repetitive four to the flour madness the youth love nowadays. Nah, keep it real with Jah-Shaka, Saxon Soundsystem and the deep meditation vibe. Yes-yes, hear me now, the truth. Nothing comes close to the echo chamber, heavy dub-basslines and youths toasting over the top about real tings, real issues, thought provoking musings on inner-city strife.

UNTIL...

I go over to catch up with Marlon and he plays me a whole heap of House music, like what I heard in Spain at the Olympic. From Detroit, Chicago and New York City he said, each has it's own special characteristic, Detroit is harsh, Chicago soulful and NYC is disco. Man, I totally get it. I'm in love with the jack-your-body-love-can't-turn-around vibe mixed with the harsh but melodic acid squelchiness and thumping eight-o-eight four-four kick drum. I get the contrast between human and machine, the harshness and the softness of society, the battle between youth and the establishment, the transition between young and old, old and new. Makes complete sense, and I'm well and truly hooked. I decide right there, sitting on the edge of Marlons sofa, from now on my promotional nights will be House music nights. No funk, no soul, no electro, no hip-hop, only House. Initially, it doesn't go down well with my regular punters, but, pretty soon, they catch on as House music explodes, and when I say explode, I mean ex-fucking-plode! Clubs, pubs, mainstream radio stations are playing House music. Later in the year, fuelled by House, I hear about illegal House parties, similar to the all-night blues parties we had back in Brixton, but these are much bigger in scale. Instead of roots and culture, they play House, and rather than terraced houses up and down the Frontline, they're held in industrial units, multi-story car parks or abandoned warehouses. The venues mirror the music, the mix of old and new and the vibe is about brotherhood and togetherness in the backdrop of long forgotten and decrepit industry. The contrast isn't lot on me. Intrigued, Me and Claude go on a scouting mission. Man, what a night...

DERELICT WAREHOUSE
YORK WAY
KINGS CROSS, LONDON
1987 or 1988 (or whenever…)

Takes about thirty minutes to drive up there and another ten to find a parking spot but eventually we find the derelict warehouse backing on to the railway tracks near Kings Cross station. Soon as I climb out, the top of my head tingles as I hear the muffled thuds of the four-four from inside. Quick chat with the bouncers on the door, who Claude knows through a mate of a mate, and we're shown through to a long narrow warehouse littered with old papers, half-broken chairs and a few battered desks. An iron crane contraption hangs across the ceiling at the far end, just above what looks to be a heap of bass-bins, horns and tweeters with a hoard of punters moving and grooving in front. No lighting other than a single strobe light pulsating quickly. It's a visual assault on the optic nerve but man, it's harshness is effective and oddly in-keeping with the industrial backdrop. Looking around, illuminated by the ultra-white flashes, it's a shit-hole, literally pretty much an empty warehouse, the dirty fucks hadn't even swept the floor. However, the sound system is good, really good actually. Getting closer, the echoing resonance of the large space subsides as the frequencies gain definition. God damn, it's so loud, the bassline tightens around my chest and I'm sure I'm struggling to breath, while my eardrums feel like they'll implode at any minute. It's busy too, with maybe five hundred punters inside huddling around the stack of speakers, with a couple of hundred more expected later on, apparently. Over to the left-hand side, a bar of sorts, a few old desks pushed together with bottles of water and kids lolly pops on top, with a couple of long-haired white boy weirdos behind taking money. They don't serve real drinks, just water and lollies, and the punters pay good money for these. God damn, paying for water? The fellas Claude knows out front charge a tenner to get in though, which is different to my nights where I need to maximise the bar take to make any money. Claudes bouncer mate ushers us away from the speaker-stack and towards one of the bars, and introduces us to the organiser, can't remember his name now. A surprisingly young, well-spoken and super confident chap, positively gobby, he's absolutely full of himself. Handshakes and smiles, he introduces himself as the "pioneer" of these types of warehouse dance parties and tells us all about it in forensic detail. He has no clue who we are, yet he's in full-on self-promotion mode giving it large. Not sure about being a promoter, this guy could sell ice to Eskimos and sand to Arabs. Anyway, I ask him about the water, and why he doesn't sell beer or rum. Says the majority of punters are off their tits on Ecstasy and can't stomach beer or "hard liquor" as he calls it. I've heard about Ecstasy but, being a lover of the Herb, it doesn't interest me. Then, out of the blue, Claude tells me he's been dropping pills every Saturday night for six months or more, selling them for about a year. He says it helps him through the drudgery of working on the doors and dealing with the stupid-as-fuck-shit-for-brains punters. Man, I haven't got a clue, I feel old and completely out of touch. First off Marlon and House music, now Claude with a whole new drug scene I know fuck all about.

Life is passing me by.

I drop my first Ecstasy pill ten minutes later, a "white dove" Claude says. Forty minutes later, I'm overcome with a feeling like no feeling ever, and I mean EVER. Almost like being pissed-up-drunk but without the world-spinning, sick-as-a-parrot, fight-the-world feeling beer or rum brings. Instead, shivers rush up and down my spine, a permanent tingling sensation at the back of my skull while my jaw and cheeks ache from the grinning and teeth grinding. Grooving and moving, the music takes me, transporting me into a whole new world, a new dimension, a new plane of existence. Immersed in a kaleidoscope of amazing colours, I'm dancing through a rainbow on fluffy clouds of warmth and safety and unconditional love. Sounds corny and a bit crazy, but it's true. Heart racing, I feel an enormous amount of love for everyone, people I don't even know, faces I've long since forgotten, and, they love me back too. With hugs and kisses from vaguely familiar known-you-all-my-life strangers, the whole world's fondling my balls and stroking my cock. Shit man, I've found total loved up happiness in a dirty warehouse in Kings Cross through an unmarked illegally produced white-dove pill. Yeah man, my up-till-then-futile life changes that night, I have an epiphany, yeah man, god speaks to me, the whole entire human race has eventually reached the next stage of evolution. Centuries of raping, pillaging and killing each other, arguing over bits of meaningless land and who's god is the best god are over.

Ecstasy can solve all our problems.

This shit is the future.

This shit will bring peace on earth and save mankind.

I love this shit.

This shit, is the shit!

Five or six in the morning with the sun piercing the black horizon, the crowd are still mad-up for it with no sign of slowing up. Although still loved up, buzzing and chewing my own teeth, my feet and lower back ache with the dancing and the swaying, so head back to Claudes to chill out, well, try and chill out at least. Turns out, Ecstasy is a long-term buzz, not an immediate pick me up like coke. I'm on one for the whole day for fucks sake, wide awake, grinding my teeth, smiling at myself like a sad-sack. Plus, I'm constantly horny, horny as fuck, cock the size of a broom-handle horny. Ten wanks later, reflecting on the night, I realise I've learnt a few important things. Firstly, House music is the future. Secondly, Ecstasy will save the human race and deliver utopia here on Earth. Thirdly, much to my regret, I've learnt the come-downs from Ecstasy are nothing short of a massive head-fuck and never to be under-estimated. Most importantly though, the single most significant thing I learn is that Ecstasy's now officially my recreational drug of choice. I love the Herb, but wow, Ecstasy is a perception warping, mood altering, life changing buzz like no other.

After my monstering of the duplicit-duo-of-doom, otherwise known as Paul and Shirley, I move in with Claude. He actually suggests it, saying he owes me one from when we took him in after the Snakehead war. From then on, we hook up big time, become best buddies, really tight. He'd properly sorted himself out by then, in fact, he runs one of the biggest security firms in London. Yeah man, he runs the doors of most of the decent nightclubs in the West End and a few football grounds, and increasingly, illegal parties dotted around the suburbs. Then, he has his other business, his real businesses, the business of moving large amounts of cocaine along with the Greek. He only does the doors as a "route to market" as Paul says, allowing him free access to a rapidly growing market of punters. Pumping iron and necking steroids too, he's massive, like a fucked-up version of the Incredible Hulk. Kids cry when they see him while wanna-be-gangster-types cross the street rather than catch his eye. He's changed in other ways too, the dreadlock Rasta from the Brixton Frontline is well and truly dead and buried. He reinvents himself as a gangster, a geezer, a wrong-un, a chap to be feared, the heavyweight champion of the world in a world of bushido mercenaries and kamikaze warriors. Him and the Greek are dealing, smashing, fucking, pumping and robbing anything and everything. Yep, full-time crazies, ducking and diving and dealing everything to everyone while ripping-off whoever they can. Both out of control to be honest, drugged up to the eyeballs the time, coke for breakfast, steroids for lunch and heroin at bedtime to help them sleep.

Ah, the brownnnnnnnnnnnn…

Here me now, if Ecstasy is my teenage crush, then brown or skagg or heroin or opium or diamorphine or whatever you want to call her, she's the true and utter love of my life, my soul mate, my one and only better half. To begin with, I dabble just a bit, trying it a few times with Claude after a heavy night out, chasing just a bit at bedtime to help me get to sleep. It helps with the come downs from Ecstasy, and, weirdly, I never think of it as "heroin", I never think I'm a full-on druggie, a "Zammo" type character from Grange Hill. Nah, not me, I'm a professional nightclub promoter and all-round business-man. Sure, I'll snort a few lines of coke during the day just to keep me going, drop a few Ecstasy pills during the evening to feel the vibe and, in need of a few hours sleep at night, I'll chase a little brown. I'm no acne-ridden-skinny-wretched-tramp of a skagg-head, shaking and trembling, giving blow-jobs for a five-quid fix.

The low-life life is not my life.

'Oh, come on,' the Interrogator teases.

Fuck off.

I remember my first ever time chasing, yeah man, I remember it like it's yesterday. They say you never forget your first time and man, it's so true, (like most clichés). After one of my parties at Cheeks, Claude picks me up on his way home from a heavy night at fuck knows where. Driving along, he's smiling and happy and whistling a tune to himself which is odd, he's usually a grumpy shit-bag. Anyway, we turn into the car park outside his block and he gives me a wink. Fuck knows what's on his mind, I suppose he's snorted a few lines of coke or maybe downed a few pills. Into his flat, he's straight on the weights bench and grunts out one-hundred bench presses while I skin up. Ninety-nine, one-hundred, he jumps up and presents to the air a little paper wrap, maybe a couple of inches long. Carefully unwrapping it, he taps out a sprinkle onto his scorched teaspoon. Gently pursing his lips, he allows a glistening ball of spit fall onto the light brown powder, zipping his Zippo, he dances the flame underneath. My heart races as he reaches for the remains of a biro-pen. Dangerously exciting, I love it. Quickly, the spoon sizzles and bubbles as vapour emerges. Cock tingling, I know what this is, I'm both disgusted and excited at the same time. Closing his eyes, he sucks in the fumes slow and steady. Putting the lighter down, he lowers the spoon and takes the biro from his mouth. Head slowly tilting backward, his mouth falls open and a plume of thick white smoke swirls and drifts out. Statue-like for a minute or so he whispers, 'fucking-hell Dev,' before handing me the spoon. I look down at it, scorched and dark and dangerous and disgusting. My heart races quicker than it's ever done before. Do I really want to try the drug of druggies and dirty skagg-heads, made by gypsy farmers in rural Afghanistan? Looking deep into the remains, my heart flutters. I love being high and looking across at Claude, he's higher than high. Observing his apparent trance-like orgasmic high, a massive pang of jealousy hits me.

FUCK IT.
I MUST HAVE IT.
Tap-tap-tap.
Spit.
Lighter.

The powder slowly falls into the saliva and dissolves, like the fall of Rome or the last day of Pompeii. The powder fades and merges with the spit, increasingly more with each stoke of the flame. So delicate, so beautiful, I'm completely mesmerised as it shimmers and moves and tiny small delicate bubbles appear around the edge. Here it comes. Lighter down, I grab the biro and lift the spoon towards my mouth, as I do, I hear Claude groan in delightful agony. Closing my eyes, the caramel-toffee-sour-vinegar aroma stings my nostrils, disgusting but alluring at the same time. Sucking hard, fumes flow deep into my lungs.

Hmm, yeah…
Warm and familiar…
Love…
Momma…
Warm milk…
Cold winters morning…
"Be safe now Devon…"
Warm and safe…
Familiar and comforting…

Hugs and kisses…

"I love you my son…"

Opening my eyes, I look toward Claude, head still tilting back, his eyes are closed and he's snoring like a pig on Valium. Shuddering warmth creeps towards my brain and, looking down, I notice a black puddle forming around my ankles. It grows wider and bigger and begins to pulsate. After each pulse it proceeds up my legs until I'm in chest deep, then consumed fully. Slow-motion, I'm drifting through time, weightless and calm and mellow and happy and definitely not scared. It's not euphoric, like with cocaine, nah, it's more contentment and at peace with the entirety of the universe. It's not the orgasmic rush I imagined, nah, it's more like the five seconds after an orgasmic sex session, the "humm" rather than the "ahhhh", if you know what I mean. I feel centred and whole, care-free and worry-free, free of anything and everything. Glorious and beautiful and peaceful and serene, it's deeper, more intimate and more meaningful than coke or Ecstasy, yeah man, it's all about me, and only me. I'm tiny small and insignificant, and I love it.

I wake up fuck knows how long after, with Claude sitting next to me, smiling and stroking my face ever so softly. Dry as a nun's fanny, wiping my mouth I swallow hard and taste the most rancid and vile taste ever.

Oh no, no-no-no-no-no. Panic rushes through me.

Please-God no.

Mouth fucked by a skagged-up-horny-as-fuck-not-knowing-what-he's-doing Claude?

'You alright dred? Don't worry 'bout dat, it's perfectly normal,' Claude says, as I screw my face up. 'All man puke first time.'

Vomit, not Claudes monster cock spunk.

Thank god.

Puking is a price worth paying because god-damn, from that very moment, I'm in love. I understand what I call love, you might call being a dirty junkie hooked on heroin, but I don't care, don't give a shit actually. Gradually, the vomiting stops and chasing becomes normal, a nice nightcap or a small treat to end the day with, just like respectable folk downing a shot of brandy or whiskey before bed. Plus, it helps me forget about poor Ashley, and about Paul and Shirley and what they did and what I did to them. Helps me forget about what I've become.

A pair of drug-fuelled villains, me and Claude lose touch with the hooligan scene. A new breed of younger hooligan has emerged, kids who care more about the fashion and looking good than the violence or the football. "Designer hooligans" the press calls them. Rumour has it the Albino got shot dead, while Lacy, Shirleys brother, is planning "something big" for the world-cup, or some other bullshit. The Greek's moving on too, teaming up with a millionaire old-school villain in Essex and some dodgy fuck in Amsterdam, doing wholesale drug deals apparently. Claude don't want anything to do with the Essex-Gangster thing though, says it's cowboy-land over there with Range Rovers and shot guns and we're better off out of it. So, this is the new me, cocaine, Ecstasy, nightclubs, uppers, downers, slags, toms, punters and, of course, skagg. At the same time, I put Shirley and Paul well out of my mind, fuck them cunts, and focus on my son. I go see Shirley's old man, Stan, about me seeing the little man. We have a right old barney on the doorstep, with him giving it the big-un about kneecapping me after what I did to Her. I don't get angry or vexed, nah man, I understand, I'd be fucked off too if some random motherfucker hurt my kid.

I don't get to see my boy at all after that, haven't seen him since. Breaks my heart, I miss him, miss him so much, miss him big time. It's for the best though, I know that, he's better off without me. Damn, that's hard to say, but if I'm honest, it's tragically true. Since the very first moment I held him, I've loved him with all my heart, beyond love, he's me and I'm him. I've such high hopes for him, just like my Momma had for me, once.

I miss him, I miss me, I miss the man I once was…
Sadness.
Tears.
Sorrow.
Regret.

Flick the switch, turn the dial.
The radio station.
Yeah-yeah, Devious Dee in the house, you're listening to Dream FM, keep it locked. Marlon runs things day to day, which suits me just fine. I don't listen to it anymore and hardly ever visit the studio. My entire involvement see's Marlon handing me a fist full of cash once a month, my share for the station running maybe ten minutes of adverts per hour. Deejaying more and more and working in the record shop during the day when he wasn't at college, he surrounds himself with music. Earning good money, he gets himself a tidy girlfriend and is properly happy. Meanwhile, I'm busy with what's quickly becoming my full-time job, consuming taking copious amounts of drugs while trying to run the promotions business. Club owners can't get enough of my nights. House music is the "in" thing, the only thing, and everyone and I mean everyone's into it. By Christmas eighty-eight, every back-street nightclub's doing "house" nights, so competition's fierce. BBC Radio One and even Top of the Pops are playing House music, and, in turn, every high street discotheque, commercial radio station, in store elevator music and even little kids birthday parties are playing House music too. But, I am the one and the only Devious-fucking-Dee for fucks sake and more than up for the challenge. Yeah man, greater competition means more of a fight which means the victory is even sweeter. I'm a big thinker yeah, ideas and concepts explode around me, I can see possibilities where other people see problems, at least I could, once, way back when. My attitude has always been reach for the stars and at worst grab the moon.

Around that time, near Christmas I think, after a heavy night of Ecstasy, coke, herbs and skagg, me and Claude sit chatting. Not the normal blah-blah buzzing our tits off chit-chat, but a serious man-to-man talk. He tells me he's had enough of his security business skirting around the edges and helping other people make shit-loads of cash. Says he wants total and complete control, he wants to make big-money. After a couple of hours, he convinces me to help him put on an illegal party. He'll sort the venue, pocket the door money and have free reign to sell whatever drugs he wants direct to punters, a "vertically-integrated monopoly", Paul calls it. Claudes plan makes perfect sense and, to be honest, in my more lucid moments, I thought about the exact same thing. I'll sort the music, the party and the promotions, while he does the doors and the drugs. A few days later, without even mentioning it to me, he signs a short-term lease on a warehouse in Stratford, slap bang in the middle of an industrial estate, everything nice and legal.

UNIT 11
THREE MILLS ROAD
STRATFORD, LONDON
EARLY 1989

The industrial estate is eerily quiet and desolate as we pull up outside a roller-shutter door, maybe twenty feet high. Similar units either side, Claude unlocks a door to the right of the shutters and we step through. Small office straight ahead and a door leading through to the main warehouse. The small office is perfect for a cloakroom, I think. Peeking through the cloakroom I see another room behind, perfect for my office and for counting and storing the cash. Through to the warehouse, I see it's wide and long and big. I feel my arsehole twitch with panic, it's too big, we'll never fill it and the night will be utter shit and Claude will lose his money. Nah, can't risk this, he's emotional at the best of times, let alone if he lost a couple of grand because I fuck it up. To be fair, although he sorts a proper lease, the stated use is "storage and logistics", so putting on a party represents a risk. From the off I've got bad vibes, but, I know how much money's made elsewhere by other promoters doing unlicensed parties, so get into promoter mode pretty damn quickly.

First thing I do is tour around most of the independent record shops in London, picking up flyers for various parties to see how they promote it, and to check the best date. We chose a Saturday when there's only a couple of other parties planned. All the parties have weird and mystical names, Genesis, Sweatshop, Bohemia, Future, Dawn-Chaser, Earthquake, Apocalypse-Now. The more intriguing the name, the more interest and presumably more through the door. We call our party "Mental Logic", fuck knows why. I get some flyers printed with an outline of a head with a brain inside with "mental" above and "logic" below in black with yellow outlining. I must say, it looks really good and surprisingly professional. As soon as they're printed, we start running adverts on the radio station, getting the deejays to mention it during their shows. The deejays call it an "exclusive-invite-only" launch party, where punters pay twenty quid for their "exclusive" invite. Right up to the actual day, we keep the location secret to avoid the attention from the Police, other party promoters and, as Claude points out, mother-fucker villain gangs who might try and rob us. The main reason for keeping the location secret is that punters get off on the whole adventure of it. Yeah, heading off on a Saturday night in search of thrills and spills, ending up fuck knows where, dancing the night away until the break of dawn, high as fuck on Ecstasy and coke. Marlon sorts the music, a few of his deejay mates together and a couple of local artists who are releasing own-label records using a pressing-plant down the road in Stratford. He arranged for them to perform a couple of tracks so we can at least deliver on the promise of a "launch party". I want to stand out from other promotions, deliver something different to the normal deejay sets all night long. Yeah man, I want to be upfront and recognised as a promoter of great, totally up-for-it, no bullshit allowed nights. Next job, the sound system. I ask Skyrocket to help out, the guy who we bought the radio station from. More than happy to help, for a fee of course, he calls a few old-school reggae sound-system buddies, who bring their systems too. Man, full circle for me, the dub-reggae sound systems I listened too in the seventies now being used to feed the illegal party scene of the nineteen-eighties. On the night we have twenty or thirty, (yes thirty), eighteen-inch bass bins and a whole heap of horns and tweeters, plus a dozen or so amplifiers and pre-amps. Marlon gets hold of a few strobe lights and a smoke machine but the best thing is a Jedi-knight green laser, can you believe it. It's got five settings and pulses in time with the music, but my favourite setting is the tunnel, god damn, I stare at that thing for ages. Claudes security guys build a bit of a stage at the opposite end to the entrance, using a few sheets of plywood, milk creates and broken up pallets they find knocking around outside. They also knock up a couple of bars, one on each wall either side of the stage, where we will sell water and candy-bars and lolly-pops. I pick up some parachute silks from an old Army and Navy store in Lewisham, draping them over the ceilings and walls, with ultraviolet lights behind them. A young kid Marlon knows called Pax or Drax or something comes with fluorescent spray paint and does some graffiti on the walls, tagging "mental logic" everywhere along with the head-brain logo.

The day before the party we plan a sound check. Standing in the middle of the warehouse, spinning three-sixty, everything looks absolutely top notch, even though I say so myself. Before a single needle touches vinyl, I'm proud of what we've achieved. With Claudes heavies to run the door, Marlon's deejay mates and some tasty girls from Cheeks in Deptford to run the bars, there's about thirty of us in total. Firing up the amplifiers, Marlon drops some tunes. The sound system's loud, so loud I can feel the bass rumbling through my stomach, exactly what I wanted. Feeling the vibe, we drop a few pills, share a few lines of coke and have a bit of a rave up. Around ten o'clock the Police turn up saying they've received complaints about the noise, which is odd because we're in the middle of an industrial estate, probably at least half a mile from any houses. Anyway, I deal with them because Claude will lose it and end up in prison for assault. I tell them we're a record label launching two new artists and rehearsing for the launch party the following night. Buzzing my tits off, I'm loved-up and grinding my teeth together, struggling not to hug them. I show them the lease and give them a tour of the place. Nodding away, taking it all in, they seem happy, almost impressed by how professional it looks. The one in charge, a kind old chap with grey hair and a flat-top cap tells me to keep up the good work and keep the fire exits clear. He promises to pop back tomorrow.

Keep up the good work? Yeah man, good work fella, nice one, pat on the back for you Devon old son. As soon as they leave, we're bang on it again, even more joyous and euphoric than before. We're now holding a legal-illegal party and have just seen off the Police without even a crossed word. This is awesome, I'm awesome, we are all fucking awesome, and loving it. Leaving Claude there with his cronies and a few of Marlon's mates, I get back to his flat in the early hours, still buzzing my tits off. Can't sleep, so, of course, do some brown. Yeah man, slept so well, probably the best sleep I've ever had, safe in the knowledge that in less than twenty-four hours we'll be throwing a brilliant party.

Waking up about twelve-noon, I head to the radio station. Soon as I walk through the door, I know the day is going to be crazy-mad. The transportable phone we bought, (less hassle than using the pay-phones outside the tower-block), is hammered all day long, with hundreds of punters ringing in for details of the party. Marlon uses a formula to work it out and reckons we have around twenty or thirty thousand listeners, basically one-hundred listeners for every punter who calls in. Meanwhile Claude, wanting to maximise our publicity and therefore the amount of cash we'll make, has a fantastic idea to take the other pirate stations off air, giving us exclusive advertising rights. Our two main competitors are based in the Nightingale Estate near Hackney, so he heads there tooled up along with a few of his meathead mates. They find the antenna no problem but can't get onto the roof to smash it to bits, nor find which flat the studio's in to do the same. Any deejays inside will have the shit kicked out of them at best, thrown over the balcony at worst, thank god he didn't find them. Him and his men end up trying to break into the electricity sub-station to cut off the electricity for the entire estate and silence the stations that way. The fools rob a car and drive it straight into the power station, ending up beaching it on top of some bollards just outside. Luckily, Claude's in the back seat unharmed, but the driver plants his head into the windscreen, ending up in the local hospital with cuts, bruises and concussion, plus serious questions from the local Police.

Amateurish arseholes.

Not a brain-cell between them.

Around six in the evening, I head back to the warehouse and wait for Claude to return from his power-station shenanigans. He gets back and we're back on one, coked-up to the eyeballs in preparation for dropping several brown-biscuit-white-dove- nuns-on-horseback or whatever-the-fuck pills later on. We decide to announce the location and the magical mystery tour later on, a little before twelve midnight. First, we'll get the punters to drive out to Thurrock services, to the east of London on the north side of the river Thames, right on the M25 motorway. Marlon arranges for some wanna-be kids, a few fit girls and a couple of Claudes heavies to be over there waiting. They'll tell the punters to drive a few junctions north and head to Epping tube station, while keeping it locked to Dream FM where our deejays will be hyping the event. At the tube station, we have another crew there filtering out the plebs, potential trouble-makers or plain clothes Police. Man, these dumb fucks always stand out like sore thumbs, all the gear but no idea, with standard issue flat sole shoes to avoid somehow nullifying their pension. Any Police will be sent thirty miles across London to some motorway services near Brent Cross where they'll search around and find fuck all. Genuine, honest punters will be sent on to Stratford.

The venue fills up from midnight and by two a.m. it's completely full, with a couple of thousand or so inside. The performers Marlon sorted go down really well. First up, a fit girl singing over a deep sounding house tune while a couple of young guys dance around the stage with her. Afterwards, two dreadlocked brothers rapping over a heavy hip hop tune which goes down an absolute storm, with the crowd jumping and raving all over the place, it's utterly crazy and absolutely the dogs bollocks. Sun rising at about five, by seven the crowd thins out so I head back into the office to re-count the cash. Best part of twenty-five thousand from the door, and just shy of two thousand from the bar. Doing some quick sums, I work out, after the expenses, we'll easily clear north of eighteen. Wow, eighteen thousand, in one night, one blinding night, for doing something you love, something you'll probably do for free given have the chance. Plus, that doesn't include the wads of cash Claude makes from punting out fuck knows who many Ecstasy pills and wraps of heavily cut coke. He comes in to check on me, (to be more accurate, check on the cash), and his face beams. Even though my cheeks ache an Ecstasy-induced ache, I can't help but smile back, we both know we've nailed it. We stare at each other for fuck knows how long, both feeling proud of what we've achieved, then…

SWITCH.

I shit myself.

Jones, the ex-undercover-now-police-gangster walks in, just behind Claude, looking deranged, pumped up with eyes bulging. I hadn't seen him since the lets-mess-with-Devon-night round at Claudes flat ages ago, and he still freaks me out. Eyeing the cash, they're like starving wolves, almost dribbling from the edges of their mouths with their eyes on stalks. Oh crap, I know what this means, I'm about to get ripped off. Shit. Can't believe Claude will do this to me, not him, not now, not after this long, not after what we've both been through. My buzz wobbles and starts to turn sour, oh no, I'm heading for a downer. Pulling the chairs out, they both sit down and stare at me with poker-face-stares.

Claude starts asking me questions about the cash, 'is it light, has anyone taken any, am I sure, am I positive?' While Claude rabbits on with his barrage of machine-gun questions, I can't help but stare at Jones. He has a mesmerising aura about him, a power, a magnetic attraction or something. He just sits there quiet, brooding, staring. I can't work it out, am I being robbed, or is this yet another fuck-with-Devon session?

'Relax yaah, re-fucking-lax,' Jones sighs, eventually, looking deep into my eyes. 'We're on your side yaah, we're not here to rip you off.'

This mother fucker can actually read my mind!

'Yeah man, why so tense brother,' Claude adds with a grin. 'Jones help me square tings off wid a few of der local rude-boys. Everything's cool, man.'

They can both read my mind, it's voodoo-magic shit.

'So anyway Dee,' he cuts across Claude. 'Me and me cousin want to put on a party, just like this one.'

'Yeah?' I say, already knowing where this is going, fucking entrapment or something.

'Yaah, like this, but much bigger. A massive, one-off, never to be repeated monster rave. We know how much money is to be made with this shit, I reckon a couple of million if we do it right. Just look at tonight, easy money, a piece of piss,' he says, animated and energised and enthusiastic, talking at a million miles an hour. 'Listen yaah, we got serious connections who are up for it too, but we need your help buddy, sorting out the promotions and all that, being the public face of it, yaah. The punters love you, fuck knows why, but to them you are the fucking man, yaah.'

'It's true Dee, this is big time now,' Claude grins.

Nodding along, I know I don't want to get involved in something so high profile, and definitely not with this meat head ex-police-potential-deep-undercover-police from the Brixton riots. No chance. 'Listen, I appreciate the offer, but it's not for me, I really can't do it justice,' I say delicately, not wanting to offend either of them.

The smile on Jones' face falls and he looks towards Claude.

'T'cha, don't be a dick,' Claude spits, all up-tight with a do-what-I-say-or-else tone to his voice.

'Claude, Claude, easy my man,' Jones steps in with a reasonable tone. 'It's okay, it's cool yaah. He just needs some time, don't yaah Dee?'

I nod, like a sap.

'That's the ticket, just needs to think it all through, yaah. Take his time to see what a wonderful opportunity this is.'

I nod again, like a pussy-hole little kid.

'Tell you what,' Jones says, nodding me along. 'How's about I come see you in a week or so yaah, see how you're feeling about it all then.'

'Yeah, alright,' I shrug. I'll have told him anything for him to leave without robbing me or giving me a beating.

Without counting, I roughly split the cash into three. Claude grabs his share, the biggest share by the way, and stuffs it into a dark blue coin bag then the inside of his black leather jacket. Him and Jones share a glance, rise together while both giving me a death-glare before heading back out of the door. An hour or so later, I usher the last of the punters out and pay the deejays and bar-girls. Skyrocket and his sound-man mates arrive at lunchtime, pack their stuff away, collect their cash and do one too. The more I think about it, the more gutted I am Claude put me in that situation with Jones, and, even worse, it looks like he and Jones are in league together. I can't go back to his flat, can't face seeing him so I head over to Tottenham and see Marlon, hopefully stay with him for a few days, keep my head down and think things through. I love staying with him, his flat's clean and tidy, his bird even tidier, and a top notch cook too. The best thing is spending time with him, seeing how he lives and what an awesome man he's turning into. I'm so proud of him, so happy for him. At the same time, I'm so regretful, so disgusted and so sad about what happened.

The following Wednesday I decide to face the music and go see Claude. On the way I stop by here, this flat, otherwise known as the tomb of the ghost that was once Devon Walters. Door's still locked. Looking through the window, I can't see any sign of life. Not sure why, but I decide there and then I need my own space and need to get out from under Claudes claustrophobic and suffocating feet. I walk the mile or so down to Deptford market and pick up a new lock. Get back here and kick the door before fetching the toolbox from under the stairs, the one Pops gave me when I first left home. I mend the doorframe best I can and fit the new lock, not a bad job, even though I say so myself.

After that, I go see Claude.

CLAUDES FLAT
MAPLE HOUSE, ADOLPHUS STREET
DEPTFORD, LONDON
APRIL 1989

Deep breath, I walk in and he's busy snorting coke and lifting weights. Sweaty and pumped, he's groining and straining but when he sees me, his face morphs into a wide grin. Arms open, he gives me a hug, yep, a big manly-man hug. 'Where you been mate, not seen you since the warehouse, didn't know where you were,' he says, holding me by the shoulders and staring into me.

Surprised, looks like he actually cares. 'Went to see Marlon yeah, stayed with him for a bit.'

'Safe man, safe,' he says before tapping a small mountain of coke onto the back of his hand and snorting it up super quick before picking up his dumb-bells.

'So anyway, I've been thinking I should sort myself out.'

'Alright,' he grunts, straining his biceps.

'Yeah man, I've been back to Shirley's flat. Reckon I'll move back over there. Give you your flat back,' I laugh, trying to lighten the mood.

'Makes sense Dev, got to sort yourself out, right.'

I can't believe it. I thought he'd be please-don't-go needy, or indeed angry that I'm leaving him. I take my normal seat next to the weights bench and skin up a very tasty joint while he continues to snort and pump.

'So, what's the score with Jones then, where's all this rave stuff come from,' I say, keeping it light.

'Oh yeah, he big time now. Reckons his cousin just got out of prison after a stretch, wants to go steady, needs some start-up cash. Wants a villa in Spain or something.'

'Sounds like a plan,' I say, and it did sound like a plan too, bank a couple of hundred then fuck off into the sunset. 'What's he in for?'

'Fuck knows, got a fourteen stretch though, out in eight for good behaviour. Stand-up guy apparently, steady job and all dat, just unlucky.'

'Right, right, yeah,' I say. Fourteen is a stretch though, you don't get that for shop lifting, do you?

'Jones says you know him,' Claude says, matter-of-fact.

'What's that?'

'Jones's cousin, you know der man.'

'Yeah, course I do.' Here we go, another Claude piss take.

'True,' he says, screwing up his face. 'Kenneth or something, worked with shit-cunt Paul in the City, back in the day.'

Time stands still as his words echo and drift away.

Kenneth?

Kenny?

Fat Ken?

Ken the bastard?

The ground beneath me shudders and shakes like in a disaster movie. I'm instantaneously transported to the top a tower block, right on the edge, a thousand feet up looking out across London. Arsehole twitching, the soles of my feet tingle as the wind rushes through me. Frozen, I want to move but can't. Have to get out of here and off the edge, don't care where, anywhere but here.

Shit man, Kenny?

Who threatened Paul?

Kenny?

Who bullied Paul into giving him a wholesale amount of coke?

Kenny?

Who we fitted up and grassed on?

Kenny?

Who we got arrested and sent down?

Holy shit.

KENNY!

I hadn't thought about him for ages, years.

Truth be told, I'm ashamed of what happened.

Story goes like this…

Leaving school, Paul goes to work at his Dad's firm in the City of London, a finance company or something. Paul would tell me stories of him buying companies on the verge of bankruptcy, then selling-off their assets and plundering their pension funds, (the mother fucking crook), and in the process making shed-loads of cash. Pauls old man is an old-school self-made guy and wants Paul to do a proper apprenticeship, learn the business from the bottom up. He doesn't want Paul to be seen as a daddies-boy nor a lazy fuck who just swans about collecting a monthly pay cheque waiting for his inheritance. Paul's placed with a junior broker to learn the ropes, who turns out to be the lumbering piece of shit, Kenneth. I first met Kenny in nineteen-eighty, I think, at a wine bar near Saint Pauls Cathedral. Paul promised to introduce us to some fine city-slicker girls if we met him after work one day. Kenny's there too with a few other spivs, talking yeah-yeah-yeah about all manner of bullshit. Kenny latches on to me and bombards me loads of questions about being from Brixton and about drugs. He gets it into his mind I can sort him out with wholesale cocaine and starts bugging me to hook him up with our "dealer". The idiot, he must think he's an extra on Starsky and Hutch or something. I give him the brush off, but for days after he's bugging Paul at every opportunity about hooking him up, hassling him and threatening to hurt him. Weeks later, it ends up with him and Paul fighting in the marble-tiled toilets at their offices near Liverpool Street. Paul, as usual, gets a pasting and Kenny threatens to get us fitted up by his "mates in the Police" if we don't sort him out.

Yeah man, I get it now, Jones is his "mate" in the Police.

Super, well, he's up for steaming in and hacking into Kennys head with his favourite tool, his "baby", his two-foot machete, but, after much deliberation we conclude this will lead to either serious gang-warfare-bloodshed, or intense scrutiny by the Police. Instead, we hatch a plan where we get hold of some coke, deliver it around to Kennys flat, then snitch to the Police who, acting on information received, will raid his flat and lock him away. I especially like the irony that he'll be getting done by "my" mates in the Police. It all make complete sense, but the plan gnaws at me, from getting hold of an ounce of coke from a taxi-cab office in dirty Bermondsey through to dropping it off at Kennys flat to grassing to the Police. When we drop it off, funny, Kenny tries to rip us off, refusing to pay what he called street prices. An argument ensues and he breaks Pauls nose with a tasty head-butt and threatens us with a shotgun, the nutter. On the way home, we stop at a pay-phone near Tower Bridge, dial Scotland Yard and do our civic duty, snitching on the fat mother-fucker. Early hours of the next morning his flat gets raided, Flying Squad, sub-machine guns in the face, get-on-the-floor-get-on-the-floor screams. They find the coke, along with knives and coshes plus a few grams of amphetamine and an shotgun with several rounds of ammunition. Six months on remand, he eventually gets sent down, Paul gets promotion and we don't think twice about him, the mug. The shotgun added ten-years to his sentence, the stupid dickhead.

As usual, echoes from my past rear-up and bite me on the arse. Kenny must have known we got him locked away, probably disclosed at the trail, and now wants his revenge. And, as a crazy twist of fate, his cousin is Jones, the head-case who put Super away all them years ago?

Fuck.

This can't be a coincidence, it must be orchestrated and planned, a long-term, deep undercover thing. In fact, this feels way beyond Police, it must be a Government or military thing. Yeah man, the establishment want to take back the streets, reclaim the urban wasteland and build flash new houses and flats and shopping centres and corporate headquarters, generating even more wealth for themselves, (the greedy mother-fuckers). Yeah, makes sense. They'll rid the country of the scourge of hooliganism, the plague of Ecstasy driven illegal parties sweeping the nation. Yeah man, they'll put us commoners back in our place, render us easy to command and control.

Wow, deep man…

Sitting next to me, Claude puts his overgrown arm around my shoulder. I'm Jesus, he's my cross. Bewilderment spreads across my face as confusion fills my eyes. I can't believe it. A fucked-up twist of fate, I'm somehow locked into this path, this particular course of events, this life. No matter what I do, no matter what choices I make, it's all inevitable. I would have always ended up here, linked somehow to Claude then to Jones and then, eventually, back around to Kenny.

'It's okay brother, dey on a level,' Claude whispers softly.

'Yeah?' I say, not believing him for one minute.

'Hear-me-nah-man, I don't trust dem one-hundred percent, dat much true, but I don't trust no man one-hundred percent,' Claude says, anti-empathy oozing from his voice.

Charming. What am I, chopped liver?

'But, I do know they are all about the money, all about starting over. Dey don't have time for revenge, Dey got bigger shit to deal with.'

Sounds reasonable, maybe all them years in prison is enough to turn Kenny, teach him the error of his ways. I don't believe it though, nah, I remember his face that night in his flat when we dropped the coke off. Closing my eyes, I see his warped, fucked up fat face laughing at us, laughing at me, revelling in the chaos, loving the conflict. After eight years locked up there's no way on earth he's willing to forgive and forget. Me, I'd want revenge, big time. Dirty, evil, sadistic revenge, blood on the carpet, guts on the stairs, skulls on lamp-posts and body parts through letter boxes. Tales of the atrocities will be front-page news and feature length News at Ten coverage. Yeah man, I'd yearn for Al Capone and Elliott Ness levels of revenge, Kane and Able grudges and payback on a biblical scale. We'll be living in night-of-the-living-dead-zombie-land, damn, it'd be nuclear winter revenge, the maimed and deformed survivors will write folk-songs about it in a hundred years time. Claude is persistent though. Eventually, he convinces me to meet with Jones to at least hear him out. He said a flat 'no' is likely to piss him and Kenny off, and nobody wants to piss him off. It don't feel right, not by a long shot, but, if they are on a level, I'll maybe make some serious cash and get some of my life back. If not, and they want carnage, at least I'll know and maybe have some time to prepare. Either way though, I'm fucked. A week or so later…

GREASY-SPOON CAFE
HIGH STREET
WOOLWICH, LONDON
MAY 1989

Speeding east along the Thames towards Woolwich, I'm sitting in the passenger seat gazing across the Thames towards East London. Claude has a dark grey Ford RS Cosworth. God dam, it's a nice car and unbelievably fast, with massive air intake grills on the bonnet and a big kitchen table of a wing on the back. It's aggressive, mean and moody, a car version of Claude. Before we set off, knowing I'm biting my nails nervous, he takes me around to the boot and lifts the spare wheel. He's smiling and nodding to himself while I'm looking at an ornate, old-fashioned shotgun, It's barrels are sawn down with a load of black-gaffer tape wrapped around it's stubby handle, with maybe a dozen red cartridges dotted around next to it. He tells me not to worry, if things get out of hand, he'll sort them out. Fucking hell, "not to worry", gangsters and guns, why need a gun if they were, as he said, "on a level?" I'm worried, more than worried, scared shitless truth be told. The drive to Woolwich takes about twenty minutes. We park in the leisure centre car park and head for a greasy spoon café on the other side of the roundabout. After a few agonising minutes, Jones walks in, looks all around before plonking himself right beside me, opposite Claude.

Wall, table, Jones then me.

I'm trapped.

SHIT.

Jones has a kind of power, an energy, like Darth Vader or something. Easily six-foot-six and at least eighteen stone of muscle, he's no neck with veins-popping out of his temples and sweat oozing out of his sunbed perma-tan. 'Thanks for coming,' he says, slow and low. 'Claude tells me you're nervous, yaah?'

I can't work him out. Someone so powerful and clearly crazy, talking in an almost caring way. Man, he freaks me out. I look up at him like I'm a tiny little kid and he's the school headmaster giving me a lecture about running in the corridor.

'Listen Dee, Kenny don't want you dead, yaah.'

'Nah?' I say, watching his reaction.

Staring deep, he weighs me up. 'Listen, you know what I've got here?' he says, patting the inside pocket of his jacket. 'Browning nine-mill yaah, 13 rounds, army issue. I can off you right here, right now, if I really want to.'

Trying not to look, his stare's like a tractor-beam, drawing me in like some kind of Jungle Book giant cobra snake with cartoon kaleidoscopic eyes. I look at Claude, what does he think of this? This "getting out of hand" yet? Fuck me, he's sitting there sipping his tea and chomping on his bacon sandwich, calm and relaxed, like we're talking about last nights' television.

'Big-boy-Cee aint gunna help,' Jones says, more forceful now. 'What you did was a fucking cunts trick. Down to me, you'd be long gone, head cut off and fed to the pigs on my uncle Tommy's farm in Suffolk.' Looking up, his eyes tell me he can see it playing out inside his warped mind. 'Yaah,' he chuckles. 'I wanted to do you when I first met you over at Claudes flat, you remember?'

Yeah, I remember. I remember being freaked out, knowing something's not right.

'But, lucky for you, prison changes a man, fresh perspective yaah. All Ken wants now is some decent wedge to start afresh, get his life back together. You understand what I'm saying?'

I actually do understand, of course I do. I want the same, a fresh start, get my life back on track, get Shirley back.

'But, you fucking snake, you owe him, right.' Jones spits in a stage whisper, saliva flying from his mouth as he over-pronounces every word.

'I know I do,' I sigh the sigh of a condemned man. He's right, of course he is. 'I'm sorry about all that, but I've got fuck all, nothing.'

'Bollocks,' he says, killing me with his eyes. 'We know what you've been up to yaah. The radio station, the raves, the loot.' Moving super-quick like a ninja on speed, he grabs me around the back of the head and pulls me into the centre of the table. 'If you don't help us, have no doubt, we'll fucking destroy everything about you,' he growls, anger ripping through his whispers.

I nod as the opening bars to Mike Oldfield's "Tubular Bells" play in the background of my mind.

He smiles his sadistic smile. 'Yaah, your bird and your kid down in dirty Bermondsey, throats slit, gone. Your folks over in Brixton, tortured and chopped up. Your little brother and his tasty-fit bird in Tottenham, she's raped, he watches, both skulls caved in, gone. Your homo-mate from the riot, the one I did good and proper, the one doing life for the Deep River thing, stabbed to fuck in the showers. Your flat in Greenwich, petrol bombed. Your folks place, Railton Road, blown to fuck-up, gas explosion yaah. Everything about you and your life, gone. You fucking understand me, boy?'

'Easy Jones, he gets da picture, don't you?' Claude interjects, eventually.

'Do ya bread-bin, do you understand where I'm coming from you fucking dirty snake?'

I nod.

'We'll wipe every trace of you from the face of the fucking earth,' he seethes, releasing me and sitting back in his seat, smiling like the mother-fucking bastard he is.

Announcing he'll kill my whole family, yet, he sits there completely calm and mellow, arms folded and smiling. Adrenalin surging, heart beating out of my chest, I struggle not scramble over him and do one. 'Yeah, I understand,' I nod in a scared whisper.

'Don't worry yaah, it'd be easier to kill you and dump you in a fucking hole,' Jones laughs. 'Like I say, if we want you gone, you'd be long gone. Make no fucking mistake.'

'Alright, alright, calm der fuck down,' Claude says, putting the remains of his bacon sandwich down, dabbing the corner of his mouth with a napkin as if this is a polite business meeting. 'Let's have it straight, what he did was out of order, but he understands dat now, don't you Dee?'

Not looking up I nod.

I feel ashamed.

I never told Claude about any of this. He'll judge me and I don't need no judging by him.

'How about dis den,' Claude suggests, positivity etching through his voice. 'We start small, another warehouse first.'

Practicalities? Stomach sliced open, my intestines are resting on the table and he's taking about plans.

'We're not interested in a couple of grand,' Jones spits.

'Me neither, fook dat,' Claude says, confidently, almost signing. 'But, we got to build a lickle bit of trust, dat right. Need to understand how we all work together.'

Staring at Jones, I wait for a sign, a twitch of acceptance.

Chewing on a wasp, I can see the cogs whirring inside his thick skull. 'Right, let me be crystal-fucking-clear, yaah, we don't give a shit about the music or the punters or any of that bullshit. All we care about is the money. Do what you need to do to put the rave on and we'll keep out of the way, but, make no mistake, by the end of the summer, we want the big one sorted yaah.'

Claude nods.

I join in.

'Another warehouse by month end then,' Jones continues. 'We'll sort the location, probably our place in North London, Edmonton. We own the place, it'll be fully legal.'

Looking down into the table, I nod even though every part of me screams get out, leave, fuck off back to Spain or somewhere. But, some sick part of me keeps me here, thinking about somehow playing this to my advantage.

'Alright, nice one,' Jones smiles, his spirits lifted. 'Right then. Kenny wants to meet yaah, clear things up, get it over and done with so we can all move on.'

'What der fuck Jones?' Claude splits.

'He's over East, waiting at the other side of the Ferry.'

I get it, all the bullshit about monster raves and warehouses and building trust is just to lure me into a false sense of security, making sure I go willingly to face my fate, the sadistic wankers. They must take some kind of sick pleasure out of it, or it's some type of Police psychological tactic. Claude goes with the flow though, relaxed and at ease the with the situation whereas, I'm completely shitting myself knowing in a matter of minutes I'll meet my fate. We walk the dead-man's walk across the round-a-bout towards the small jetty leading to the Ferry. I hate the ferry, only ever been on it once. It's a rickety old piece of shit relic from the nineteen-twenties and only ever used by lorries that can't fit through the Blackwall Tunnel. Bouncing like a bad-man, showing zero fear, I glance toward Claude and he's doing the same. We're both cool-in-the-gang super cool, taking it literally in our stride like we're back in the day, back in Brixton, back on the Frontline running errands for Crissy. Jones though, he's pensive, nervous even, maybe he's getting cold feet, maybe he expects some form of resistance, maybe he planned to do it in the café but thought twice, too many witnesses or something.

We get to the jetty and I watch the ferry as it slowly sets off from the north side, spinning around then heading across the Thames to take me to my destiny. As it approaches, I play out a series of sick scenarios in my head ranging from long-lost friend let's let bygones-be-bygones bear-hugs through to full on decapitation with a three-foot long samurai katana. Boarding the Ferry, I'm in between Claude, who's in front, and Jones, who's behind. I look towards the skipper or deckhand or whoever the fuck it's ushering the other foot passengers on and scream "help-me" with my eyes. Looking sideways, he doesn't know what I'm on about though.

Nobody knows.

I'm fucked.

WOOLWICH FERRY NORTH SIDE
PIER ROAD
CANNING TOWN, LONDON
MAY 1989

Docking at the north side, we disembark and make our way along the approach road as the cars drive off and stream by into the East End. Heading toward a dark green Range Rover, my stomach does a double back-flip. Getting closer, a lump of a bloke climbs out, stretches his back and pushes his arms out wide. Heavier than before, he's weathered and hardened with even fairer hair than I remember, beginning to thin-out at the front too. He looks old, much older than me even though we must have been similar ages, man, prison hasn't been kind to him. No emotion, he stands there looking through me with dead eyes. Slowing, we stop maybe ten feet from him. As the last car pulls away from the Ferry and speeds away, an eery silence descends on the now deserted approach road. The sky's getting dark and the wind's getting up, dust and litter dance around our ankles as we stare at each other like in an old spaghetti western movie or something.

Then, silence.

Waiting for the other to blink first, the tension kills me.

After an age, he holds out his hand, fingers straight, thumb up. His face doesn't change, he's dead inside, and I'm dying right here on the outside. I step forward, raise my hand horizontal to his, then, we shake. 'Been a long time, Devon,' he says slowly, then, ding-dong, stars spin around my head as I stumble to the left before he yanks my hand backward, stopping me from falling. He's landed one on me, the fat fuck, and I never saw it coming. Another blow crashes into my head and I know this is it. I don't fight back, I know what I did was, as Jones so eloquently put it, "a cunts trick". After Ashley, Paul and my princess Shirley, I am a cunt so I'll just let fate play out and allow destiny wash over me. If today's the day I die, then so be it. Submitting to him, I wait for him to put me out of my misery. Yeah, I get it, I'm a whores gaping pussy waiting to be fucked by his ex-convict cock. Well, bring it on, end it once and for all.

Why fight fate?

Can you even fight it, if it is indeed fate?

Grabbing me by the throat, he throws me onto the bonnet of the car. He's nearly on top of me now, his face in mine, evil-anger and eight years of hate in his eyes. 'I'll fucking kill you,' he screams, gripping my throat even tighter, forcing his thumb into my adams-apple, his mouth touching my ear. 'You owe me, you owe me big time,' he whispers before releasing me.

Coughing, I cradle my neck. Stinging, I feel my right eye swelling. 'I'm sorry,' I say, like I'm a little boy apologising to the head teacher. What do you say to someone you've fitted up for an eight stretch? I am sorry though, I really am, I'm ashamed of what I've done. Sure, he's a dickhead who deserves it, but, a snitch is a snitch, and, on that night, I was the biggest snitch of all time. Kenny lumbers back to the car, opens the door and looks back. 'All I wanna do is make some serious cash, right,' he yells. 'After that, you can fuck off back to Jamaica or wherever the fuck you're from. Strictly business yeah.' He and Jones climb in, engine roars, wheels spin and they're gone.

On the Ferry back…

Claude's upbeat, positive and decidedly jovial, says he wasn't sure how it would pan out. What the fuck? He knew about the meet, knows what they're up to? I'm supposed to be his mate, his long-time friend, the one who saved him from the Snakehead oblivion and he knowingly puts me in that position, unsure if they wanted to kill me there and then. Confused, my mind's a puzzle. Life's quickly turning into a spider's web, knotted and tangled and nasty and evil. Yeah man, I'm the fly stuck in the middle waiting for the big hairy eight-legged bastard called Kenny to come along and bite my head off. More worrying than the threat of Kenny is my lack of fight, my submission to him, my acceptance of fate. Claude don't give a shit about any of it though, that's for sure. I don't know him no more, he's a completely different person to the person I knew back in Brixton or the broken man me and Shirley took in after the Snakehead war. The Claude I know, Crissy's right-hand man on the Frontline, is long-time dead and friendship clearly means jack-shit to him. As the Ferry crashes through the waves on our journey back to South London, Claude goes into hyper-drive about the next rave. His jib-jabbery words fade into the Thames as I begin thinking about a way out. If their "monster" rave is going to be as big as they said, then there will indeed be mountains of cash. Maybe I can settle my debt with Kenny, make a tidy sum and get out of this madness, then somehow get Shirley back. Driving back from Woolwich, we get talking about the next party. We agree to use the same format as our first "mental logic" event, Marlon and his deejay mates, Skyrocket and his sound-system buddies, meeting points, magical mystery tours, everything. We call it, "Logical Progression, a new beginning," a bit poncey for my liking, but, it's Claude's idea and I can't be bothered arguing with him. Kenny and Jones keep their word and keep out of it, apart from the cash side, of course. They control that side alright, posting meatheads all over the entrance and in the cash counting office. They have the Ecstasy and coke dealing locked down too, banking a tidy sum no doubt. The party itself is a pretty good, all things considered. The venue turns out to be decent, and we don't get any attention from either the Police or any of the local gangs. Most importantly the gruesome twosome keep their distance, as they said they would. At the end of the night we split the cash three ways, a third for expenses, a third for them and a third for me and Claude to split between us, about three thousand each.

A couple of days later we met up with them again.

THURROCK SERVICES
JUNCTION 30, M25 MOTORWAY
ESSEX
LATE JUNE 1989

Kenny and Jones are already there when we arrive. Me and Claude sat directly opposite them, adjacent to the windows, overlooking the motorway. Kenny's vague and distant, quiet too, whereas Jones, on the other hand is on fire. Rabbiting on, he tells us he's sorted a venue for "the big one", a small place called Halstead, rural Essex, (thank god they stopped referring to it as the "monster-rave"). I've never heard of Halstead or wherever the fuck-stead. Jones says it's a couple of miles past Braintree, maybe thirty miles outside London. He goes on to say it's a farm out in the middle of nowhere, says it can take up to twenty thousand punters, maybe more. Shit, that big, that is indeed a monster. I heard the stories about some public school-boy promoter doing warehouse raves out in Kent, at an old airfield hangar with eight thousand punters, and ten thousand punters in some in old movie studios in West London. The thought of putting on an outdoor rave, in the countryside, with twenty thousand punters is daunting and way bigger than anything else, ever. Kenny and Jones don't seem one bit worried though, in fact, they appear to be revelling in it, enjoying it even. I can tell these guys are deadly serious and, as Claude suggests, are all about the cash. I'm just an insignificant part of their big plan, which is fine by me. They want to do their rave on the Bank Holiday weekend at the end of August, which means we only have a couple of months to get it sorted. With the lack of time and the sheer scale of their ambition, this has the potential to go seriously wrong. Man, if it does go tits-up and those two mentalists don't make what they expect to make, I'm dead. As much as I hate myself for how I hurt Shirley, I'm not ready to die, but, at the same time, I don't much want to live either.

After explaining it in minute detail, Jones suggests we go and have a look at the venue, there and then. There and then is the last thing I want to do, nah, no way. The Essex countryside's a notorious burial ground for failed gangster-wannabe's and plebs who get too close to the flame, plebs just like me. Claude, of course, is totally up for a day-trip in the countryside, jumps up to follow Jones out to the car park. I look at Kenny who shrugs before following Jones and Claude.

Oh crap.

We follow their Range Rover for maybe forty minutes north through Braintree and out into the Essex countryside. I tell Claude I'm worried about being alone with them in the secluded middle of fuck-knows-where, and we should stay in a public space like the motorway services. He tuts and tells me to stop being a pussy, to man-up and go with the flow while there's big money to be made. He goes on to say if they try anything, he'll deal with them. As a precaution, still driving, he gets me to climb through to the back seat and rummage through the trap-door thing into the boot to fetch the shotgun. This is quickly turning into a big-boy game, and I can't turn back, even if I want to.

OLD FARM
SUDBURY ROAD, HALSTEAD
ESSEX
LATE JUNE 1989

Eventually, we pass through a quaint little village, which I presume is Halstead, and, about a mile further down the road we slow and turn right onto a dirt track. Up the hill and we stop just before the top. Fuck, a deserted track in the middle of nowhere, shit man, this is it. Playing it out in my head, I see us dragged from the car, hoods over heads, hands tied behind our backs and several un-traceable bullets shot into the back of our heads. Thirty seconds later, the crazy twins are dancing around on our deformed remains, Jones crying with laughter and Kenny has his cock out taking a piss on my lifeless body...

Break lights shining bright red, I'm jerked from my day-nightmare and see the Range Rover glide to a stop. We do the same but Claude keeps the engine running, I can tell he's as tense and nervous even if he doesn't show it. Shit, they're getting ready, loading their guns, waiting for re-enforcements. Looking over my shoulder back down the dirt track, I can't see any sign of assassins creeping from the tree-line, or a back-up car approaching from the main road.

So, what are we waiting for?

Heart beating fast, this is it.

Climbing out, they wave us over. No shotguns, no assassins, just both of them waving as they head over the top of the hill. Engine off, Claude gets out and I follow. Approaching the apex of the hill, I can see for miles and miles, the view is amazing. From the top, the hill rolls down to a flat plateau, then back up a steeper but smaller banked-hill on the far side. On the right, a little picture-book farmhouse and on the left, luscious green fields stretching into the distance towards a small wood. I hate to admit it, but it's a great venue, almost a purpose-built amphitheatre. As Jones suggested, it is indeed a big sit and can easily accommodate way more than twenty thousand, more like forty or fifty thousand, it's truly massive. Thoughts jump to practicalities, it'll need a truly massive sound system and lighting rig. Skyrocket and his sound-system pals won't be enough for this one, nah, professional help is needed. Maybe it's the warm, early summer breeze, the relief of not being killed, the venue or the herbs I've smoked on the journey here, but I'm feeling good about this, excited almost. Inside my head, I've already transformed the area into a parallel universe and the world's biggest and baddest rave. Yeah man, a big old stage on top of the smaller hill and a dance floor on the plateau with more dancers on the banks of the hill we're standing on. Yeah man, middle of the night, pitch black, the mighty sound system booms as bright green lasers scan across the gyrating silhouettes dancing in front of a glowing neon background. A wave of excitement washes over me, and although delicious, I hate it. Must keep my distance, keep some perspective, maintain an emotional detachment from this and them, especially them. But, me being me, I'm trapped in a vortex of exciting, exquisitely beautiful deadly danger. It takes me an hour or so to stroll around the site while the loony-tune twins and Claude sit in the Range Rover smoking resin and snorting coke, the dirty fat fucks. At the other side of the small banked hill, (where, inside my mind, the stage is), is a wide meadow, leading to a wood or forest or something at the bottom. It's lovely and beautiful and quiet and serene. Closing my eyes, just for a second, pictures of Shirley flood my mind. We're here, enjoying a picnic in the meadow, with scones and jam and strawberries and strong-sweet tea. My boy's here too, rolly-pollying in the long grass while me and her share loving smiles and delicate kisses. My heart physically aches with sorrow and pain and regret.

Opening my eyes, I see the Range Rover in the distance and instantly feel empty and hollow and disgusting. Walking back I find Claude and Jones arm-wrestling over the bonnet as Kenny, sporting aviator sunglasses and looking super-cool, leans casually leans against the door. 'What ya' reckon then?' he asks, straightening himself out.

'It's alright Ken, yeah. Actually, it's fucking perfect.'

'Good stuff, champion,' he smiles.

'What about the farmhouse,' I ask, pointing over.

'Don't worry about that my man. Bunged farmer-Gilles five-grand to take a long weekend in the south of France. Says we'll have the run of the place, but, we can't go anywhere near the house. We'll need to make sure no fucker messes with it.'

'We can't use it as an office, to count the cash?'

'He said leave it, yaah. Take a fucking hint rude-boy,' Jones spits, slamming Claudes arm down into the bonnet.

'Easy-nah Jones,' Claude protests, rubbing his wrist. 'What the fuck man it won't be a problem. We'll fence it off and I'll put a couple of my men on sentry duty.'

'Look at you two, already working it all out? Good work guys, good work,' Kenny says with a warm smile.

I look deep into him. If he wasn't such a dickhead and

clearly mentally deranged, he'd be a good leader of men, a general in the army or captain of industry or something. Jones, now sweating like a dirty pig says he has a 'present for me', oh fuck. He fetches an ordnance survey map from the back seat and we stand around as he spreads it over the bonnet. We agree Claude will sort security, I'll look after sound, lighting and promotions and they will sort the local Police and, more importantly, the local gangs. After a short but heated argument, we agree they will supply all the Ecstasy and coke on the night, with Claudes men punting it out. We'll split the gate money, after expenses, three ways, just like before, and they'll share the drug money between them and Claude. Sounds reasonable, very reasonable in fact, way too reasonable actually. Listen, I'm no mug, neither are you, and we both know I won't see a penny of the cash, if indeed I made it out of this madness in one piece. I know, right there, I'll have to out-clever these clever bastards.

Driving back to London, we sit in silence and I find myself staring into the mid-distance as the blur of random colours zoom by. I try working through all the angles and options, trying and find a way out. Meanwhile, Claude sits there chewing a wasp, gripping the steering wheel like it's a scrawny neck he's draining the life out of. As we approach the docks in the East End, a couple of miles before the Blackwall Tunnel, he breaks the silence. 'You know what,' he says. 'I reckon we skank dose mother fuckers and take der cash, all of it.'

He's thinking of ripping them off? Sure, I'm looking for an angle, looking to make something out of it, getting out in one piece, but ripping them off? Nah, no way, too dangerous.

'Shoot dem both, dump der bodies in the woods, pants around their ankles and dildos up their arses.'

'Eh?'

'Police will put it down to rival gangs and dat Essex-gangster bullshit,' Claude says, drifting into a giggle.

'What?' I say, not believing what I've just heard.

'Dey got enough enemies, nobody will be surprised,' he smiles. 'Anyway, dey got it coming yeah, I haven't forgotten about Jones and his part in der riots. Cristobal got deported because of dat fucking fool.'

Damn, seems he's thought about this a fair bit, this is no spur of the moment plan. He hardly ever talks about Brixton or his previous life on the Frontline and never about Crissy. It's like the Brixton-Claude and the pumped-up geezer-Claude are completely different people. I'm glad he never opened that particular Pandora's box though, shit man, if he lost it, it'd be like a nuclear bomb detonation with, no doubt, my head splitting like an atom and my blood as the mushroom cloud.

'Serious tings you chatting brother. Careful what you wish for,' I say, hopefully putting a lid on his ambition.

Not responding, he grips the steering wheel harder.

I'll have to watch him, don't need him starting no war with these two fools where we all wind up dead, although, a war might be the diversion I need to grab some cash and slip away without anyone noticing. Can it be that easy, that simplistic?

I got to think this shit through.

Next day Claude and I mess about with the map, planning where the stage should go, the car parks, the toilets and all that. We use match boxes and cigarette cartons it to signify where the stage, main gate and speaker towers will be positioned. Takes an hour or so, but we eventually agree the layout. Nipping down to Deptford market, I get some felt-tip pens and a ruler and draw all over the plan. It looks the dog's bollocks, professional too. Claude reckons he'll need a hundred or so men and a couple miles of fencing to fully secure the site. Said he'll hire a couple of security firms he trusts to do general crowd control, while his own men run the important stuff, the entrance gate and the cash box. The last thing any of us want is for some other gang of villains to storm the place and rob us blind. Meanwhile, I'm struggling to think about a decent sound and lighting rig so Marlon asks around at a few of the clubs where he deejays, and a friend of a friend put us in touch with a company called "SLS Audio Visual." A professional firm who do stuff for the BBC and loads of commercial pop acts. I give them a call and arrange a meeting.

STADIUM LIGHT AND SOUND
INGATE PLACE
BATTERSEA, LONDON
1989

Taking about an hour to drive across London, eventually I pull into a small industrial estate and park in front of a set of closed roller shutter doors with a massive sign above, "Stadium Light and Sound." Walking through the main entrance, I'm surrounded by a load of big hairy bastard roadie types putting scaffolding together, messing with cables and taking the piss out of each other. A tidy looking girl, blonde hair and a purple baggy hooded top with a black and white Indian symbol on the front greets me with a mona-lisa bored smile and takes me through to an office out the back. Two young guys are sitting there, cool and casual and chilled-out. All first names and smiles, they introduce themselves as Tony and Phil and I introduce myself as a dance music promotor, and reel off a few of my nights including the Mental Logic and Logical Progression raves, as well as Dream FM. They say they know about the station and a couple of our deejays, Deejay Marley, (aka, Marlon, big up my man!), and Groovestar, (Marlons buddy from college). I tell them I'm planning a "dance music festival", organised in a way to mimic the current illegal parties, taking advantage of the raving culture and bring it to a mass-market, (exactly what I did in Spain, with Big Geoff). I explain the site, the lease and the agreement with the Farmer before showing them the map. Nodding away, totally getting it, Phil, short with cropped hair, has a look, (ironically), of Phil Collins about him, gets his calculator out and starts tapping away. I thought he's sorting out a price, but, turns out, he's working out the likely power needed to run a site that big and what size sound and lighting rigs we'll need. Tony, tall and lanky with long centre-parting hair gets a glossy brochure out. He starts showing me different types of stages and what he calls, "A.V." towers, basically elaborate scaffold erections with speakers and lights on. For the stage, he recommends twelves metre, with a huge spherical covered roof, along with three A.V. towers. One right in front of the stage, in the middle of the dance plateau with speakers facing in all directions, the other two at either edge of the slopping large hill, mid-way up focusing the sound inwards. Phil draws on top of the map, showing the direction of lights in yellow while Tony draws wavy lines in blue marker to show the direction of the sound. He says the natural amphitheatre will accentuate the frequencies making it sound really loud and scribbles down some kind of square-root formula to explain it, but he might have been taking Chinese for all I know. Excited and enthusiastic, they say they'll love to support our event and it'll take a few days to work out a price. Helpfully, they remind me end of August is a Bank Holiday which happens to be "peak time" for them. Yeah, yeah, I know the score, they're getting me ready for a high price, but, I'm not about to be ripped off by two cock-suckers from Battersea, I see them, see their game. Driving back here, pleased as punch with myself, feeling every part the professional big-time promoter, I catch myself smiling in the rear-view mirror. Although shitting myself and anxious about the future, I'm secretly loving it. Must keep sharp, keep my focus, seek out an angle and a way of getting out of this in one piece.

Next day, I go met Kenny and Jones at Claudes flat to talk them through the plans. They say they've squared things with the two main gangs in Essex but need to pay a "loyalty" of five percent to each. Kenny and Jones aren't about to pay ten percent to nobody, no chance, they'll be taking it for themselves. Even more bad news, the local Police are intent on playing hard-ball, demanding ten percent, apparently. Twenty percent in total, the greedy fat fucks. I know what Kenny's doing though, and I'm pretty sure he knows I know too. In reality, they'll give the gangs and the Police twenty thousand each if that and pocket the rest for themselves. Still, their elaborate bullshit makes me feel a little bit better, in that they go to the trouble of making this up when they can easily just take the cash and tell me to fuck off, or worse, just dump me in a shallow grave. Claude agrees they are indeed taking the piss, but says we don't have much choice, so best just to go with the flow, for now. "Go-with-the-flow" has quickly become his catchphrase, surprising, because normally is attitude is to kill everyone and rob everything no questions asked. His cocaine and steroid consumption has increased, and his mood swings are even more erratic, whereas I'm becoming more and more serene and steady. As chaos grows, calmness flows, and, right in the middle is me, dodging a bullet and winning this crazy game.

A week later, Tony from SLS calls, asking for my address and company registration number, to send the quote to. Always dealing cash, I never needed a formal business or anything like that, so, thinking fast, I give them Claudes security business name and his home address. Let me tell you, Claude is vexed when I tell him, says I've done it deliberately to incriminate him, threatens to kill me if any shit comes back on him. I must admit, while incrimination never crossed my mind, and it really hadn't, this is a stroke of accidental genius. He's now as deep in the shit as me, which is good. Couple of days later we receive a two-page letter from Tony and Phil on SLS letter headed paper, quoting a price of sixty thousand. Sixty thousand, sixty big ones, sixty large, damn, this is way more than I expected. The price includes the stage, towers, rigging, sound and lighting plus setup and dismantling and generators. Sixty thousand is the most I've ever paid for anything by a long, long way, it's the price of a flat around here, or a decent house in Brixton for fucks sake. The letter goes on to say a credit check on Claudes company suggests a "cash flow risk" so, they need a ten-thousand deposit within a week, and half of the balance up front before they even enter the site. God damn, thirty-five thousand up front, that is serious cash. Kenny and Jones will be seriously pissed off, thinking I'm trying to rip them off, like they are with me and their fictitious twenty percent.

I meet the gruesome twosome again a few days later. Kenny's busy totting up the finances, expenses and what we'll charge to get in. After a few minutes of head scratching and frowns, a broad smile spreads across his face. Says we stand to make three or four hundred thousand through the gate, so after expenses, that's maybe a hundred thousand each. That's without the cash him and Jones will make selling maybe ten thousand Ecstasy pills and a couple of kilos of cocaine, I reckon another hundred, maybe two hundred thousand. While Kenny's doing the sums, Jones keeps reading the SLS letter over and over, with the occasional growl and tut. None of us have that amount of cash to hand, so, playing up to his stereotype, Jones says we head over to SLS and "sort-the-little-pricks-out". I convince him they'll be straight to the Police and we'd be left with no sound system and unwanted attention from the flying-squad. After an age of wasp chewing, Kenny suggests he and Jones will stump up half the cash, but me and Claude will have to do the same. Promising Kenny we'll get it sorted, we agree to meet again in a few days time, meanwhile, Claude and I go into panic mode.

I've a couple of thousand left from the two previous raves, but most of Claudes cash is tied up by "dickhead" club owners and outstanding unpaid invoices, a large stock of cocaine due for delivery next week and, a not insignificant amount of heroin on top of his wardrobe at home. Says he's about the same as me knocking around at home, and he can lay his hands on another five or so if he calls in some debts. Even so, we're still about ten thousand light.

Later in the week I visit Dream FM, maybe get some from

them. Even though Marlon isn't there all the time, it runs like clockwork. The studio's like a mini rave-set with a few youths lounging on the old brown sofa at the back, smoking what smells like tasty weed, while, at the other end of the room, the deejay and two fit girls dance away in front of the turntables. All three of them are wide-eyed with massive grins, obviously feeling an Ecstasy rush. I know that feeling, I fucking love that feeling, I god damn yearn for that feeling. Pissing down with rain outside, I stay an hour or so, share a couple of joints before heading to Claudes to tap him up for a little bedtime brown. Pulling into the carpark outside, I spot a bright red Porsche sitting outside the stairwell.

What. The. Fuck.

CLAUDES FLAT
MAPLE HOUSE, ADOLPHUS STREET
DEPTFORD, LONDON
1989

Heart sinking, stomach does a backflip. You've guessed it, Paul, the cunt, king snake himself. Climbing the stairs, I go to knock the door, but it's already ajar. Fuck, something bad has happened, Claude never leaves his door open, never. Gently pushing it open, I quietly tip-toe in and hear murmurs of a conversation. Sounds cordial, no shouting or wailing or violence. Edging into the front room, I see him sitting on the sofa, opposite Claude smiling his highly manicured arched eyebrows.

'Hey,' he says with a smile, the cheeky cunt-bastard. Best part of a year not seeing each other, me catching him fucking my baby-mother and all he can manage is "hey".

'I had to call him,' Claude says, seeing how pissed off I am. 'We need him.'

Need him?

Fuck off.

How the fuck can Claude call him, after what he did to me? God damn, I'm upset and hurt, actually, no, I'm angry and fucked off. But, I can sort of understand why Claude called him, if I'm honest, the thought vaguely crossed my mind too. Whereas now, just looking at him sitting there makes me feel sick. Crossed legged, suited and booted with slicked back hair and a perma-tan tan, just the look of him makes me want to finish what I started when I found him and Shirley together and smash his head in then drill his highly groomed skull into the floor. My life's ruined because of him, the sharp-suit-wearing shit-cunt. I'm on my knees while he's winning at life.

Just thinking about him makes me feel like a cunt.

Why am I the cunt?

He's the fucking cunt.

10. Killer

"You want to be free, to live your life the way you wanna be. Will we live or will we die, tainted hearts heal with time. Is there still a part of you... that wants to live?"

Adam Tinley

THE FRONT ROOM
17, HAMILTON HOUSE
GREENWICH, LONDON
LATE SUMMER, 1989

Stranded in a semi-conscious no-mans land, somewhere between drowsy drunkenness and coma-level deep sleep, I lay here with one eye open. Shards of laser-sunlight chisels through the dirty grey window and ripped net curtains. Piercing my retina, the light slices through my optic nerve, but, I don't close my eye, I don't even squint, the pain's exquisite and I love it, makes me feel alive. Igniting my imagination, the sensory stimulus kick-starts my brain and the black and white retrospective dream-state inside my mind bursts with colour.

Knock. Knock.

Eyes wide, I look towards the hallway. Who the fuck? Nobody's knocked that door in months. Sitting bolt upright, looking for a tool, I scan the shit-tip that was once the front room. Eyes darting everywhere, nothing, other than broken bits of sideboard.

Shit, un-armed, weak, vulnerable.

Knock, knock-knock, knock.

Cold lino beneath my feet, I tip-toe through to the hallway and see a silhouette through the mottled glass panel running down the right-hand side of the door. Nah, can't be? Heart pounding, adrenalin racing, is it really her, after all this time? God damn, look at me, look at this place, she'll understand though, she'll realise how much I need her. Breathing deeply, I reach for the lock. This is it, get my life back, get sorted, start living again. Door opening slowly, the beautiful chorus of angels singing engulfs me as heavenly light floods into my heart. Soul lifted, joy, hope and happiness swirl around me. Staring deep into each other our thoughts merge, both replaying forgotten loves, buried regrets and wasted years. Wow, she looks good, better than ever, great even. Then, she does it, throws me the killer smile, the angelic, beautiful, heart-stopping smile. Forgiveness in her eyes, her head shyly tilts left in a Princess Diana way. Wearing the sexy blue wrap-around satin dress, falling around her breasts, I can see her vanilla-soft cleavage heaving in and out. Breathing deeply, she's excited, nervous and anxious. I can tell, I can always tell, all the madness has been worth it, like "He" said it'd be. Wearing that "Babe" perfume, the one she saves for special occasions, she smells hot, gorgeous, sexy. Gently biting her bottom lip, just at the side, she has a let's-fuck-all-day look in her eyes. For the first time in years I feel my cock swell and loins stir. God, I've missed her, I miss us, I miss me.

"Twinkle…"

Thank god, eventually come to her senses, realises I'm sorry for everything and, at the same time, realises she needs me, like I need her. I've missed her, I want to tell her I love her, tell her all the secrets I've kept from her, all the deep-dark historic skeleton's in the cupboard. I want to open up to her, merge with her, get inside her and her inside me.

"Twinkle-twinkle," the Interrogator whispers. *"Little-star?"*

No, no, no.

Fucking hell no.

Please, no. NO.

Tears fill my eyes.

It can't be. I rise and head toward the kitchen.

I was saved, for just a moment, redeemed, but now heartbroken. Turns out I'm still here, with you. When's this going to be over, when we going to be done? I want you gone, need you gone, I need peace. Can't think straight, can't think about anything else, this nightmare has to end soon. God damn, I need some brown, need something, anything to ease the pain.

"Brown?" the Interrogator says, surprise in his voice. *"It's been a week since you chased."*

A week?

"It's true bread-bin," the Interrogator says, sincerity in his voice. *"I told you getting all this out would help. Listen, you think*

I'm some type of evil mother-fucker, some type of crazy sadistic bastard?"

He's sadistic, a bastard and a cunt, but, this must be helping. A week without the brown, I can't believe it. Maybe it's not really been a week, maybe he's messing with my mind, again, like he always does. Elbows on the table, head in hands, I rub my aching temples like an Aladdin's lamp, seeking inspiration rather than wishes. Then, whizz-bang-poof-shazam, the genie delivers. The Interrogator circles me, pacing around and around while staring into me, working me out bit by bit. He places the gun onto the table, right down beside me.

What the fuck?

His first mistake.

Don't react, I tell myself.

Be cool, easy does it.

"Go on then," the Interrogator says, enticing me to be deviant, daring me to be naughty, urging me to defy him.

Maybe I can grab it, I might be quicker than him then threaten him, get him out of my head for good, or…

Kill him.

"Yeah right, as if!" the Interrogator tuts, slamming the door shut on my daydream fantasy. *"Tell me about Paul and his bright red Porsche."*

I know what he's doing, I can see it, I'm no mug. Provoking me, teasing me, making it so tantalisingly close I can taste it. Can't let him see it's affecting me though, that will hurt him even more, drive him mad, madder than me. You see, I'm in control, I have real power, I decide what stories to tell, I run tings, tings nah-run me, ya-hear!

Closing my eyes, I finger through my mental notepad stopping at the page marked "cunt."

Here we go…

Paul agrees to put-up the rest of the cash, of course he does. Strictly between him and Claude though, I'm having nothing to do with him, and I tell him as much. Even so, he can't part with his cash quick enough, claiming it's a "good investment". Investment my arse, he's the last person on earth who needs "high yield returns" on a couple of thousand, the fucking cunt. Nah, I know, and I know he knows I know, he's doing it to make amends. Yeah, I can see it in his eyes, a kind of "I'm sorry" glint but I can't be done with him, can't bring myself to get close to him. I miss him though, of course I do, friends from the first day of school, but, and it's a fucking big "but", he ripped my heart out, pissed on it then kicked it around a dirty whorehouse floor. He probably don't even get what he did, can't appreciate the pain he's put me through, nah, she's probably just another easy lay for him, another notch on his headboard of a million meaningless fucks.

Anyway, three weeks to go and I'm in promotion overdrive. As well as the standard adverts, Marlon arranges for the Dream FM deejays to mention the rave during their shows, teasing the listeners, dropping the odd hint and giving away a few not-so-secret secrets. I want to build genuine interest and real excitement, I want listeners to be chatting about it and deejays and producers gossiping about it too. I take out adverts on two other pirate stations as well, Energy FM and Moonshine. Both robbing bastard crooks, demanding best part of four hundred quid a week for an advert on the hour, every hour. Marlon sorted a great advert though and gave it to them on a cassette tape. With that "Voodoo Ray" tune as the backing track, it has an official sounding bloke putting on an American accent…

> *"Logical Progression brings you the worlds' biggest and baddest dance-music festival… Held at a purpose-built, top secret location, you'll be treated to home-grown deejays and special guests from Chicago, Detroit and New York City… Through to the break of dawn, you will be treated to podium dancers, fire-eaters, jugglers, lasers and a one-million watt bass in your face state of the art turbo-sound sound-system… Keep it locked for tickets details and meeting points."*

I get ten thousand flyers printed and drop them round the record shops in the west-end of London, I'm in full-on promotions mode, keeping busy and love it. To be honest, I'm not too bothered about the actual rave, Marlon can deal with the SLS guys and book the deejays and artists and all that. The music scene's changed over the past year, with soulful house tunes now competing with the relentless thumping electronic mish-mash "Acid" House made by young foolish or genius kids in Chicago who can't work out how to use a drum-machine or something. The cool Ibiza beach party scene has morphed into the rave scene, and that's gone mainstream. Everywhere I go, I see smiley face hooded tops and kicker-boots, dungarees and baggy pants along with centre parting curtain haircuts for the white kids and funky dreads for the brothers. Keeping my hair a bit longer, twisting it into small dreads is easy, and looks good, even if I say so myself. News of these "Acid-House" raves reaches the press, and on the television too. An evening news bulletin features some footage of a big rave held near Wembley stadium, with a reported ten thousand punters raving their tits off chanting "ahh-seeeed". The middle-aged reporter stands in foreground in a trench-coat, (a fucking trench-coat for fucks sake), with the rave raving in the background while he's rabbiting on about kids "tripping out" on Ecstasy and biting the heads off pigeons. Damn, nearly as ridiculous as your fucking trench-coat, you mug!

The week before our rave is absolutely manic. Kenny and Jones are all over us checking, double and triple checking what we're doing. "Are you sure... show me this... show me that... what if this... suppose that..." the relentless questions and queries drive me mad. Without checking with me, they get some tickets printed, the amateurish, clueless pricks. No mention of a price, no location, nothing. Just said "keep it locked to Dream FM for further details". If we're raided by our DTI friends and taken off air, we'll be fucked, more importantly, these piece of shit tickets are easy to copy with nothing to stop joe-public-punter from spending a couple of quid getting them photocopied and selling them on to his friends and their friends too. The terrible twins of doom give the, (bullshit), tickets to the record shops around London on a "sale or return" basis, which, to be fair, wasn't a bad idea. By the Wednesday before the rave, they've sold best part of eight thousand tickets and we're on course to sell all ten thousand by the weekend. With that, I know our rave's going to be massive.

As for Claude, man, he's hyper, beyond hyper actually, crazy-hyper, manic-hyper, rip-your-fucking-head-off hyper. Coked up to his eyeballs twenty-four-seven, he pulls his "team" together earlier in the week and fucks off somewhere in the countryside for what he calls a "training camp". We both know this means a blade-sharpening, red-meat eating, teeth-grinding grunt in a muddy bog to get his men ready for what they're expecting to be a war, meatheads versus the ravers. Keeps him out of my hair though which is great, but, I can't seem to get Kenny out of my mind. Every minute of every day I see him when I close my eyes and hear his voice whenever there's a silence, he haunts me, I'm obsessed with him. I keep replaying the first time I saw him after being released from prison, at the Woolwich Ferry. The way he looked at me, a tiny glint in his eye or something I cant quite put my finger on, it's a little window into his subconscious mind haunts me, I know something isn't right. After thinking things through, I decide to box Kenny off and keep Paul as far away from everything as possible. He's bad news and bad luck and I fucking hate him. I don't tell him Kenny's involved and don't tell Kenny or Jones about him neither. If they know he's involved, they'll definitely rip us off and at least give us a proper hiding, if not, something far worse.

Just when I think things are going well, Paul comes around here the Thursday before the rave making up some bullshit excuse about him looking for Claude, but, I know he knows Claude's gone into the countryside. I see him through the front door and wonder whether to answer or not but, me being me, I can't resist the temptation to take the piss. Soon as I open it, he's apologising, sincere and genuine and worthy, tears in his eyes too, the fucking sap. Tells me, on that day of days, he only went around to see Shirley to check how she and my boy were doing, and he never wanted to get involved in any domestic, especially with my missus. According to him, soon as he gets there, she breaks down crying, spilling her heart out. According to him, she tells him about what happened, about what I did to her and that she wants out, doesn't want me no more. Man, that's painful to hear, it properly hurts, especially coming from him. Can't let it show though, I simply cannot and will not allow him see how much I'm hurting. He goes on to say she invites him to stay for dinner, and he pops out to the local off-license to get a bottle of wine and some sweets for the boy, then, one thing leads to another. Yeah right, like it's a set of dominos lined up, a certain inevitability about it, it's just meant to happen? No way. Even if it is fate, you got to have some fucking self-control, yeah. You save that shit up, hurry yourself home, grab your steaming-hard cock and bang-one out with your eyes tight shut, thinking about fucking her in the mouth. What you definitely do not do is fuck your best mates' women, the mother of his child, the shit-cunt-bastard. He goes on to say when he woke up the next morning, he's not sure whether they actually fucked or not. Yeah, right, blind drunk on a couple of bottles of wine, the guy that can snort a pound of coke in a single night, the dirty lying piece of shit slag bastard. He wanted to fuck her from the off, of course he did. Yeah man, I'm out of the picture in Spain, so he moves in like a vulture, going around there to have her, that's his plan. He can't get in there quick enough, the cunt.

Staring deep into him while he's chatting crap, I remember going back into the bedroom, after all that time, with the smell of dirty, stinking, snake in the grass sex, not a drunken did-they-didn't-they fumble in the dark. He's a fucking liar, and I know he knows I know. In any case, fuck the circumstances, the fact is he fucked her which meant he fucked me in the process. Crying, he says it's been the worst time of his life, work's shit and he never wanted to fall out with me, friends from school and a whole load of sentimental crap. He stands there, tears and snot everywhere with his hand hanging out wanting to shake hands. Shit, what else can I do? Like a mug, I feel for him, so shake his limp, sweaty, cunty hand and hate myself straight away. After more tears, he says he won't come to the rave, says all he's interested in is being mates again. Eventually, when the tears dry up, he fucks off home or wherever snakes go.

He's not seeing a penny of the cash, he can fuck right off.

I love seeing him cry, gives me a sense of achievement, a feeling of real satisfaction. So, in a good mood, I spark myself a nice five-skin and muse on dark ideas, twisted, political concepts along with cunning, contorted and calculating thoughts. That's when everything falls into place, yeah man, Devious Dee in the house. I want him to hurt like I'm hurting, for him to feel the pain I feel. He's ruined my life, literally ruined it and I can't let that go, no matter how apologetic he says he is.

Nah, I'll fuck him up, just like he fucked me.

This is how I'll play it…

I'll persuade him to come to the rave, tell him it's cool, tell him I want him there just like old times, tell him we all make mistakes and life's too short to hold grudges. Then, once there, I'll give him to Kenny and Jones, yeah, just hand him over like a baby calf at a cattle market and tell them he's the shit-bag who got him an eight-stretch, not me, definitely not me. Yeah man, what a plan. Kenny and Jones will see me as the hero and I'll be saved, while cunt-face Paul will be well and truly fucked. That's right mother fucker, evil, devilish, Devious Dee's at it again, I'll stick it in him like he did with her. With a bit of luck Kenny and Jones, especially Jones, will give him a good going over while giving me a pass and hopefully a reasonably large wad of cash. Now, you have to admit, this is a proper plan. Killing two birds with one stone, if you know what I mean. Save me, by fucking him, beautiful! Kenny gets a boat-load of cash and gets his revenge on the real villain of this story, mister-slick, mister-fuck your best mates missus, mister-cunty Paul Richardson.

That's a plan and a half my friend.

Plan of the century.

THE PLAN OF ALL PLANS.

I'm pleased with myself, but, deep down inside it don't feel right, of course it don't. I've known him nearly all my life but, I'm mad, crazy mad, not thinking straight mad. I want vengeance, I need revenge, I must have my satisfaction. I realise now back then I was bitter and twisted and confused with warped and distorted thoughts. The cocaine and heroin upper-downer-rollercoaster blurs shit up, mixes realities together, somehow makes the rational irrational. Even so, my life's permanently frozen in a state of shitness while his life is sweet as a nut, roaming around the City in his Porsches and Saville Row suits with cash falling out of his arse and birds hanging off his dick. Then, I consider the very real possibility of Kenny and especially Jones might actually kill him. Sure, I want him hurt, I want him in serious pain, cuts and bruises and maybe some broken bones, but, I don't think I want him dead, or do I? Let's face it, he killed me, my life as it was anyway. He killed the handsome guy that was once Devon Walters the moment he slid into Her. If they do kill him, maybe I'll go to the Police and turn informant, queens' evidence and witness protection. Get them both locked up, get me a new identity and get therapy for my addiction too, then get Shirley back. Yeah, we can run off together along with our little boy and start again, quite literally, a new me, a new her, a new us. That's the spirit, the creative juices are flowing, this is a most excellent plan. God damn, I'm on a roll, the roll of all rolls. Yeah, if it goes tits-up, I'll become a snitch, a dirty snake in the grass, a gutter-snipe. I've done it before with Kenny in eighty-one, and that was okay, so what's the difference? At last, everything's falling into place. It's easy when you're in the right state of mind and I'm in a fuck-everyone-save-Devon state of mind.

Clarity, at last.

So, in summary, the plans of all plans sees Paul getting quite rightly fucked-up and maybe killed, Kenny and Jones thank me for the pleasure and bung me a few grand, or, get arrested and banged up for murder and I'm off sunning myself in Spain with a new identity, a bag full of loot and my beautiful princess back in my loving, never-hurt-her-again arms. Man, that's perfect, or, "perfecto" as they say on the Costa del "I'm-a-genius" Sol.

I ring Paul later and tell him I've been thinking about what he said, about when we were kids and about us not speaking. I suggest we let bygones be bygones and I want him to be there, at the rave, to share our success, for us to be mates again, just like old times. Rather helpfully, I suggest the rave will be a good opportunity to impress his City pals, just like our nights down at Bonny Boo's and the after-show fuck-fests with dirty prostitutes. Yep, yep, yepping away, he says he's been thinking about it too, and he'd love to come, he was always easy to convince. Now, I'm a piece of work, you and I both know that, but, he is the original sneaky bastard, oh yeah, you'll see. Tells me he's been thinking that with the likely sums of money involved, it's sure to attract "unsavoury gangster types", (he talks like nowadays.) Says Claude and his men might not be able to deal with it, so perhaps we need some additional protection. I literally laugh out loud, he obviously has no idea what a monster Claude has become. However, rather than suggesting we hire some ex-SAS or Navy-Seal mercenary types to protect us, he suggests we invite some newspaper reporters along, maybe a television film crew too. He says cameras on us, the rave organisers, will be the best deterrent and scare off any villains from doing us harm. The press are all over the illegal parties right now, so no doubt will be totally up for it. He goes on to say he knows a mate of mate on Fleet Street who can hook us up.

Damn, that's clever.

Funny, there's me trying to work out who'll be heavy enough to deal with Claude and the looney tune twins, while he's scheming with the press. To be fair, his plan sounds like a good idea, in fact, the more I think about it, the more I think it's a blinding idea, and a useful add-on to my plan of all plans. I'll cling onto the press gang while ensuring he gets lost in the sea of punters, then, with my help, he'll be found by Kenny and Jones who will royally fuck him up. The press guys will be my alibi with physical evidence I'm not involved in any dodgy shit, and definitely not involved in any beatings or killings or drugs. Nah, I'm just some naive Joe putting on a party, hoodwinked by a gang of utterly despicable villains.

A genius plan, I surprise even myself.

Mastermind, University Challenge?

I'll shit em!

With my devious-genius planning, everything's set and the inevitability of our combined fates sealed. Right there, the beginning of my end had started. Safe to say, the fate-train from hell has begun it's long and tortuous journey and I'd bought a non-returnable one-way ticket.

Day before the rave...

I wake up early to get up to the venue pronto. The SLS boys will be there mid-morning to start setting up, Kenny and Jones will be there too, no doubt lording it over everyone, checking, double and triple checking everything. We plan to sleep at the site ready for the big day tomorrow so pack the car up with a quilt, pillow and a change of clothes. Takes over an hour to get up there so I listen to Dream FM for as long as I can before the signal fades into garbled white noise. Marlon brought in a high-powered transmitter built by geeky David to boost our range, but Halstead's in deep countryside and fucking miles away. I get a signal until about Romford, so figure we have about a twenty-mile radius, taking in most of London. Sweet.

OLD FARM
HALSTEAD, ESSEX
AUGUST, 1989

After winding through the great British countryside for ages, I bring the motor to a slow and steady stop near the top of the dirt track. Jaw dropping, tongue out, mouth-watering goodness, the view is the absolute dogs bollocks, the Eiffel Tower, the Taj-Mahal and the fucking Pyramids wrapped up into one magnificent scene of beauty. The stage is built and has this big snail-shell shaped roof on. Damn, those SLS guys don't waste any time in setting up. Closing my eyes, time speeds up, time-lapse fast-forward style. Sun go down and the venue fill up with more and more and more punters. The search lights and lasers scrape the sky and it's perfect, the rave of all raves, a truly legendary party the punters will be talking about in twenty or thirty years time. I've done it, I've created something truly legendary, something to be proud of, I'm Michael Angelo finishing David, Christopher Wren finishing St Pauls, Leonardo da Vinci finishing the Mona Lisa. A wave of emotion sweeps over me and I get a bit emotional. Wiping my eyes, I'm back in the here and now, staring at the stage and still in awe. Engine in gear, clutch releases, I set off over the brow of the hill and spot two Transit vans either side of the track, with four meatheads in between, spread side by side. All four have black bomber jackets on with "Best Guard" stencilled on the left-hand side. I explain who I am but they just stare at me with a "we-don't-give-a-fuck-who-you-say-you-are" look spreading across each of their fat faces. One of them walks away talking into a walkie-talkie while the others stand firm, screwing me with their dead-eyes. I'm nothing to them, just a clueless punter, a day too early. Right there and then the scale of what I've done really hits me. I'm the architect, the creator, the mono-god of this whole shooting match, yet, at the same time, I'm the most insignificant person on the planet. Bigger than me, bigger than any of us, it's grown into its own sentient being with its own personality, own mind, own energy and its own Jedi-life-force. A minute later, the walkie-talkie geezer comes back and waves me through with knowing nods and winks. Although a little upset nobody knows who I am, I'm pleased Claudes team have this place locked down. Driving slowly around the left-hand side of the hill towards the back of the stage, I spot two dark green Portakabins, yep, full-on temporary single-story buildings, in the countryside. Turns out Kenny had them delivered on the back of an articulated truck, along with a mobile crane. One will be our "office" where the cash will be counted and held, the other a staging area for the deejays, the acts and Claudes men.

Also wearing a "Best Guard" black bomber jacket, but with the word "BOSS" etched underneath the logo, Claude strolls over with a beaming smile. 'Oi, oi, wha-gwan Devious, come nah man, let me show ya 'round,' he says before taking me on a guided tour of the stage and the cabins. He points towards the wood at the other side of the field behind the stage and a flat-bed lorry moving slowly dropping off concrete blocks and wire fence panels. A team of men / ants are spread out behind, erecting the fencing panel by panel. Like a dog with two dicks, he's loving his work and, for a change, he's actually smiling, almost like he's happy. Quite right too, he's pulling this off and being professional, he's grown and I'm proud of him. Next up I see Tony from SLS. Draping an arm around my shoulders, he takes me up to the centre of the stage. Looking out across the empty field with the sloping hill in front, I feel like a rock star. Smiling ear to ear, he points over to where three scaffold towers are nearly fully erect ready for the sound and lighting gear. Says it'll be ready for a sound check and lighting test tomorrow afternoon. His eyes go wide when he mentions the lighting rig, like he's wrapped up a Christmas present surprise for me. Then, my eyes zone in on Claude running diagonally across the field and up the hill in the direction of the two transit vans on the dirt track / front gate. He's followed by half a dozen black-bomber-jacket-meatheads. Adrenaline rushing, panic surging, I shout over to a meathead who's just below the stage with his ear glued to a walkie-talkie. He tells me there's an incident at the front gate. Incident, no shit. Jumping down from the stage, me and the walkie-talkie meat head follow Claude while Tony slips out to the back of the stage.

Top of the hill, (I'm panting, out of breath, sweating like a pig), we see a full-on travelling carnival parked up way down the dirt track, right back to the main road. Claude's having a nose to nose argument with what looks like the leader or elder of the clan, an older guy with a dark green cardigan on and a flat cap. We don't need the complication of a whole heap of Travellers with god-damn fairground rides. Just then, I hear a huge roar behind me. Swinging around, I see the big green Range Rover bouncing over the grassy horizon at top speed. It races towards me before hand-brake skidding to a stop right in front of Claude. Kenny lumbers out and starts pointing towards Claude and then the Travellers. Jones follows and joins in the shouting and pointing. Holy shit, it's going nuclear, run for cover, protect the children, pray to God. But, the pointing quickly turns into smiles which turns into arms around shoulders and pats on the back. Turns out, Kenny invited the Travellers, he says he thought it might be a tidy earner, and extra muscle if things get out of hand. Huge Ferris big wheel, an umbrella twisty thing and a waltzer, three burger bars, an ice-cream van and ten caravans. What the fuck's he thinking, we don't need this shit, he's quickly turning the rave, (my rave), into a complete joke. Anyhow, the Travellers park their caravans behind the Portakabins before moving the Ferris wheel to the top of the biggest hill and positioning the waltzer to the left of the stage and the umbrella ride over near the entrance. As it turns out, and I hate to admit it, it looks iconic and distinctive, plus, at two quid a pop, just as Kenny predicted, turns out to be a nice earner too. Kenny says we'll go fifty-fifty with the Travellers, which of course, is a load of crap. Yep, we can kiss goodbye to that, that's for sure, but fuck it, it looks good.

The rest of the day is pretty uneventful, with a mix of wandering around checking on things, dealing with odd query from the SLS crew and dealing with a thousand and one questions from Kenny and Jones. Claude loops around now and again to check on me, but mostly, I'm left to my own devices. Early evening, I go for walk down through the trees behind the Portakabins, just needed some time on my own and some peace and quiet if I'm honest. Stunningly beautiful, the dense trees are separated by a little stream gently rambling side by side with a small dirt track leading to fuck knows where. Just as the sun begins to set, bless them, the Travellers offer us some dinner, old-school shepherd's pie and boiled to fuck peas, but, the sentiment's appreciated. After dinner, Kenny, Jones and Claude hold court, giving it large to Travellers, Claudes men and anyone else who'll listen about their hooliganism and drug dealing and loads of other tall stories. We sit around a camp fire and get fucked up on beer, Irish whiskey and harsh as fuck resin. Surprisingly, there's no sign of any coke or brown, apparently Claude banned his men from snorting cocaine on a "school night", as he called it and the Travellers hate any type of drugs, so even the resin was frowned upon. After dinner, some drinks and no end of highly exaggerated tall stories, I slope off to my motor and skin up some, (proper), weed and listen to an old roots and culture cassette I found in the glove box. Wrapped up on the back seat in my quilt, with a full belly, the country air, mellow weed and some roots, I peacefully drift off to sleep.

NEXT UP…

RAVE DAY

Feels like a dream now, like I'm reading it from a book or watching it on television or in a movie, a fading memory or a twisted long-forgotten echo from my fucked-up mind. The whole day, start to finish, is totally trippy and surreal and complete and utter madness. Up early with the cold, it's misty and damp and magical and mystical with an air of excitement about the place. Anticipation and nervous energy surrounds everyone, so real it's palpable and tangible. Expecting to shift five to ten thousand Ecstasy pills at fifteen pound a piece, Kenny's off early to get his stock for the night, which suits me fine. Marlon turns up around lunchtime with a few of his mates to do the sound-check. Man, it's storming, the sound-system is the absolute dog's bollocks, super loud with a deep, stomach rumbling bass. In an open air field, deep in the middle of nowhere countryside, it's louder than the loudest club I've ever been to. Kenny gets back mid-afternoon with a couple of blue and white cool-boxes, each about two feet square and full to the brim with little milk-chocolate colour brown pills. Dropping them at my feet he tells me to grab a few for later and heads back to the Range Rover. Reaching into the back seat he pulls out a small black and grey machine, about the size of a kettle with his left, and a small cream coloured briefcase thing with his right. Holding his left aloft, says it's a note counting machine, and has another one in the back too. In his right, he says it's a transportable telephone, in case he needs to call a taxi. Ha-ha, what a joker he is, the prick. But, I understand it now, he is indeed all about the cash, all about the business and I'm now positive he'll rip me off, of course he will, but, right now I don't know how or when.

Either way, I know I got to get in there first.

The fuck-Paul-save-me plan is most definitely on.

The rest of the day, man, it's really, really, really boring, all I can do is check and double-check the arrangements. Marlon calls the deejays and artists, checking they're still on, which they are. Most of the deejays are getting three hundred quid each for a one-hour set, but Marlon books two big-time American deejays. Yeah, I can't remember their names now, Mando and Tony I think, and they both get five hundred plus a thousand for flights and a hotel. Not a clue who the fuck they are, Marlon tells me they're oldschool deejays who both played at a club in Chicago called the "Sound Square", where House music first came about. He also books three artists to do live performances too. First up a fit singer called Rosie, I think, then the two rapping dreadlocked brothers we used at the first warehouse rave in Stratford. He also booked a young white-boy keyboard player and his tall, funky-dread mate singer. Friends of Marlon, just starting out in the business, they don't have a record deal or even a name but fuck it, lets give them a go. Early evening, the SLS guys kick off the lighting test which, holy shit, is quite simply out of this world. All of us, the meathead security, the SLS guys, Kenny, Jones, Marlon's crew and the Travellers stand and watch like little kids. Each of the three AV towers has green, blue and red lasers plus loads of other lights and a couple of huge searchlight things. Those, plus with the fairground rides lit up against the increasingly black darkness of the countryside sky, the whole scene looks unbelievable, something I couldn't never have imagined, like the final scene in a Star Wars movie.

As for Claude, man, he's pumped-up and hyper all-day long going on and on about having an "escape route", in case things go tits up. He'd found the track through the woods I spotted the day before on my beautiful walk, and one of his men tracked it over a field and on to another dirt track which eventually leads to a local B-road. This is the escape route and serves as the VIP entrance. Marlon arranges to meet the artists and deejays, (aka the VIPs), at a hotel in Braintree, about five miles away, where he'll ferry them into the venue through this back-route in a mini-bus the Travellers lend us. The last couple of hours before kickoff are absolute agony. I can't wait for the night to start, and then, for it to be over. I end up playing cards at a fiver a hand with some of Claudes men, not the hired help, but the original Millwall boys who I sort of know from years back. Relaxed and chilled out, to them, it's just a job, they're not into the rave scene so any excitement washes over them. I, on the other hand, feel more and more excited and, at the same time, more and more nervous. Later in the evening and forty quid lighter, I call Paul and tell him to meet Marlon along with the deejays and artists at the hotel and follow the them in through the back roads. Claude can't know he's coming, no way, in his drugged-up-pumped-up-paranoid state he might spill the beans to Kenny. I tell the Millwall boys I have some personal guests coming through along with Marlon and the talent and ask them to call me when they arrive. They're cool and tell me know problem.

Back in London, Marlon gets a few of the local younger kids deejaying on Dream FM. He plans to announce the first meeting spot at nine pm, Gateway Services on the M1 motorway, near Wembley. From there, they'll head to the second meeting spot at Thurrock Services on the M25 maybe an hour later. With the magical mystical tour, I reckon punters will get here around midnight. The deejays and artists arrive around ten thirty, minus Paul, he's late, he's always late. Anyway, Marlon introduces everyone with handshakes and smiles before showing them around the venue. The consummate host, I see he's grown into a professional guy, confident, self-aware and in control, he's not a little kid anymore who idolises his big brother. Yeah man, bittersweet feelings, he's no longer my baby brother, he has a career of his own, a life of his own, he's his own man.

I'm so proud of him.

I'll always be proud.

As one of the warm-up deejays mixes and scratches his way through some bouncy tunes, the punters begin to arrive. At the same time, the other deejays and artists are having a right old pre-rave party in the Portakabin next to the cash-counting office. Feeling like an outsider, I slip away, especially as Marlon has them eating out of the palm of his hand. I head up to the main gate which is the highest point so I can see all around and check on the punter numbers. Watching the trail of cars backed up all the way down the dirt track and queuing along the local road toward Halstead village, a shudder of excitement flows through me. I call Paul on a transportable phone Kenny brought. Out of breath and frantic, he says they missed the mini-bus by ten minutes, the idiot. I give him directions to the front gate and tell him to call me once he arrives. I feel on edge again, nervous and anxious and begin over-thinking everything. If Paul doesn't show up with his newspaper reporter chums, I'm definitely fucked, what do I do then? I start thinking about the exit route, maybe slip away now, straight to the airport and a flight to Acapulco or wherever the fuck away from Kenny and Jones. Devious Dee, going loco down in Acapulco, yeah man, that's got a ring about it.

Punters are streaming through the gate, some with tickets but most paying cash. Claude's standing at the other side of the track, collecting cash and directing cars down behind the stage and Portakabins, charging a fiver each to park, the cheeky, enterprising bastard. I hang around near the gate until about one a.m. Must have maybe fifteen or twenty thousand in by now, if not more. No sign of Paul though, so I go back down to the office which is now a mini Fort Knox. I count ten black bomber jacket meatheads plus Jones, lording it around the place with a sawn-off shotgun in his fat hand, it's stubby barrel resting over his forearm. Subtle as a baseball bat around the head, but, I must admit, he's effective, no gang in their right mind will try to turn us over, no chance. Heading for the cabin, I catch sight of the field-come-car-park behind the office, and it's absolute chaos. Cars everywhere, punters raving, dancing on top of cars, on the bonnets and roofs. Eyes scan for my car, shit, blocked in, surrounded, trapped.

This is a monumental problem.

No. Way. Out.

The back-up plan is well and truly fucked.

A quick pat down from a meathead and a nod from Jones, then I enter. Kenny, with thin little reading glasses on the end of his nose and piles of cash all over the place, doesn't even look up. I've never seen so much cash. With the counting machine whirling away, he looks like a bank manager, a fat-bastard-pig-in-shit-smug-as-you-like bank manager, all grins and smiles. 'Told you we'd make a mint,' he says, nodding. I'm distracted though, over his shoulder I spot a mound of beautifully white cocaine on top of one of the cool-boxes. 'Go on me-old son,' he smiles. 'Grab a toot. Help yourself to some pills too, check the other box.' I look down at the cool-box at the left-hand side of the cocaine box, the lid slightly ajar. Looks to be a couple of thousand chocolate-brown pills inside. I look back towards Kenny, he looks happy, no sign of any sinister I'm-going-to-kill-you-later vibes so grab a couple of pills and slip them into my back pocket before cutting a few lines. Sniffing and snorting, nose tingling, rushes shoot across my brain. After some yeah-yeah-yeah small talk, I tell him I'll pop back in a couple of hours to see how we're getting on. He nods without looking up.

Back outside, tunes are banging, punters raving and the fairground rides are going down a storm. I spot a couple of blokes with long lens cameras walking about, either Police or reporters, but, either way, a good sign, Paul must be here. I make sure I'm pictured a few times, smiling just-in-case-evidential smiles then go for a wander around. I'm moving and grooving through the crowd, feeling the vibe and, with a cocaine haze around my brain and the good vibe smiles from Kenny, I'm feeling good. Maybe I've been playing this out in my head through a negative and dark lens, maybe he's on the level and does indeed just want to make some cash. Maybe he appreciates my help and can see I'm trying to make amends. Damn, maybe, just maybe, I can get out of this in one piece after all. After some more wandering, I find myself at the back of the stage looking out at the sea of punters stretching out right up to the edge of the horizon. The lasers look amazing, scanning across the crowd, particles of light being broken by the silhouette of a thousand hands in the air, each grabbing a memory of the best night of their lives. All the hassle and tribulation from the past, the racists, the fascists, the hooligans, the dodgy gangsters, the drug-dealers and complete wrong-uns are all at one. No violence, no threats, no sideways looks, just peace and happiness and music. Shit man, I'm loving it, loving what I've created, loving this high, loving the buzz. Then, this "salsa-house" tune comes on, "you used to hold me, you used to touch me," rings around my mind and across the ocean of togetherness in front of me. The soundwaves connect us together, our brains synchronising and becoming one. I can literally feel their love, their contentment, their happiness ooze towards me, engulfing me. Man, that is a blinding tune, blinding, the vibe completely takes me. I'm coked-up and loving it. You to get high on a high, go super-high, turbo-high, higher than high you can touch the sky, so I drop my couple of Ecstasy pills then and there.

Buzzing.

Then.

I'm grabbed from behind.

Panic-panic-panic.

Fuck.

Arms over my shoulders, I'm spun around.

Shit.

It's okay though, it's Marlon, my not-so-baby brother hugging and kissing me, telling me he's loving it. Buzzing, his eyes are like plates and his pupils massive. Sweat is literally pouring out of him and he's hyper, loved-up and buzzing his tits off. Dancing with arms around each other shoulders, we look out toward the crowd. I'm buzzing too with an intensity I've never felt before, I'm totally in love with what I've achieved, yeah man, standing on top of Mount Everest, I'm king of the world, master of the universe. I love it, the punters love it, the Travellers love it, Claudes men, now moving and grooving, head bobbing and shoulders swaying, love it too, the whole god-damn world loves it. Punters are on the stage dancing, pulsing and pumping with their arms out in front of them, oblivious to the outside world, trapped in their own microcosm of love. I don't mind them being on stage, in fact, fuck it, I love it. Yeah man, I'm proud we can do this, proud of the vibe, proud the freedom, proud of the togetherness of the night. We don't need no rules or Police or Government bullshit, nah man, left to our own devices we can all get on just fine, work as a team, as a single unified mono-entity. We're just human beings who simply yearn to belong and be loved, and tonight, we belong to each other.

After fuck knows how long, the white-kid keyboard player and his funky-dread mate are shown onto the stage by Tony from SLS. Damn, they rip the place up, I've never seen a reaction like it. Whistles and cheers and screams for more and more and more. Dropping this "solitary brother" tune, heavily electronic sounding but the dread's vocals are deep and meaningful. I get it, the juxtaposition between the soulless microchip future and the honesty of his voice is deep man, deep. Grabbing Marlon, I hug him knowing as long as we have each other, we'll never be alone, never be solitary. I'm so lucky my little brother's here, sharing this with me and it's perfect. To be honest, for a moment, I forget about the cash and Paul and Kenny and Jones and the plan of all plans, I'm taken by the vibe and just rave and rave. Fuck the time, fuck the predicament, fuck the consequences, life's for living, and tonight I'm living like I've never lived before. But then, reality grabs me once again, changing me from buzzed-up Raver back to Devious Dee the promoter. Life is indeed for living and I love life, yeah man I really do. I want to extend my life, I don't want to be dead so, the fuck-Paul-save-me plan is back in action, it has to be.

Leaving Marlon trance-like on the stage, I call Paul again.

Surprisingly, he answers, says he's been here for a couple of hours so we arrange to meet-up, near the big wheel. Takes an age to get up there with every wide-eyed-joe-public-punter hugging me and shaking my hand. Eventually, reaching the big-wheel, I spot him before he spots me. He's with a couple of posh looking types who are smiles and yah-yah-yah's, trying to fit in with head-bobbing-pigeon-style dancing, both obviously buzzing their tits off, probably dropping their first taste of Ecstasy tonight. One of them, a dickhead with a blue woollen jumper over his shoulders, Nigel or Jeremy or Sebastian or something shakes my hand furiously, way too much for my liking. All over the place, he tells me the rave's unbelievable, life changing and the beginning of a new youth movement. Complete crap, I see through his platitudes which are nothing more than Ecstasy induced, cocaine fuelled public-school-insincere-clichéd crap. Pulling Paul to one side, away from the dickheads, I ask him where he's been, but, before I can get a word in edge-ways, he tells me a few newspaper reporters are here as well as an ITV "News-at-Ten" camera crew.

'Don't matter mate,' I yell into his ear, trying not to grind my teeth as the Ecstasy rush begins to take me. 'We're fucked.'

'What doesn't matter,' he says, eyes wide.

'Reporters don't mean jack-shit, we're fucked yeah, fucked.'

'Eh?' he says,

'Kenny and Jones.'

'Who?'

'Fat Kenny, who we fitted up.'

The colour drains from his ugly face and he's transported back to when he's ten years old, receiving a royal telling-off from the headmaster. 'Kenny?' he says. 'From the firm, who we, you know, round at his at the Barbican?'

'Yeah, that's what I'm saying, we're fucked.'

'He's here, tonight, where?'

'I don't know mate.'

'But how? Why?'

I'm loving his confusion, he hasn't got a fucking clue the clueless piece of dog shit.

'Claude got them involved in the security side and they've sort of taken over. I only found out earlier.'

'But, how the fuck Devon, how?'

'I dunno, not a clue.' I'm compelling and utterly convincing, plus, the best lies always contain a fair element of truth, something I learnt a long time ago. 'Listen, don't panic, but they know we're here.'

Frozen to the spot, his face is shape-shifting between saucer-eyed Ecstasy-driven baby-boy-dimple-smiles and an I've-seen-a-ghost-I'm-going-to-die frown.

I like that, I like that a lot.

'Fucking hell, no. He'll know we grassed, he'll know it's us.' The prick doesn't even ask how they know, just starts shaking and panicking, eyes darting everywhere.

'Yeah he does and he's gone fucking mental, Tony Montana crazy. He's coked-up to the eye-balls and wants revenge Claude reckons.' I see a bolt of panic literally sear through him as fear fills his puppy-dog-help-me eyes. Someone once told me, fear is guilt in disguise, and, right here right now, I see this truth in action. I'm fucking loving his panic, feasting on his fear, the more scared he is, the more powerful I become.

'Oh fuck, oh fuck. We have get out of here, back to London,' he spits, grabbing at me like a frightened little kid.

'They'll be watching your car,' I suggest, helpfully.

'Yeah, yeah, of course, of course. Shit-man, shit.'

'Best thing to do is mingle,' I say, acting my arse off. 'Keep your head down till later.'

'Yeah, yeah, yeah, blinding Dev, blinding,' he says.

'Hold tight around here, get on the big wheel and stay on, they'll never look there, never mess with the Travellers.'

'Yeah, yeah, Travellers, big-wheel, yeah, cheers,' he says rubbing my shoulder affectionately.

Cheers, after he fucked my missus and fucked my life?

Cheers mate, cheers pal, cheers buddy, cheers old chum, cheers boyhood friend, cheers you cock-sucking mug? I see straight through him, the stinking piece of dog-shit. This is all coming together nicely, the plan is now in action and my pass to freedom sorted.

I promise him I'll be back later, when it's safer, then make my way back down to the cash-counting office. Even busier than earlier with maybe thirty thousand punters in, the crowd are going mad for this soulful and melodic "promised land" track. Approaching the cabin, I spot Jones, still patrolling outside the cabin with sworn-off slung over his shoulder, now looking even more demented. Suddenly, I'm aware of movement at the edge of my peripheral vision, adrenaline punches it's way into my brain, I see Claude charging toward me. Spinning around, I move into a defensive stance but he's too quick, too strong. Grabbing me by the shoulders he's screaming and shouting, but I can't hear a thing, talking in tongues his voice doesn't match the movement of his mouth. 'Marlon, blah-blah-blah, Marlon,' he screams, pulling me by the arm we head toward the back of the stage where a crowd has gathered. Getting closer, I see they're standing around a body.

No, no, no.

NO.

NOOOO.

Tearing through the crowd, I see it's him. Panic, panic, panic. Writhing around on the floor, he's foaming at the mouth and flipping back and forth, spinning like he's possessed. Confusion surrounds me, engulfs me, drowns me. Claude's on the walkie-talkie and at the same time telling me to be cool, the ambulance is on it's way. On my knees, I'm shouting into his face, hugging him, trying to stop him fitting. The thumping baseline and jeering crowd fades into the distance, all I can see and hear is my brother, my baby brother. His distorted face morphs between a demonic monster and a frightened little boy, his eyes roll back and white foam seeps from his mouth. Cradling his head, he writhes around uncontrollably, his fragile and tender body spasming and jolting. Glance up at the surrounding crowd, I spot old-school friends from years ago and memorable strangers I've never met before. I'm tripping through this massive dé-jà-vu moment while reality disintegrates right in front of me.

After God knows how long, blue lights bounce off the tarpaulin at the back of the stage and Claude pulls me away. A couple of Ambulance men get in beside him, one holding him down and the other shining a torch into his eyes. Claude pulls me close, controlling me, squeezing me, comforting me. Within a minute, Marlon's strapped onto a stretcher, oxygen mask over his face and is packed into the back of the ambulance. Setting off slowly, it weaves it's way through the chaos of cars out towards the VIP entrance. Claude takes hold of me, spins me around and hugs me tight. I'm sure he's crying too. 'He be okay, don't worry, be strong,' he whispers.

I'm listening, but can't really hear.

'Seen dat before brother, dodgy pill or some-ting,' he says.

I'm numb. Shock or something.

'Stomach pump and fluids, no worries,' he says, calmness growing through voice.

I can't take any of this in.

This isn't real.

'Right as rain tomorrow, no worries,' he says, his words echoing into nothingness. He's trying to help but I'm a night of the living dead zombie.

I take myself off down to the woods, need to get away. Why didn't I go with him? I've let the single most precious thing I'm my life disappear to fuck knows where. Sitting under a tree where the roots disappear into the rock-hard soil, I look back towards the rave, while the punters rave on in full force they are oblivious to the horrors I've just witnessed. It's cold and wet and dark down here, just like me, freezing cold, shivering and drenched in guilt. Totally detached, I'm having an out of body experience or whatever they call it. I'm a spaceman looking back towards Earth from the Moon, lonely, solemn and abstract, a real life solitary brother. What have I done? I should have been there for him and looked after him, not been scheming to get my boyhood friend fucked up by two demonic gangsters, just to save my sorry skagg-head ass. Momma will blame me, of course she will, hating me, cussing me, never forgiving me. Same with Shirley, she'll be judgemental, looking down her slaggy cute-as-a-button nose.

I'll never get her back now.

What have I done?

What's happening to me?

Marlon's in an ambulance, Paul's about to receive some serious pain and I'm going to be ripped off, then fuck knows what, maybe killed. All of a sudden, my plan isn't going to plan, not by a long shot. Got to salvage it, must get something from it, need to be positive, seek an angle, discover a way out. Got to think it through, reason it out and apply some emotionally detached logic to the most highly emotional of all emotional situations. Claude said they'll pump his stomach, it's a dodgy pill, happens all the time, nothing to worry about. Marlon's young and strong and tough, maybe he'll be okay. Maybe I'm just being dark and negative, thinking the worst, as usual. Dodgy pills are just part and parcel of being a full-time raver, besides, I'll find out where they've taken him and go see him tomorrow. Yeah man, the negativity is just the down-curve of my cocaine-Ecstasy buzz. Need to be positive, think of the up-curve. Positivity breeds positivity, right. Not sure how long I'm sitting there, but, eventually, feeling refreshed and more positive, I head back.

PORTAKABIN / OFFICE
HALSTEAD
ESSEX
AUGUST, 1989

'Stop right there, yaah.' Spinning around, Jones faces me, frown down with both barrels pointing into my face, poised like a military sniper. 'Thought you'd fucked off,' he says through narrow, suspicious eyes.

'Me? Nah, jobs not finished,' I say. We stare at each other, weighing each other up.

'Your brother, he alright?'

'Yeah, yeah, he'll be okay.'

'Good kid, yaah,' he nods, barrels still pointing.

We both nod "fuck-you" nods.

'Right as rain tomorrow,' I say while the voices in my head are shouting, screaming, disagreeing, blaming him and his crazy cousin for their mother fucking baby brother killing dodgy pills.

Pointing the gun towards the door, he nods me in.

Edging in, I keep my gaze on him as long as I can. As I turn, I see Kenny still at the desk. The piles of cash from earlier have been transformed into neat, elastic band bound bundles. The door closes behind me.

'Heard about your brother,' he says not looking up.

'Yeah,' I say, dying inside, hoping for some sympathy.

'Shame, nice kid.'

We both nod at each other.

'You okay?' he nods.

I look to the floor, I'm not okay, I'm as far from okay as you can possibly be. I want to tell him everything, get it out of my system, confess my sins, maybe his sympathetic tone. He's like a truth magnet or something, shit, I'm about to pour my heart out to this evil monster, telling him about my grand plan, the fuck-Paul, fuck-them, save-me plan.

'You holding it together, Dee?'

'Yeah man, sweet. I mean, all things considered.'

'Yeah?'

'Stomach pump or something. Right as rain tomorrow.'

'You sure?' He looks up. 'Need you on top form.'

'I'm cool,' I smile, even though behind my smile I am the exact opposite of cool, a mess, a walking disaster zone.

He stares at me for what seems like ages. 'Good, good,' he nods, laser beaming me with his sunken dead eyes, maintaining his stare deep into me, reading my mind, reaching into my soul. Reading me like a book, he knows, yeah, he knows alright.

THEN SILENCE.

'So,' he says, eventually. 'Cleared north of four hundred on the gate already, on for five, maybe five and a half by dawn.'

A wave of guilty, exciting, disgusting relief washes over me. I knew we'd make a proper mint, even if he did fiddle it and under-report the gate by a couple of hundred thousand. Breathing out slowly trying not to let him see my relief, I crack a fake smile. 'Four? Sweet, sweet,' I say, steadying myself. Got to act fast, it's time to sort this out, put an end to my never-ending slow death.

'So,' I say.

He looks up over his glasses. 'So?' he asks.

The tension is palpable.

Transported to dusty gold-rush Texas, we're cowboys facing each other on Main Street with tumbleweed softly bouncing away into the distance. The locals have run for cover and window shutters and doors are slammed shut. Hands hover over our guns while we screw each other through slitty who'll-blink-first eyes.

Tiny movements, iris contracting.

Silence.

'Me and you,' I say slowly, blinking first.

He doesn't say a thing, just takes his glasses off. Eyebrows arch down towards the bridge of his nose, the bank manager version of Kenny fades away, replaced by serious-as-shit-you-owe-me-a-lifetime Kenny.

'We're cool, yeah,' I say, mixing a statement with a question. 'I know you said we're straight, but it don't feel straight. It can't be straight, not after eight years, Ken.'

'Nah?' I see the anger building in his eyes, his bloodshot blood-vessels widen and go a deeper shade of red.

'Reckon later on you and Jones gonna to take my share.'

He stares through dead eyes. I need him to say something, anything. His lack of emotion makes me feel even more emotional and scared-shitless.

Pursing his lips like he's kissing a fanny, he nods. 'Yeah, that's the plan. Like you say, eight years is a long time.'

Struck dumb, I literally can't say a thing. I've always known deep down in side, but to hear it confirmed is gutting. Left knee shaking, I can't control it.

'So,' he says. 'Where does this leave us then? Your move.'

'All I want is to walk out of here intact.'

He nods slowly.

'Maybe with a few quid in my back pocket,' I add.

He tilts his head like it's a reasonable request. 'Yeah, I get it,' he nods. 'But, your debt's a fucking debt and a half. Jones was up for killing you when you and him first bumped into each other over at Claudes.'

Fuck.

'You can't take a man's liberty for eight fucking years without retribution,' he says, getting angrier. 'A couple of hundred cash don't come close, what's that, twenty-five a year? I was earning more than that when you fucking snitched,' he spits, anger cracking through his voice.

Leg still shaking, the truth dawns on me. I must have been mad to think just the cash could settle it. Then, the cold, stark reality of the situation washes over me, freezing around my ankles, anchoring me to this very spot. We both know where this is going…

In my mind's eye I see Momma standing over an open grave, crying her eyes out, weeping and hollering. Pops is there, Shirley, Marlon and my little boy too. Paul, the cunt, he's there with Super who's chained in between to two prison guards. Crissy and Claude and a few other Railton Road rude-boys are standing in the background looking melancholic and sad. I'm there too, but, rather than standing over the grave with tears in my eyes, I'm stretched out in a six-foot wooden box being lowered into the ground. I'm deader-than dead, beyond dead, dead and gone to hell dead.

'Paul,' I blurt out. No turning back.

'What?' Kenny queries through narrowing eyes.

'Paul. He's here, tonight.'

'What you on about?'

'Paul, Richardson.'

'Richardson's here, tonight?' he says, disbelief spreading across his face. 'You sure?'

'I understand the debt Ken, I really and truly do. It's Paul though, he's the one who fitted you up, not me.'

Confused, he shakes his head. 'Posh-Paul, the daddies-boy-gay-lord is here, tonight?'

'Yeah,' I nod, waiting for a pat on the head for a job well done, just like Crissy used to do when I was a little boy.

'And, he's the grass, not you?'

'Yeah, that's right.' My words echo forever. I've done it, sentenced my boyhood best mate to fuck knows what.

'Let me get this clear,' he says. 'You reckon Paul snitched and got me locked away, not you?' Standing up, he shakes his head, holding the bridge of his nose. 'You'd drop your best mate in it, so you can walk away?'

'No mate of mine, he fucked me, like he fucked you.'

'He fucked you?' he screams, his face screwed up, full of confused. 'Jones, get the fuck in here.'

Door crashing open, Jones leaps in. 'Yaah Ken, what the fuck, what?' Eyes bulging, his head darts everywhere as he points the shotgun towards my head.

'Daisy here reckons we should give him a pass.'

'Yaaaahhhh?' Jones sings, disbelieving what he's heard. Stepping forward, his teeth grind together as the barrels push into the side of my head, aggression etching across his face. 'No fucking way this piece of shit walks.'

'Reckons Paul Richardson's here, from the city firm. Says he's the one who fitted me up in eighty-one, and not him.'

'Yaah?' Jones queries his anger and aggression fading into confusion. I see his two brain cells working overtime trying to work it out, the thick fuck.

'Says he'll give him to us, if we let him walk. That's about right, isn't it petal?'

I nod slowly as the barrels probe further into me, forcing my head to tilt to the left.

'Fuck-ing-hell, you'd do for your own, yaah?' Jones says, prodding my head.

I nod again, unable to speak.

'Can you believe it?' Kenny says, like he's cracking a joke.

'Dirty fuck-yaah, snake in the grass this one Ken,' Jones laughs before banging me on the head with the barrels.

'You don't know what that prick did to me,' I blurt out uncontrollably.

'Shut the fuck up, boy?' Jones grunts.

'What you on about?' Kenny says, his frown dipping.

'Alright, alright,' I hold my arms up patting the air. 'He fucked my misuses, didn't he. She fucks off taking my boy with her. I've lost everything, become a fucking skagg-head addicted to the brown.' Unimpressed, I step it up. 'Known him since we were little kids.'

Laughing, Jones, the mug, chuckles to himself, no doubt wallowing in my despair. Kenny though, he's stone-cold sober, calm and measured. 'You're taking the piss.'

'He's got everything, job, cars, cash, fanny galore, and he fucks my missus?' I plead.

'A looker yaah, bit of a stunner?' Jones smirks, the wanker.

Kenny glares at him.

'Right then, let's sort this out once and for all,' he says, reaching into the holdall behind his chair before shoving a pistol down the back of his trousers. 'Where is he?'

'On the big wheel, with a couple of public-school boy pals. Mugs, nothing to worry about.'

'Right Jones, let's go. Lock the snake in here. You're not going anywhere, are you dickhead?'

11. Long Bad Saturday

"I'm setting up the biggest deal in Europe with the hardest bastard since Hitler stuck a Swastika to his jockstrap. If I were you, I'd run for cover, otherwise, you're gonna wind up on one of those meat hooks, my son."

Harold Shand

PORTAKABIN / OFFICE
HALSTEAD
ESSEX
AUGUST, 1989

Locked in a Portakabin with an army of meatheads outside is not part of my masterplan, not by a long shot. Jones, the mad-man with a sworn-off and Kenny with murder in his eyes and a pistol in his pants, are definitely not part of the plan either. At least they've gone to sort Paul out rather than in here kicking seven bells of shit out of me, or worse. I wait and wait and wait, fuck knows how long, pacing back and forth, thinking things through, waiting for my fate and my future to converge. Ear to the door, I hear shouting in the distance, movement of sorts, maybe running and chasing, but nothing for sure, nothing definitive, nothing certain. Turning around, my eyes gravitate towards the cash, beautifully still, it rests majestically on the desk, clean and crisp and beautiful. It talks to me, quiet and covertly, whispering seductively, every character on every little note talking all at once. The chorus of historical figures urge me to touch them, fondle them, stuff them in a bag and liberate them. Although trapped in this Portakabin, helpless, I'm not dead just yet. Looking around the small, sparse cabin, there's a narrow horizontal window at the back, high up about two feet from the ceiling. Too high to get to, too small to fit through. Fuck. Maybe I can drop some of the cash through and fetch it later, if I'm lucky enough to get out in one piece. Yeah man, it's dark out back and the grass pretty long, any meatheads walking around probably wouldn't spot it. Reaching up on my tip-toes, I try and force it open but it's nailed shut for fucks sake. I look inside the two holdall bags behind Kenny's desk, empty as fuck apart from some loose screws and half a roll of gaffer tape. The lazy fucks haven't even bought new bags, probably stole these from some honest, decent hardworking plumber guy, the dirty shit-cunts. Think-think-think, think outside the box, time is of the essence. Hang on, hang the fuck on, brainwave coming. The Portakabin's made of flimsy plywood and fibreglass, maybe I can kick through? But what about the multiple meatheads outside, nah, they'll be in here before I can get out or, or, if I do manage to get out, they'll be on me pronto and I'll end up in the woods minus some limbs or worse, dead.

SHIT.

Thoughts turn to the super-hero villains I've known through the ages. Maybe they can come save me like a massive reveal at the end of a movie…

The Greek, a fucking madman? He'll shit on Jones surely, (but, man, what a fight that would be), but he's probably retired now, as he predicted, superseded by a young-upstart from a shithole estate in Deptford or somewhere.

Crissy, from the Frontline? Maybe he's served his time in Jamaica and come back to reclaim his crown, simultaneously saving me, anointing me as his right-hand man and we get back on the up from this mother fucking down.

Samurai Sam or even Snakehead? They both love money, love selling drugs, love violence, why aren't they involved in this scene? Maybe they both shot-up dead or locked away or supplying the drugs to the dealers who sold to Kenny.

Turkish from Spain, yeah man, he's a fucking bad-man gangster, he might have done with Spain, wants some of the English action. Maybe he's been turned on by his Algerian associates, stripped naked, bummed and fed to the vultures.

Or, what about my one and true hero, Super. Maybe he's been let out early on appeal, followed me here and been keeping an eye on me ready to jump in at the last minute.

Finally Claude, maybe he can save me, yeah man, strong, brave and masculine, we go way back, back before the madness. I see him bursting through the door, guns blazing, Jones gets one between the eyes, his brain splattered across the wall, Kenny, reaching for his pistol is too slow and gets two in the chest. Claude grabs me, I grab the cash, and we do one. Yeah that's it, we're out of here, go find Marlon and get back to London before sun-up, pack our things and get at the airport by lunch time, sipping rum on the beach by tea-time. Maybe, maybe, maybe. Claude doesn't come though, nobody does, it's just me here now. No matter how hard I think, the only way out is to sit tight and sweat it out. Maybe Kenny will be satisfied with the cash and Paul, doing me in is just an unnecessary burden, another body to get rid of. Yeah man, true, I haven't thought about it that way before, plus, they haven't killed me so far, maybe that'll be it, maybe he likes me. He does seem genuinely concerned about Marlon, and he checked I'm okay…

Wait, what?

SMASH.

Door disintegrating, the bottom hinge and half the door frame spins through the air as a massive dullness explodes inside my head like a nuclear power station powering down. Time slows down and Paul enters the room, floating head-first through the air like he's underwater or something. Colliding with the side of the desk, cash explodes like a million-pound snowfall. Gravity defying, notes float around the room and I'm in the middle of a giant cash-filled snow-globe. Mesmerised, bewildered and shitting myself, I look toward Paul, crumpled up on the floor, I can't see his face properly for all the blood, but I see his right eye's bulging, closed over and purple. Looks like he belongs in a nightmare or a horror movie, god damn, the whole situation is a nightmare, my own, personal, warped, fucked-up nightmare. Adrenalin pumping, heart pounding, panic surging, time speeds back up. Kenny leaps in, face screwed up with veins popping out everywhere. Demented, murderously crazy, I can't look at him. Jones stands behind him in the doorway, seething with a kill-kill-kill glint in his eye and sworn-off in his hands. Mad-dog on a leash, blood red eyes, his forehead bulges and top lip splits over his vampire-dagger teeth.

Fight or flight instinct kicks in and I bolt for the doorway.

BOOM.

Jones steps forward, catches me with what must have been

an upper cut. A super-massive ding-dong sound crashes around my skull and I land on my back, just to the right of the desk. Dazed and confused, my nose feels inside-out while stars spin and pop around me. 'Nobody in or out.' Kenny yells as Jones pushes what remains of the door back in it's frame. The baseline and snares and cheers and jubilance from the rave outside fade as the room fills with silent fear and echoing dread. The starkness of the single strip light above sears my skin like liquid nitrogen while the darkness at the edge of the room creeps forward, ripping through my stomach, delving into my soul.

This is it, the end.

Memories of every single dream and nightmare and dé-jà-vu moment flood into my mind and I glimpse the future and the past at the same time. Standing over Paul, Jones locks onto his prey, his next victim, his sacrifice to the God of cunts. Nodding his head, smiling, licking his lips, standing side on, he points the sworn-off diagonally down towards Paul's head. Legs astride, total control, he's the master of doom, guardian of the inevitable and the god of gangsters.

He's so fucking cool.

'No, no, no, wait, wait,' Paul screams, desperation scraping the back of his throat as horror fills his eyes.

'Don't fucking move, slag,' Kenny points at me.

Freeze-frame, nobody moves. Piercingly painful silence hangs heavy in the air. I can literally taste the toxic cocktail of fear and masculine testosterone, sour and bitter and disgusting and sweet and delicious.

'I have money Ken,' Paul pleads, snorting through broken teeth and twisted cartilage.

'Fuck the money, we don't need hand-outs,' Jones hisses.

'Can't buy your way out of this one, slick-fucking-rick,' Kenny seethes through gritted teeth, shaking his head slowly while continuing to point at me.

'Everyone's got a price,' Paul whimpers apologetically.

Then...

SILENCE.

'So anyway,' Kenny says, thankfully breaking the uncomfortable silence. 'The old gang's back together, just like old times, eh?' Revelling in it, he's loving it, savouring it, the mother fucking bastard.

Looking at Paul, our eyes awkwardly meet. Immediately I turn away, can't face what I've done, can't face what's happening to him, can't face what might happen to me, can't face my future.

'What's wrong Paul, can't work it out?' Kenny teases. 'Oi, oi, Devious, tell him what you told us?'

'Yaah-yaah, give him a piece of your mind,' Jones chips in.

The words are buried deep inside, my throat too dry. Shame washes over me as I plunge into an ice-bath of regret.

Turning, Jones points the gun towards me. 'Do it, slag. Tell him yaah,' he grunts. I can tell he's playing out pulling the trigger, visualising my head being split wide open with blood, bone and brains splattering against the wall.

'Alight, alright, for fucks sake,' I say, looking across at Paul. 'I told them.'

'What?' he groans. I look away.

'He's done for yaah,' Jones laughs, swinging back around to Paul. 'Dropped you right in it.'

Looking at Jones, then Kenny and then me, Paul shakes his head slowly. 'Nah, nah, no chance.'

Kenny and Jones both look at me, and I die inside.

'It's true.' I say, absolutely gutted. Never thought I'd feel this way, but Pauls eyes do for me, judge me, remind me of when we were kids, when we were mates, real mates. 'You fucked Shirley.'

'What?'

'You fucked me.'

'Shirley?' he shouts, high pitched, not believing what he's hearing. 'They're gangsters, they'll kill us both, you idiot.'

Guilt churns in the pit of my stomach while inevitability scratches across my brain. He's right, I know he is, suppose I've always known.

'Right then my beauties, enough of the school reunion, eh.

What a crazy conundrum,' Kenny says, rubbing his hands together.

Paul looks up at Kenny. I know that look, he gave Super that look all the time

'A no-mark like me, knowing multi-syllable words?' Kenny nods, arms wide open. Paul looks away. 'You arrogant piece of shit. Eight years gives you a lot of time to read, to think and contemplate life. EIGHT FUCKING YEARS.' Kenny roars. Stepping forward in front of Jones, he points his pistol towards Paul's head.

'I'm sorry,' Paul yells, seeming to be genuinely sorry for costing a man eight years of his life.

Kenny stares into the distance, replaying his lost life…

The raid on his flat, torches in his eyes, sub-machine guns in his face. Getting sent down, the indignity of being strip searched on arrival at Wormwood Scrubs. The fighting, the scheming, the watching your back and the visits from his mum crying her eyes out and weeping with her broken heart for the lost life he never had. The birthdays, the parties, the first dates, first kisses and one-night stands. The horrors of prison, the yells and screams and constant noise in the dead of night, the cheap resin they're forced to smoke and the sight of grown men bumming each other in the showers with tears in their eyes. His cell mate crying and bawling into his pillow and never shutting the fuck up and him swinging in the morning, all blue and stiff and suicidally dead with a belt round his neck.

I can see he literally hates Paul.

He's going to kill.

This is the end.

'Right,' Kenny says, breaking himself out of his trance, sanity resuming inside his head. 'Let's get this sorted. Jones, tape him up,' he says, pointing at me.

Placing the sworn-off on the desk, Jones reaches into one the holdalls and pulls out a roll of dark grey gaffer tape. I stare at the shotgun and grab-it, grab-it, grab-it voices scream inside my head. My chance to take control, my chance to get out of there and save myself. Grab-it. There's something stopping me though, a force-field or something, just can't force myself to do it. I wimp out, like the dirty coward that I am.

'Yaah, like you've the arsehole for it, you fucking pussy,' Jones seethes, spotting me looking, before pushing the gun further into the middle of the desk. 'Nah-then, come here you snake piece of shit,' he growls, kneeling on my stomach before wrapping tape around and around my head, covering my mouth and my eyes before rolling me over to my front. Like the pussy he said I am, I lay still, accepting being gaffer-tape-raped by this meathead psychopath.

It's pitch-black darkness now and I'm struggling to breath, hands are bound behind my back, ankles too. Then, I'm picked up by my wrists, shoulders cracking, pain surging. Using my knees I stand up straight, then, WHACK. Stomach imploding, I bend double and stumble back against the wall. Hearing myself moan like a dying dog, I slide down the wall so that I'm sitting on my arse with my knees near head. I tense up, expecting a boot to the head or worse.

'Jones,' Kenny shouts. 'Leave him alone for fucks sake.'

More silence.

Excruciating, never ending silence.

Glued to the spot, back against the wall and a gaffer-tape balaclava over my head, my ears are on red alert for movement, noises, clues to my fate. Tuning my head-radio to the BBC World Service of doom, I can just about make something out, something sinister, something dark. Whispering and murmuring, plotting and planning, it's subtle, secret and discreet but definitely something. This is nothing short of excruciating, just waiting for the inventible. Expecting the end has to be worse than the actual end.

Eventually, the not-so-honourable-judge-dread, Kenny himself delivers his verdict. 'Right then daisy,' he shouts. 'We're gone at four, got a lot to get through,' he says, his voice calm and calculated and matter of fact, zero emotion.

Then, more silence.

Painful, never-ending silence, until…

An ungodly scream tears through the tension, followed by thuds and slaps. Paul's in pain, suffering big time. Even though my eyes are taped up, I squeeze them even tighter shut. I can't stand it, can't stand to think what he's getting right now is coming my way very soon.

'Yaah,' Jones grunts, triumphantly as Paul groans in agony. More cracks and thuds follow, lots more. 'Yaah Ken, yaah,' Jones yells as they giggle, egging each other on like vampires feasting on Paul's carcass.

This can't be happening, it can't be real.

My mind drifts to Shirley and then to Momma but it's no use, I can feel every impact as the grunts and thuds grate through me.

'Hold him, hold him,' Kenny giggles, the sadistic bastard.

More blows follow, more violence, more screaming, more pain, more pleading for mercy, I hear Paul crying please, please, please pleads from the pit of his soul. I see Shirleys gorgeous, beautiful, innocent face smiling at me and tears force their way through my gaffer-tape mask, slowly streaming down my cheeks, stinging like ice cold acid. I don't want this, none of this, I thought I wanted revenge and retribution, for him to feel my pain, but, right here and right now, I know I don't. More slaps and thuds and giggles follow the begging and pleading morphs into muffled whimpering and then into silence.

Ears on high alert.

What's happening?

Have they gone?

Me next?

Then…

Eardrums are pierced with 'noooo, pleeeease,' screams ripping through my rib cage into my heart. This scream's different, medieval, prehistoric, more like a snared animal than a man.

'Yes treacle, YES,' Kenny grunts, excited hate, poisonous pleasure and delightful death filling his voice.

Another scream tears through me, this time it's long and drawn-out, the tell-tale sound of a soul detaching itself from it's worldly body, vacating this place of horror.

Then silence and darkness.

Heart racing.

Me next.

'You mug,' Kenny breaks the silence, whispering just loud enough for me to hear. 'Look at him.'

'What?' Jones whispers back.

'Shit,' Kenny sighs. 'Get him stripped, then get the plastic.'

Plastic? Eh?

'You okay there rude boy?' Kenny says, raising his voice.

I nod slowly.

I'm shaking, left leg first then my entire body. I strain to hear something, but only hear the dull thud from the rave outside. A few minutes later, five, maybe ten, I hear footsteps then the crinkling sound of plastic.

Then…

'What. The. Fuck?' Jones says, over pronouncing every word. 'The sneaky fuck.'

'Eh?' Kenny says, puzzlement in his voice.

'Recorder, yaah, strapped on.'

'The dirty slag,' Kenny spits, disbelievingly. 'Police issue?'

'Not one I've seen, proper though,' Jones says, admiring the engineering or build quality.

I can't help but smile, just a little. The scheming little shit, there's me thinking I'm the snake, yet he's gathering evidence with a tape recorder strapped to his chest.

'Shush. Not a word,' Kenny whispers in an even lower tone. 'Get him sorted and destroy that. Burn it or something.'

The sneaky, devious, clever little shit. Even now, he impresses and surprises me. Ears aching, seeking out morsels of sound I just about make out more plastic crinkling, then gaffer-tape ripping. Poor Paul, what have I done, what have they done? I'm so sorry I've caused this, I've killed him, done him in, taken his life. I've become a vampire, turning to the dark-side, completing the transformation from man to snake. I've ruined him and poor, fragile, defenceless Ashley too. Shit, in the space of a few years I've ruined both brothers and in effect fucked a whole family, destroyed an entire generation. Thoughts turn to God as my last salvation, then, inevitably, my thoughts turn to the Devil. With the pain and suffering, the lost souls and lifetimes of regret, I am the Devil, I must be. Born bad, born wrong, born not right, born off-key, born with the sign of the Devil scraped into my soul, the number of the beast.

I'm evil. I hate myself.

Whatever fate awaits me, bring it on.

I accept whatever the universe has in store for me.

Listening hard, I hear only muffled sounds of movement and murmurs of whispering. I'm delirious, hallucinating, drifting in and out of reality. Thoughts turn to Super and Crissy and Claude and my past life in Brixton. Come to think of it, where the fuck is Claude anyway? Why hasn't he come check on me, check on Kenny, check on the cash? He loves cash. Maybe he's in on it? Maybe he's outside waiting to share the cash and rob my share? Yeah, fuck me up and leave me for dead. I did implicate him with the SLS contract thing, so maybe he has his own fuck-Devon-save-Claude plan, the total and utter bastard. But, perhaps Kenny and Jones have a plan of their own that deals with Claude, a fuck-Devon-fuck-Paul-fuck-Claude plan to bag the loot and sort us out once and for all. Fucking hell, never mind my plan, what about their plan, kill Paul, kill Claude, kill me, kill us all, take all the cash with no loose ends.

'Right then my man, your turn,' Kenny says, solemnly with monstrous undertones lurking deep within his voice.

THIS IS IT.

I'm grabbed, stood up and launched. Floating through the air I'm free, weightless and released from this hell-hole. I'm flying now, swooping out of the door and over the stage, doing a lap of the rave. Even though it's not real, it feels surreal and lucid and maybe real. Whizzing in and out of the fairground rides, I loop-the-loop near the waltzers before diving down to skim the heads of the raving masses, their hands in the air caressing me as I glide by. It's lovely, like a recurring dream or something. Maybe I'm dead and this is heaven? Maybe when I stood up, they killed me, gun to the back of the head, nice and quick and painless.

The feeling doesn't last long though.

Crunching into what must have been the desk, searing pain shoots through my shoulder and down spine. Rolling off, I hit the floor, shoulder cracking, even more pain surging, the reality of this x-rated movie embraces me once again. I hear the muffled sound of the rave outside, still going strong. The sound increases slightly and I sense the remains of the door opening and someone has entered.

Claude?

The Police?

'All sorted yaah,' Jones says, out of breath.

Damn.

No saviour, just Satan.

'Nice one,' Kenny says, matter of fact. 'Now, his turn.'

Grabbed to my feet, I'm sprawled over the desk chest first. The tape around my wrists is cut off and my left arm held down flat. Trying to pull away, it's no good, he's so fucking strong and I'm so fucking feeble and weak. Grabbing my hand, he tries to uncurl my curled-up fingers. 'It's a finger, or the whole fucking hand,' Kenny whispers into my ear, an inch from the side of my head so close I can feel the warmth of his cigarette stained breath. Not the whole arm, or my hand? I'm half relieved, partial mutilation has to be better than full on amputation.

'You've had a touch, you fucking snake,' Jones yells, his words stronger and deeper and louder. 'Finger or hand?'

It's about me choice, choosing to submit to the inevitable, choosing to accept fate, admit defeat. They're literally taking everything from me, this is the real torture, worse than any beating or cutting. I drift back to when I'm a kid, with Crissy in the Windsor Pub when I chose between Super or Paul to get a beating from Samurai Sam. I chose back then, I can choose now, choosing Super to receive the beating saved Paul, way back then, can't save him now though. Without thinking, my fingers spread apart. Hand on top of mine locks me in position and I feel a line of coldness across the top of my little finger, just below the knuckle.

Calmness engulfs me.

I don't attempt to pull away.

I accept it.

Paul's dead and I've killed him.

I deserve this.

I need this.

THUD.

'Yaah,' Jones yells triumphantly.

I wait.

No pain, a surgical cut.

Sweet.

I hear them both giggling and laughing together like little girls in the playground, the fucking pansies.

Still no pain.

I'm released.

Maybe they haven't really done it? Maybe they're taking the piss out of me, like when I first met Jones around at Claudes flat. Wiggling my fingers, I check they're all there. Mistake, big fucking mistake. Red hot searing pain shoots up my arm like a bolt of lightning, ten thousand volts straight into my heart. Screaming out through my gaffer-tape-gag, every nerve ending in my hand cries out in unison. Pulling my hand closer, I cradle it like a baby, like I did with my little boy the day he was born. My mind darts to Shirley, then to Momma and then to Marlon, poor tube-up-his-nose-on-life-support Marlon, then...

CRACK.

Complete blackness.

Shivering and shaking uncontrollably, I'm in complete darkness and struggling to breathe through my gaffer-tape hood. Petrified, I stay statue still, listening for movement, expecting a boot in the stomach, a blade through the heart or a hack across the head from a machete. I hear the rave in the distance still going strong with that "french-kiss" tune playing, the tempo slowing down beat by beat as the sexy vocals moaning and groaning echoing into the distance. Tentatively, I move slowly. Hand in pain, with the other I seek around my head to find the end of the tape and unwind it slowly, ripping my skin as it peels off. Squinting, the light above my head is ultra-bright. Rubbing my eyes, I look around and see Paul's gone, Kenny and Jones have gone, the cash too, in fact, the entire room is completely empty. Pain washes over me, ice cold at first, then fiery-hot, starting with my hand then moving up my arm to my whole body. Unwrapping my ankles, I wedge my injured hand under my right armpit and although it's tight and warm and safe, the pain stills throbs. Looking at my watch, my vision zones in and out, but I see it's quarter to five. Eyes adjusting, I scan around, zoning-in on the spot where I last saw Paul. A dark red bottomless pool of despair remains, along with what looks like skid-marks and smears as if a child has attempted to clean it up but gave-up mid-way through. Damn, I can't look at it, can't face it, can't accept what has happened, what I've caused.

Need to get out of here.

Quietly opening what remains of the door, I sneak a peek, expecting an army of bomber jacket clad meatheads to be waiting for me, showing their teeth, snarling, glints of hate in their eyes, but, they're gone. All I see is the silhouette of the stage, illuminated by the strobing lights and scanning lasers, no meat heads, not even Claude, he must have fucked off with Kenny and Jones. God damn, I knew he'd do the dirty on me. Feeling ten times its normal size, the cold air makes my hand throb even more, but, the pain's intoxicating and sooths my real pain. Edging toward the back of the stage, I see the rave going on strong, the fairground rides are spinning, the tunes rocking while the punters rave their tits off. Heads bobbing, arms jerking up and down, they're having the time of their lives, oblivious to the horrors that have just happened on this night of a thousand deaths. Confused, light-headed and trippy, doubting myself, I query what's just happened. The stark, cold and clinical realisation splashes over me, clearing my mind and waking me up from my dream-state. The truth dawns on me, I'm a witness, witness to mass-drug dealing, witness to money laundering, witness to murder. They know I can pin it all on them. They're fools, we both know that, but not idiots, they're not likely to leave any loose ends or liabilities like me hanging around. Nah, they'll want everything neat and tidy, boxed off and sorted. They can't leave it like this, no way. Holy shit, maybe they haven't, maybe they're coming back for me, maybe they've gone to get more plastic or something, maybe they've gone to get rid of the body, bury it deep in the woods at the bottom of the car-parking field, maybe they've gone to stash the cash before coming back to sort me out.

Got to get out of here.

Walking quickly, but not running, I head around the perimeter towards the main gate, don't know why, maybe looking for Claude. Wedging both hands under opposite armpits trying to force warmth into my freezing body, I'm shaking like a leaf. Nearing the top of the hill and the dirt track, I spot a few guards and ask where everyone is, and, more importantly, where the fuck Claude's gone. They tell me there's been an "incident" down by the back gate, and he's gone down there to sort it out. Sort it out? Yeah right, you fucking idiots, he's done the off's along with the demonic twins of doom, dead body and best part of a million quid in tow. These main gate suckers haven't got a clue, the thick fucks. They go on to tell me about the numbers of punters passing through. A keen looking guy with a chrome handheld clicker says they stopped counting hours ago, when they hit twenty-seven thousand, and since then he's seen another couple of thousand passing through, plus an additional two thousand who he reckons will have bunked in over the fences.

Thirty thousand, maybe more?

I find myself smiling, the sick bastard that I am.

THEN.

A young scraggy girl approaches through the pack of meatheads. Long, no-style dark hair with a centre parting wearing a baggy light blue tie-dyed hoody top, she's pretty, in an ugly kind of way. Sporting an Ecstasy induced cheshire-cat grin, I see a hint of recognition in her saucer shaped eyes. Handing me a blue cash bag, she asks me if I'll do her a favour take it back to the office. Taking it with my good hand, bringing it close to my chest I turn and start walking. Heading back down the hill, my eyes drift from the raving masses, to the deep blue sky and the rising sun streaming through the treetops while hazy mist hovers above the ground. Getting closer, I see the office is still deserted, no meatheads and thankfully, no sign of Kenny nor Jones. Without stopping, trying hard to be invisible, I pass the cabin and head towards my motor. Still blocked in by dozens of abandoned cars, cash bag on the roof, I fumble the keys and eventually get in. Shoving the blue cash bag into the glove box, I exchange it for the half empty pack of cigarettes. Lighting up, I close my eyes. The searing pain in my hand has dulled, feels like throbbing waves now but still, I know I need to get it seen to. Yeah, I've got to get out of here, have to find poor Marlon.

Poor, poor Marlon.

Poor Paul.

Poor me.

What have I done?

Tilting my head back I can feel myself relaxing.

Peace at last...

Opening my eyes, the sun's fully up and the cars around me have thinned out. Shit, I've slept. Looking sideways towards the portacabins and the back of the stage, the fairground rides are still turning and thousands of ravers are still raving and the music's still pounding away. Key in, twist and the engine coughs into life. Steering with my knees and changing gear with my right hand, I weave through the field, slow and steady. I spot a couple of bomber jacket meatheads near an open gate through the woods. They're not checking any of the cars, just hanging around, chatting and laughing, Ducking my head I drive by. They don't notice me and don't give a shit, they're thinking about collecting their couple of hundred quid wages and downing a full-monty fry up later on at a greasy spoon cafe. Head down, eyes not meeting theirs, I nod my way through and follow the slow convoy of punters along a dirt track, eventually reaching the main road.

I'm out.

Alive.

Just.

Following the road-signs, I head towards Colchester and follow the signs for the Hospital. Forty minutes later, I'm sitting in the accident room along with a few drunks sobering-up, a couple of back street brawlers with bumps, bruises and black eyes, plus several little kids in pyjamas along with worried mums and dads. Looking around, I shake my head and look myself up and down, a complete state. A sorry, pitiful sight with blood smeared over my shirt and bumps and grazes over my head, plus no little finger on my left hand. The journey of my life has led to this, shivering in an accident room waiting to get my mutilation seen to, hoping for news on my little brother. The lady behind the counter eyeballs me with suspicious, judging eyes. I ask her about Marlon, "young guy, messed up, possible drug overdose?" Not a clue, no idea what I'm talking about, she looks at me like I'm an alien taking Martian. Worried, depressed and melancholic, thoughts turn dark, maybe Marlon's not in the hospital at all, maybe he's lying on a slab in a mortuary, next to Paul. Tears roll. I've fucked things up, yet again, whatever I touch turns to shit. It's hard to admit, but it's true. Eventually, I'm seen by a nurse who's matter of fact and business like, no loving bedside manner for the likes of me, no chance. She asks inquisitive questions about what happened, how I managed to do it, where did it happen and all that, questions the Police might ask. I tell her I'm working the nightshift on a cabbage farm, (a cabbage farm, for fucks sake), and get caught my hand caught in a machine. Not sure where the fuck that came from, but I'm in the countryside and it's all I can think of. The dumb fuck buys it with a doubting "humph", and stitches it up, injecting it with some nerve-numbing shit before putting the biggest dressing on you've ever seen. She says I need to see a plastic surgeon and will make an appointment for me to see a consultant in a few weeks. I don't give a shit about that, these country-bumpkin mother fuckers won't see me ever again, that's for sure.

Ten minutes later…
I'm gone, heading south, back to London.
The worst drive of my life.
Everything's gone.
Brother gone.
Best mate gone.
Wife gone.
Family gone
Finger gone.
Dignity gone.
Pride gone.
Manliness gone.
Money gone.
Ambition gone.
Wanting gone.
Hurting gone.
Humanity gone.

Feeling gone.
Emotion gone.
Drive gone.
Passion gone.
Love gone.
Life?
Gone.

All fucking gone.

12. Catch Twenty-Two

"Destiny is a good thing to accept, when it's going your way. When it isn't, we don't call it destiny, we call it injustice, treachery, or... simple bad luck."

Joseph Heller

THE KITCHEN
17, HAMILTON HOUSE
GREENWICH, LONDON
LATE SUMMER, 1989

All these pages of re-playing, re-living, re-dying, re-telling, re-writing, re-wishing, re-gretting, re-thinking, re-dwelling, re-gurgitating, and yet, it still doesn't feel real. Hearing it out loud, reading from the page, it sounds like an elaborate story, a tall tale or a fable, more like watching it on television or in a movie or something. So much pain, so much heartache, so much waste, it's all I ever think about. You know what, now I've spilt the beans, you can leave, do one, get out of my head, leave me alone.

"I can't though, you know that. We're not finished," the Interrogator says, inevitability echoing through his voice.

For fucks sake.

'So, crack on dickhead' the Interrogator prompts, urging me on.

No fight to disagree, can't be bothered to argue otherwise. I just need closure, get you out, end this tale of woe…

After the hospital, I come back here. No way I can go to Claudes, he might be there with Kenny and Jones celebrating the success of the let's do for Devon plan. Maybe I go back to Mommas, but, she don't need me there bringing unwanted criminal attention, plus, how will I explain what happened to Marlon, or my hand. Nah, I can't face her, can't look her in the eye, it's always in the eyes, man. I come back here and take a shower with my bandaged hand sticking through the shower curtain to keep it dry. Later, I open the blue cash-bag stashed in the glove box and find best part of seven thousand, nice. Not quite the half-million I thought I'd bank, but fuck it, better than nothing. As I'm doing now, I sit here at the kitchen table on edge and nervous, fully expecting Kenny or Jones or Claude to turn up at any minute and tidy up their loose ends. Still can't sleep, even now, nah, I just lay here on the flee-bitten sofa, all day and all night thinking it all through, replaying what happened, recalling the sounds, the noises, the smells, the waiting for the inevitable. I see Pauls cut up face, hear his groans, the slaps and punches and sadistic giggling, his deathly screams and pleads for mercy. I see poor Ashley curling up on the floor and the bastard Police jumping on him and hear him screaming in pain all those years ago. I see my baby brother Marlon fitting and writhing around like a snared crocodile doing a death roll and hear the foam gurgling in his throat as he chokes and sputters. I see my beautiful princes, cowering in front of me, blood dripping from everywhere, fear and disgust in her eyes and her shouting at me to get out-get out get-out. It's all too much, I seriously consider ending it and play out a few different scenarios in my sick warped head. Down a heap of pills, rope around the neck, jump off roof, electric toaster in the bath, head out of a train, leap off a motorway bridge, head on the oven, exhaust pipe through the window. I can't do it though, I'm a coward. Instead, I just sit here trapped in this purgatory hell, too scared to live, too pussy to die.

A few days after getting back, I find myself heading down towards Deptford and Claudes girlfriends flat. She's a skinny ugly mother-earth bitch with unwashed fading-out bleached blonde hair and hairy armpits, which is disgusting by the way, she has an absolutely stunning body, with an insatiable sex drive. Claude tells me when he's high as a kite on coke they'll fuck for literally hours and after that she'll play with herself while he snores through a post-coke-post-orgasm sleep. Anyway, while she's not sexing herself, she stores the majority of Claudes drugs under the floor boards in her bathroom, and small-time deals to friends and friends of friends to fund her own habit. Opening the door, in her olde-world cockney accent and nicotine brown front teeth, she rabbits on about not seeing Claude for a couple of weeks while, at the same time, asking me loads of questions, Where is he? Why hasn't he been around? Where is he? Have I seen him? Where is he? Who's going to pay the rent?

Sounds like an interrogation, formal and over-pronounced with leading questions, like it's being recorded for future evidence. The only thing worse than not wanting to live and not wanting to die is living in the perpetual night-of-the-living-dead, otherwise known as at Her Majesty's Pleasure, locked up in the Scrubs or some other non-descript prison. Nah, I get my stash of delicious brown and get the fuck out of there double-quick time. I reckon the Police will be all over this now, organised crime unit or something. Pirate radio, raves, wholesale drug-dealing, money laundering, villainy and gangsterism, killings on an industrial scale, yeah, for sure the Police will be all over this, possibly MI5 or MI6 too, James Bond level shit.

Takes me about an hour to walk back here through the back streets, double-backing on myself a few times in case I'm followed. All the while I tease myself with thoughts of cooking-up some delicious brown, shooting that shit-up and falling into a deep, peaceful, orgasmic sleep. Around the corner into the car park, I look up across the balcony and see the front door's wide open. Shit, I definitely locked it when I left. Heartbeat jumping, adrenaline pumping, veins enlarging, pupils dilating, danger-danger-danger. Should I run, hide, disappear, merge into the never to be seen again nothingness of everyday urban life? But, where will I go and, more importantly, how will I cook the brown, man, I'm clucking with excitement and that shit needs shooting. Ninja-like, I creep up the stairs and edge along the balcony. Action-Man with the bionic eye, I peek through the kitchen window. Can't see anything so turn an ear to the crack in the door, nothing but deadly silence. Robbed? A dirty bastard mother fucking crook has robbed me, stolen my blue cash bag, absolute cunts. Slowly, edging my way in through the door, I shimmy along the hallway and, leaning in, spy through into the sitting room. Nothing. Slowly I push the door open and see a pair of bright white Reebok Classics.

Shit, there's only one double-hard bastard I know who rocks Reebok. Dum-dum-dum…dah-dah-dah…dah-dah-

dah War of the Worlds stabs echo around me. It's him, it's Claude, sitting right here, where I am right now. He's fucked up with a line of butterfly stitches across his cheek and his right eye bulging like he's squeezed a tennis ball inside his eye-lid. He's taken a beating, that's plain to see. Without moving his head, his eyes lock onto me and we both stare at each other in silence. I open my mouth, but, before the words come out, he launches toward me, grabbing my throat.

'Where's my fooking money?' he yells.

'What,' I plead.

'Money cunt, da money,' he screams, not making any sense. 'Quarter mill you slag.'

I can't speak he's gripping so hard.

'Fooking money, where der fuck is it,' he spits, slapping me around the head with his left, gripping my throat harder with his right. 'You fooking did for me, cunt.'

No I didn't.

He fucking did for me.

More blows land.

'Rip me off, ripped der shit,' he screams, centimetres from my face. 'You, you and Kenny, bunch of slags.'

I try and plead with my eyes.

'I'm gunna fooking kill you, fooking cunt, fooking slag.'

Insanely strong, I can't fight back and, to be honest, I don't want to. I deserve a beating, I deserve much more if I'm honest, so, I just take it like a pussy. Yeah, punch-fucked by this pumped up steroid fuelled monster, a stranger I don't know anymore.

'Cunt,' he screams before pushing his forehead into mine then releasing me. Out of breath like he's just orgasmed after a mammoth sex-session he slumps back onto the sofa, head in his hands. He's weeping and whispering to himself about his kid and his missus who he hasn't seen for years, ever since they were placed into witness protection. Looking up, he stares at me. 'You not got any clue,' he says, shaking his head.

'What?'

'You just a boy, a pleb, a come-de-go-day mother-fucker.'

'I'm sorry,' I say, but he cuts be dead.

'Shut der fuck up or I'll fooking end you, you cunt. You still don't get it, after all dis time, you still clueless. Dey connected man, you don't know shit, dey fooking set, untouchable, beyond the bloodclat law.'

'But.'

'But nothing, nobody's safe, not me, not you, nobody.'

'More fucked than now?' I plead.

'Yes more dan now, dis just the beginning, like you don't know.'

'I don't know shit,' I say, sitting down next to him. 'All I know is I tried to scheme my way out of this shit, and it back-fired. Marlons gone, they did for Paul then they mutilated my hand then fucked off with the cash.'

'Don't try and mug me off cunt, old school or not I'll fooking cut ya open.'

'T'cha, believe what you want. I gave them Paul, literally handed him to them on a plate hoping they'll let me do one.'

'What?' he laughs. 'Sneaky snake mother fucker, you'll never change, you a born bad wrong-un.'

'That's harsh man.'

'Fook off harsh. Listen, whatever happened wit duppy boy lemon, he deserve it. He snitched way back den.'

'True,' I laugh.

'I aint fucking laughing, shit-cunt. Make no mistake, we'll never be straight, never be right. You're a fucking Jonah, rotten at the fucking core.'

'What?'

'You fooking stay away from me, you hear.'

'But.'

'But fook off, don't believe a single word you say. You bladed your own hand and did Marlon too, left him to overdose on dose moody pills dey punting.'

'Nah man, nah.'

His words hurt.

'Nah man nothing. You a dirty low-down snake. What happened to you dred, Crissy like you you-nah, had time for you.' Hand cupping his head, he looks to the floor and shakes. 'If I didn't think I'd be hexed or something, I'd off you right now.'

It's hard to admit, but, half of me, maybe more than half, wishes he would put me out of my misery.

Then, leaping to his feet, he starts ripping the place apart, looking for cash. 'Where der fook is it then, come on, where?'

'Where's what, come on man.'

'Fuck come on man, how much dey pay you.'

'Claude, please.'

'You owe me, cunt, dey were gonna kill you in Canning Town, you know that? I stopped dem, you know dat? Like a mug I fooking help you.'

He doesn't find the cash bag, nah, I hid it in the pressure cooker under the sink, you can never be too careful. He rips this place apart though, doors off cupboards, beds tipped upside down, toilet seat ripped off, god knows why.

'You listen and fooking listen good cause dee's are der last words you'll ever hear from me,' he says, eyes darting everywhere, nervous to fuck. 'You ever set eyes on me again, you see me walking down der street or think you spot me in da crowd, you fucking turn around and walk der other way because as sure as shit, I'll fooking kill you, no matter the consequence. You understand me, boy?'

Then, he gets up and leaves. No looking over his shoulder, no wink or smile for old-times-sake, nothing. Haven't seen him since. Fuck knows how he ended up cut with that mad thing with his eye, but, he's taken a beating, the beating of all beatings. I can only think Kenny and Jones did for him, fucking him up like they fucked me, and how they fucked Paul up. Whoever gave him a pasting is someone I don't want to meet, man, if they can do him like that, imagine what they can do to me.

Fuck. That.

A few days later…

Next up, a lovely visit from couple of plain clothes Police, say they're with "Serious and Organised Crime Unit", otherwise known as the "Flying Squad". Classic good cop, bad cop, 'we can do this the easy way or hard way,' clichéd crap. Doing for Claude crosses my mind, yeah, telling them he's the mastermind, he's the organiser and king-pin in the whole escapade. I don't, of course, what good will it do, other than incriminate me even in a small way. They go on to say they know for sure I organised the rave and have signed confessions from both the SLS guys along with the printer who printed the tickets. Damn. They know I used to run Dream FM, (used to, when did that change?). They even know about the meeting points. After that, they keep firing loads of pointless questions at me, where are the monetary proceeds, who supplied the drugs, who'd helped me, what about the drugs, who's behind it and who put up the cash, where did the drugs come from. They say it's only a matter of time before they pin everything on me and I'm sent down for the rest of my life. Yeah right, so why not arrest me there and then, the fucking saps. But, I hate to admit it, I'm surprised at how much they actually do know, I always assumed Police are clueless dicks but, in fact, turns out they're Sherlock fucking Holmes in disguise. Then I start thinking, are they indeed exceptional investigators or maybe I've taken too much for granted and been sloppy? Then, even darker thoughts, maybe someone snitched, maybe Kenny or Jones turned Queens Evidence, maybe they were the ones with the tape recorder and not poor Paul, maybe they switched around the fuck-Paul-save-me plan to their own fuck-Devon, fuck-Paul, fuck-Claude and save-Kenny-and-Jones plan? Claude says they're connected, plus, I always had nagging doubts about Jones being actual or ex Police. Shit, maybe he's still undercover, yeah, that makes sense. I fucking knew it, I always suspected he's ex-police-now-deep-undercover-police, a fucking sleeper cell or something. My mind spins. In any case, there's no way I'm telling these flying-squad dicks a thing, no way, they'll use it against me and fit me up for sure, they probably working for Jones in any case. Yeah, I'm someone they can use to take the blame, be their patsy, take one for the team.

The two officers go on to mention reports of a missing person, a white male in his thirties, (obviously Paul), and a young girl in a coma from a dodgy pill, I don't know anything about no white girl. They don't mention Marlon though and I don't ask because if he is dead, they'll surely question me about it, or, at least, it'll be all over the news. Yeah man, with an unexplained death and potential murder charge they won't be chit-chatting to me here in this flat, nah. I'll be stripped naked, arrested, fingerprinted and be in a forensic white suit with photographs, written statements and the right to remain silent bullshit. Yeah man, a death is a hundred times worse than an illegal rave, even if drugs are being sold. After a couple of boring hours, tweedle-dee and tweedle-fucking-dumb fuck off, promising to be back in a few days, leaving a business card in case I remember anything and need to turn super-grass.

After that, deep breath, I go see Momma…

Driving over to Brixton, my mind wanders and I feel trippy and surreal. I've been through these streets a million times, but, today, they look completely alien to me, grey and beige and old fashioned. Eventually, when I reach the Frontline, it's all changed too. The Caribbean shops have closed, the meat patty and root-beer stalls gone, the record shack on the market closed up, derelict. What the fucks happened. Normal everyday folk are busying away, commuting and going about their business and there's no sign of any doom mongers hanging around preaching about the end of the world or even any rude-boys hustling outside the tube station.

Everything's different.

Knocking the door, I hear Momma behind, taking an age

to open up. Eventually, the door creaks and I take a step back. Man, she looks old and short and grey and fragile. Looking me up and down, she kisses her teeth. 'What'am,' she tuts, folding her arms.

'It's me Momma, Devon.'

'T'cha, you not welcome 'ere.'

'Momma, please.'

She kisses her teeth before heading into the kitchen.

I follow.

'Why you nah look out for your pickney bruddah,' she yells, turning to face me, her eyes full of disappointment.

That kills me.

'He dropped some pills, I didn't know.'

'Didn't know what? Bwai, he's there because of you, ya idiot-fool.' She pulls out a chair and slumps over the table. 'He in Saint Thomas' ya-nah. Twelve days in a coma, intensive care unit, enough tube and ting down his throat. They say a stroke or something'

He's alive!

'Momma.'

'Don't Momma me-nah, bwai, ya-get no get no forgiveness no nothing. You a fallen soul, you nah no son to me.'

'Momma, please.'

'T'cha,' she kisses her teeth.

'But I am your son.'

She's killing me way worse than any gun or knife or bat.

'Listen, no son of mine'll allow his own blood to be hurt, nearly killed. T'cha, the bwai can't even walk nah-man. Only yesterday they remove the feeding tube ting.'

'Shit.'

'A stroke, at twenty three.' Tears roll down her face.

'God, Momma, I…'

'Nah take the lords name, you don't mutter a ting about Him,' she spits, angry now. 'Leave this house, leave nah man, and don't come back. You broke me heart, broke it into a thousand pieces. You not wanted here.'

'Please,' I say, reaching for her hand.

'Go!' she screams, slapping my hand away. 'Be gone, leave man, leave.'

Turning, I head slowly to the front door, glancing to the left to see the front room, where we weren't allowed to go when we were kids. Still pristine, still neat and tidy, still super clean.

I hear her weeping.

I'm crying too.

Worst day of my life.

Remember it like it's yesterday.

But, he's alive, just.

Sounds fucking horrific though.

A stroke.

All because of me.

A stroke, at twenty-three, because of me.

His whole life in front of him, ruined.

BECAUSE OF ME.

ALL BECAUSE OF ME…

I hear a massive roaring sound echoing around the room, bouncing off the inside of my skull. Louder than before, much louder, deafeningly loud! I hear myself roar, like a lion, a lion caught in a man-trap.

"It's you who's the fuck up," the Interrogator says, telling me what I already know. *"The world will be a better place without you, you should be crippled like Ashley, dead like Paul, bruised and battered like Shirley or laying in a coma instead of poor Marlon."*

He's right, of course he is.

But, I can't accept he's right, can't let him win.

Sanctimonious monologs?

Fuck off.

"You should be hobbling around on crutches, life ruined or six-feet under wrapped in tarpaulin or in hospital, tubes up your nose, close to death," the Interrogator spits, damming me with every word.

Fuck the fuck off.

"It Should be you," the Interrogator says, telling me what I've told myself my whole life. *"You should be dead."*

DEAD…

Jumping to my feet, fists clenched, teeth biting together, I've had enough, this is it.

THIS.
    IS.
        IT.

Let's have it you cunt.
He's strong though.
Too strong.
Head smashes against the kitchen table.
AGAIN. AGAIN. AGAIN.
SMASH. SMASH. SMASH.
Deep red blood spurts everywhere.
Without thinking, I'm literally picked up.
Launched across the room.
Land on my shoulder.
Pains urging, taking my breath away.
I skid across the floor, banging into the kitchen cupboards.
"The end is coming," the Interrogator yells theatrically, foreseeing the future like Nostradamus on speed.
Louder and louder, the roaring's now deafeningly loud, so loud blood seeps from my ear-drums.
'Mother fucker,' the Interrogator screams.
Gun cocked, safety off.
PANIC.
Bolt for the balcony door.
Trip, head first.
SMASH.
Head colliding, smashes through the bottom panel. Flesh rips against the wire mesh impaling into the safety glass. Hair, skin and bone entwine into the window as dark black blood pumps out. Shards of glass and broken wire point in all directions.
I scream, the pain's incredible.
The roaring engulfs me, controls me, it's so damn loud.
"You," the Interrogator screams. *"YOU should be dead."*

Wrenching my head free from the glass-wire mess, I spin around. Come on then.

COME ON!

I scan the room.

Empty.

And quiet.

Roaring gone.

"Shhhhh-nah-man," the Interrogator whispers, quiet and secretive and intimate.

Eyes gravitate to the gun resting on the table.

Where is he? Where's he gone?

WHERE THE FUCK ARE YOU?

"Here," the Interrogator giggles.

Standing in the centre of the room I swing around, spinning three-sixty. Around and around, guard up Muhammad Ali style, the crown of blood forming around my head glistens as it slowly seeps out of the multiple cuts and gashes.

WHERE THE FUCK ARE YOU?

"Here," the Interrogator says, seriousness in his voice.

Ear cocked, eyes slanted, I struggle to locate him.

"Here," the Interrogator says, again, guiding me to my fate.

Tentatively, I step slowly towards the sink.

Heart beating incredibly fast, I'm scared of what I'll find.

Scared of what I might see, even though…

I know what I'll see.

Deep down inside, I've always known…

Just like you, you've known too.

"I'm here," the Interrogator says, in a familiar tone.

A silent energy fills the room and I see shadows reflecting across the council-issue stainless steel sink. I catch a glimpse of myself in the mirror above the taps. Frozen to the floor, eyes fixing and pupils wide, the past few weeks race by in a millisecond. All the events, all the feelings, all the regret, all the sorrow come racing back.

"It can't be?" I question out loud, slowly and lowly, even though nobody can hear and only I know the answer.

"It can be."

Early morning golden rays of sunlight splitter the dark horizon of my mind, on this day of truth. The clouds part and, for the first time in years, I see clearly now, (the rain has gone).

Me?

You're me, and I'm you?

"What?" he says.

Don't you get it?

I get it.

Mad, a nutter, mental, a raving nutcase.

You've known or at least suspected it ever since I came here, you've always known.

Pictures of my life zoom through my head-fucked head, replaying freeze frames of my life over and over.

I can't believe it.

It can't be.

Me, mad?

A raving lunatic, talking to myself?

Nah man, nah, how can I be mad if I know I'm mad?

"I am you, and you are me."

Shut up.

SHUT THE FUCK UP.

A trick, yeah, must be a trick.

The drugs?

Yeah, what do they call it, psychosis or paranoia or something?

The little kid running errands for Crissy, the little man looking out for his baby brother, the best mate there for his mates, the father, the lover, the dad, the husband.

It can't be.

Sitting down, slowly and steadily, every muscle strains, every ligament tightens. Elbows on the table, palms cupping temples, tears form a puddle in front of me. Confused thoughts smash through my mind, loss, regret, sorrow, confusion.

Poor old Devon.

Devon the nut-job.

Devon the crazy.

Had everything, ended up losing the lot.

Envy of everyone.

Made his Momma proud…

"So, I'm mad," I say to myself, for the very first time hearing my own voice echo around this hell-hole of a deserted kitchen. I've been talking to myself, all this time, keeping myself prisoner? I can't believe it. Thoughts turn to Pops, poor old Pops. All he wants if for his kids to do a tiny bit better than he did, nothing flash, no doctor or lawyer or architect, just a tiny bit better. Happy and healthy he'd say…

I hear myself groan as more sorrow-tears flow.

Arms wrapping tightly around my body, I hear the roar of England fans in the background, cheering the winning goal in the nineteen sixty-six world cup final. Paul's there, Super too, both are young and innocent and kids. We're all jumping around, celebrating and having young naive innocent fun.

Happy times.

Hand move towards the gun.

Shit man, it's cold and heavy and real. At least he, or I, or us, or we didn't imagine that, I'm not completely mad. A broad smile grows across my face and I open my eyes. I'm still here, in the flat, all alone, apart from me.

Mad?

"Surely not, no way."

My other hand floats towards my head. The wounds are sticky and warm and wet, with fragments of sharp glass sticking out. I feel the pain, yeah, love the pain. Grimacing, I push my index finger into the wound on top of my forehead. Vision wobbling, I flinch, but I must feel, I must know I'm still me.

And it is me.

A mad version of me, but still me, I think.

Don't act shocked or coy, like you don't know. I know, of course I do but, even now, can't admit it, especially to myself. Fucking hell, it makes sense now, of course I'm mad. Normal, non-mad, sane Devon would have done things differently.

Hit Shirley?

No chance.

*"Very convenient, gets you/*me off the hook."

Fingers trace the outline of the barrel, then toward the trigger. Smooth and precise, cooling and beautifully simple. Who am I talking to? Me, that's who. I'm mad, that's why. The roaring, the thousand voices inside my mind scream and yell. Chit-chattering together, they're loud, too loud.

Thoughts turn to Marlon, my baby brother…

Tears and mucus glisten on my top lip, but, the steely coldness against my temple sooths my pain.

I blink and see Momma's face, smiling. She's proud of her son, proud of what he's achieved. Breaking out of Brixton, he made something of himself. A million pounds in one night. Earned, not robbed or swindled or conned, but earned through hard work and graft. Now, that's something to be proud of.

Breathing deeply, the coldness of the barrel eases the pain, cools my throbbing brow. I see Paul and Super in my bedroom at Mommas house in Brixton skanking to the latest "Mad Professor" tune, Marlon's there too, in the doorway, little and skinny and shy and nine years old. Ashley's behind him on the landing trying to copy and join in, he's naïve and innocent and fragile. Something's not right though. He's not skanking, he's struggling with metal calliper things around his legs. Falling over, he's in pain. Paul bends over to pick him up but something's not right with him either. His head, at the back, it's dark and red and wet with blood oozing everywhere from a hollow indentation. Moving, like it's alive, maggots fall out as a swarm of bluebottles appear from nowhere and buzz around the room. The rancid, putrefying smell explodes through my nostrils and I retch to be sick…

Eyes open I focus on the table, on the here and now and

not the x-rated snuff movie from the past.

Knock, knock.

The door?

Knock-knock-knock.

Is it her?

I've come to my senses and now, so as she. We've been waiting for this day to come and eventually it's arrived, this day of discovery and clarity and truth.

Knock-knock.

No way.

Soon as I see what's happening, so does she and she wants me. She's here, come to save me, rescue me, be with me. I hear the key in the door, it's her, it's really her. Gliding in like an angel floating on a cloud, she's smiling, happy and sexy and with that blue silk wrap-around dress. I see the tease of her cleavage, the curve of her breasts and the shape of excited nipples. God, she's sexy, I've missed her. Like watching the television with the sound muted, she's talking but I can't hear. Then, little man, my boy, my son and heir chases past with his arms out ready to give his daddy a massive hug. He's grown up now, handsome and beautiful.

Thank god, I'm saved.

All this madness, the craziness, the regurgitating of the past has been well worth it. A wave of excitement fills my heart and instantly I know everything's going to be alright. I'm saved, we can get back to normal. The madness will go, Marlon will be fine and Paul will turn up not-killed. Smiling, I can't stop smiling, this story does have a happy ending after-all. I wait with my arms out-stretched, waiting for my daddy cuddle, waiting for the closeness, the warmth, the love. Joy fills my fragile heart as my boy gets closer. He doesn't look happy though, he runs straight by me.

WAIT.

Out to the Balcony.

No, no, no, wait.

Over the side, head first, heels follow.

He's gone.

Panic. Screams.

NOOOOOOOOOooooooooooo.

Got to wake up, this isn't happening, it's a dream, a bad dream, a nightmare, a snuff movie, and video nasty.

Frozen to the chair, I can't move.

Please. No, no, no.

I spin around to Shirley, she's gone.

No.

Please.

I feel an incredible gut-wrenching loss, like the last light in the universe has just been extinguished. I need her, I'm addicted to her, I can't live without her…

Eyes open slowly.

I'm still here, at the kitchen table.

Why torture me, please stop this madness.

"Do it then."

Heart beating faster than ever before, beads of sweat pump from my forehead. I know none of this is real, it's madness, a crazy construct inside my heroin warped mind.

"Do it, do it, fucking do it, *pussy."*

I stare straight into the barrel. It's a dead weight. After all this time I've been threatening myself, locking myself in, keeping myself prisoner with this here with this gun?

Shit man, at least this is real.

"Please, please I can't," I say, pleading with myself.

But, I know I can.

Destiny, you see.

I've always known, since a little boy, since I ran errands for Crissy. I realise now, for the first time in my wasted life, I was indeed born bad and I am truly a bad man. I can try and blame circumstance, my upbringing, the environment, the economic context, the Government, but, if I'm honest, I've always known it would end this way.

Heart exploding, sweat streaming, my eyes transfix on the metal embodiment of my fate.

"It's inevitable."

I know it is.

The world will be a better place, I know it but I'm a coward. Even though I won't miss this world, not for one second, I hope I'll be missed, even if just a little. I'm born bad, rotten to the core, and bad can't ever be good, I know that. Redemption is a myth created by do-gooders trying to stop the chaos, so, logic dictates, the world will be a better place. Look at what I've caused, the misery, the pain, the ruin, the waste.

I need peace…

The roaring starts again.

Loud, really loud.

Make it stop. PLEASE.

I'm screaming, screaming to myself. It's inevitable. I'm all alone in the world, nobody wants me no more, nobody needs me. The world will be a better place. The lion roars, and not just one brave lion-heart, but hundreds and thousands, every lion on earth roars and screams, louder and louder, ear piercingly loud. Everything's been leading to the single point in time, we both know it, we've always known.

Slowly, I lower my forehead and bow to the majesty of fate, the queen of destiny. Say a prayer for me, remember me for me, Devon Walters, not the vampire-monster me that wasn't really me. Closing my eyes, my screams merge with the lion's roars and we become one. The incredible noise infects my brain, cutting deep into my inner most thoughts and fears.

Screaming, crying, screaming.

Love is the key, must fight the darkness…

Love.

    Is.

        The.

            Key…

My strobing freeze-framed hands punch the air, illuminated by high frequency super-bright flashes. I sway side to side as the tie-dyed dungaree ravers chant "ah-seed" to the never-ending four-four kick drum and acid-house squelches. War of the Worlds style, the pitch-black countryside's ripped apart by two high powered light-sabre green lasers sweeping toward the brightly lit big wheel and spinning waltzers. A smile stretches across my face as my teeth grind and cheeks ache. Scanning the multi-coloured silhouetted horizon, a sense of love fills my heart as the euphoric Ecstasy rush caresses my spine and tingles my skull. I'm alive like never before, loving life and loving everyone. I realise now I've lived a half-life, surreal and unreal and make believe, an urban daydream surrounded by a haze of chemical cocktails. Tonight though, on this night of nights, this is the real life. Eyes closing, my thoughts drift into the night-time darkness. God no, heading for a downer I'm faced with black-and-white snap-shot pictures of tower-blocks and skinheads, riots and Police brutality. My nostrils flare with childhood smells of ginger-bread spices, stewing tea and curried goat. Guilt, remorse and regret creep slowly from the shadows of my mind. Shit man, this is heavy, got to fight the darkness, fight the fear, get back on the up from the down. Squeezing my eyes shut, the "move-your-body" music echoes around me and takes me up, moves me higher. My smile stretches as the rushes recommence. Ah yeah, better, much better. Eyes open, I see ravers raving way out into the distance, right up to the big wheel lit-up like a Christmas tree on top of the grassy hill. Yeah man, this is it, this is life, this is love. Yeah man, focus, focus, focus. Love is the key, need to fight the darkness. The voodoo ray melody echoes in the distance and begins to take me again as the rushes come on stronger.

Oh yeah, that's better.

This is it, this is life, this is love…

Blinded by a super-nova light-burst as multi-coloured strobing neon-green lasers pierce deep into my eyes. Struggling to swallow, the acrid taste stings the back of my throat. Feeling warm, tingly, nice and happy, every muscle relaxes and the tension eases. I feel a smile spread slowly across my face as little fluffy cloud memories float through the deep blue sky of my mind. The soft chorus of early morning bird-song dances around in the background while the beautiful sound of kids playing in the playground reverberate through my sub-conscious. Closing my eyes, I'm transported back home to Mommas house in Brixton. I'm in the bath, nice and warm and peaceful. Floorboards creaking, Momma climbs the stairs, telling me not to use all the hot water, just like she always does. Final score blares from the television downstairs while Pops ticks off the no-score draws on his football pools coupon. Stretching out, I allow myself a small groan as the warmness soaks over me. I haven't felt this relaxed for ages, years maybe. Safe at last. Bang, bang, bang. Time to get out, already? Reaching for the towel, I can't move. The water turns ice cold and the familiar noises from downstairs fade as silence surrounds me. The light flickers, then dims and my breath hangs in the air as ice crystals form on my top lip and around my eyebrows. The ice bites deep into my legs as my fingertips tingle. Head spinning, I feel dizzy, light-headed and queasy. Nose twitching, the dark, dirty rancid smell hangs in the back of my throat. The light flickers and dims some more. The room becomes stained with a dirty brown half-light.

So dark.
So cold.
I'm shivering, shaking.
I'm scared.

13. Voodoo Ray

"I'm a big thinker yeah, ideas explode around me, I can see the possibilities. My attitude is reach for the stars and worst case, grab the moon…"

Devon Walters

SHIRLEY'S NEW FLAT
SCOTT LIDGETT CRESSENT
BERMONDSEY, LONDON
PRESENT DAY

Heart racing, he faces the door, staring at the letter box just below the two feet square frosted glass panel. He can hear the radio on in the background and a girl singing along. He's nervous. Should I, shouldn't I thoughts fill his mind.

Knock-knock.

Radio off.

'Won't be a minute,' the girl yells.

Knee shaking, he never thought he'd feel like this. Lock clicking, chain sliding, the door swings open.

She stares opened mouthed, disbelief in her eyes.

'Alright Shirley,' he says.

'Come here, come here,' she says, her arms out. Stepping forward she embraces him, pulling him close. It feels good, warm, welcoming. She hangs on to him tightly.

'Who is it mummy?'

'Uncle Marlon,' she says.

'Marlon, yay.' Pushing her out of the way, his small arms clutch around his uncle's waist.

'How've you been, where've you been, you okay?' she says, placing his face between her palms. Thinner than before, he's lost weight, looks older too.

'Can Uncle Marlon stay for dinner?' the youngster sings.

'Course he can,' she says. 'You want some dinner?'

'That'll be nice, cheers.'

Through to the front room, he sits down on the edge of the sofa as she disappears into the kitchen to plate up fish fingers, chips and beans.

'What we watching?' he nods toward the television.

'Blue Peter, innit.'

'Alright, cool,' he smiles, remembering when he used to rush home from school when he was about the same age.

'Where you been Uncle, you not been around in time.'

'Time? Talk properly, yeah. Ages man, not time,' Marlon says before sharing a giggle.

Minutes later, plates on knees, they're dipping hot chips into tomato ketchup as the TV presenters build play-fort from toilet roll tubes and sticky-tape. Ten minutes later, the front door slams shut as the youngster heads off to the shops to get an ice lolly.

'So, what happened?' she says, her voice full of concern as she reaches over to turn the television off.

'Dodgy pill they reckon.

'Shit,' she whispers.

'I remember feeling dizzy, got to the back of the stage and puked up. Can't remember anything after that. Woke up in the back of the ambulance with a tube down my throat.'

'Oh my God,' she says, staring deep into him.

'Liver failure or something, they said my brain swelled. Can't remember any of it to be honest.'

'So where was "he" when all this is going on? He should have been looking after you, you know that, right?'

They share a knowing look.

'Haven't seen him since. Came around to Momma's when I was in hospital though. She got angry, sent him packing.'

'I can imagine, been on the receiving end, remember?'

They laugh.

'Yeah man, yeah. So, you seen him then?' Marlon nods.

'Not for months.'

'Right, right. Just my deejay mates are chasing me, they haven't been paid yet so…'

'You sound surprised Marlon. You do know him, right?'

Her stare burns into him.

'Anyway, I'm off down to your old flat,' he says, motioning his head towards the front door.

'Stopped paying the rent months ago,' she shrugs. 'I know he's your brother and all, but I can't afford it with the boy and this place. Anyway, he'll be with that muscle-bound freak, browning or chasing or whatever they do.' She pushes her thinning lips together, forcing herself to stop.

'I know he's a fuck up, but he's still my brother. Anyway, I was hoping to take the little man down there with me.'

'No chance,' she tuts, dismissively.

'I'll have him back in an hour, two at the most.'

Not breaking her stare, she shakes her head slowly.

'Shirley, I'll look after him.'

'I know you will, it's him, I don't trust him.'

He stares deep into her tear-filling eyes. 'I know what he did to you and it's not right, not right at all. I can't forgive him for what he did. He won't hurt his boy though, I know that for sure.'

'Yeah, right.'

'Anyway, I won't let him, no chance.'

'Marlon, you're a good guy, I know you are, I just…'

'He must ask about his daddy.'

A single tear rolls down her cheek. 'Don't do this, please.'

His hand surrounds hers. 'Listen, I promise he'll be okay, I swear on my life. Seeing his son might be just what he needs to sort himself out, get him back on track.'

Silence fills the room.

'Come on Shirley.'

'Marlon, please.'

'You can come too, wait in the car or something.'

'Oh god.'

'Please Shirley, he needs this.'

'Just have him back by seven,' she says, wiping the tears away. 'Any sign of trouble or drugs or anything, I want him home. You understand me Marlon?'

'Yeah, course I do. I love the little guy, I won't let anything happen, I promise.'

DEVONS FLAT
17, HAMILTON HOUSE
GREENWICH, LONDON
PRESENT DAY

Pulling into the estate, they park near the bins, just outside the entrance to the stairwell. Laughing and joking, they climb the stairs and walk along the walkway, the youngster skipping along beside him.

Knock-knock. No answer.

Looking over the open walkway around the estate, Marlon can hear the opening bars of that Guy Called Gerald track echoing from an open window in the other block, "ooh-who-who, ahhh-ha-ha-yeah, voodoo-ray, voodoo-ray." A smile curls at the corner of his mouth as he remembers moving thirty thousand ravers to that very tune just a matter of weeks ago. He knocks again, harder this time. Looking through the window, he can tell someone's inside. 'Devon, open up nah-man,' he shouts through the letter box.

No answer.

'What do you think, maybe your old man's asleep, the lazy sod. Shall we surprise him?'

'Yeah, yeah, let's surprise him,' the youngster says, excitement cracking through his high-pitched voice.

'Got to be quiet though, like spies or ninjas yeah. Listen, do me a favour, go get my jacket from the car, yeah. I'll watch you from up here.'

Grabbing the keys, he skips back along the balcony before disappearing down the stairwell. Turning back to the door, Marlon leans against the lock and pushes. No joy. Turning his back on the door, he looks down to the car park and sees the youngster rummaging around on the back seat.

'Ah-say, what ye' doing?' a thick Irish accent comes from further along the walkway.

Marlon spins around.

'What ye' playing at?' yells the overweight fat guy with fair gingering hair, his forearms covered in blue swallow tattoos.

'Remember to lock it yeah,' Marlon shouts over the balcony before turning back. 'My brother lives here.'

'Devon's ye' brother?'

Marlon nods.

'Not seen him in ages, so I haven't.'

'Right-right.'

'Gave her a fair beating. In a right state she was.'

'That's ages ago mate,' Marlon nods. 'And, none of your business neither so do yourself a favour and go back inside.'

The Irishman looks Marlon up and down. 'Listen now,' he says. 'We don't want any trouble around here. Any shenanigans and I'll fetch the Police.'

'Yeah?' Marlon squares up.

The Irishman shakes his head, throws his hands in the air and slams his door shut. Marlon faces the door again and smashes his foot against the lock. Bursting open, the door slams against the inside wall before bouncing back. Turning away he covers his mouth as an unbearable smell burns his nostrils. Edging in, he can just about see through the kitchen door, three-quarter closed. His eyes zone in on the balcony door, smashed and bloodied. Slowly pushing the door ajar, he freezes. 'Oh god, no,' he whispers as he kneels beside the lifeless body. Old and grey, skinny and frail, a large crown of black-blood surrounds his head. 'DEVON, NO.'

'Daddy?'

His eyes dart to the doorway and the small boy standing with a coat in one hand, car keys in the other with a big beaming smile.

'Don't come in, don't come in,' he shouts, jumping up.

'What's happening?'

'Nothing mate, he's just tired. Sleeping on the kitchen floor. What a mug, eh?' Marlon says, leading him outside, through the front door and back onto the open walkway.

'Yeah?' the little boy says, his trembling voice not matching his forced smile.

'Listen buddy, you stay here, don't come in. Let me wake him up. You know grouchy he gets when he wakes up.'

The boy nods slowly as Marlon returns to the flat. 'What the fuck happened,' he whispers out loud, his eyes floating around the torn apart room. Signs of a struggle, maybe he's been killed? Claude? The heavies behind the rave? He spots a pile of papers on the table, chewed up with scribbles all over them.

Stories.

Devon's stories.

Stories about growing up, about Paul and Super and Shirley. Flicking through the pages, he spots his name and memories from when he's a little boy, when Devon used to pick him up from school and they used to walk home hand in hand through the park. Flicking further through, he sees they are stories about Devons life, fond, loving and gentle memories.

'Why Dev, why?' he says out loud looking back to the body on the floor. Lump in the throat, tears roll down his face.

'You okay uncle Marlon?'

He turns to see the youngster poking his head around the kitchen door. 'He's not waking up, is he?'

Marlon goes to him, hugs him and spins him around so he's facing into the hallway. Pulling him closer into to his chest he feels him sobbing softly as he hears Police sirens echoing in the distance. 'Listen little man, he's sleeping with the angels now. Sleeping with the angels.'

Devon Walters
1955 - 1989
R.I.P

MORE FROM THE AUTHOR

"Riot", the prequel to Raver, join Devon, Paul and Super in the story of the 1981 Brixton Riots.

&

"Yuppie", the sequel to Raver, where we pick up the story in Wall Street, New York City.

PLAYLIST

"Madness" by Prince Buster

"Rudeboy dub" by The Mad Professor

"Paint it black" by The Rolling Stones

"Suspicious minds" by Elvis

"In the air tonight" by Phil Collins

"Number one" by Princess

"Shout" by Tears for Fears

"Clear" by Cybotron

"Hip hop be bop" by Man Parrish

"Let the music play" by Shannon

"Show me" by the Cover Girls

"I-O-U" by Freeez

"I can't wait" by Nu Shooz

"Don't let the sun go down" by Elton John

"Relax" by Frankie Goes to Hollywood

"Tell it to my heart" by Taylor Dayne

"How soon is now" by The Smiths

"Tubular Bells" by Mike Oldfield

"Give me a sign" by In-Dex

"A Day in the life" by Black Riot

"Move your body" by Marshall Jefferson

"Come get my loving" by Dionne

"Love can't turn around," by Farley 'Jackmaster' Funk

"French kiss" by Lil Louis

"Salsa house" by Richie Rich

"Acid trax" by Phuture

"Acid thunder" by Fast Eddie Smith

"Stakker humanoid" by Humanoid

"Killer" by Adamski

"Voodoo ray" by A Guy Called Gerald

Printed in Great Britain
by Amazon